NO[THING]
TO LOSE

Yours to Keep
Withdrawn/ABCL

ANGELA
WINTERS

Dafina
BOOKS

Kensington Publishing Corp.
www.kensingtonbooks.com

DAFINA BOOKS are published by

Kensington Publishing Corp.
119 West 40th Street
New York, NY 10018

ISBN-13: 978-0-7582-8657-4
ISBN-10: 0-7582-8657-0
First Kensington Trade Edition: December 2013
First Kensington Mass Market Edition: May 2016

eISBN-13: 978-0-7582-8658-1
eISBN-10: 0-7582-8658-9
First Kensington Electronic Edition: December 2013

10 9 8 7 6 5 4 3 2 1

Printed in the United States of America

1

Everyone in the room at the Marriott hotel on Pennsylvania Avenue in Washington, D.C., thought today was a great day for the governor of the state of Maryland, Jerry Northman. Twenty-nine-year-old Sherise Robinson knew better. Today was a great day for her. And although all eyes were on the man standing at the podium, who had just announced his decision to run for president of the United States, Sherise was feeling like the center of the universe.

It was a fault of hers, really. She knew that. She was too often overconfident and self-centered for her own good. That's what her friends had always told her. But she was no fool. Having been a player in the game of D.C. politics, in some role or another since she was a teenager living on the southeast side, Sherise learned that if you don't make it all about you, no one else will.

That lesson never became more clear to her than when she'd taken time off from her career as a communications professional with the White House's Domestic Policy Council to focus on saving her marriage to her lobbyist husband, Justin, and having a second baby.

She had lost her way and allowed another man to convince her he was worth risking her marriage for. It was a terrible mistake, but Sherise didn't want to put herself down for it. After all, the man was Jonah Nolan, one of the most powerful men in the country.

Fortunately, she was able to keep this indiscretion from blowing up in her face and ruining the charmed life she had with her husband and baby girl, Cady.

What she wasn't able to keep from imploding was her career. Out of sight, out of mind, was the way of Washington power brokering. You can jump ship for another or go off on your own, but you can't disappear and expect people to care about you. Sherise was a woman whose stunning beauty usually made her the most memorable woman at any event she attended. Being forgotten was not a space she was willing to occupy.

This was why, when the Northman campaign offered her a chance to showcase her press management skills eight months ago, just as he was forming an exploratory committee, Sherise jumped at the chance. She didn't bother asking Justin because she knew he would be against it. Their marriage was becoming a mess because of her unhappiness with her stay-at-home mom status and inability to get pregnant. Oh yes, and there was that part about Justin having an affair.

Details, Sherise told herself. A bright smile lit up her beautiful face, the highlight of her flawless appearance. She was a golden caramel stunner, with silky dark brown hair that went to her bra strap. Her high cheekbones, full, sultry lips and piercing green eyes caught every man's eyes, as well as her trim figure with killer curves.

She watched Northman smile for the pictures, just the way she'd taught him. She was wicked for finding joy in the fact that he was wearing the red tie that she gave him instead of the blue one his wife, Ginger, standing next to him with a saccharine smile, had given him earlier that day. Yes, even though this ball had gotten rolling long before Sherise joined, she knew she could take a lot of credit for where it was now.

That fact was also obvious in the look of beaming approval from LaKeisha Wilson, Northman's deputy campaign manager, as she joined Sherise at the far side of the podium.

LaKeisha was a very average-looking woman, but she had chocolate skin as smooth as a baby's bottom, despite being in her late thirties. She barely wore any makeup and dressed sharp, as any woman who had spent her life on Capitol Hill in D.C. did. She had recently cut her long braids and was now wearing a short, stylish cut.

"What are you so happy about?" LaKeisha asked.

"Same thing you are," Sherise responded in that smooth, soft voice she had. It was a tone that made women suspicious of her and men want to buy her a drink.

"It is exciting, isn't it?" LaKeisha asked. "We work well together."

That might not have always been the case. When LaKeisha first came to Sherise, it wasn't because the younger woman's name was mentioned in the power circles of D.C. communications. Despite having a husband who was an active and successful lobbyist, Sherise was having a hard time getting invites to the power events in D.C.

No, Sherise's name was on the tip of LaKeisha's tongue because Jennifer Ross had placed it there—the woman who was having an affair with Justin. Jennifer had been the wife of Ryan Hodgkins. Hodgkins was a man Sherise had slept with early in her marriage. It was suspected he might be the real father of Sherise's daughter, Cady. It was only one night, and both Ryan and Sherise cut all ties the day after, but Ryan eventually spilled the truth to Jennifer during their messy divorce.

Instead of finding Sherise and trying to beat her head into the ground, like most women would do, Jennifer decided to get back at Sherise by sleeping with her husband. With the way things were between Justin and Sherise at the time, he was ripe for the picking.

It was during this madness that LaKeisha approached Sherise. Despite taking her up on the offer to help out the Northman campaign, Sherise was more distracted than ever before. Her reputation for being immaculate in her work style took some blows, which LaKeisha was around to witness firsthand. Although she never found out the truth behind Sherise's momentary lapse of professionalism, there were times when LaKeisha doubted Sherise still had it.

Those doubts had been obliterated. Sherise had gotten Jennifer out of the way, via exposing her plan to Justin and ruining her reputation beyond repair in the *Washington Post*. After that, Sherise was able to focus once again on her job. LaKeisha, Northman, and the rest of the team had nothing but impressive words to say since then.

"You're taking too much credit for this," LaKeisha said with a sly smile.

Sherise laughed. "I didn't even say anything."

"You don't have to," she answered back. "That smug expression on your face looks like you just made the entire press say your name before sitting back and smoking a cigarette."

Sherise had done an amazing job. She was able to increase Northman's exposure and make him a national name. No one outside of Maryland had even known who he was in the beginning. Now, even the prime minister of England mentioned him to the British press when discussing the future of American politics.

More important to Sherise, her name was being mentioned in the press, as she was giving several quotes a week. Now that Northman was officially announcing, Sherise's life was going to go into hyperdrive. This is what she'd wanted forever. She had fought and clawed her way up the ladder—sometimes playing by the rules, but more often by not obeying them. Either way, Sherise was an "end justifies the means" type of girl. When the "end" was her gaining more power and influence, the "means" were a mere afterthought.

"Let's go," LaKeisha ordered the second that Northman ended the conference and headed behind the curtain.

As Ginger darted off to her eagerly waiting grandchildren, LaKeisha latched onto Northman to inform him of the interview he was to do next with *Washington Life,* an interview Sherise had set up for him. She noticed Northman glance in her direction. He smiled and she smiled back, with a thumbs-up, keeping a bit of a distance. LaKeisha was very possessive of him and Sherise had learned to wait a few minutes before showing up. Whenever Sherise did show up, she immediately got Northman's attention. He was no different than any other man. This always bothered his wife and sometimes bothered LaKeisha.

As her phone vibrated in the pocket of her navy

blue suit, Sherise shrugged her shoulders at the fact that women were always jealous of her beauty. She was going to use what she had, to get what she wanted, for as long as she had it. At least to an extent, she thought as she saw that the call was from her husband, Justin.

The end didn't always justify the means, she had to remind herself.

"Hello, baby," she said cheerily as she answered. "Did you watch it?"

"The TV is on in my office right now," Justin answered in that supportive tone he was so good at. "I saw you in the corner there. Looking good."

"As always," she said flirtatiously. He was in a good mood and that made her happy. "What's up?"

"Don't be angry," he said cautiously, "but I've got a late night at the office. You'll have to pick Cady up from day care."

Sherise's first instinct was to complain, but she bit her tongue. It wasn't fair, but she had to pick her battles. When their marriage was in a better place, its best place, Sherise could get whatever she wanted. Justin would bend over backward to accommodate her, to compromise for her. She was demanding and spoiled, and that was the way she liked it. That was the way it was supposed to be. She made Justin happy, and he gave her everything she wanted.

Things changed after her affair with Jonah Nolan. Almost getting caught, she realized what she could lose and focused on trying to make Justin happy. She lost herself and he lost interest in her, making it easy for him to stray. After he'd found out about Ryan and the possibility that Cady wasn't his, Justin wanted nothing to do with Sherise. At least for a while.

Sherise had spent a lifetime getting what she wanted. She always got what she wanted, no matter what she had to do to get it. She used every trick in the book and set aside her own pride to repair her marriage. It seemed as if Justin was trying hard too. They saw a marriage counselor once a week for a few months. They both needed to be forgiven, and they were both willing to do just that for Cady.

Sherise knew as soon as she'd gotten Justin back in her bed, he would be hers again. She could always distract him with sex and mold him in the way she wanted. Now that no one else was distracting him that way, he would be all hers again. She didn't expect it to take another four months before he'd move back home. However, what was important was that he was there and the three of them were a family again.

Sherise knew things were still raw between her and Justin. She felt immense guilt for not revealing her affair with Jonah to him. She just couldn't. With his affair with Jennifer exposing what she'd done with Ryan, Sherise could play both their mistakes as equal. If she revealed she'd had a second affair after that, Justin would have left her forever. She wouldn't let that happen. Cady was going to grow up with an intact family—a family with two loving, supportive parents. It was everything Sherise never had.

So Sherise bit her tongue. Justin was hers again, she knew that, but there was still that little voice in the back of her head that told her there was still work to be done. Too much had gone wrong.

"When do you think you'll be home?" Sherise asked in a sweet, loving voice.

"Can't say," he answered. "We have some new people on the team from our L.A. office, and . . . well, just don't wait up."

"I'll wait up," she said, "because I love you and can't go to sleep without you by my side."

This was true. After sleeping alone for a while, Sherise remembered how much she hated it.

"I love you too, baby."

Just then, Northman emerged from a crowd of people and made his way toward Sherise, with LaKeisha nipping at his heels.

"I have to go, baby," Sherise said quickly. "Northman is calling for me."

She hung up before he could say good-bye; she hoped he wasn't upset about that. She knew that Northman wasn't going to wait for her to finish her call—he never did. He'd just start talking; and if you missed, that was a problem for you. By the time he reached her, she had already shoved her phone into her pocket.

"That was great, don't you think?" he asked.

Jerry Northman was a tall, distinguished-looking man in his early fifties. True to his last name, his Nordic heritage was evident in his blond hair and blue eyes. He was a handsome man, and he looked as if he'd been on the lucky side of everything his whole life. His only visible flaw was an extra fifteen pounds, but Sherise had done a lot to conceal that with the new wardrobe she'd gotten him.

"You were great," Sherise said proudly. "They're lining up outside for interviews. Can I assume you want Fox News first again, or shall we go with NBC?"

"Whatever you suggest," he said, waving his hand. "They only get ten minutes. My family and I want to go out and celebrate."

"Of course," Sherise said.

"Go get the first reporter," LaKeisha ordered.

Just as Sherise turned to leave, Northman called after her. When she turned around, she saw a wide smile on his face. Not the usual political smile, but a real one—it was one that was rarely seen.

"Sherise, we'll be getting a lot more funding, now that I've officially declared." Northman reached out and placed a hand on her shoulder. "I think it's time you stop acting as a consultant and come on board full-time."

Sherise realized what he was asking and her eyes lit up with excitement. "Um . . . do you—"

"Yes," Northman said as if sensing what she was going to ask. "I want you to join our team formally as my communications chief. What do you say?"

Sherise noticed that LaKeisha wasn't at all happy at the sight of his hand still on her shoulder, but she ignored it.

"Well, I . . ."

"She's been wanting this forever," LaKeisha said. She stepped closer to the two of them, which forced Northman to remove his hand to make room for her. She looked at Sherise, seeming annoyed with her hesitation. "Haven't you?"

"Of course," Sherise answered, but things were different now.

She had to consider Justin. In the past, she did what she wanted and just convinced Justin—sometimes with a nice dinner or great sex—to go along. They had a new dynamic now.

"I'll have to discuss this with my husband," she said. "I assume this will require more of my time and hours."

"And travel," Northman said. "All of that. We're on

full go now. No stopping us on our way to the White House."

As he turned to leave, with LaKeisha rushing after him, it really hit Sherise what had just happened. Of course, she'd expected Northman to ask her to join the campaign formally. However, now that he had, it dawned on her. If he won, he would be the president of the United States, and she would be in the White House. That was the top. That was the height of everything. She would be one of the most powerful people in Washington, D.C.

Not bad for a girl from Southeast D.C. whom everyone expected to be another sad statistic.

"Are you gonna finish that?" Lane Redmond asked as he pointed across the table at Brasserie Beck on K Street in D.C.

Thirty-year-old Billie Carter laughed as she slid what was left of her croque-monsieur with French fries across the table to her friend and client.

"It's like law school all over again," she said. "You used to eat all my food then too."

Billie and Lane had met when they worked together on the *American Criminal Law Review* at Georgetown Law. She hadn't expected to have much in common with Lane at first. She was a poor African-American girl from southeastern D.C., who had to fight and scrap for everything she had. She had committed herself to fighting for the voiceless and powerless who were railroaded by a flawed criminal justice system.

On the other hand, Lane was a blond-haired, blue-eyed trust fund kid from private schools in New York, who wanted to follow in his rich daddy's footsteps defending the richest of the rich, who were "unjustly targeted by a flawed justice system."

Despite coming from, and intending to go into, two different worlds, they clicked instantly and had kept in touch since graduating.

"I was doing you a favor," Lane said. "I wanted to make sure you kept that perfect, little, petite figure. I see you have. I'll take some credit for that."

Billie had to laugh at that. Yes, she was still the petite, dark chocolate, beautiful woman she had been back in school. Her looks were defined by fine, feminine features, large, mesmerizing eyes, and short, curly hair. She didn't look much older than she had when she'd graduated either. She had aged immensely on the inside, though. Some of that, Lane knew about. Some of it, he didn't, and he wasn't going to.

It had been a rough year for Billie. After trying desperately to move on from her divorce with celebrated D.C. lawyer Porter Haas, whom she had also met in law school, Billie continued to find herself caught in his web. This was mostly because Porter, despite cheating on her with a blond bimbo from his law firm, refused to let her go. It was also because of Porter's teenaged daughter, Tara. Billie loved Tara and refused to cut her out of her life, despite the problems it caused with Porter.

Her ex enjoyed making her life miserable, manipulating situations and circumstances to keep himself in her life. He wasn't above using his daughter to keep it going. When he realized that he couldn't get Billie in his bed anymore, he turned on her and sent Tara away at a crucial moment in the girl's life. Porter had practically destroyed her relationship with the child she thought of as her own daughter.

Meanwhile, Billie compounded her messed-up personal life by placing her career, which was promising and successful, in the gutter as well. She'd been so excited last year when she'd gotten her first pro bono case through the prestigious big law firm that she worked at. It brought back her days of being a public defender just out of law school—days she had to leave behind for a job that paid the bills her divorce had left her.

Why did her first client have to be the seductive and handsome Ricky Williams? He'd flirted with her from day one—and she hadn't discouraged it as much as she should have. She knew it was an ethical disaster, but she assumed she had the willpower to resist the man who reminded her so much of the father she'd loved and lost. Not to mention the fact that she was passionate about defending him against the local housing authority, which was using its power to steal the property that he used as a shelter for immigrants, who were seeking asylum, in order to shut it down.

She'd won her case and Ricky was able to keep his shelter. In the meantime, she'd allowed her emotions to get the best of her and had slept with him. This was just before she found out that he was involved in local gang and drug activity. It was an ugly situation, only made uglier by her impropriety.

She had a chance to walk away from this clean, if she never told her bosses. She'd told her best friends, her girls, Sherise and Erica, of course. She told them everything. They had both encouraged her to thank God that she'd won the case and Ricky was on his way to jail. Although Billie couldn't reveal what she'd known about him, the district attorney's office was able to turn one of his drug mules against him.

With him out of the way, Billie would keep her mouth shut; and if Ricky said anything, she could always deny it. But that wasn't who Billie was. She couldn't keep lies and secrets. She knew what was right and what was wrong, and she needed to sleep at night. She was a lawyer who knew she had a moral, ethical, and legal obligation to tell her bosses. So she did.

She wasn't fired and she wasn't disbarred, but she was reprimanded. Her standing at the firm was never going to be the same. Once she'd come on, they had all thought Billie would be a partner there, but there was no chance of that now. Just going to work every day was painful for her—embarrassing. She'd lost respect and trust; and it was clear to her that it would take a very long time, if even that, to gain those back. So she did what she'd assumed her bosses had hoped she would do and quit.

It had been pretty difficult for her since then. She was taking on contract work and ad hoc public defense cases. Public defense cases paid about $1,200 each. The few bright spots were some old friends from law school whom she'd kept in touch with, like Lane, who hired her for high-paying jobs. She'd just completed an arbitration agreement for his financial services company, Agencis.

"I can look after my own figure," Billie said. "You wanna help me out, just hire me again. That sounds like a better deal."

"Well, you did great work," Lane said. "They signed

the agreement right away. Can't really calculate how much you'll save us if anything comes up and we can avoid court."

"It was easy," Billie said confidently. "I've been either fighting or enforcing arbitration agreements for quite a few years now."

"It shows." There was a short pause as he leaned back in his chair. He brushed his expensively tailored suit with his napkin before setting it down. "Just how much work do you have now, Billie?"

Never let them see you sweat. Billie knew that. She finished the sip of her lemonade and smiled. "I'm keeping busy, but I can take on more."

He leaned forward, looking into her eyes. "I think you're unhappy, Billie."

"You don't know me that well," Billie said, even though he was right. She'd had a rough six months . . . a rough year.

"Okay," he said. "Then you're probably too busy to accept the associate general counsel position we have open."

Billie lost her cool for a second as her eyes widened. She pulled herself together quickly, but it was too late. He'd caught her.

"Don't play games with me, Lane," she warned.

"I know you've been waiting for the dust to settle before looking for a permanent job," Lane said. "I think six months is long enough, don't you?"

Rumors had been swirling as to why she'd left her firm. Despite an endless amount of law firms in Washington, D.C., it was still a pretty small community— especially in white-collar criminal defense. She wasn't talking and, hopefully, her former employers hadn't talked. "Starve a rumor and eventually it will go away" was what Sherise had taught her and she'd listened.

"I don't know," Billie said. "Do your bosses know about this? Sorry to be blunt, but you're just an associate general counsel yourself, Lane. Do you have the power to make an offer?"

"That's fair," he said. "But, yes, I've discussed it with them. We need another person and they all like you. You've proven yourself. That means more to them than anything."

"Well," Billie said, trying her best to seem uncertain, "it's something I'd have to consider."

"Salary plus bonus potential could reach two hundred grand," Lane said matter-of-factly. "But, yeah, go ahead and take some time to consider it."

Billie rolled her eyes. She wasn't fooling him. He knew she needed the money and needed back in the game in a more permanent, stable basis to get her mojo back. Her life was out of whack. Although she was hopelessly unlucky in love, she could at least have her career back on track.

When twenty-seven-year-old Erica Kent walked into Oyamel, an expensive Mexican restaurant on Seventh Street, downtown D.C., she'd felt immediately out of place. She looked fine in her black boatneck tunic top and khaki pants, coupled with black pumps, but everyone there was dressed in designer suits. Everywhere she looked, she could see D.C. power and money, something this girl from Southeast D.C. was still not used to.

As she approached the hostess—a pretty black girl,

with a side ponytail and a smile that seemed frozen in place—Erica was about to give her name, but it clearly wasn't necessary.

"Hello, Ms. Kent," she said in what sounded like a Haitian accent. She quickly came around her stand to greet her. "You are Ms. Kent, right?"

"Um . . . yes." Not a trusting soul, Erica didn't like that this woman assumed she knew who she was, but she was sure it was only because she had been described to a tee so as to be rushed hurriedly out of view.

"Your party is waiting," she said. "Please follow me."

Her assumption was right. As she was rushed through the restaurant to a private corner booth, Erica knew exactly what this was about. The person in the booth waiting for her—her father—didn't want anyone seeing him having a private lunch with her. She found it hilarious, considering he'd been begging her to meet him for weeks now.

"Hello, Erica." Jonah Nolan leaned up from his seat on the other end of the booth as the hostess gestured for Erica to sit down.

Jonah Nolan, U.S. secretary of defense, was one of the most powerful men in the world. He was incredibly popular among D.C.'s power circle. He always looked the bit. He was a very attractive man in his fifties, with a powerful presence. He was tall, had a warm pink hue to his skin, and dark hair, which was graying at the temples. He had a firm jawline and thin lips, which made him look very serious all the time.

Erica sat down before responding. "Hi, Jonah. Nice and private, I see."

She could tell from his reaction he was tired of her saying things like that, but she didn't care. If he was intent on her being his little secret, she was going to make him suffer for it. He was lucky she even agreed to see him.

Erica hadn't wanted much to do with Jonah, ever since finding out almost two years ago that he was her father. He'd been a rich, privileged kid who had volunteered at the same hospital where Erica's mother was a nurse. They'd had a brief summer romance, which Erica's mother never told her about, and it wasn't more than a fling to Jonah. Jonah left for the military and never looked back. Her mother had never told him she was pregnant, so Erica had spent the first twenty-five years of her life believing her real father was the same deadbeat no-gooder as younger brother Nate's.

It was chance that Jonah found out about her. He was assistant secretary of defense and his office at the Pentagon, where Erica worked, was looking for a new assistant to his administrative manager. Erica's middle name was Achelle, which was her mother's first name. That, plus the same last name as her mother's, piqued his interest.

He'd realized she was his daughter; but by then, Jonah was a powerful man with a political future, a blue-blooded socialite wife, and two kids. He was rumored to be on the path to the White House. A biracial love child was not a good look.

But, according to Jonah, he wanted his daughter near. He had Erica hired, but immediately she knew something was wrong. He was too nice to her, too involved in her life, especially too disapproving of her boyfriend of several years, Terrell Nicolli. Curious as to why Jonah was so eager to have him out of her life, Erica did some investigating and found out that Jonah was her father. Prior to this discovery, Erica had already found out Jonah was having an affair with her friend Sherise. She'd lost respect for him and was devastated to find out the ultimate truth.

She also found him to be a ruthless, calculating man—a person who did whatever he wanted. Anyone who crossed him paid a serious price. Erica hated him for it, but she couldn't ignore that she was curious to find out about him. All her life she had dreamed of having a relationship with her father, but she never imagined this.

"This secrecy is to avoid rumors of an affair," he said. "You're an attractive young woman and I'm a very public man."

"With a reputation as a ladies' man," she added. "Well earned."

"Let's not pretend I'm the only one here who would like to keep our relationship on the down low," Jonah said.

"Down low?" Erica laughed as she spread her napkin on her lap. "What is that—an attempt to sound street so you can connect with me?"

"Isn't that the right phrase?" he asked.

Erica shook her head. "Hasn't been for a while now."

The waiter approached their table with shrimp, chicken, and pork *tortas* plates. He began laying it down on the table.

"I took the liberty of ordering for us," Jonah said. "Speeds things up."

"Of course," Erica said as the plates were placed in front of her. "What does it matter what I want?"

"Not fair," he said sternly. "Much of this has been

on your terms. We agreed that you would let me be a part of your life."

Erica made a deal with the Devil—that Devil being her own father—a little over six months ago. She'd found out that Terrell, the man whom she loved and tried to work with on a fractured relationship, had returned to his hustler ways. Even though she'd ended their engagement, Erica worked hard to forgive him a year ago when he tried to blackmail Jonah over his affair with Sherise. She loved him and wanted a future with him.

That was before she'd found out that he had been acting as a mule for drug dealers. That was enough to make her cut him out of her life for good. But the fact that he'd also involved her younger brother, Nate, with these crooks was the last straw. Nate was using and selling for a little extra cash on the side. She would never, ever forgive Terrell for that. He'd broken her heart for the last time.

Desperate to save a quickly spiraling Nate, Erica went to the only person she knew who had the power to protect him. That was Jonah. He came through, making sure that Nate was kept out of trouble as the police came down on the dealer and those involved. He also helped Nate get into rehab. This was all in exchange for Erica agreeing to let him be a part of her life.

"You aren't holding up your end of the bargain," Jonah said.

"You make it hard to," she responded.

No, she hadn't been as open to him as she'd promised. To be honest, she was somewhat afraid of him. He'd shown her how far-reaching his power could go and how effortlessly he wielded it. There was a part of her that knew the closer she let him get, the more he could hurt her if she ever crossed him.

"You can't expect me to forget all the things you've done," she added. "You threatened Sherise and Terrell. You've—"

"That's old news," he said dismissively. "Besides, none of that matters now. I am glad you're here. It's been almost a month since we've seen each other. How are things going for you?"

She knew what he was asking. In addition to letting Jonah be a part of her life, his help was also conditioned on the promise that she never let Terrell in her life again. It wasn't necessary. After what he'd done to Nate, Erica wanted nothing to do with Terrell.

"No," she answered. "I'm not seeing Terrell. Why don't you just ask me what you want to know? I haven't seen him in almost four months."

"He's not begging and pleading for your forgiveness anymore?"

"He gave that up," she said.

She was glad when he did. Jonah had done her a favor and spared Terrell from jail. There was a part of her that hated him, but the part that had once loved him—the part that once expected to marry Terrell—didn't want him going to prison.

"Are you seeing someone?" he asked.

Erica stopped just before placing a fork filled with food in her mouth. With a sarcastic tone, she said, "I would tell you, but I'm sure you know already. You know everything that's going on in my life, even though I've told you to stay out of it."

He smiled as if he appreciated her boldness. "You're my daughter. I'm going to look out for you, whether you want me to or not."

"Fine," she said, "just don't ask questions you already know the answer to."

"I think," he offered, ignoring her tone, "you need to get out of a funk. I know a couple of choice young men that you could meet and—"

"Really?" she asked. "We've already had this discussion, Jonah. No and no. The answer is always 'no' to you setting me up with anyone."

He sighed, showing rare frustration. "You need to elevate your standards. The young man you went out with last week isn't much different than Terrell."

"Are you having me followed?"

"You like the thuggish type, don't you?"

She rolled her eyes. There was probably a hint of truth to that. She didn't like thugs, but she liked the kind of guys that are from around the block. She wasn't interested in the polished perfection that Sherise and Billie went for. Erica liked boys who reminded her of the good things about where she came from, but she didn't want anything to do with the bad things about where she came from.

"That was my first date in six months," she said. "I'm rusty."

The truth was, she hadn't had much of an appetite for dating since breaking up with Terrell. She hadn't imagined a future without him and wasn't looking forward to giving another guy a try. She wasn't trusting by nature, and relationships were scary. She had agreed to go out on a date with the son of a new coworker, mostly just to get her coworker off her back. The date was a disaster.

"Besides," Erica said, smiling, "how would Juliet feel if she knew you were trying to set me up with someone from your social set? Does she even know you're having lunch with me?"

"Yes, she does." He glared at her, making it clear he didn't care for her playful tone. "Juliet isn't happy about all of this, but she's dealing with it."

Erica had only met Juliet Nolan a few times, but each time the woman had nothing but disdain for her and had treated her coldly. Erica knew that she was a chink in that smooth plan that Juliet had to become first lady of the United States.

"I'm trying to encourage her to get to know you better." Jonah reached into his pocket to get his ringing phone. "I think you would like each other."

"I doubt that," Erica said.

Erica returned to eating and watched as Jonah's face darkened and looked bewildered. This was such an uncommon look for a man who was always confident and so assured. Whatever it was he was hearing on the other end of that line had shaken him.

Just then, Erica realized that she was hearing more phones ring, more than usual at the same time. Something was up. This was Washington, D.C., and that usually meant a really great thing, or, more likely, a really bad thing.

Jonah placed the phone down on the table and looked off into the distance.

"What is it?" Erica asked eagerly. "What's going on?"

Jonah looked around the restaurant and gestured for someone to come over to him. Erica peeked around the booth and noticed one of the two men walking toward them as Jonah's security detail.

"I have to go," Jonah said slowly. "Don't worry. This is on my account. I have to go."

"Jonah, what happened?" she asked as he started to slide out of the booth.

"It's the vice president," he answered. "He's had a serious heart attack. It's not looking good."

Just then, both men reached Jonah and swiftly led him away from the booth.

Erica stayed where she was, listening to all the buzzing around her. Chairs squeaked against the floor as more people left their seats. She sat back in her booth, looking at her plate, her appetite completely gone.

2

Sherise was in the middle of her conversation about the newest restaurant in the West End that she wanted to try when she realized she was talking too much and too fast. Justin had been sitting across from her at their eat-in kitchen table. He had that barely awake, early-morning look on his face. Suddenly his dark eyes started getting smaller. He'd noticed just before she did.

She stopped talking and turned her attention to Cady, her two-year-old baby seated in the high chair next to her. Sherise tried to take her fork to feed her some of her scrambled eggs, but Cady was stubborn and squeezed tight. She was determined to feed herself, even though 90 percent of her food ended anywhere except for her mouth.

"Let Mommy help you," Sherise pleaded, "if you actually want to eat something."

"No," Cady said, stubbornly clutching her tiny little fork to her chest.

"What's going on?" Justin asked.

Sherise laughed. "She'll die from starvation if I leave it up to her."

"I'm not talking about Cady," Justin said in a stern voice.

Sherise turned to him and could tell from the look on his face that he wasn't interested in any games. The smooth, dark brown skin of his sturdy, handsome face highlighted the lightness of his brown eyes as he stared at her. He'd given up the glasses he'd worn since he was twelve and was now wearing contacts. In his thirties now, he'd also recently lost those last ten extra pounds he'd been holding on to his entire adulthood.

Sherise loved the new Justin. He was already a good-looking man, but the changes to his six-foot-tall frame made him even more handsome and distinguished.

"So do you want to go?" Sherise asked. "To the new place? I could probably get reservations even at this late date."

Justin placed his fork down and leaned back in his chair. This impatience with her was just another sign of how things had changed. Sherise used to be able to string Justin along all she wanted, at least until she could distract him from what he wanted to know.

Sherise sighed, knowing that she had to come out with it. With Vice President Ben Shaplin hospitalized for a heart attack, the last two days had been crazy for both of them. Sherise had used that as an excuse not to tell him about her job offer. But how bad could it be? It wasn't as if it wasn't expected.

"We agreed, no more surprises," Justin said. "We don't do well with surprises."

"Depends on the type of surprise," Sherise added. Was she really joking about this? That was progress, wasn't it? "Okay," she conceded. "I wanted to tell you, but with Northman's formal announcement and Shaplin in the hospital, things have been crazy."

"I know," Justin agreed. "I'm sure things will be okay."

"They could be better than okay," Sherise said.

Justin frowned. "You aren't actually suggesting this is a good thing for you? The man almost died, Sherise."

"No, of course not." She was angry he'd think she'd be that cold. Yes, she was willing to win at any cost, but even she had lines she didn't cross. "This isn't so much related to Shaplin."

"What is it then?"

"Northman has offered me the chief communications job."

There, she'd said it. It sounded so wonderful! How could anything bad come from this? Of course the look on Justin's face told her how.

"Formally," she added. "No more consulting from my home office and sending them a bill. It's a formal title, a real job. He's going to the White House and he wants me to be his voice."

Justin managed a half smile as he nodded, as if he just now understood. He swallowed hard and looked down at the bagel on his plate.

"This isn't a surprise," Sherise said. "I'm excellent at what I do. There was no way he'd want someone else."

"You are great." He looked up at her and smiled proudly. "But it's not true that it isn't a surprise. This was a consulting gig, and it had been from the beginning. You're already spending almost thirty hours a week on him."

"And now it's going to be much more than that," Sherise said. "I'll be working full-time again and traveling."

Justin sighed. "Since you said, 'it's going to be,' I take it you aren't interested in my opinion."

"Of course I am," she answered. "I told him I would talk to you first. But, Justin, you can't expect me to turn this down. It's the White House."

"You seem more confident than the polling."

It was true that in a poll of possible contenders, Northman was trailing well behind incumbent president, Mark Matthews, but Shaplin's heart attack was going to change everything.

"At least more confident than you are in me," Sherise said. "Justin, we've discussed this in therapy. Part of the reason our marriage fell apart, and you ended up in Jennifer's bed, was because the spark had gone out. I'm not happy as a housewife, and you aren't happy if I'm not."

Justin sat up sharply, his face contorting in anger. "Is that your plan? You bring up Jennifer so I feel guilty and agree to whatever you want?"

Sherise was shocked. "What? No, I just . . . I'm just trying to explain how—"

"That is so you, Sherise." Justin shook his head. "I might not give you permission to do something, so you try to guilt me."

"'Permission,'" Sherise responded loudly. "I wasn't asking *permission*. I'm not your daughter. I have just as much a right to a career as you do."

"What about Cady?" he asked. "What does she have a right to?"

Sherise looked down at her daughter, who was trying to eat some scrambled eggs she had gathered in her tiny palm.

"She has a right to a happy mother," she answered

angrily. "She'll have to go back to day care full-time. It's not ideal, but she'll be fine. And thank you for making me feel like a bad mother."

Justin's eyes blinked, showing a hint of guilt before looking away. "I don't think you're a bad mother."

"Yes, you do," she said quickly.

Sherise watched him as she wondered what was going on in his mind. She used to be able to read him so well, predict his every move.

"I was being a bad mother by making the horrible mistakes I made."

"Don't," he ordered. "We agreed to stop bringing up the past."

"We did," she acknowledged, "but it manages to find its way into every argument we have."

"I know you're a good mother," he said. "And no matter what has happened, you've never *not* loved Cady."

"I've never not loved *you,*" Sherise said.

It was the truth. Despite Ryan and Jonah, Sherise never stopped loving Justin. She didn't appreciate him, but she loved him. She loved him more now, since she'd almost lost him.

"Do you think I stopped loving you?" Justin asked. "I never have, Sherise. Even when I was angriest, I still loved you."

Sherise felt the tug at her heart as she quickly rose from her seat and came across the table to him. He looked up at her as she sat in his lap and wrapped her arms around him.

"We almost lost everything," she whispered to him.

"We did lose some things," he answered back sadly.

"But we're getting trust back," she said. "We'll be

okay. You remember what Dr. Gray said. We can't be happy together, if we aren't happy on our own."

"I know." He was shaking his head as if he was already regretting what he was about to say. "You're happiest when you're trying to conquer the world."

She ran her hand over his head lovingly. "And when I'm happy—"

"Everyone is happy." He smiled, looking up at her.

She leaned down and kissed him. Her soft lips pressed against his. He kissed her back, and their lips molded together. She loved the familiarity of this, more now than ever.

When their mouths separated, he leaned away and shook his head. "How can I resist that?"

"You can't," she insisted. "And I can't resist the chance to take Northman to the White House."

"So, since that decision is made," he said with a resigned tone, "let's talk about what we're doing this weekend. This new restaurant sounds—"

Just then, Sherise's phone, which was on the table next to her chair, began ringing the tone of "The Battle Hymn of the Republic," a tone reserved for Jerry Northman. She was stunned at first. Northman rarely called her directly from his phone.

After a short hesitation, she jumped up from Justin's lap and rushed to the phone. Justin's expression changed from annoyance at being interrupted to curiosity as he saw the expression of extremes on Sherise's face as she spoke to the governor. She said good-bye and slowly lowered the phone back to the table.

"I take it our weekend is canceled," Justin said.

"Vice President Shaplin died two hours ago," she said, still amazed to hear the words come out of her mouth. "The vice president is . . . dead."

* * *

Billie hopped on the Metro train at the last minute, just as the doors closed behind her, almost crushing her. She had to chance it.

Having gotten caught up in the morning news reporting the vice president's death, she was already running late for a court date. She was defending a young man accused of robbing a carton of milk from a local convenience store. Considering he was caught on tape, walking out of the store with the milk, she had her work cut out for her and wanted to present the best defense she could. That would be hard if she showed up late. The last thing this eighteen-year-old defendant needed was to believe his lawyer didn't bother to get up early enough in the morning for him.

"Careful there."

She looked up to see the words had come from a man standing near the door, less than two feet away from her. She noticed right away that he was very attractive. He was around six feet tall, with smooth cocoa- or cinnamon-colored skin and deep black eyes. He had thick eyebrows and full, dark lips. He was wearing an expensive black suit, tailored perfectly enough to let you know that he was very fit.

She smiled nervously and giggled a little bit, feeling like an idiot for doing so. He smiled back.

He looked around the very packed train car they were in before turning back to Billie. "Sorry that none of these guys is offering you a seat. If I was sitting down, I'd offer mine."

She detected a slight Southern twang, making him even more attractive.

"That's okay," she offered. "I don't really expect that kind of thing anymore."

He frowned. "You should."

Before she could brace herself, the train came to a quick stop in the middle of the tunnel. Billie was holding on to the rail, but the force of the stop forced her tiny body to fall forward . . . right into the Southern gentleman.

He grabbed her with his hands to stop her from falling. His grip was firm and tight, but not too rough. Her arms were bare and she immediately felt the heat from his hands against her skin. Her free hand went to his chest, over his shirt, to help her stay upright, but she quickly removed it when she felt his muscles underneath.

The train started again immediately.

"I'm so . . . I'm sorry." She was so embarrassed as she leaned away from him.

"It's okay." He laughed, seeming not at all bothered. "I've learned that these trains stop whenever they want."

"Thank you." She smiled.

His smile was pretty addictive and hard to look away from, but she already felt like a clumsy idiot after coming across like a giggling schoolgirl. The last thing she needed was to creep out some guy on the Metro, so she looked away.

Although she basically had turned her back to him, she felt like he was still looking at her. It made her uncomfortable. Considering her recent track record, she had no luck with men and wasn't really interested in another disaster at this point in her life. But she couldn't ignore how attractive he was and that she was sure she felt a little something when his hand took hold of her arm.

The train came to a more reasonable stop this time at the next station, her station, and although Billie had

never been reluctant to get off the train during morning
rush hour before, she was today.

She was tempted to look back and get one last look
just before the door opened, but she thought better of
it. This was just a random train encounter. One could
have many over a lifetime of taking the train in D.C. It
didn't mean anything, so she did nothing, said nothing,
as she stepped off the train and headed for the escalator.

"You're late" were the first words that Erica heard
the second she showed up in her department.

She was only a few feet from her desk, so she ignored the voice and kept walking. It didn't matter. She
knew whom the voice belonged to and that it wouldn't
go away.

Caroline Billings was the head administrator of the
communications division within the U.S. Defense Department. She was Erica's most recent boss at the Pentagon in Arlington, Virginia, and she was by far her
worst.

Erica had been working at the Pentagon since she was
eighteen years old. Unlike Sherise and Billie, she couldn't
afford to go to college. When Erica was a teenager, her
mother died and Erica had to figure out how to provide for
herself and her twelve-year-old brother, Nate. She had
been in various administrative roles since.

After learning that Jonah was her father and that
he'd slept with Sherise, and went on to threaten her and
Terrell if they'd told his secret, Erica quit her job in his
department. Jonah refused to accept her resignation
and instead had her transferred to the communications
department. Considering Terrell had moved out of their

shared apartment after she ended their engagement and Nate was away at rehab, bills that were being shared three ways were now all on her. She couldn't afford to be out of work, so she accepted the new job.

Everything was fine at first, but just one month into the job, her boss quit and moved to Alabama. In came Caroline Billings, a Pentagon veteran of almost thirty years. She immediately clashed with Erica. For the last several months, Caroline made Erica dread coming to a job that she used to like. If the job market hadn't been as tight as it was at the moment, she would have quit already.

It wasn't that Caroline was just a mean boss. She was way too nosy for her own good, in Erica's opinion. She wanted to know everything about Erica and how she'd gotten such a plum position in the communications department and why her stint with Jonah's office was so short.

Erica was evasive and nonresponsive in general. Caroline told her she would find out what the real deal was, whether Erica told her or not. This was a mistake. Erica wasn't sure what happened, but she imagined that Caroline's snooping reached Jonah's office and she was shut down immediately.

For someone like Caroline, who thought she was more powerful than she actually was, this was frustrating and humiliating beyond words. So while she stopped inquiring about Erica's past at the Pentagon, she decided she would get her revenge by making her miserable.

"Nice of you to join us," Caroline said as she reached Erica's desk.

Caroline's appearance fit her personality. She looked gaunt and angry, with dark circles around her beady eyes and her salt-and-pepper hair in a severe bun. She wore clothes two sizes too big for her excessively thin frame and walked around with a constant frown on her face.

Erica sat down and placed her purse in the drawer. "I'm ten minutes late, Caroline. I couldn't get in. There was some tour group or something blocking the entrance and—"

"Excuses, excuses," Caroline said. "You're going to have to stay fifteen minutes late to make it up."

"I know" was all Erica said.

Caroline eyed her for a second as if she was begging for Erica to offer some sort of protest so she could exert her authority and just be an overall bitch. She seemed very disappointed when it was clear that Erica wasn't going to play into it.

It wasn't that she wasn't tempted. Erica thought of saying something sarcastic, because she knew Caroline couldn't do anything about it. So many times she'd wished that she could tell her who she was and who her father was and put her in her place. She wanted Caroline to try and fire her and see what happened when she couldn't. She sensed that Caroline knew that she could only push her so far, but she sure made a practice of doing just that: pushing Erica as far as she could every day.

Erica wasn't proud of this little fantasy she had, even though the woman clearly deserved it. She had promised herself that she would never take advantage of Jonah's status as her father. There was just something about this woman that annoyed her so much that she was tempted to go back on that promise.

But wouldn't that make her just like Jonah? He used his power to hurt others who crossed him and manipulate their lives to his pleasure. Was this who she would turn into if she let him be a part of her life?

Billie and Erica both thanked the waiter after he brought them their drinks. They had gotten a prime table in the bar area, just at the window, so they could watch the Capitol Hill crowd that gathered at the many restaurants in the area after work.

This area was the part of Southeast D.C. that people loved. It was just off the Eastern Market Metro stop, blocks from the Capitol, and was vibrant. The neighborhoods were nicer here, unlike only a few blocks away in Southeast, which no one liked to talk about. That was the part that Billie, Erica, and Sherise had come from.

Their neighborhood had been rough and full of blight. Nothing good was supposed to come from where they grew up, all three girls living on the same street. Despite the slight differences in their ages, they all made quick friends and formed a bond based on their mutual desire to be better than everyone expected them to be. Despite the challenges they faced—and there were many—they relied on each other to stay strong, stay focused, and make it in life. They had formed a bond stronger than sisters; and although they clashed often, some of them more than others, their love was unbreakable and always reliable.

"Where is this bitch at?" Erica leaned against the window, trying to look as far down the street as she could.

"Sherise is always late, lately." Billie took a sip of her cherry martini. "I'm just glad it's someone other than me. I used to always be the late one."

"I'm the one that came from Virginia," Erica said. "If I can make it on time, so can she."

"She's been all over the place lately," Billie said. "Her world is crazy right now. Besides, you know she's trying to focus more on Justin."

Erica nodded. "I guess that's 'better late than never.' "

Billie looked at her sternly. "You need to check your attitude."

"I'm happy for her," Erica asserted.

It was true that she and Sherise had been at odds more than usual in the past year and a half. They were both opposites in a lot of ways—Sherise was always reaching for high-society status, while Erica tried to keep it as real as possible. Sherise's disdain for Terrell, whom she'd always referred to as a "hood," didn't help either.

"Despite everything," Erica continued, "you know I want her to keep her family together. Cady deserves to have her daddy around. Every little girl does."

"It may not be a perfect situation," Billie said, "but at least she is getting her shit together."

"Do you remember six months ago, we were at this very place, having drinks, and we agreed that our lives were a mess?" Erica asked. "We gave ourselves six months, Billie. We said we would all get our shit together in six months."

Billie started counting with her fingers, doubting that Erica had it right. "Has it really been six months?"

Erica nodded. "It looks like Sherise is the only one who has even come close. She's got a great job offer and her husband is back home."

"I doubt she'd say she's securely back on track," Billie argued. "But she sure as hell is ahead of me. At least personally."

"You and me both," Erica added. "Being single sucks ass."

The girls clinked their glasses in agreement just as Sherise showed up at the table.

"I'm sorry," she said, exasperated, as she took a seat between the girls. "I swear I got here as soon as I could."

"What's going on?" Billie asked, noticing how frazzled the usually perfect-looking Sherise was.

"Things are crazy!" Sherise emphasized her words with her expression of exhaustion. "I need a drink, now!"

"Finish this." Billie shoved her martini at her. "I'll get a waiter."

Sherise took a sip and felt herself start to calm down. "You guys don't even know what's going on."

"Well, we kind of know," Erica said.

She pointed to one of three big-screen televisions behind the bar. The reporter was discussing the death of the vice president. It was all anyone, everywhere, ever talked about now. It was shocking and scary. The nation was officially in mourning and funeral plans were in full swing with leaders from all over the world coming to D.C.

"I'd put together a pretty detailed press campaign against Shaplin," Sherise said. "He was honestly more popular than the president. Now that he's going to get replaced, I have to start over again."

"That's horrible," Erica said sarcastically. "Why did he have to go and die and cause you more paper-work? How rude of him."

"Shut up." Sherise shot her a warning glance. "I don't need any of your shit tonight. I know this is about more than me. I'm just dealing with what I can."

"Well, you're at an advantage, aren't you?" Billie asked.

"How is starting from scratch an advantage?" Sherise finished what little was left of Billie's drink.

"President Matthews's biggest weakness is defense and foreign relations," Erica said. "Shaplin was the guy who made up for all of that. Matthews looks much weaker without him."

Sherise's eyes widened as she looked at her, not sure of how to respond.

Erica was offended. "Yes, I do know about politics. I pay attention. Don't be so surprised."

Billie laughed. "I have to say, I'm honestly surprised too. You never show an interest in politics."

"I can't help it now, can I?" Erica asked. "Our vice president is dead. I mean, I know he wasn't killed or anything, but he's dead and it's pretty shocking. I've been paying attention to the news a lot lately, trying to find out what it means for our country."

"Is that your precious daddy rubbing off on you?" Sherise asked, with a look of disgust on her face.

"Speaking of Jonah rubbing someone," Erica started, knowing it would piss off Sherise.

"I will cut you right now," Sherise said, only half kidding. Any reminder of her affair with Jonah made her sick to her stomach. In fact, she was suddenly not feeling too good.

"Girls," Billie, always the mediator, stepped in. "We didn't come here to fight. We came to catch up."

"On what?" Erica asked. "My love life sucks. My job sucks. My life sucks. I just came here to drink and feel sorry for myself."

"Well, I actually have some good news," Billie offered. "I've got a job."

"Where?" Sherise asked, half paying attention to her and half watching the television screen.

"At Agencis." Billie placed her phone, which had the company's website showing on it, in the middle of the table. "I told you about them. Lane works there. They really liked the work I did for them and they wanted me to join as an associate general counsel."

"Congrats," Sherise said. "Now you can leave all those scrubs and degenerates to lawyers who need the money."

Billie rolled her eyes at Sherise being Sherise. "I'm never going to stop helping people who can't afford me. There's no point in being a lawyer otherwise, in my opinion."

"I admire that," Erica said. "I assume you're getting paid. I know those bills were piling up."

Billie nodded. "Honestly, it was getting rough. I can't believe I let things get as bad as I did."

"You're lucky," Erica said. "Your career is about to kick back into gear. Wish I could say the same. I hate my job so much."

"Why don't you quit?" Billie asked. "If you asked Jonah, he could get you a job in any department at the Pentagon. He's running that place. Honestly, Erica, you could probably get a much higher-paying job, even outside of the Pentagon."

"By using my connection to him?" Erica asked. "I thought you both hated him."

"Doesn't matter," Billie said. "You can't let your relationship with him depend on us. He could open up a lot of doors for you."

"With how many strings attached to each one of them?" Erica asked. "Besides, I'm afraid the closer I get to him, the more I'll become like him. Doesn't that seem likely? What do you guys think?"

"We'd never let that happen," Billie said. "Would we, Sherise?"

They both turned to Sherise, who wasn't paying either of them any attention. She was looking at the television screen, which was showing the U.S. Senate voting on President Matthews's nomination to replace the vice president. It was House Majority Leader Leonard McGarry. The House had already voted, by majority, to elect him vice president. With this vote in the Senate, it would be a done deal. The country would have a new vice president.

"Sherise!" Billie yelled at her.

She swung around. "What? What did I miss?"

"Erica needs our advice," she urged.

"Never mind," Erica said. "She hates Jonah more than anyone. She can't be objective."

Sherise's expression went grim. "Fuck Jonah Nolan. Fuck everything about him."

She saw Erica's mouth open and pointed directly at her. "Say one word!"

Erica quickly shut her mouth, but she let a smile escape as she looked at Billie, who just shook her head.

"You're both ridiculous," Billie said.

"I don't like this choice," Sherise said. "McGarry."

"He's harmless," Billie said.

"He has no interest in national politics," Sherise indicated. "He's only serving for the rest of this term. He's not going to be on the ticket for the second term and it's an election year. We need to know who we're fighting."

"You're not fighting anyone right now," Billie said. "We're united under our president right now."

"Yes, but it's all a waiting game." Sherise's tone expressed extreme agitation as she glanced down at the phone in her hand. "I hate waiting. It's a position lacking power."

It was someone else's job to find out who the most likely candidates would be, people with stronger connections than her own. She scrolled her e-mails and saw no new updates. She needed to call and check in.

"I have to make a call," Sherise said as she slid back her chair. "It's too noisy in here."

As she stood up, Sherise felt a sudden rush to her head and the room started to spin. She grabbed the edge of the table as she felt the phone drop out of her hand. She heard one of the girls—she couldn't tell which—say her name before everything went black.

3

"Justin!" Billie yelled his name the second she saw him enter the hallway at George Washington University Hospital. When she got his attention, she waved him over.

Justin rushed over to her like lightning. She could see the look of pure anguish on his face as he reached her.

"Where is she?" he demanded. "Where is she?"

"Calm down." Billie placed her hand on his arm to try and calm him, but he jerked away.

Things were weird concerning Justin and the girls. From his end, he knew they learned about Sherise's affair with Ryan and the possibility that Cady might not be his daughter before he did. He knew that they would have never told him, as long as Sherise asked them not to.

From their end, both girls still knew about Sherise's affair with Jonah. They knew they could never tell Justin, although there was a part of them that believed he deserved to know. It all made for awkward interactions; but right now, all anyone was thinking about was Sherise.

"Where is she?" he repeated.

Billie pointed to the room just a few feet away, where Erica was standing, trying to see through the small window in the door.

Erica jumped aside just in time as he reached the door and swung it open. She snuck a quick peek and noticed Sherise was awake and sitting up in the hospital bed with the doctor standing beside her. That was a good sign, wasn't it? When the door closed, Erica turned to Billie and gave her a thumbs-up sign.

At the bar, it was Billie who first noticed something was wrong as soon as Sherise stood up. She stumbled back quickly and the phone fell out of her hand. Billie looked at her and noticed she looked confused. Billie called her name and reached out to her just as Sherise began to fall.

Erica screamed and jumped to catch her, getting her just before her head hit the floor. Erica fell flat on her butt, with Sherise in her arms. Everyone around them became alarmed. Billie screamed for someone to call 911 as she got on her knees and tried to wake Sherise up. She was out like a light; Erica started to panic.

"Someone help!" Erica called out. "Is anyone a doctor?"

The ambulance was there in less than ten minutes. Neither Erica nor Billie was allowed to ride with her. They were angry, but relieved that it seemed as if Sherise was moving her head as the doors to the ambulance closed.

It wasn't until then, when a waitress ran up to Billie to hand her Sherise's phone, which had been left behind, that Billie thought of Justin. She called him right away. By the time she got off the phone, Erica had hailed a cab and they were on their way.

Once at the hospital, they were not allowed to see Sherise at all. They were only told to get family there. Justin arrived a few minutes after they had.

A very tense Sherise calmed immediately the second she saw Justin rushing toward her. He reached down and hugged her tightly, kissing her on the lips.

"I'm fine, baby," she reassured him.

She could see the love in his eyes and it warmed her heart. He and Cady were all she could think about since coming to in the ambulance.

"What's wrong?" he asked as she rubbed his cheek to comfort him.

"I'm sure it's just exhaustion," she answered, turning to the doctor.

Dr. Deepa Gupta was standing by the bed. She was a young doctor, with a very smart, serious look on her face.

"Everything seems fine," she said slowly as she read over the paper in front of her. "We'll have to wait for the blood tests to come back."

"Did you not eat or something?" Justin asked.

She shook her head. "I had a sandwich for lunch. I had less than half of one drink at the bar, but that's it."

"Wait a second." Dr. Gupta looked at Sherise. "You told the nurse your last period was the middle of last month."

Sherise nodded. "Yes, I think it was . . . I think maybe the fifteenth."

"Well," Dr. Gupta said, smiling, "it's the twenty-ninth."

"What does that . . ." Justin stopped midsentence as he seemed to grasp what the doctor was suggesting.

Sherise's stomach clenched and she gasped. She looked at Justin, who looked like a deer caught in the headlights. He started shaking his head as if not believing, and she did the same, turning back to the doctor.

"That's not possible," she said. "I'm on the Pill, every morning at eight."

"You mentioned that you've been under a lot of stress," Dr. Gupta said. "You've been running all over the place. Trust me, busy schedules are the leading cause of pregnancies among working mothers. You don't think you forgot, but you probably have."

The doctor laughed, but she stopped as soon as she realized that neither Sherise nor Justin joined her.

"Well," she offered, her voice returning to a more professional tone, "we don't know anything yet. The blood test will be checking for pregnancy and I'll have a nurse bring an at-home test down so you can do some preliminary testing of your own."

She waited a moment, but after not getting a response from the dumbfounded couple, she continued. "I'll just leave you both alone for a little while."

After the doctor left, Sherise and Justin just looked at other.

"Do you really think?" she asked.

He shrugged. "I'm sure it's not, though."

"But . . . what if it is?" she asked.

Justin leaned up from the bed and looked straight ahead.

Sherise watched his reaction and wondered what was going on in that mind of his. Over a year ago, they had been trying so hard to have a second child, but it wasn't working. While Sherise wanted to spend a couple more years focusing on her career, Justin seemed adamant that they continue growing their young family.

After the disaster with Jonah Nolan, Sherise refocused herself on her family and did everything she could to get pregnant. It just wasn't happening. It scared Sherise to death because it fed into her worst fear: Cady, who had been conceived around the same time she'd had a one-night stand with Ryan Hodgkins, might not be Justin's. She was afraid they would find out that Justin was shooting blanks and then everything would fall apart. Finding out Cady was, in fact, his solved so many problems.

But there were a million problems left; and while they worked on their marital issues, they agreed to put having another baby on hold. Well, actually Justin suggested putting the baby making on hold. Sherise had thought it would be a great way to regain the closeness they once had, but Justin wanted to focus on other things. So she went back on the Pill.

"Justin?" Sherise reached out and placed her hand on his chest, looking up at him.

He looked down at her and sighed heavily. "It's . . . It's probably not that."

He didn't answer her question, and that was a problem. The man who had been hell-bent on having another baby with her looked scared to death of that prospect now. What did that mean about how he felt about her, about their marriage? Were things worse than she'd thought?

Lane Redmond arrived in the lobby of Agencis with an excited look on his face. He retrieved Billie from an attentive receptionist and led her to the elevators.

Once inside, he said, "I'm excited that you're here. We really need the help."

She laughed. "You sound like I'm starting today.

I'm just here to sign my employment papers. I won't be starting for another week."

"I know," he assented. "It just feels official, now that you're here. The workload has been brutal. I feel like I'm a big law associate logging all these hours."

"Well, hold on for another week," she said. "I'll come and save the day then."

"This will be quick." Lane stepped out of the elevator on their floor. "It'll take less than twenty minutes to go through all this stuff."

Billie followed him down the hallway. "I've brought copies of my passport and everything else you wanted. Do I need to talk to anyone?"

Lane looked at her for a moment and cleared his throat. "Okay, this is the thing."

"Oh no." Billie didn't like the sound of that.

"You don't have to interview with anyone," he said. "Everyone down here is in human resources and they know you've already been working for us because they process your consulting fees."

"But—"

"Michael Johnson," Lane said. "He's not employed here. He works for himself. He's our headhunter on retainer. He usually finds all our people and he's very close to the CEO. He's been working for us since we formed almost ten years ago."

"Let me guess," Billie said, pulling from her experience working with headhunters in the past. "He doesn't like that you went around him to hire me."

"Not at all." Lane laughed sarcastically. "He was pretty pissed, actually. In addition to the retainer, he gets a nice fee for every hire we make that he sends our way."

"You have to keep these guys under control," Billie

suggested. "They'll start thinking they're running the show. You're the client. They don't get to throw a hissy fit because you found someone good."

"Easier said than done," Lane muttered quietly. "Michael is buddies with the most powerful people in this company. He gets his way."

"Why are you telling me about him?" Billie asked.

Lane stopped just as they reached a conference room door. "Well, he wanted to meet you. I think he'd like to believe you're subpar, because he thinks if you were any good, he would have found you. Just say hello. You don't have to answer any questions. Just don't be intimidated."

"I won't be." Billie was determined to give this Michael Johnson a fit if she could. "I can handle headhunters. Let's go."

When Lane opened the door to the conference room, the first thing Billie saw was a woman sitting at the large table in the middle, with several sheets of paper laid out in short stacks. The woman was on the phone. It wasn't until she turned her attention to the left, where there was a man standing at the floor-to-ceiling windows, did she have to catch her breath.

It couldn't be.

She blinked, wondering if she was seeing things. She had actually thought about the man she'd encountered on the train last week a few times since then. But this wasn't her imagination. This was real life and he was standing at the window, looking at her with just as much surprise as she was.

"Billie Carter," Lane said, walking over to Michael, "this is Michael Johnson, our headhunter. He was eager to meet you."

Lane stopped midway as he realized that Billie

hadn't moved from where she was standing. She forced herself to recover from her shock and pull herself together. She took a deep breath and headed over toward him.

Michael took a few steps to meet her halfway. By this time, the look on his face, clearly caught off guard, was composed and unreadable. He held his hand out to her.

"So you're Billie Carter," he said, no hint of that Southern twang from before.

"And you're Michael Johnson." She took his hand and gripped it as firmly as she could.

His hands were warm and strong. Fortunately for her, the shake was quick and done in a second.

"Um . . ." Lane looked from one to the other. "Am I missing something here?"

"Mr. Johnson and I ran into each other on the Metro a while ago," Billie informed him.

"So you remember that?" Michael asked. "It was a very brief moment you seemed eager to get away from."

Billie found that to be an unexpected reaction. Was that how it seemed?

"Well, it was my stop," she said.

He nodded. "Of course."

"I hear you wanted to meet me to prove to the company how much of a mistake they made in hiring me."

"Well . . ." Lane wasn't sure how to recover from that. "I wouldn't say that. . . ."

Michael smiled wryly. "I wouldn't say that is exactly what Lane is trying to say."

"Wouldn't you?" she asked.

Michael lifted his head just enough to seem haughty as he crossed his arms over his chest. "Well, I'm sure you're a good lawyer, but I know for a fact that I had several excellent candidates for this position—the tops in their field."

"But I'm here and they're not." She smiled, making sure her tone was playful so as not to seem too bitchy.

"I guess the best person isn't always the right person," he said as his dark eyes bore into hers.

"Or," Billie offered, "maybe the best person doesn't need help from a recruiter to get the right job."

She knew she'd hit a nerve. That confident smile flattened a bit, just a bit.

"I don't think anyone here would question the process I have," he said. "You'll see that the turnover at this company, at most of the companies that I work with, is directly related to people *not* hired through me."

"So you're already predicting a quick end to my tenure here?" Billie's tone couldn't hide that this offended her.

His left hand went to his hip as stared at her intently. "I'm just saying that my candidates at this company have always been the most successful long-term and others haven't."

"Well, I'll just have to prove you wrong, Mr. Johnson." Billie smiled just sweetly enough to make it seem fake. "It's been so nice to meet you."

"Same here," he offered flatly before turning and walking away.

Billie watched as he walked out of the conference room, not bothering to look back. She felt herself breathe a little now that he was gone.

It was too bad. She had imagined running into him a few times since first seeing him. In her mind, though, it would have gone very differently. He would be so excited to see her again that he'd ask for her number. She would give it to him and discover that she'd met her dream man.

Oh, well, she thought. That fantasy was shattered now. There was a 0 percent chance of it turning out that way, anyway. Considering her luck with men, one might consider that encounter successful. She didn't intend on ever seeing Michael Johnson again, and it was probably for the best.

Sherise wasn't quick enough. She was trying to get rid of all of the signs of her work before Justin reached the bedroom. Either she had miscalculated or he had run, instead of walked, up the stairs of their town house. The latter would seem strange, considering he hadn't seemed to be in a rush to get home to her this past week since the doctor's office confirmed that she was indeed pregnant.

"What are you doing?" he asked as soon as he entered the bedroom and saw what was going on.

"I'm just trying to tidy up," she said nervously. "This place is a mess."

There were papers strewn across their king-sized bed and she was trying to put them together and get them back in their respective folders.

"You've been working?" he asked.

He approached the bed, placing his briefcase on it. His frustration was evident on his face. "For Christ's sake, Sherise. You're supposed to be resting for another week. What's the matter with you?"

Those were the doctor's orders, but Sherise wasn't trying to hear it. There was nothing wrong with her. It was just first-trimester light-headedness and her stressful schedule. A visit to her ob-gyn prescribed two weeks of bed rest. Sherise tried to explain to her that she had just accepted a position on a presidential campaign and needed to work. Justin sided with the doctor; and although she was touched by his concern for her, since he'd seemed very distant the previous few days, Sherise's career was foremost on her mind.

"Don't start with me, Justin." She finally got the papers out of the way. "I've only been drafting some statements and doing opposition research right here from the bed, in my pajamas."

Justin grumbled. "Didn't you tell them that you need no stress for the next week?"

"Work doesn't stress me out," Sherise said. "I thrive on it, and you know that. What does stress me out is starting a new, extremely important job on the wrong foot. Trust me, baby, working is much less stressful."

When Sherise told the campaign heads that she was unexpectedly pregnant, it was clear that they were disappointed. It was too late to rescind the offer, but she could tell that at least LaKeisha was wishing she could. After a short, surprised pause, Northman congratulated her and told her everything would be great. He was good at faking it, so Sherise wasn't sure if he meant it or not. All she could do was promise to keep working, just from bed. She would have to Skype into their meetings and use her surrogates to fill in for her.

"Sherise, I'm not taking any shit from you on this." Undoing his tie, Justin walked over to the dresser against the wall and began pulling things out of his pockets and placing them on top of it. "I'll take your phone and your laptop away if I have to."

"Don't be ridiculous."

"Damn it!" He slammed his fist on top of the dresser.

Sherise gasped, startled at his reaction. When he turned to her, she could see there was real anger in his eyes. It was definitely about more than her working from bed. She couldn't let this go on any longer.

"We need to talk about this." She patted the bed, gesturing for him to join her.

Justin stayed where he stood. "There's nothing to talk about. You're supposed to be resting, and that's all there is—"

"Not me," she responded. "You've been terribly concerned about me, and I love you for that. You keep saying what *I* need to do for myself and what *I* need to be careful about. You won't mention this baby at all. You don't want to talk about it."

"There's nothing to talk about," he retorted. "You're pregnant. That's that."

"*We're* pregnant," she corrected. "And you're acting as if a blessing is a punishment."

"That's not true," he said. "I'm happy. I am. I just need time to adjust."

"So do I," Sherise argued, "but we should do that together. This is just as unexpected for me as it is for you."

"Look," he said, holding up a hand to stop her. "This isn't . . . I don't want to do this right now."

"Then when?" she asked.

"Right now, we need to just focus on you staying calm, safe, and healthy."

He turned and headed for the bathroom. She called after him just as he reached the door. He reluctantly turned back to her.

"I'm fine," she insisted. "I want to talk about us, about our family."

"Our family is fine," he assured her, although the

expression on his face was more of annoyance than anything. "Just take it easy, Sherise. I don't want anything happening to you."

As he walked into the bathroom, closing the door behind him, Sherise felt like crying. She wasn't sure if it was hormones or the ridiculousness of what just happened. Maybe she was pushing too much. They hadn't been expecting this child, so it was a surprise. She was having a hard time adjusting to the idea of another baby too. After Justin had shot down the idea, she'd let it go. After all, it wasn't as if she didn't have her hands full working on their marriage, caring for Cady, and doing her job. Another baby could wait.

Now that she found out she was pregnant, she was concerned about the effect on her career, but mostly she was happy. Knowing her own boundless love for Cady, she warmed at the idea of having another baby to love the same. It made her more hopeful for her marriage, for her family.

Things were back on track, weren't they? With a second baby, they'd have to make things work. Why couldn't Justin see that? Or was it that Justin did see that and wasn't sure about it? This baby was going to be a blessing for them. Sherise would make sure that it was.

Just as Erica was about to reach Jonah's office at the Pentagon, the door opened. Out stepped an olive-skinned young man, with a smile on his face that went from ear to ear. He was tall and attractive, with an athletic build, dressed in preppy college-boy clothing.

Erica wasn't sure what to do. His smile made her feel awkward, as if she was supposed to recognize him.

"Hi," he finally said, holding out his hand. His eyes were light brown and his hair was dark and cut conservatively short. "Are you Erica?"

"Yes, I am. How did you . . ." Erica realized that she'd left him hanging and quickly reached out to shake his hand. "I'm sorry. Hello."

His shake was firm and quick. Erica appreciated that. She hated long, drawn-out handshakes with strangers. Although, truth be told, this young man didn't seem like much of a stranger.

"You know who I am," she said kindly, "but who are you?"

"I'm Alex," he answered. "Alex Gonzales. I just know your name because Mr. No . . . I mean, Jonah said he was meeting with you next."

Erica nodded. "It was an unexpected call. Seemed urgent. Do you know what he wants?"

She hadn't intended on coming to his office, but he'd called her three times already that day. The last time he'd called, she was almost on her way out, so she agreed to stop by very quickly. He'd only get five minutes she warned, especially since he refused to tell her what he wanted to talk about.

Alex's smile widened, if that was even possible. It was contagious, making Erica smile as well. She could tell he was a very likeable person. He looked around her age as well, maybe a little younger. It was odd for her, since she usually did not warm to people right away, but she liked him immediately.

"I can't tell you," he said sheepishly. "He'd kill me. What I can tell you is that you and I will be seeing more of each other, and I look forward to it."

Erica's jaw tightened in anger. The nerve of that man!

"Look, Alex." Her tone was becoming extremely serious. "I don't know what Jonah told you, but I'm not looking to be set up with anyone. I'm not really dating right now, so I don't think you will be seeing—"

"What?" He leaned away, his face racked with confusion. "I wasn't talking about that. Jonah didn't say anything about me dating you. Why would Jonah Nolan be setting you up with guys, anyway? How well do you really know him?"

Erica realized she'd just made two huge mistakes. One, assuming that this was a setup by Jonah; and two, revealing their unusual relationship to a stranger.

"Look, I . . ." She stepped around him quickly and headed for the door. "I'm sorry, I didn't mean anything. I'm just playing. I'm joking around. Just ignore me. I have to go. . . . See you around!"

She knocked rapidly on Jonah's office door, not waiting for permission to enter. She escaped into his office and quickly shut the door behind her. She was embarrassed beyond words, hoping to God she would never run into him again.

Jonah, who was on his phone, frowned at the rudeness of letting herself in. She knew she must have looked embarrassed and he wouldn't have any reason to understand why. Whatever the case, he waved her toward his desk as he hurriedly finished his phone conversation.

Erica sat down in one of the plush leather chairs on the opposite side of the massive desk in his office, trying to recover from her humiliation. Was Alex now suspicious of her relationship with Jonah? Would he ask more questions? Would he jump to conclusions? Was Jonah going to be mad at her? Should she even tell him? Who the hell was Alex, anyway?

"Hi, Erica," Jonah finally said after putting the phone down. "I'm glad you finally agreed—"

"Who is Alex?" she asked, too anxious to realize she was being rude.

Jonah looked confused.

She pointed to the door. "Alex Gonzales."

"Oh, Alex," he said, nodding. "You met him? Good. Do you like him?"

"Who is he?"

"I'll get to that later." He waved his hand as if the matter was unimportant. "I wanted to know if Caroline was still giving you a hard time."

"Well, I . . ." Erica leaned back in her chair, not sure what to say. She imagined the less said to Jonah, the better. "Why are you asking? I've never complained to you about her."

"I know she's had it out for you," Jonah said. "She's tried to write you up before, and I've put a stop to it. She's tried to find out why you left my office, and she was slapped down. We've discussed this before, Erica. I want to make sure she's still not giving you a hard time."

"She's a horrible boss," Erica said. "But if you're asking is she asking me questions about you—no, she isn't."

Jonah looked away, his expression doubtful. "I think she may still be sticking her nose where it doesn't belong."

"A government administrator has you spooked?" she asked. "I find that hard to believe."

Jonah Nolan was not one to be worried about much. He'd made it more than clear in the past that people who had gone up against him had suffered the consequences. Sometimes those consequences were severe, but they were never traceable to him. He was extremely confident and excessively connected. He made the things that he wanted happen, and he prevented things he didn't want from happening.

Jonah sighed as if annoyed by the entire thing. "I'll just have her fired. That will be easy. Strip her of all her clearances. That should do it."

"Wait." Erica shot forward in her seat. "Are you serious? You would do that?"

"I don't like these annoyances."

"She's not an annoyance, Jonah. She's a person. She has two teenaged daughters and a mortgage or . . . whatever."

"So now you care about her?" Jonah seemed confused.

"No, I don't care about her." Erica wasn't sure how to talk to this man. This seemed so easy to him. It shouldn't be. "I don't like her, but I don't want her to lose her livelihood."

"She makes you miserable," Jonah said.

"I never told you that."

"I know what goes on everywhere in this building," he said. "She's a nosy bitch. That's a fact."

Erica couldn't deny that. "It's not right, Jonah. Does that matter at all? That it's not right?"

"Of course it does." He hesitated as if trying to find some explanation, but eventually gave up. "Fine, you don't want me to fire her, I won't."

"Good." Erica grabbed the arms of the chair, ready to lift herself up. "If that's all, then I—"

"I have another solution," he said.

Erica moaned, slumping back into her seat.

"That's enough of that," he warned.

"I'm listening," she said.

"You come work for me," he said.

"Been there, done that," she responded. "Not happening."

"Not here," Jonah said. "My campaign. I want you to come join me on my campaign."

"For what?"

"Vice president." Jonah smiled proudly in response to Erica's stunned face. "There are some things to take care of first, but President Matthews will be announcing next week that I'll be his running mate for the upcoming election."

Erica wasn't sure how long she was speechless, but Jonah waited patiently for her to find the words.

"What about . . . What's his name, again?"

"McGarry has already said that he will only serve out the rest of this term because of his respect for the president and his lifelong friendship with Shaplin. He will not be on the ticket."

Erica shrugged as she said, "Um . . . congratulations?"

"This is a great thing," he said. "If we win . . . When we win, I'll be poised for the presidency four years from now."

"I thought you . . . I mean, what about your privacy?" she asked.

"I'll protect everything that needs to be protected."

"What about Sherise and—"

"No one will ever know about that," he said forcefully. "No one will ever know anything I don't want them to. I'm not stupid, Erica. I didn't get this far by just hoping things worked out."

"What does that mean?" she asked, feeling an ominous tone.

"Speaking of Sherise," he said, ignoring her question, "you can't tell her. Do you understand? I know you're still close to her, but until this announcement is made, no one can know."

This was the last thing Erica wanted to tell Sherise. She would be livid. She would feel exposed. No matter what Jonah said, if he ran, the press would turn over every stone. They'd be looking to find any skeletons in his closet. Sherise was pregnant and her marriage was still in a sensitive state. She could lose everything.

"I don't know if this is such good news," Erica said, noticing his disappointment. "I'm sorry, but that's my opinion. It exposes me, you know."

"I won't let anything happen to you," Jonah said. "No one will know about you. I've hired people to make sure that no one looks into anything that could lead to you . . . to us."

"Why would you want me to come work with you?" she asked. "Wouldn't that just increase the risk, us being close like that?"

Jonah smiled and his usually stern face softened considerably. "You've worked for me before, so it won't seem weird that I've brought you on. Other former staffers of mine will be offered the chance to join me. I will pay you just as much as I pay others doing the same job, so no red flags. I won't treat you differently. It will be fine."

"But—"

"Most important," he said, "this is the most amazing thing. I have a chance to be vice president of the United States. I want you near me."

Erica couldn't help but feel touched by the sincere tone in his voice and the compassionate look on his face. He could be so convincing, but she had to remember who he was, what he'd done, and what he could do.

"Alex," she said. "He's working on your campaign? That's why he said he'd be seeing me."

"Yes. Alex is an amazing legislative aide on the Hill and he's going to be your boss. You'll like him. He's a great kid."

"You're assuming that I'm coming to work for you," she said. "But, Jonah, I just don't think that's a good idea."

He didn't hide his disappointment. "It's an exciting opportunity to be part of something incredible—something that people dream about. It will open endless doors for you and it pays well. You would be stupid not to take it."

"Insults aren't really a motivator," she said in a sarcastically observant tone.

"You shouldn't need motivation, Erica," Jonah stated. "This is something on a national scale. Hell, it's a global scale. You're meant for greater things than making copies of press releases. It's time you start realizing it."

4

Being the wife of one of the most important people at Justin's firm had its benefits. Sherise didn't have to go through all the hoops that most people did in the highly secured building. The security guard Alvin was basically in love with her. All she had to do was smile and she was let in the elevator that went to the twelfth floor, the top of the building.

She bypassed the receptionist, a new one she didn't know and who was easily intimidated by her refusal to "check in" before going ahead. Down the hall, to the left, was the corner office belonging to her husband who was a principal on the lobbying side of one of the largest law firms in the country.

She'd been prepared to bypass his administrative assistant, Candy, as well, but she wasn't there. All the better for the element of surprise. Sherise wanted to catch Justin off guard so he couldn't dismiss her so easily. She wanted to talk to him, needed to talk to him.

However, she was the one caught off guard when she entered the office and saw Justin sitting at his desk, with a beautiful young woman leaning over him from behind. Both of them looked up immediately as she entered. Sherise tried to hide how much this scene irked her. Who in the hell was this woman?

She was a strikingly beautiful woman, who looked to be in her midtwenties. She had a classical type of beauty, and she looked to be of Italian or Spanish descent, with warm olive skin, dark hair, and large brown eyes. She was on the thin side, but she had enough curves to make her the kind of woman you wouldn't want to find hanging over your husband's shoulders, with her cleavage in full view.

"Sherise." Justin said her name as if he had just remembered it that second. "What are . . . Um, what are you doing here?"

"Nice to see you too," she answered, closing the door behind her.

She approached the desk as the young woman stood up. At least she no longer had her breasts all up in her husband's face.

"You're supposed to be in bed." Justin quickly got up from his chair and came around his desk.

He opened his arms to her and she hugged him. She reached up, grabbing his face gently, and brought it down to her. She kissed him passionately and he hugged her a little tighter. It was important to set the stage.

"We'll talk about that later," she said as they finally separated.

Sherise knew how to deal with her husband's attractive coworkers. She took the ignore approach. They were unimportant. She would never make them think they even mattered, let alone were a threat. So, after the initial moment of seeing them together, Sherise kept her attention completely on her husband, who seemed, at the least, confused to see her.

"I came to take you to lunch," Sherise said. "And don't protest, because I called Candy this morning and she told me your lunch was free."

"Well, that was before," he said. "I have a working lunch now."

Sherise wasn't about to be turned down by her husband in front of this woman. She gently caressed her husband's cheek. "We've worked around working lunches before."

He smiled at her and this made her confident. Justin used to be so weak to even the most simple of her flirtations, but that had gotten lost in the mix of their madness. She knew he still wanted her, so she made sure to look amazing before coming over here to make it harder on him if he considered resisting.

They hadn't talked since the brief argument they'd had the other night; she wasn't going to let things lie like that.

The woman, still standing behind Justin's desk, made a sound clearing her throat. Sherise smiled at Justin, but she still paid her no mind. It was Justin who, having forgotten about her (to Sherise's delight), remembered there was another person in the room. He swung around.

"Oh, Elena, I'm sorry."

"It's okay," she said, smiling. She came around the desk, preparing for her introduction.

"Honey, this is Elena Nichols, one of our new associates."

Elena laughed flirtatiously. "I'm not that new, Justin."

Sherise didn't like the way that woman said her husband's name. Way too familiar for her taste.

"Basically off the boat from Cleveland," Justin said jokingly. "Just kidding. She's been here a few months, right?"

Sherise thought the girl had a little more polish than she expected from the Midwest. She was trying to impress someone. Better not be her husband.

"Six almost," Elena corrected.

Justin slipped his arm around Sherise's waist. "Elena, this is my wife, Sherise."

"It's nice to meet you," Elena said with a sweet voice as she held out her petite hand.

"Yes." Sherise kept her expression unaffected as she accepted her hand and shook it briefly—very briefly.

She could tell that Elena didn't really appreciate the fact that it seemed as if Sherise couldn't be bothered.

Sherise turned and headed to the plush leather sofa against the wall. "Justin, I'm not leaving until you give me what I want, so let's make this as short and painless as possible."

Justin smiled down at her as she sat on the sofa and winked at him. He turned to Elena and asked, "We'll pick this up later, okay?"

Elena looked annoyed for a second, but she smiled and excused herself from the room. She didn't say another word to Sherise, and Sherise understood that. She'd made the girl feel invisible; and for a beautiful girl like Elena, that was upsetting.

"You need to be in bed," he said as he joined her on the sofa.

"So she works for you?" Sherise asked, placing her hands gently on his lap.

Justin rolled his eyes as if he knew what was coming. "Don't try and control this situation. Yes, she works under me. Yes, she is attractive. No, she doesn't flirt with me. You should be nicer to her. She's a bright young woman."

"She doesn't flirt with you?" Sherise responded. "When I walked in, she had her breasts in your face and you weren't protesting at all."

"You need to go home and get in bed," he said, ignoring her complaints. "We can discuss Elena at a different time."

"I don't want to discuss her anymore, Justin. I want to discuss this baby."

He sighed, looking away. It bothered her that he was so reluctant.

"We can't leave things like they were the other night," she pleaded. "If anything, therapy has taught us that. We have to deal with our problems immediately. Letting them fester is what tears us apart."

"I told you I need time," he said.

"And I told you, we both do, but we need to take that time together. Neither of us expected this, and—"

"Is that really the truth?" he asked.

He blinked, his expression showing that he immediately regretted what he had said.

It took Sherise a second, but his words, coupled with the look on his face, made it clear to her what he was thinking. It was clear why he was behaving so strangely. The truth horrified her.

"Oh, my God!" she exclaimed. "You think . . . I did this on purpose? You think I got pregnant on purpose!"

"Sherise, just let it go." He held up his hand to gesture that he wanted this to end. "I didn't say that, so just don't get all upset."

It tore at her that he'd think she'd be so underhanded. There was a lot she would do, but even she knew some things went too far.

"Why would I do that, Justin? I'm focused on my new job. We agreed that we weren't going to try at having another baby until later."

He sighed as if resigned to this conversation. "You aren't sure you tried to speed that timeline along?"

"Why?" she asked. "To trap you? To make sure you feel obligated? Have I ever seemed that desperate to you, Justin?"

"I know you'd do anything to get what you want," he said.

"I thought I had what I wanted." She stared at him, feeling very shaken by this turn. "I thought things were working out so great between us."

"So how did this baby get here?" he asked.

"It was an accident!" she yelled.

"How do we get pregnant by accident?" he asked. "We tried for six months and nothing, but you're on the Pill and, all of a sudden—*bam*—baby is here."

"We weren't trying when I got pregnant with Cady," Sherise argued. "This is just like that time. When we don't try, it happens."

He shrugged and got up from the sofa, walking over to his desk. "I don't want to talk about this."

Sherise followed right behind him. "I don't give a shit what you want, Justin. This is our baby. We're talking about this. You can't just—"

"Isn't that the point?" he asked, turning to look at her. "You don't give a shit about what I want. You never have. I said I wanted a baby and you miraculously couldn't get pregnant. I say I don't want a baby and now you're pregnant."

"So now this is all me?" she asked. "Not just this time, but since the beginning?"

"You were the one who said that another baby would be good, remember?"

"Yes," she agreed forcefully, "and then you said that you didn't want that, so I went back on the pill."

Sherise couldn't believe this was happening. The one time she didn't try something underhanded, this is what she got accused of.

"You're stressing yourself out unnecessarily," he said. "We can deal with this later, when you're better."

"Don't you get it?" Sherise asked. "The only way the stress will go away is if we work this out, Justin. Delaying it only makes it worse."

"I have to work, Sherise!" Standing behind it, he pushed his chair toward his desk. "And you need to go."

"Of course," she said sarcastically. "Fuck your wife and your new baby. Must make those billable hours with your new, slutty associate."

"Now you're just being ridiculous," he said.

"I must be," she said. "It's the only excuse for me thinking that we were doing great. I would have no reason to get pregnant to trap you. Clearly, I was wrong, because we're in a lot more trouble than I thought. But, by all means, you have to keep your priorities straight."

She ignored his calling her name, satisfied that his voice seemed weighed down in regret. Her stomach was tied in knots and she felt like she wanted to cry. This was all made worse by what she saw the second she left his office.

Elena had been standing right outside the office all along. She met Sherise's stare with a blank smile, one that told nothing but everything. How much had she heard? Sherise had been so upset that she'd forgotten where she was. She wasn't so sure how loud either of them had been.

"What are you doing out here?" Sherise asked, even though she would have been better off acting as if she didn't care.

"I'm waiting for Candy to come back," Elena said innocently. "You wouldn't happen to know where she is?"

"You work here," Sherise said. "Not me."

Sherise brushed past her quickly, dismissing the coyness of Elena's attitude. She didn't have time to worry about little peons right now.

Where had she been living, in a wonderland? She knew things weren't perfect, but she couldn't have even thought they were so bad that Justin would accuse her of this. She had to figure out a way to fix this, but she couldn't do it alone. Justin wasn't going to help her out. Sherise needed her girls to shed some light on this situation. The future of her family depended on it.

Billie's first day at work started early and fast. She went straight to her new office, which had a nice wooden desk already beginning to get covered in folders. The bookcases on the wall had several law books in it, and there was even an empty frame, sitting on the spare chair against the wall, waiting for her diploma.

The paralegal named Evelyn, a twenty-two-year-old cute redhead with freckles, kept her busy until around nine in the morning, when Lane showed up to take over. Billie had been happy to see him; but the second he walked into her office, he looked a little stressed to be there.

"What's wrong?" she asked, right off.

"Um . . . nothing." He tried to play it off. "By the way, love the way you handled Michael last week. Usually, people don't talk to him like that."

"You guys talk to him a lot?" she asked. "He doesn't work here."

Billie had gone over that conversation more than once in her head. Part of her was proud of how she handled herself, but she was regretting that she might have been a bit of a bitch. She'd let herself get defensive. It didn't feel great to have someone doubt your skills before you've even started a job.

"For someone who doesn't work here," Lane said, "he sure as hell is here a lot."

That wasn't what she wanted to hear. She figured it would be best if she never ran into him again. It would likely be just as awkward as the last time.

"But enough about him," Lane said. "Check your e-mail. I've sent you a copy of the Federal Trade Commission subpoena we received."

"I was reading it when you walked in."

The Federal Trade Commission, FTC for short, was the government agency that oversaw consumer products and competitive business practices. One of the issues it oversaw were vertical restraints, agreements that businesses made with each other, in order to make sure they didn't stifle competition.

In the case of Agencis, as a financial commercial buyer, an agreement made with a supplier, a financial software company, was being investigated after some competitors said it gave Agencis an unfair business advantage and excluded them from like software.

"The powers that be want you on it," Lane said. "You've done a lot of vertical work, right?"

Billie nodded grudgingly. "That's pretty much all I did at my last firm. I think my first act would be to call my contacts at the FTC and get this deadline extended."

"Gil already tried," Lane said. "Didn't work."

Gil Anderson was general counsel at Agencis. He was a powerful, influential guy. If he couldn't use his influence on the FTC, she had little hope of doing so. The timeline was very tight to work with, so she would give it a try. It was possible that she had a way of going about it that Gil didn't know.

"What firm are we hiring?" she asked.

"Well, your old firm is the best in the business," Lane said.

Billie knew that was coming. Her old firm—the one where she ruined her career—was, in fact, the best at this kind of law. However, that would be very awkward.

"They are the best," she agreed. "Do you want me to call them?"

Lane laughed. "Are you kidding? I think that would be awkward for you. For all of us."

Billie sighed, happy she wasn't the one to bring it up. "Not to mention that they probably wouldn't do it. I didn't leave on the best terms with them, so I doubt they'd want to take orders from me."

"Don't sweat it," Lane said. "Gil is working on finding another firm. He knows what he's doing."

"Wow!" Billie didn't hide how impressed she was. "That's actually amazingly cool of him not to want me to be in a complicated position."

"Don't think too much of it," Lane said. "That was just one consideration. Gil likes to get the job done. If he thought your firm was the only one to do it, he'll just tell you to suck it up. I don't think he likes some of the partners at your firm. He mentioned something about hating them since being classmates at Harvard Law."

"So, who is he considering?" Billie asked.

"Well, that's what I came to tell—"

Before Lane could finish his sentence, there was a knock on the door. It was Evelyn returning, but this time with a bouquet of flowers in her hands.

"These are for you," she said in an excited voice as she laid them down on the desk.

The flowers were a beautiful mix of stark blue and white orchids.

"Here you go." Evelyn handed Billie the card, before turning to Lane. "Gil wants to see you now. He's been looking for you."

"In a second," Lane answered.

"Fine," she said, "but he seemed pissed."

Lane groaned, as if he'd already dealt with a pissed-off Gil that day. "I hate Mondays. Glad you're here, though. We'll talk later?"

"Sure." Billie waved good-bye.

Evelyn followed him out of the office and closed the door behind her, but Billie didn't think a closed door was a good look on a first day.

Before she got up to open it again, she opened the card. She was admittedly nervous. The last time she'd gotten a bouquet of flowers on her first day of work, they were from her ex-husband, Porter. It was just another passive-aggressive way of him letting her know he knew all about her life and he wasn't going anywhere.

But the flowers weren't from Porter. She didn't know if this was much better, but she still smiled when she read it: *Hope I get a third chance to make a first impression—Michael Johnson.*

Erica had just taken her purse out of her desk drawer and was ready to lock everything up when Caroline sauntered out of her office and over to her desk. From the satisfied look on Caroline's face, Erica knew the older woman was about to give her some shit. Erica wasn't in the mood; she had something very important to get to.

"What are you doing?" Caroline asked.

"It's five." Erica pointed to the clock on the wall. "I'm going home."

"Not today," Caroline said. "We've got to prepare for the Bring Your Child to Work event. We've got a lot of work to do."

"I'll do it tomorrow," Erica said, standing up.

"You'll do it when I say," Caroline corrected, placing a skeletal hand on her hip. "I've been approved for overtime all week, so it's really my say."

Erica wasn't about to get into it with this lady. How could she possibly have known that today, of all days, Erica couldn't work late?

"Sorry, Caroline," she said as politely as she could. "But my brother is coming in on the train tonight from New York. He's been gone for a long time and I'm picking him up."

"Last I checked," Caroline interjected, "your brother was an adult."

"Last time you checked?" Erica asked. "What the hell does that mean?"

"Watch your tone with me," Caroline warned,

pointing a finger at Erica. "I'm your boss. I can write you up."

Erica took a deep breath, trying to stay calm. "Caroline, I can stay late the rest of the week, but not today."

Today was too important. After Nate got involved with drugs last year, Erica, with Jonah's help, was able to get him into the best rehab facility in the country. Unfortunately, that was in New York. After getting out, Nate had decided to stay with some friends he'd met in rehab. Erica wasn't happy about it, but she needed a break from the difficult year they'd had. She knew that Nate wasn't her baby brother anymore; he could do what he wanted.

Eventually he tired of New York and announced that he wanted to come home. A friend of his who ran an electronics store in the Friendship Heights neighborhood offered him a job when he got back, much to Erica's delight. She was excited to have her brother, her only real family, back. And even though he'd already told her that his goal was to get his own place, he was moving back in with her for the time being. Things could be like they used to be. Well . . . almost.

"Your brother is a grown man," Caroline said, with a stone expression on her face. "He can catch a cab. We'll be here till nine, probably."

Erica gasped as Caroline turned and started to walk away. Her blood began to boil over at this woman's audacity. She'd had enough.

"I'm going to pick up my brother," she stated in a very certain tone. "I'll be in at nine tomorrow and will work late then."

Caroline swung around, her face turning as red as

wine. "How dare you? I told you that you have to stay. Do you want to keep your job?"

Now it was Erica's turn to laugh. Her laughing only incensed Caroline more.

"That's funny to you?" Caroline asked. "You're in for it now. I'm writing you up. And if you walk out of here, you shouldn't bother coming back."

"Do you really expect me to believe you can fire me?" Erica asked. "Your poker face is awful, Caroline. I'm done playing along."

"How dare you speak to me like that? I'm your boss!"

"I know what you've been up to," Erica said. "You've been trying to get dirt on me to get rid of me. I never did one thing to you, but you've had it in for me ever since you showed up here."

Caroline's mouth was agape. "What are you afraid I'll find out, Erica?"

"Nothing," she said, "but I know what you've found out so far. You've found out that your power is bullshit here. You got your hand slapped for trying to screw me over and poke your nose where it doesn't belong. But you didn't think I knew, so you kept up this façade of having power over me."

Caroline's mouth flew open as if she wanted to say something, but it wouldn't come out. She was clearly livid; Erica loved it.

"The truth is," Erica continued, "you need to be thanking me. Because while you keep talking shit about getting me fired, I'm actually the one with the power here. If I wanted, I could snap my fingers and you'd be out of a job."

"I have seniority here," Caroline sneered between grinding teeth, her nose jutted in the air. "I have tenure. I've been here forever. People like me never get fired."

"You're still just administration," Erica said. "You're still replaceable. The people who keep slapping you down will do whatever I want, when I want. You think you're powerful, Caroline? You have no idea what real power is. If you don't stop fucking with me, you're going to find out."

Caroline stumbled back a bit as if she'd had the wind knocked out of her. She looked as if she was a minute away from having a heart attack.

"I'm going to pick my brother up from the train and we're going out to dinner." Erica leaned in, looking into Caroline's astonished eyes. "And that's the end of it."

Caroline started vehemently shaking her head. Enraged, she yelled out, "No, it—it isn't! I—I . . . This is not the last of it. You just . . . You just wait, Erica!"

With that, she turned and stormed off to her office, slamming the door behind her.

Erica sighed, realizing just then how tense her body was. She took a deep breath as what had just happened settled into her. She'd lost her temper and let it loose. What had she just done? In her mind, she quickly reheard everything she'd said. She gasped at how revealing it was. She knew she'd done something really wrong when she ended up feeling sorry for Caroline.

How could she be so mean? How could she so easily flaunt an influence she was supposed to be ashamed of and wanted nothing to do with? Who was Erica turning into?

* * *

"Sherise." Billie used the most calming voice she could manage over the phone. "You need to calm down. This stress isn't good for the baby."

"Are you listening to what I'm saying?" Sherise asked. "My husband thinks I got pregnant to trap him!"

As soon as Sherise had gotten home, she called her girls, but she had been unable to catch either of them. Billie finally called her back, and Sherise told her about the fight she and Justin had earlier that day. She was still sick over it as she lay in bed, waiting for him to come home and wondering what was next.

"He knows you," Billie said. "I'm just being honest. You know I love you, and you know he loves you to death, but you play games, Sherise."

"This is how you show your support?" Sherise asked. "I know I play games, but this is too much, Billie. I wouldn't bring a baby into this world to trap him. Besides, I didn't think trapping him was necessary."

"It's not," Billie said. "Justin is yours, and you know it. If he was going to leave, he'd have done it by now. The only problem is, he wasn't being as honest in therapy as you thought. He still has some trust issues, and this is just a shock to his system."

"That's what I thought," Sherise said, "but the look on his face today. It was like he'd already decided why I'd done this and wasn't even interested in hearing another explanation."

"Or maybe he's avoiding this because he loves you and doesn't want you to hurt yourself or the baby." Billie checked her watch. She loved Sherise and wanted to help her, but it wasn't a great idea to spend her first day at work on the phone with her friends.

"Look," Billie continued, "it's just fear. He's scared.

Think about it. You know this man. He isn't going anywhere."

"It's not just about him leaving me," Sherise said. "It's about him loving me and trusting me."

"You doubt that he loves you?" Billie asked. "Come on, now."

Sherise smiled. "I know he loves me, but I want everything to be right."

"That takes time," Billie said. "Clearly, more time than you thought. Sherise, you're going to have to accept that you can't have everything you want in the timeline that you want it."

"And that little bitch working under him isn't making things better." Sherise made sure to mention Elena to Billie as well. "I know she heard us arguing. She's going to use that."

"You have no reason to believe she is after your husband," Billie said. "Just because she's a pretty girl working with him doesn't mean she wants him. She might have a boyfriend or be after someone else— someone without a wife and all the trouble that comes with that."

"Did you have reason to believe Claire was after Porter?" Sherise asked.

That hit hard. Billie would love to forget that her marriage fell apart after Porter had an affair with Claire, a younger associate at his law firm. He later moved her into the home she had once lived in with him and Tara, even though he was still sleeping with Billie. Office affairs were common, and her marriage wasn't the first—and wouldn't be the last—destroyed by coworkers who spent too much time together.

"You forget," Billie assured her, "Porter is an asshole. He's always been an asshole. Justin isn't. Justin is a good guy who lost his way, and not completely from his own fault."

This was true; it made Sherise feel a little better. One of the main reasons she married Justin—in addition to loving him and desiring the connections he had in D.C. politics and power—was that he was a genuinely good guy, one of those rare animals that seemed to be extinct. She'd never known a guy like Justin. Until she met him, she'd mostly known only thugs, playboys, betrayers, and abandoners. Justin wasn't perfect, but he was the best man she'd ever known.

"Leave him alone about her," Billie said. "You don't need that extra stress between you two. Keep an eye on her, though. Use your contacts at the firm. You know Candy will tell you anything."

"It's just one more thing for me to be worried—"

Suddenly her phone made a *pinging* sound and a text came up. Sherise read it and was horrified: Urgent! Matthews picks J. Nolan as VP! Call me now! LaKeisha.

"Holy shit" was all Sherise could muster.

"What?" Billie asked. "What's going on?"

Speaking into the earplug mic, Sherise repeated the text. She heard Billie gasp on the other end of the line.

" 'Holy shit' is right," Billie added.

"How could this be?" Sherise asked. "He wasn't on any of the short lists. He was supposed to run for president after being promoted to secretary of defense. He's not even a Republican! How is he running for VP on the Republican ticket?"

"It's not that much of a stretch," Billie said. "Matthews is weak on defense without Shaplin. Nolan is a defense icon and he's supposed to be a pretty conservative Democrat. You didn't suspect this even a little bit?"

"No!" Sherise yelled. "Do you think I would still be sane if I thought that we would be campaigning against Jonah Nolan? Do you think I would have even gotten into this game?"

"What are you going to do, Sherise?" Billie felt for her. The last thing she needed in her condition was more stress. *This can't be good for the baby,* Billie thought.

"I'm going to kill myself," she said. She was only joking; but in reality, this was a nightmare. "You have no idea how much I hate this man, how much of a threat he is to me."

"But Erica won't let him act on any of those threats," Billie said. "As horrible as he is, he doesn't want her cutting him out of her life. And now that he's running for office, he won't want to risk her revealing their . . . you know, their secret."

"That's not the secret I'm worried about," Sherise said. "If he's running, the press is going to pore over his personal life, hoping for a sex scandal. He has a reputation as being a ladies' man. I can assure you, I wasn't the first woman this man has cheated with, and I probably wasn't the last. They'll be looking for anything."

Billie sighed. She didn't know what to say. After all, if Erica's boyfriend, Terrell, who was nothing more than a limo driver, could find out about their affair, couldn't the press figure it out?

"Like you said," Billie offered, "he's probably slept around a lot. Your affair was really very short, basically nothing. He's probably had longer affairs with more prominent women that the press would be more interested in."

"More prominent than the chief of communications for the Democrat candidate for the presidency that he's running against?"

Billie couldn't deny her position made this worse. If found out, the discovery of the affair would be the worst possible outcome for many more people than just Sherise. If the connection could be made, she'd be a global household name for all the wrong reasons.

"For all the things that Jonah is," Billie said, "he's a man who works in his best interest. He has power and influence. I think he'd use all of that to assure he'd make it to the White House."

"What if it's not enough?" Sherise asked, feeling ready to throw up at just the thought of it. "What if even the great Jonah Nolan can't stop the relentless press machine? Do you know what happens to me if this comes out? Everything is ruined—my marriage, my family, my reputation, my career . . . all of it! My life will be over."

Billie was still reeling from her conversation with Sherise when she heard a knock on her door. She looked up, amazed to see Michael Johnson standing in the doorway. She had to laugh when she realized he was waving a small white handkerchief in his hand. He looked handsome and humble in a casual blue suit.

She waved him in, wondering what she looked like right now. She knew she'd looked professional and sharp when she'd started today. But it was almost six in the evening and she'd been rushing all day.

"I just came from a meeting and thought I would risk it and drop by." He pointed to the chair on the opposite side of her desk. "May I have a seat?"

"I promise I won't bite you," she answered, nodding. She told herself to behave.

He pointed to his flowers, which had been placed in a vase and now sat on the small windowsill of her office. "I'm glad to see they didn't go straight into the garbage."

"Why would they?" she asked. "They're lovely."

He sat back casually in the chair. "I know I didn't make the best impression last week. I was still a little angry about the whole thing."

"Don't." She held up her hand to stop him. "Neither of us was on his or her best behavior."

"I have an idea," he said. "Can we act as if our first meeting on the train was the only other time we've met?"

"That would be nice," she said. "But you didn't seem to like that encounter so much. I remember you believing I was too eager to get away from you."

"I was a little disappointed," he said. "I thought there was a . . . I don't know, something. Then you turned away and never looked back. If you had, you would have seen a very pleased smile on my face. You were a bright light that morning."

Billie felt her cheeks warm to his compliment. "What I was that morning was late and preoccupied. I actually enjoyed our brief, albeit clumsy, encounter."

His expression lightened even more and his charming smile widened. Billie had to fight the urge to flirt with him, even though he didn't seem to bother fighting the same urge. It wasn't professional, was it?

"Don't you find it odd?" he asked. "That we would meet on the train like that and then, a week later, have this . . . connection?"

"'Connection'?" she asked.

"Maybe that's the wrong word," he said with a short laugh. "I've lived in D.C. for a decade and I don't really believe in coincidence. I hardly ever ride the Metro. I usually drive or cab it, but my car was in the shop. Maybe there was a reason I was supposed to be on that train that day."

"You just said the reason," she stated. "Your car was in the shop."

He squinted as if trying to read through her blocks. "You're not going to make this easy for me, are you?"

She wasn't, even though she wanted to. Billie couldn't ignore that she was attracted to Michael, despite their most recent encounter before this. He was very handsome and clearly interested in her. However, the last thing she needed was to get involved with someone who was in any way connected to her job. That was what got her in trouble with Ricky. He was a client and her inability to keep things professional led to horrible things.

"I've lived in D.C. all my life, Michael, and I do believe in coincidence." She shrugged. "Sorry."

"Don't apologize," he said. "You're a sensible woman. You probably like playing it safe and being careful."

If only you knew, Billie thought. She used to be that person and wished she could go back to it. Seemed her life made more sense then.

"Glad you understand," she said.

"I didn't say that," he quickly added. "I don't know a lot about you, Billie, but I suspect there is a part of you that believes in fate, and that part thinks about that train encounter a little bit."

More than a little bit, she wanted to say, but she didn't. He was looking into her eyes right now, searingly, as if searching for what was on her mind. Billie wanted to look away, but she couldn't. He was a compelling character. The more she was getting to know him, the more trouble she realized he was going to be.

Fortunately, there was a knock on her door. The sound allowed her to tear her gaze away from his. It was Lane; he walked into the office with an odd look on his face at the sight of Michael.

"What are you doing here?" Lane asked.

"I had a meeting," Michael said, standing up.

Lane seemed a little confused by that; Billie thought for a second that Michael had lied to her. He hadn't been there for a meeting at all. He'd come just to see her. This was flattering and worrying at the same time.

Looking as if he had other, more important things on his mind, Lane let it go. He turned his attention to Billie.

"We have to talk," he said. "Privately."

"I was just leaving," Michael offered. He turned to Billie. "I'll see you around, I'm sure."

"Thank you again for the flowers," Billie added, wondering if he was really going to keep that gorgeous smile on his face every time she saw him. It made her knees feel a little weak.

Lane and Michael said their good-byes before he left, and Lane closed the door behind him.

"What is it?" she asked. "You look a little anxious."

Lane leaned against the wall closest to the desk. "I was going to tell you this morning when you asked me about the firms we were looking at to handle the FTC case, but Evelyn came in with the flowers. What is Michael doing here, by the way? Did he come here just to—"

"What is it, Lane?" Billie didn't want to talk about Michael anymore, but she was also getting a little nervous. "What did you want to tell me? Has Gil decided to go with my ex-firm?"

"No," he said, "but that is an amazing choice of words you just used. I mean . . . 'ex.' "

It hit Billie like a brick. If she hadn't been sitting down, she would have fallen.

"I told Gil that could be a problem," Lane offered. "But he felt like he accommodated you enough by not hiring your old firm."

Billie was shaking her head, not able to find the words she needed. When he mentioned "ex," she knew. She just knew. They had hired Dinklett & Williams, a large New York–based law firm, which she knew all too well. It was the firm that her ex-husband, Porter Haas, worked at, in their D.C. office. Porter was the star of their finance practice and would likely become a partner later this year.

"The good news," Lane said, trying real hard, "is that Gil said he has enough confidence in you to handle it. He has faith in you. That usually takes a long time to earn here. You've earned it just through two consulting gigs."

"This is a finance case," she finally said when she found her voice. "Porter will definitely be working on this."

"Shouldn't he be?" Lane asked. "He's one of the best, right?"

Porter was well known in D.C. circles as a genius in finance law. If any company hired the firm, they had to demand he work on the case. It was as simple as that.

"You still want me on this case?" she asked. "It might be easier to give it to someone else."

"You really want to do that?" Lane asked, concerned. "That's not a way to start your career here, Billie. I know that it might be awkward, but handing over a case, your first case, is not going to go over well with Gil. He wants you running head on this."

She nodded, knowing that Lane was right. The last thing she needed was to come across to another employer as weak. She could handle this. She *had* to handle this.

"You've been divorced for a while now," Lane added. "It's still not that bad between you, right?"

"Yeah," Billie lied.

Lane had no idea. He didn't know that Porter cheated on her, screwed her over financially in the divorce, continued to seduce her, using his daughter as a tool even after they were divorced. He wasn't aware that Porter had tried to blackmail her into his bed and had used a paralegal at her old firm to spy on her and give him information he could use to exert control over her life. He wasn't aware that Porter broke her heart again by sending his daughter away and threatening Billie with legal action if she tried to contact her.

Yes, she had gained some ground by matching him at his game and threatening to expose his many bad deeds to even the playing field. She had taken Sherise's advice and decided to play as dirty as he did. She didn't like the way she felt afterward when she realized that Porter's reputation had been tarnished and his promotion to partner had been put on hold for at least a year. But it worked, and Porter had less power over her. He worked less at ruining her life. That was until he sent Tara away. She would never forgive him for that. She hated him now—the man she once loved, had wanted to have children with, and spend the rest of her life with.

"We're good now," she said with a smile. "We'll work together fine."

"If it makes you feel any better," Lane said, "you won't really be working together. He'll be working for you. Not bad, huh?"

Billie thought about it for a second. That was true. This might be better than she thought.

5

"Nate!" Erica yelled from the kitchen. "Dinner will be ready in a few. Gonna be ready?"

"I'll be there!" her little brother yelled back from his bedroom down the hallway.

Tonight was going to be low-key, just dinner at home. Last night, after picking him up, Erica treated Nate to a dinner celebration at Art and Soul, a restaurant only a few blocks away from Union Station.

They had a great time catching up with each other. It had only been six months, but it seemed like longer than that to Erica. It was bittersweet, because while Erica realized that she finally had her baby brother back, she knew right away that she had lost him. He was more independent now, having spent time on his own, getting to know what he wanted. He had come home with her, but his new job started in two days. He already had lined up a few apartments to look at this weekend.

There was a part of her that wanted to get back some of what she'd had when the three of them—Nate, Erica, and Terrell—all lived in the apartment together. They fought often, but, all in all, they had a ball. Those few years were some of the happiest of Erica's life. She thought it would be nice to get some of that back, but it was just reaching for a promise that wasn't meant to be. She was supposed to marry Terrell and have children with him; and Nate would move on, get married, and have children of his own. They would all be one big, happy family. They would be what she knew their mother had always hoped for them.

But things didn't turn out that way and it broke her heart. At least she had Nate back, but she knew he was moving out and he'd probably get a girlfriend soon. She'd hardly ever see him. Erica couldn't use Nate to make herself not feel alone.

Stop it, she thought. *There is no point in feeling sorry for yourself.*

Besides, she was already upset with the way things had gone yesterday with Caroline. Then, when she found out that Caroline had called in sick today, she knew something was wrong. She doubted Caroline had come down with a sudden illness; and with all the extra overtime work she had lobbied so hard for, it made no sense that she would not come into the office. She hated being worried about someone as distasteful as Caroline, but she was.

To add to it, Jonah had tried to contact her three times already that day. She'd ignored each one of his calls. Now that the news of his vice presidential appointment was out, it was all the talk pretty much everywhere. She wasn't feeling it and didn't want to hear it.

When the phone rang again, she expected to see Jonah's name, but it was Sherise. She'd been waiting all day for his phone call; she wasn't looking forward to this conversation.

"How long did you know?" was the first thing Sherise asked as soon as Erica picked up the phone.

"I couldn't tell you," Erica explained.

"How long?" she repeated loudly.

Erica was stunned by her tone. "You need to calm down, Sherise. This isn't good for your baby."

"You wanna know what's not good for my baby?" Sherise asked. "Her mom being exposed as Jonah Nolan's mistress to the world. Just tell me, how long did you know?"

Erica sighed. "It's been about a week, but I couldn't tell you. I promised him."

"Since when does he deserve promises?" Sherise asked. "A week. Oh, my God. Do you know that I could lose everything? Do you even care? If you'd told me, I could have been prepared. I could have done something."

"Like what?"

"Anything," she said. "I don't know. I have the press at my disposal. I could have thwarted it, made it look messy or something. I would have done anything to discourage them from picking him. I never got that chance."

"I wanted to tell you," Erica said. "I knew what it could mean for you, but I didn't want to betray him. He made me promise."

"Fuck him," Sherise said. "That man is an asshole and deserves to be betrayed."

"He's my father," Erica retorted. "No matter how much you hate him—and I know you have a right to— he's my father. I'm not going to do that. Besides, it could easily be linked to me and I don't want to be on his bad side like that."

"Listen to you," Sherise said. "You're scared of him and protecting him at the same time."

"He's protecting himself," Erica said. "He's not going to let anyone find out about that stuff."

"How?" Sherise asked. "How is he going to keep a ravenous press from finding anything out?"

"I don't know how," Erica said, "but he seemed confident that—"

"Confidence isn't enough! You need to find out how exactly he plans on keeping this secret, Erica. My life depends on it. Cady's future, this baby's future, they both depend on it."

"He didn't tell me," she said.

"Find out!"

After being hung up on, Erica put the phone on the kitchen counter and took a deep breath. As always, Sherise was being insane, but Erica couldn't say she was overreacting this time. The second Jonah told her, Erica knew exactly what this could mean for Sherise. She had compassion for her friend, despite all of their clashes. She loved Sherise like a sister and didn't want her friend's family to fall apart. This would be global, not just national. It would ruin Sherise's life, and Justin would never forgive her. Right now, in her delicate position, the stress could have even worse consequences for Sherise.

But Erica also felt it was wrong of Sherise to make her responsible. Erica wasn't the one who had the affair with Jonah. Sherise made the choice—like many she always made—out of selfishness, ambition, and greed. It wasn't fair for her to make Erica risk getting on Jonah's bad side to save her.

So, why did she feel like she had to reassure Sherise? Erica wasn't close enough to Jonah to get these details, so what exactly was she supposed to do?

"What's wrong?"

Erica was startled. She hadn't even noticed that Nate had come around the corner and was standing outside of the kitchen. Twenty-one years old, he was tall, with an athletic build. He was the color of a brown nut, with thick black eyebrows that framed his handsome young face, which was made up of a distinctive nose and full lips. He had experimented with cornrows for a while, but he was back to the completely bald look, which flattered him more.

"Nothing." She returned her attention to the food. "Just Sherise being Sherise."

"What is that crazy chick up to now?"

Erica shook her head. "You don't want to know. Just go sit down. I'll have dinner on the table in—"

"I came to show you this," he said. "What do I do with it?"

Nate held up a Philadelphia Eagles jersey. Seeing it put a lump in Erica's throat. She remembered that jersey all too well. It was Terrell's favorite. She and Nate always gave him a hard time for wearing it in a Washington Redskins household. She remembered telling him she would not be seen in public with him with that jersey on. The last time they went to a Redskins game, where they played the Eagles, he'd waited to put it on when she went to the ladies' room. She came back and saw it and let him have it. They argued, laughed, and went home and had sex for three hours.

"I should send it to him?" Nate said, framing it more like a question.

She nodded. "I guess, but I don't know where he is."

When they were catching up last night, Erica made it clear to Nate that she had no contact with Terrell and didn't want any ever again.

"Well," Nate said, "I guess I could call one of his boys and find—"

"No!" Erica pointed a finger at him. "I don't want you in contact with any of those thugs."

Nate smiled. "It's okay, sis. I'm not that guy anymore. The last thing I want is to get involved in anything bad. I can handle myself."

He wasn't her *baby brother* anymore. "I know you can."

As he headed down the hallway, he said, "Don't worry. Whatever I find out, I won't tell you anything."

She appreciated that. It had been hard enough getting over Terrell the first time she ended their engagement and broke up with him. The second time was so much more heartbreaking. She was willing to move on, but she still felt pain at the thought of him. Seeing that jersey brought a lot back to her, but she wasn't going to let it get her down. That part of her life was over. It just was, and that was that.

The second Erica showed up at Sherise's town house for a Saturday lunch with the girls, Sherise started in on her.

"I can't believe you haven't found anything out yet," Sherise accused as Erica joined them on the plush living-room sofa.

Billie had already been there for an hour, trying to calm Sherise down, but it wasn't working. Still dressed in her pajamas and silk bathrobe, Sherise wasn't her usual self. She hadn't bothered with her appearance at all. She looked extremely tired and stressed.

"Here." Billie offered Erica a glass of red wine. "You're going to need it."

"I need that so bad," Sherise added as she took a gulp from her water bottle.

"Considering this is the first time we've been able to get together since finding out about the baby," Erica said, "I was hoping we could talk about nicer things."

Sherise placed her hand protectively on her belly. "It's because of this baby that I'm even more desperate. And in all this time, you haven't talked to Jonah at all?"

"It was three days ago." Erica looked around. "Where is Cady, by the way?"

"She's upstairs napping," Billie answered as Sherise walked over to the window that looked out onto the busy Georgetown streets.

"Sit down," Erica ordered. "You're making me nervous."

"Not nervous enough, obviously." Sherise did as she was told and walked back to the girls and sat in the lounge chair. "I won't be able to sleep through the night until I find out what Jonah's plan is to keep people from finding out about us."

"Well, there isn't anything I can do about it," Erica said. "I can't just go up and ask him."

"Why not?" Sherise asked. "He knows you know."

"He's not going to tell me," Erica argued. "He's knows I'd be asking for you. He's not giving me any information that I could give you."

"Maybe you can get it another way?" Sherise asked. "I've been thinking. He has to tell whoever he's hired to backtrack and get rid of records and all that stuff, right? That's what rich people do when they're about to be investigated. You can find out who that is and sneak in—"

"Are you nuts?" Erica asked. "We're talking about Jonah Nolan. No one sneaks in on anything that has to do with him."

"Your thug of a boyfriend did," Sherise said.

Erica glared at her. "Fuck off talking about Terrell. Besides, he wasn't running for vice president then. Now that he is, his shit is gonna be on lockdown. It's not happening."

"What if you don't have to sneak?" Billie asked as both women turned to her. "What if you had access?"

"I don't," Erica said just as she realized what Billie was thinking. "No, I'm not doing it."

"Doing what?" Sherise asked.

Erica had told Billie about Jonah's offer to come work for him. She hadn't told Sherise for obvious reasons. She didn't want to hear all of the shit Sherise would have to say to her about it. At the time, she'd assumed that Sherise would drive her crazy to keep her from taking the job, not believing that Erica would go up against her and help a man whom she hated.

"She could go work for him," Billie said. "He's asked her."

"And I turned him down," Erica maintained.

"Why didn't you tell me about this?" Sherise asked, her heart leaping in her throat. "This is . . . Oh, my God, Erica, this is it! You can get access to everything."

Erica fell back on the sofa and let out a big sigh, wanting to crack Billie in her head for letting that out.

"I don't want to go work for Jonah," she stated. "This is way too complicated. I could explain it to you, but both of you never want to hear about anything that has to do with Jonah."

"How could you be so selfish?" Sherise asked.

"Hold on a minute," Billie warned her. "It's true. This is a seriously emotional issue for Erica. It could—"

"For fuck sake," Sherise said, "you have an asshole for a father. Join the club and get the fuck over it."

"I'm not going to deal with that at your pace," Erica said. "I'm not gonna be forced because you have secrets you need to keep."

"What exactly are you being forced to do that is so hard?" Sherise asked.

"One," Erica began, "go work for Jonah, meaning being around him a lot and letting him be closer to me, which I am scared to death to do."

"Getting closer to Jonah is dangerous," Billie agreed. "Although you probably wouldn't be around him a lot. He'll be traveling and working. You'll probably be at staff headquarters."

"So that's out," Sherise said.

"Two," Erica added, "I would be working for Jonah's campaign and betraying him by giving you information. You work for the enemy now."

"Sherise doesn't want you to give her information about the campaign," Billie said.

Sherise shrugged. "Well, if she's there, why not—"

"Because," Billie said. "That's why not. You only need to get information on his relationship with Sherise and what he's doing to keep it quiet."

"Then you can quit," Sherise said, "if it bothers you that much."

"And then do what?" Erica asked.

"You just don't want to help me, do you?" Sherise asked accusingly.

"Don't be ridiculous," Billie said. "Of course she does."

"No, she doesn't." Sherise's tone became high-pitched as the realization hit her. "She wants my life destroyed. That's it. All this time, you've been fighting with me, and now this is your chance to get me for good."

"I don't want to 'get you,' " Erica argued.

"You think I deserve this, don't you?" Sherise asked, tears beginning to flow down her cheeks. "You like the idea of me just stewing in my own panic and fear, because it's what I get, isn't it?"

"I don't want you hurt," Erica emphasized. "I just want your problems to stop being mine."

"Isn't that what friendship is about?" Sherise asked. "Isn't that what we've always thrived on? Being there for each other? This is my life, Erica. This isn't just some random favor that could get me out of a bind. This is my marriage, my family, Cady, this baby, everything."

"I know what it means to you," Erica said. "You don't have to keep repeating it."

"And how much of a sacrifice would this be for you in comparison?" Sherise asked.

Billie didn't like what Sherise was doing to Erica, guilting her like this, but it was true. They were supposed to do anything for each other; and considering what pain this could cause Sherise, it didn't seem as if it was asking too much of Erica. Still, Erica had her own demons with Jonah. This would be forcing her to face them earlier than she'd wanted to, maybe earlier than she was ready to.

"Sweetheart." Billie reached over and placed her hand comfortingly on Erica's shoulder. "This might turn out better than you think. You're always talking about how much you hate your job. This could open the door to so many things."

"Jonah already gave me that speech," Erica said.

"Well, it's true!" Billie urged. "And you don't hate the man. You can be near him at least long enough to find out what Sherise needs to know, so she can be at peace or prepare—whatever the case."

Sherise moaned as she looked away. "How can someone prepare to have their entire life completely annihilated?"

Erica couldn't contain how apprehensive she felt about this. She felt a sudden urge to get up and leave; but then she heard a noise, a crackling of sound right in front of her. She looked down at the glass coffee table and saw the baby monitor. She could hear Cady making the most adorable sounds. It seemed as if she was laughing a little bit. A smile immediately came to Erica's face at the sound of it.

"Can you do it for her?" Sherise asked, jumping on the opportunity as she saw the familiar softening of the usually hardened Erica just at the sound of her baby.

Billie's phone made a beeping sound and she reached into her purse for it.

"Fine." Erica threw her hands in the air, giving up. "I'll do my best, but I can't make any promises."

Sherise jumped up from her chair and leapt toward her friend. She wrapped her arms around her, hugging her tight and thanking her profusely. Erica struggled to break free of Sherise's kung fu grip, looking to Billie for help.

"Can you get this fat, pregnant woman off me?" she asked, laughing.

Sherise slapped her on the arm. "Fuck you! Even pregnant, I'm going to be the hottest bitch in every room, just like I was last time."

"Oh, dear" was all Billie said in response to the text she read.

Both girls turned to her as Sherise finally released her hold on Erica.

"What is it?" Erica asked.

"It's a text from Michael," she said. "He wants to have dinner with me."

"Who's Michael?" Erica scooted closer to her.

Usually very interested in Billie's dating life, Sherise was too relieved at Erica's agreement about Jonah to care about Billie's social life right now. She leaned back on the sofa and took a deep breath, barely listening as Billie told them about her initial meeting with Michael on the train and then again at the office, followed by the flowers and the personal visit.

"Why are we just now hearing about this?" Erica asked.

Billie shrugged. "Because it's nothing. I'm focused on my new job."

"You need to get some, though," Erica said.

She knew Billie was having a rough time since Ricky. She wanted Billie to get back in the saddle just as much as she wanted it for herself.

"You're blushing," Erica said, laughing. "You like this guy. You say he's gorgeous. Sherise, get your tablet. Let's Google him and see what he looks like."

"No," Billie said. "Trust me, he's fine. But he's too close to where my bread is buttered."

"He doesn't work with you," Erica said. "He doesn't work for the company. He's a consultant. There's no conflict of interest here."

Billie just shook her head, not wanting to get into it.

"You're doubting yourself now," Erica said. "That's

not good. You made a mistake. Just like you got past everything that happened with Porter, you can get past what happened with Ricky."

Billie rolled her eyes. "Speaking of Porter."

"Can we not?" Sherise finally asked, her ears perking up at the sound of Billie's ex-husband. "Nothing good ever comes from a conversation about that asshole."

Billie told them about her first case and that the firm had hired Porter. Erica looked a little cautious, but Sherise managed to form a big smile on her face.

"Oh, it's on now," Sherise said.

"What do you mean?" Erica asked.

Sherise leaned forward. "This is your chance to make his life a living hell for all the mess he did to you. You're the client now. He's the servant boy and you can whip him to your own delight."

"She doesn't want to do that," Erica said, looking at Billie. "Right?"

Billie hadn't thought of it like that. She'd been so busy worrying about the awkwardness because of the current status of their relationship.

"No," she said, not at all convincing. "I mean, I definitely saw it as a dynamic that would favor me, but the last thing I need to do is allow my personal and professional life to conflict again. That's never gotten me anywhere good."

Both women looked at Billie with very concerned faces.

"I can handle it," Billie insisted. "Trust me. I'm not someone who doesn't learn from her mistakes. I can handle working with Porter."

"You mean having Porter work *for* you," Sherise corrected.

"So," Erica said, "you can handle this thing with Porter, but not Michael? Because it seems like Porter would be the complicated one. Michael, on the other hand, sounds like a win-win situation."

"There could be complications," Billie said.

"As with anyone," Erica said. "Fine, just ignore me. Ignore Sherise. What do you want to do? Do you want to go out to dinner with him?"

Billie opened her mouth to protest, but nothing came out. She stopped trying and just let the smile, which wanted to come, naturally form on her lips.

"Okay," she said. "Just dinner."

"You got this," Erica said reassuringly. "Nothing to worry about."

"Now that this is settled," Sherise said, "let's talk about this bitch in my husband's office, Elena."

Sherise had a great poker face, and she made sure that poker face was in full form when she walked into Jerry Northman's office at the campaign headquarters in downtown D.C. While she had been on the phone with the office and had attended meetings via Skype, this was the first time she'd been face-to-face with him since announcing her pregnancy.

She wasn't stupid; she knew there was doubt. She knew they probably resented giving her the offer, but the truth was she was still the best at what she did. Plus, the baby would be born before the general-election swing began. The preliminaries, when the party candidates did all their infighting to find out who would come out on top, was the focus now. Northman was the clear leader. The hard work, the general election, when he would run head-to-head with Matthews and now

Jonah, would come next year. They had to know this; if they didn't, Sherise would be sure to remind them.

So she had to bite back her paranoia and beat her value and worth into them until every doubt they had went away. She walked into Northman's office, with head held high and looking like a million dollars—a million healthy, ready-to-do-miracles dollars.

"You look good" was the first thing Northman said from behind his desk.

"I feel great," Sherise reassured. She took a seat across from his desk and nodded toward LaKeisha, who was sitting in the chair next to her. "All that bed rest was to make my husband happy."

"And is he?" LaKeisha asked. There was a pointed tone in her voice.

"As a clam," Sherise responded quickly and tersely, before turning to Northman. "I feel great. I've done this before. It's nothing. What I'm really excited about are the talking points I've been working on. You got those, right?"

"If you need help," LaKeisha continued, "you can just let me know. We'll add to your staff."

Sherise slowly turned her head to LaKeisha. With a stone stare and a bulletproof smile, she said, "The two staff members I have now are all that I need. I won't need more—"

"The talking points are amazing," Northman interrupted. "Nolan has weaknesses that most people don't know about."

"I learned a great deal about him during our short work together at the Domestic Policy Council." Sherise crossed her legs and leaned back confidently in her chair. "He's strong on defense, but he has some political weak points. I think his party switching makes him an easy opportunist target and verifies that he's not some-one who can be trusted."

"We need to work this angle hard," Northman said. "Right now, a man who looks very strong needs to be made to look very weak."

"That's exactly what we're going to do," LaKeisha assured. "Meanwhile, Sherise will be reminding every-one of what a loyalist you've been to the Democratic Party."

Northman pointed his finger to his desk and tapped a few times as his brows centered in frustration. "He's very popular. That's a problem. With the sympathy for losing Shaplin and Nolan's popularity, this isn't good. I think we'll need more."

"We're working on that," LaKeisha boasted.

Sherise blinked for a second, but she regained her composure as she looked at LaKeisha, trying her best not to give anything away. "What do you mean?"

LaKeisha tilted her head to the side with a self-assured grin. "Nolan is a very rich, very handsome, very powerful man. He's been married for twenty-five years. There's something out there."

As Northman made a muddling sound, like a moan suggesting he wasn't comfortable with this conversa-tion, Sherise gripped the edges of the folder she held in her hands. She should have just quit. She was greedy, not wanting to pass up this opportunity to ride to the White House. No, if she quit, it could come out still; but the shit storm that followed wouldn't be as bad.

It was too late. She had her chance. Sherise was in this for better, for worse, or for life-ending, apocalyptic disaster.

"Do you think that's a good idea?" she asked. "Getting so dirty, so early, generally backfires."

"We'll deal with it later," LaKeisha said. "For now, on the subject of your pick for vice president, we won't announce anything until after the primaries are finished, but I've been researching probable—"

"Before we move on," Sherise interjected, "I have to disclose something."

"Again?" LaKeisha asked, sounding annoyed.

So LaKeisha is going to be a problem now, Sherise realized. The woman who had sought her out and urged her to join the campaign seemed determined now to be a thorn in her side. Sherise understood that LaKeisha was concerned. How Sherise turned out was a reflection on her, so she had reason. But Sherise was not about to be belittled in front of the future president of the United States. If LaKeisha didn't straighten up, she would have a bigger problem than she thought.

Sherise ignored her, keeping her focus on Northman. "As you collect tabs on Nolan's staff, you'll find a young woman, Erica Kent, has joined it. Erica used to work for Nolan at the Pentagon."

"Is there some inappropriate relationship there?" Northman asked.

"No," Sherise said assuredly. "She's relevant to this conversation because she's a very, very close friend of mine."

There was a short moment of silence in the room as Sherise watched Northman process this.

"What does she do for him?" LaKeisha asked.

"Nothing yet," Sherise answered, "but she has no political experience. She's an admin, so I imagine it will be very low-level legislative stuff. Governor, there's nothing to worry about. I'm a professional and she's—"

"It's a small world," Northman said. He made a flippant gesture with his hand. "In D.C., friends work on opposites sides all the time. This isn't news. You know what you can and can't discuss, don't you?"

"Of course." Sherise's voice held no doubt at all. She had a great poker voice as well.

6

As Billie walked from the Metro, down the street toward her building, she thought of possibly running an errand or two before going home. It was nice outside, warm and breezy. She thought of picking up dinner and then remembered the chicken she'd left out late yesterday. She'd spent enough time on a budget that she'd stopped wasting money on carryout as much as she used to.

She was lucky now. While getting her financial house in order, she still could afford to splurge on takeout once or twice a week. She was thinking of all the things she needed to get back on track, now that she was collecting a steady, healthy paycheck again. All the things she'd neglected during those lean months. She was saving up to buy a home and . . .

She had been so lost in her thoughts that she hadn't noticed the figure sitting on the steps to her apartment building, looking at his phone. When she reached the gate to the stairs, he looked up and their eyes met.

"What in the fuck are you doing here?" she asked.

It had been a while now since she'd last seen

Porter, but he never changed. He was perfect as usual. He was always sharply dressed, and his hair was always trimmed tightly to his head. He was six feet tall, but his deep voice gave him a presence that made him seem taller. He had milk chocolate skin and a finely shaven goatee surrounding his full lips. He had dark, mesmerizing eyes that bore into you when he looked at you.

Things were much better between them when she'd thought of how much he invaded her life and her peace before, using her strong sexual attraction to him to keep her coming to his bed even after he'd cheated on her and moved his mistress into his home. Or they were worse, considering he'd exacted the worst punishment of all on her by sending his daughter to Michigan to live with his mother and forbidding Billie to see her.

"What are you up to?" he asked, standing up. He wore his usual accusatory expression.

She slammed the gate shut behind her. "I told you that you weren't welcome at my home anymore."

"I'm not in your home," he said as she passed him.

She reached the door to the building and turned to face him. She longed for the day when she would look at him and not wish things had been different. It was getting better, but she still wasn't there. She hated him and, at the same time, missed what he could have been to her.

"I know what you want," she said, "and I have nothing to tell you. It wasn't my choice to hire your firm."

"Bullshit!" he spat. "You kept it a secret that you were working there, and you—"

"I never kept anything a secret," she said. "I just started, and the reason you didn't know is because it's none of your damn business."

"The partner who got this account was never given

your name as being on the account. If he had, he would have told me."

"Remember," she said, "my name isn't Haas anymore."

"He knows who the fuck you are, Billie."

"You don't have to work on the case," she said. "Your practice has plenty of lawyers who—"

"You know I do FTC cases!"

She had to smile at his arrogance. "Porter, I don't keep up with your career or anything you do."

His expression said he was clearly unable to believe that she wasn't still obsessed with every aspect of his life, as he was with hers. "I don't want to hear any more of your lies. Just tell me what you're up to."

"If you think everything I'm saying is a lie, Porter, then why would you believe me when I tell you what, in your words, I'm 'up to'?"

His eyes squinted as he seethed in anger at her. "You've gotten too big for your britches."

"Excuse me?" she asked, her blood beginning to boil.

"You know—"

"Wait!" She held her hand up to stop him. Her voice got very loud. "Scratch that! I don't want clarification of what you mean by that insulting comment. You're an asshole, Porter, and I want you to leave."

"You've had a few victories," he continued, ignoring her. "I let my guard down with you, and you fucked with me."

"Oh, poor baby," she said. "The only time I ever went at you was because you went at me first and endlessly."

"You better not mess with me," Porter warned, pointing his finger at her. "Whatever you thought you were going to do by hiring my firm, get it out of your mind. Fuck with me, Billie, and you'll regret it."

With that, he turned and walked away, leaving Billie at the door. She could feel herself breathing fast and hard as she realized he'd just threatened her . . . again. How many times had he done that since she'd filed for divorce?

There was nothing about him that resembled the man she had fallen in love with. So, why did he still have the power to upset her so much? Billie could still feel her heart racing as she reached her floor. Once again, he would jump in and out of her life and leave her to recover. She wanted to be angry at him, but she could only be angry at herself for letting him get to her after all of this time.

Her mood was only lightened somewhat at the sight of flowers at her doorstep. She reached down to pick them up and grabbed the attached postcard. She read the words out loud: " 'Looking forward to Wednesday night. Michael.' "

She smiled a little bit more, thinking about Michael and hoping that things would go well on their upcoming date. It almost allowed her to forget about Porter and all of the trouble he was likely going to cause her.

For once, in all of their clandestine meetings, Erica had gotten there first. When Jonah showed up in the corner booth at the small Mexican restaurant in Alexandria, Virginia, she felt a certain sense of satisfaction in that. For the first time, she had called this meeting. It made her feel like she was somewhat in control, which was extremely hard to do in the presence of a man like Jonah Nolan.

Still, as he sat across from her and greeted her firmly, but kindly, she was already feeling like a little girl. He was just so intimidating.

"This place is . . ." Jonah looked around and sighed. "Actually, I wanted to say something nice, but it's a shit-hole. Do you actually eat here?"

"The food is authentic and cheap," Erica said. "The people here are nice. Your sort doesn't come here."

"Can we dispense with the class warfare?" he asked. "I've offered to set you up in a better lifestyle. You've declined every time."

"So stop offering," she said.

"I'll stop offering to give you money if you stop throwing in my face the fact that I have a lot of it."

"Deal," she said. "I just picked the place because you weren't likely to run into anyone you knew here. I know how important your secrecy is to you."

"Well, the security detail standing a few feet away from me at all times kind of defeats the point."

He pointed to the two men against the wall, whom everyone in the tiny restaurant was staring at.

"No more secret meetings," he said. "I won't have that option, but I'm sincerely hoping that the reason you called me here will mean we won't have to meet in secret anymore."

"Rule number one," she said, trying her best to look stone-faced. She didn't frown or smile, just stared right into his intense eyes. "You don't get involved in my personal life."

He looked annoyed. "Anytime I've gotten involved in your personal life, it was for your own good. I warned you about Terr—"

"Don't ever say his name to me," she ordered. "Never again. If you do, this is done."

"Don't threaten me," he ordered. "And I'm not to blame for his actions."

"You are to blame for yours," she said. "And they kind of go together, wouldn't you say?"

"No, I wouldn't." He paused. "Any more rules?"

"If you're not willing to treat me like your daughter in public, don't ever expect me to treat you like my father in private. It won't happen."

His expression made it clear he wasn't happy with that statement, but he seemed to brush it off quickly. "That seems fair. I know this situation isn't easy on you, and I don't deserve any better than what you're willing to give me. But I do care for you, Erica."

Erica stuck to her resolve. This was when he usually got to her. He was good at this, making her believe he was getting emotional, that there was a softer side to him. Trusting this always backfired; she had to remind herself of that. She could never really believe anything he said.

"I hope I can make you at least proud of what I can—"

"So, when do I start?" she asked, interrupting him.

He nodded as if he understood her meaning. "You remember Alex? He'll contact you soon and get you started. There is a bit of administrative and background stuff to get through, so be patient. You'll be up and running in no time. We're having a party next—"

"Let's talk about Sherise," Erica said.

A frown immediately darkened his face. "We've already discussed that. There isn't any more to say. As long as Sherise keeps her mouth shut, she doesn't have anything to worry about."

"Is she in danger?" Erica asked.

He frowned, looking confused. "Why would you ask me that?"

"You seem certain this won't come out," Erica said. "I just don't see how you can be so certain, unless you plan on making certain it—"

"That's nothing for you to be worried about," Jonah said. "That's not a part of my campaign you'll be—"

"Anything involving my best friend is something for me to be worried about!"

"Keep your voice down," he ordered calmly, leaning in. "Is there something about Sherise you need to tell me?"

"I wouldn't tell you anything about her," Erica said.

"That's fine," he said. "I don't need you to."

His tone was definitive; Erica knew exactly what he meant. All of this time, she had been worried about how he was protecting himself and Sherise from anyone finding out. She hadn't thought about how he might decide to protect himself from Sherise. Jonah found out anything he wanted to know, did anything he wanted. This could be good for Sherise, meaning she was safe from anyone finding out about the two of them because Jonah would see that no one would. Or, this could be bad for Sherise, meaning if she was the only real threat to anyone finding out about them, Jonah would make sure she wasn't a threat anymore. That was what Erica was afraid of most.

Billie was somewhat grateful that her first date with Michael was a weeknight. She didn't have to fuss over herself because she didn't have the time to go home and get dressed up. She wore a sharp ruby-red

Jones New York suit, coupled with a sleeveless silk button-down black blouse. The skirt was a little shorter than her usual skirts. Being petite, she needed all of the help she could get to appear to have longer legs than she did. Her Lanvin bow-toe patent leather pumps helped in that area too.

The smile on Michael's face as she reached the table, situated in the center of the room at Palena on Connecticut Avenue, probably matched the smile on hers as she watched him stand for her. Here was a man who would offer her his seat on the train, send her flowers in anticipation of a first date, and now this. When was the last time that happened?

"Aren't you a gentleman," she said as she approached. She beamed the most gracious smile at him.

"It's how my mama raised me." He waited for her to sit down before taking his seat again. "You look great."

"In this?" she asked, laughing. "Just work wear."

"I feel silly," he said. "I actually tried to get all gussied up and I don't look anywhere near as good as you with no effort."

No effort. She had to laugh at that. Also, he was wrong about not looking good. He looked great in a sharp black pin-striped suit, paired with a sky blue shirt and silky black tie.

"You're right on time too," he said. "I love that in a woman."

"It isn't polite to make a man wait," she said, tilting her head to the side in a flirtatious manner. "Well, at least not too long."

He smiled approvingly, only looking away from her as the waiter approached their table. The server placed a basket of warm bread and a small tin of butter at the center. After asking her what her tastes were, Michael ordered the wine for them.

"Before you came to D.C., you lived in the South, didn't you?" she asked.

"How could you tell?"

"You have the perfect manners of a Southern gentleman," she said, "but you also have an accent. One that I haven't detected since that day on the train."

"So you caught that?" he asked.

"Why don't you speak it all the time?" she asked. "Or am I being too personal?"

Michael waited for the waiter to bring their drinks and asked him for a few more minutes to decide. He nodded and left.

"No," he finally answered. "I was brought up in southern Georgia. Went to Morehouse. I'm a Southern boy at heart."

"Nothing wrong with that," she said. "Nothing at all."

He shrugged. "Well, when I moved to D.C., I noticed my Southern accent got a few side eyes. They're pretty elitist up here, you know."

"Tell me about it."

"So," he said, pausing to take a sip of wine, "I decided it was best to . . . reserve the accent for more personal situations, let's say."

"Don't I count for personal?" she asked. "This is a private dinner, right? We aren't working."

"Of course," he agreed. "It's just sometimes I'm so used to speaking carefully, it becomes the way I speak. Glad to know I can let go of all that with you."

"I think it's charming." She felt her face get flushed at the pleasing response he gave to her compliment. "Speaking of elitist D.C. folks, why would you come to

D.C. in the first place? Most people I know from Atlanta never leave."

"The *A-T-L* is great and it'll always be home. I might even consider moving back there when I retire. Honestly, I would have never left if it wasn't for . . . well, you know."

"Let me guess," Billie said, deducing from that somewhat shy smile on his face. "A woman? Yes, it was a woman. Ah, you moved away from home for love."

"I thought it was love at least." He reached for the bread, offering it to her.

She shook her head. "No, but thank you. How romantic. Did you follow her here, or did you come here with her?"

"I came here with her." He focused on the bread, seeming a little embarrassed to be sharing this information. "I was very passionate about her, but it turned out all of her passion was for activism. She came here to change the world and didn't really have any time for much else."

"You're not the activist type?" she asked, pleased that his Southern accent was coming out, more and more, with each sentence. She found it sexy.

"Not like her. I love being a part of my community. I volunteer at DC Central Kitchen, I mentor for The Making of a Man, and I give free résumé and job interview–skills training at the Brentwood men's center."

Could this man get any better? Billie asked herself. *Handsome, successful, perfect manners, and committed to giving back.* Her heart picked up the pace.

The waiter returned; and after sharing the specials, they agreed on their meal. After he left, Michael got right back to the conversation.

"I saw your résumé," he said. "As part of what I do for the company."

"You were likely looking for reasons to tell them not to hire me." She gave him a sly smile.

"I won't admit to that," he said. "What I noticed was that you like to volunteer a lot too. You made quite a reputation as a crusader during your short stint as a public defender. I take it the money was the big drawback."

Billie took a deep breath and cleared her throat. Now was as good a time as any to tell the truth. "Divorce can sometimes change circumstances."

"You're divorced?" he asked, his left eyebrow rose in curiosity.

"Yes," she answered. "For almost two years."

"Well," he offered, without missing a step, "that must be some damn fool to let you go."

She was pleased with his reaction and felt a little weight come off her shoulders. That was done and he had reacted in the best scenario she could have imagined.

"He wouldn't, by any chance . . ." Michael paused, seeming a bit hesitant to continue. "Do you keep in touch with him?"

"Do we have kids is what, I think, you're asking?"

"No, I just . . . Well, it's none of my business."

"Don't worry." Billie's tone was as nonchalant as she could manage. "We had no children together, but he had a daughter before we met. He isn't really a part of my life anymore."

" 'Really' is an interesting word use."

"He happens to be a lawyer at one of the firms I'll be working with at Agencis."

"That could be awkward."

"I've got it under control," she lied.

After her encounter with Porter two days ago, she was even less confident than before, but what choice did she have but to deal with it? She was a big girl, and big girls just deal with it.

"I hope you're good at stress relievers," he said. "You'll need it working with your ex. Do you do kick-boxing?"

"No, I'm more of a jogger."

"I'm not talking about exercise," he said. "I mean just plain good ole stress-relief fun."

"I've never done it," she said.

"We'll go kickboxing." He sat back confidently in his seat. "On our next date."

"Getting ahead of ourselves," she said, even though she was already planning their next several dates in her head.

"You have to try it." He looked into her eyes with an intensity that grabbed at her.

"I have to?" she asked, mesmerized by his gaze.

"Kickboxing will transform you, Billie. Not only is it a massive stress reliever, but also the power that you feel. . . . It courses through your veins. It takes you over and you just feel like . . . It's a passionate, sensual feeling."

Billie felt a little breathless for a few moments. She was only torn from his gaze when their appetizers came. She was grateful for the distraction.

"Sounds a little intense to me." She focused on her bowl of lobster bisque, not wanting to get caught up in those eyes of his again.

"It is," he said, "and also addictive. Once you try it, it'll become your favorite hobby, replacing whatever it is you like to do now. What is that, by the way?"

Billie tried to think and was a little surprised that nothing easily came to mind. "Well, I like spending time with my girlfriends more than anything."

"But what do you do by yourself?" he asked. "You know, not with or for someone else, but just for you."

"Um . . ." She was starting to feel embarrassed after a few seconds of not being able to come up with anything. "I guess . . . I used to love to paint."

" 'Used to'? Why don't you do it anymore?"

This perfect evening was starting to get a little uncomfortable for her. She could tell he was enjoying this, intent on her admitting that she had no real hobbies.

"I don't have a lot of time," she said, "but I used to love it. I was awful at it, though."

"That doesn't matter," he said. "If you enjoyed it, then you were great at it. Although I'd like to see one of your paintings, before taking your word for it. I imagine you're a lot better at everything than you give yourself credit for, Billie."

This boy is too much, she told herself. "Too much" usually meant "too good to be true." She urged herself to be cautious; but as the night continued, all Billie could do was find herself liking him more and more. He was funny and curious, two characteristics she loved. His laugh was infectious and he seemed to know right where the line between being suggestive and inappropriate stood and stayed on the edge.

Billie felt silly when she discussed her concern about their working relationship. By the time she'd mentioned it, it no longer seemed like much of a big deal to her. Michael reinforced that fact with his own belief that there was nothing there to worry about. He seemed determined to wipe away any doubt she had about the two of them pursuing something, but it wasn't much necessary. Before the desserts even came, Billie couldn't wait until the next time she'd get to see him again.

Sherise wasn't feeling so great. As she sat in the chair of her office at campaign headquarters, she felt compelled to complain again. This was the third chair she'd sat on in two days. She had demanded that her staff find her something more comfortable. This was ridiculous. She wasn't even two months pregnant; yet she was already feeling her body start to change. That wasn't a good sign. She wouldn't dare ask for another chair. What would LaKeisha say if word got back to her that Sherise was already complaining? No, she'd just bring a better pillow to sit on tomorrow and suck it up.

It was time to leave, anyway; but just as Sherise got up from her chair, there was a knock on her door. "Yes?"

In popped Jesse Williams, a young man on her staff who got the job because he was Northman's Harvard roommate's son. Politics was all about connections. Sherise held some animosity for people like Jesse. He was only twenty-two and as green as grass, but he was born to the right person. His circumstances were so unlike Sherise's, who had to fight for everything she'd gotten, because she didn't have any connected DNA.

"What is it, Jesse?" she asked.

"You know about Congressman Cooper, right?"

"Of course I know about him. Everyone does."

Congressman George Cooper, the pro-life, pro–traditional family Republican from Texas, was caught coming out of a Miami hotel with a rent-a-boy who was barely eighteen and more than eager for the fame that came with bagging a hypocrite. It was the story of the day around D.C.

"LaKeisha says that before you leave, you need to get a statement on her desk for Northman to say."

"He doesn't need to say anything," Sherise said. "I told him that this morning when the news broke. This is Cooper's mess. Let the Republicans wallow in it. Northman needs to stay above it."

Jesse shook his head. "LaKeisha said the Democrats are urging him to make a statement. She said something dry and unattached, but acknowledging his hypocrisy. Cooper went to Yale with Matthews."

Sherise was taken aback. How could she not know that? She'd been listening to the news reports all day and no one had mentioned that connection. This was good news. If they could imply a relationship between Cooper and Matthews, it could force Matthews to get involved in this scandal, which would put a crinkle in his campaign. No, they probably had no real relationship at all, but all one had to do was imply that they've known each other since college, more than twenty-five years. Both ended up in D.C. in national politics. The relationship would be inferred from that.

More important for Sherise, it would distract the press from Jonah for once, since he seemed to be the only person everyone wanted to talk about.

"She'll have it," Sherise said, smiling.

After Jesse left, Sherise went straight for her phone. She was supposed to relieve the babysitter within the hour, but she didn't think she'd be there in time. She was going to write this statement for Northman, but she also needed to create some hints she could leak to the press that insinuated a stronger connection between Matthews and Cooper.

Her momentary excitement at this new opportunity was immediately shattered when she heard a woman's voice say "hello" on the other end of Justin's cell phone.

"Who is this?" Sherise asked tersely.

"Oh," the voice said after a few seconds. "Hello, Sherise. This is Elena."

Sherise's eyes narrowed suspiciously as she gripped the phone more tightly. "Really, Elena? You're calling me 'Sherise' and you're answering my husband's cell phone. Since when did we become such good friends?"

Sherise heard what she thought was a chuckle, which only made her more fuming mad. *This bitch is about to get an earful.*

"I'm sorry, Mrs. Robinson." If Elena was trying to veil her sarcasm, she was horrible at it. "I just thought—"

"You thought wrong," she corrected quickly. "Why are you answering my husband's private phone?"

"I was just here," she said. "I'm in his office. We're working and he stepped away."

"Where is he?" Sherise demanded.

"He just stepped away to go to the bathroom. I didn't think it would be a big deal if I answered it. I was just trying to be—"

"Save it," Sherise said. "You know cell phones are private, and you knew when you picked his up that I was calling. My name was clear as day on the phone."

"I picked it up without looking at—"

"Elena, you're not fooling anyone. Answering a man's private phone when you know it's his wife calling is a classic territorial move."

"Sherise, stop it."

Sherise was halted by the sound of Justin's voice. She paused for a second as she heard him ask Elena to give him a moment.

"Justin, I—"

"What's the matter with you?" he asked.

"Where is she now?"

"She's gone," he said.

"Are you sure?" Sherise asked. "Because last time she was gone, she was actually outside your damn office listening in on us."

"Sherise," he said as almost a sigh.

"I don't appreciate that bitch answering your private phone. She knew it was me. My name is lit . . ."

"Sherise, you can't go around yelling at my coworkers. You just can't. Look, I'll tell her not to answer my phone again, but—"

"Why are you working alone with her, anyway?" Sherise asked.

"The other two are out getting dinner."

"Dinner?"

"Yes," he said. "I was just about to call you. I have to stay tonight and do a working dinner. I'm sorry, but—"

"You can't, Justin." Sherise didn't feel up to another "who makes the sacrifice?" argument. "I have to stay and work on an emergency here. Kenya can only babysit until seven."

"It's out of my hands, Sherise."

"I sincerely doubt that," she said. "You're the boss of your team. If you wanted to go home and leave the work to them, you could do it. But you want to stay. You want more time with your young coworker who knew damn well what she was doing by answering your—"

"Can you get off that already?" he asked, sounding annoyed. "I'm not going to listen to this. I have to work.

The sooner I can get back to it, the sooner I can be home."

"What difference does that make?" Sherise asked. "It's not like you'd be willing to discuss it then either."

"Because it's ridiculous, Sherise. There's nothing to discuss. I have to work late. If you're working late too, just call Kenya. Offer her double for another hour."

"That's your solution?" she asked. "And, of course, I'm the one who has to do it because it's my responsibility, right? I'm the one making this a problem by having the nerve to want a career, so I have to fix it while you have dinner with your little—"

"I'm hanging up, Sherise."

"You hang up on me, don't you even bother coming home tonight, late or not!" she warned.

"Are you kidding me?"

"Do I sound like I'm kidding?"

"Look," he said in that voice that is always meant to defuse a situation where she'd gotten too angry to be rational anymore. "If you want me to call Kenya, I will. I just—"

"Fuck it," Sherise said. "I'll call her. I'll do everything as always. You enjoy your dinner and then come on home, where we'll act like nothing is wrong. The perfect family."

She hung up the phone and slammed it on her desk. She knew from the moment she laid eyes on Elena that the girl was going to be a problem. A problem her marriage couldn't afford at this point. Something would have to be done.

Billie was overseeing Evelyn as she set up the presentation on the computer when the lawyers from Dinklett &

Williams came in. Porter was the third lawyer to enter the main conference room at Agencis, looking right out of a *GQ* magazine cover. When Billie looked up, her eyes met his before he quickly looked away.

This didn't bother her. The less attention Porter gave her, the better. This was awkward enough; and after their encounter last week, Billie's stomach was tightening with every second. What she was bothered by was when the teams shook hands and introduced themselves; he glossed right over her like she wasn't there. Everyone noticed it. Everyone there knew they were once married. Billie had thought, since Porter was always one for appearances, that he'd play nice. To be willing to make himself look bad, Billie realized that Porter was angrier than she had thought.

Porter sat at the middle of the table, kissing up to Gil and the other lawyers on the client team, while Billie graciously got acclimated with the rest of his team. As general counsel, Gil called the meeting to order. As he went over the basics of everything that both sides had already talked about, he was quick and to the point, which Billie liked. There were few questions. She stole a few glances at Porter, who stared straight ahead at the presentation.

Billie was ready when Gil brought up the topic of getting a continuance in order to reply. Sitting at the end of the conference table, she turned away from the presentation to the group.

"I've already spoken with David Atwood at the FTC." Billie's voice was smooth and calm, like she'd hoped it would be. She'd done this many times before. There was no reason for her to be nervous. "I've told him that we need more time for a reply. This investigation came out of nowhere and—"

"You don't actually believe you'll get a delay, do you?" Porter asked, his expression stone.

Billie turned to him, refusing to let it show that his interruption annoyed her.

"Yes, I do," she replied. "I made it clear to David that this type of notification just flies in the face of FTC tradition. As I'm sure your firm knows, there is usually prior notice of complaints and concerns, followed with meetings and then a determination on an investigation, giving ample time to prepare a possible reply."

Porter rolled his eyes and looked down at the notebook in front of him. He was writing something down. Billie told herself it was probably nothing, but there was a part of her that was sure he was taking notes on how to try and embarrass her further.

"After we get the continuance," she said, then slowing her voice noticeably before adding, "and we will, we need you to focus on the reply, of course, but we're concerned about all the document requests from the FTC. There's a five-year window here. We need to get this narrowed."

"Billie, you should know better than that." Porter's tone was clearly condescending.

Billie turned to him; this time, her anger was somewhat visible as her eyes seared into his. He seemed unfazed.

"If the FTC wants documents," he continued. "It's going to get them. Is it really a good use of your company's money to have us—"

"I'll decide what a good use of our money is," Billie interrupted him, much to his surprise. "You just do the work."

The words came out a little harsher than she'd expected, but they had the desired effect. After looking extremely offended at being interrupted, Porter pressed his lips together and returned his attention to his notepad again.

The meeting lasted another hour. The only other time Porter upset Billie again was when she was going over the schedule of updates and he acted a little irked, but he never said anything. No one else seemed to notice, or maybe they were pretending not to see.

Billie noticed and she wasn't about to forget. After the meeting ended, she made the rounds as expected, making sure to talk to everyone again and answer any questions. All the while, she kept a side eye on Porter, making sure he didn't leave before she gave him a piece of her mind.

He'd made his way out into the hallway before she rushed over to him, grabbed him by the arm, and pulled him aside. Fortunately, no one else was around at the moment. Billie knew anyone could step out of that conference room, so she needed to be quick.

"What are you doing?" Porter asked.

"I'd like to ask you the same thing," she sniped. "What's your deal? Why are you trying to one-up me during the meeting?"

He only offered an innocent smile. "*One-up you?* Funny, but no, I wasn't 'one-upping' you, Billie. I was trying to help you out. You shouldn't be running a case. You don't know what you're doing, and I didn't want you to look foolish."

"Bullshit," she said, just under her breath. "You were trying to make me look foolish, and it needs to stop now."

"Excuse me?" he asked sarcastically. "If you don't want my help—"

"I don't need your help," she said. "I just need you

to remember that I'm the client now. I'm not your peer here. You work for me. Don't second-guess me in front of anyone ever again, or you're going to be sorry."

From the enraged look on his face, she realized that her words were sinking in. Or maybe it wasn't just sinking in, but it had already been there and he'd thought she didn't know it. Now that it was out there, Porter looked threatened as hell. Billie felt a sense of satisfaction, at least enough to end it there.

She turned and headed to her office, not bothering to look back. She imagined Porter had been standing there, bowled over, as he usually was whenever she stood up to him. Only this time, he hadn't been frozen in place. He was following her.

"Don't you dare walk away from me!" he demanded.

"I'm done talking to you, Porter." Billie continued to her office at the end of the hallway.

"You're done with me?"

She stopped at the door to her office and turned to face him, waiting for him to approach. He was so livid that she could imagine smoke coming out of his ears about now. All of this time, she'd been thinking that this was going to be very hard on her, but it was Porter who wasn't able to deal. He just figured if he could strike first, she wouldn't figure that out. But she had.

"I know what you wanted," Billie said. "You were hoping you could use your textbook tricks to intimidate me and put me on the offensive. You were hoping that you could work a number on me mentally before I could figure out the truth."

"The truth?" he asked, laughing. "What's that?"

"That you're at my mercy," she said. "You thought you could distract me from that fact by making me constantly on guard against you."

Porter shook his head. "You need to be on guard against me, Billie. I'm a few months away from being made partner. You already cost me that promotion before. I'm not letting you do it again."

"I'm not trying to do anything to you, Porter. You always have it in for me, so you assume I always have it in for you."

"I'm not . . ." Porter held back as Evelyn approached. She was carrying something that was covered in silver wrapping paper, with a red bow around it.

"This came for you," Evelyn said. "It's from Michael."

"Michael who?" Porter asked.

Billie looked at her ex as though he was crazy. "Really, Porter? You really think you're entitled to know that?"

"Is this some new boyfriend?" he asked, ignoring her. He stood up straight, his shoulders arching back in his usual jealous stance. "Who is he?"

"None of your business." Billie took the present. "Thanks, Evelyn. Can you do me a favor and help Mr. Haas here find his group again? He seems to be lost."

"Um . . ." She looked at Porter nervously. "I guess. Okay, can you follow me?"

"I can find out who he is," Porter said as Billie walked into her office.

"I think you have other things on your plate." Billie gave him a cold smile before shutting her office door in his face.

Despite the anxiety she felt about Porter, Billie couldn't deny she was excited to see what Michael had sent her. They were going to have their second date tomorrow night and she'd been looking forward to it before the first date was even over. Every sensible part of her told her not to get too excited. She knew her track record and that Prince Charming just didn't exist anymore.

After she ripped the wrapping off, her heart warmed at the sight of his gift. It was a small, wood-framed, beautiful painting of an adorable little black girl. She couldn't have been more than ten years old, standing next to a window and in front of a canvas, painting a rainbow. She had paint on her nose and her arm. Next to her was a palette of various colors. She'd told him that she used to love to paint and he was listening. A man who listened and remembered? Sensible parts be damned. She was excited as hell.

7

For now, at least, the headquarters for Jonah's campaign staff was set at an ex-lobbyist's office in a building on K Street, downtown D.C. But today was the first official day the team would meet, so Jonah decided to have a BBQ at his Leesburg, Virginia, home.

When Erica showed up, after getting past the security in the driveway, her last time at the eight-thousand-square-foot traditional white-column-and-redbrick Colonial mansion came flooding toward her. She'd learned the truth from Billie and Sherise about Jonah being her father; she'd driven out here to confront him. It was one of the most confusing and painful moments in her young life.

Now she was here again, supposedly on better terms, but still cloaked in secrecy. This time, the subterfuge resulted in her being granted a leave of absence from her job at the Pentagon. Once she'd decided to go work for Jonah, she submitted her paperwork. As policy, she submitted it to Caroline, who laughed in her face. To Caroline's surprise, the top office was waiting for the paperwork and had already approved the leave, which could start immediately.

Caroline was furious, demanding it be at least pushed back until major projects the department was working on had been done, but her request was denied. Erica couldn't help but offer her boss a bright, sweet smile as she dropped by her office just to say good-bye. It was just too easy.

Now that she was here, standing at the front door of this home again after such a painful first time, nothing was easy. This would be harder than she could have ever expected. It was true that this could be a great opportunity for her. She was getting paid good money, and not having to deal with Caroline every day was worth twice what she made in actual dollars. But there was also Sherise; and although Erica still wasn't sure she could help her, she was willing to get close enough to Jonah to try.

"Erica!" Alex met her at the door with a wide smile on his face and an outstretched hand. "Finally we meet again."

Erica shook his hand. He gripped her hand tightly and led her into the house.

The inside of the house was just as Erica expected it to be. It was English-style with old, expensive things on display and mostly everything was white. The foyer was wide, with a white-and-gray-speckled marble floor, which led into a hallway through the middle, and a winding black staircase to the right. It was very mon-eyed D.C.

"Erica?" Alex asked. "Are you okay?"

Erica blinked, not realizing that she had frozen in

place in the foyer. Alex was a few feet ahead of her, seeming surprised that she still wasn't following him.

"Um . . ." Erica rushed to catch up with him. "Yeah, I'm fine. I'm just . . . It's a nice house."

"Everything here is nice," he said, leading her toward the back of the house. "I envy the kids who grew up here."

"Where did you grow up?" Erica asked.

"Herndon," he said. "You're from D.C., right? Jonah told me that you were."

She wondered what else Jonah was telling people about her. "How long have you known him?"

"Come in here," he said.

They entered the kitchen, which looked newly remodeled with white cabinets and red granite countertops and stainless-steel appliances everywhere. It was way too spacious for an original kitchen, so Erica assumed either room had been added or another room had been knocked out to expand it. There were five people working there, with plenty of room among them.

"Take this." He handed her a bottle of water. "You can come back here for snacks, but there's a whole spread in the formal dining room. We're going to wait until after Jonah gives his big speech to the team before eating that."

"Sounds good. I'm not that hungry yet." Erica knew she wasn't being that expressive, but she was feeling weird walking through this house. Alex's words about being jealous of the kids who grew up there pressed a button somewhere in her.

"My mom was a housekeeper for his sister, Emma, but after I was born, my mom stopped working for her. My dad died when she was pregnant with me. After that, she just needed to start a new life."

"I'm sorry to hear that," she said.

Erica always felt compassion when meeting other people who also had grown up without their fathers. Maybe that was why she felt she and Alex had a lot in common.

"Thanks," Alex said. "My mom went on to work for someone else, but she stayed friends with Emma. So I met him a few times as a friend whenever I was at Emma's house and he came over. But then I went off to boarding school."

"You went to private school?" Erica realized how rude she sounded as she said it, but most kids of maids don't go to boarding schools.

"I got a scholarship to a school in New York," he said. "Then I went to Columbia. I've only been back for four years, but Jonah was totally cool with offering me this job after hearing I was working on Capitol Hill."

"You know I have no campaign experience at all," she said.

He nodded. "I'm not worried. Jonah said you're great at organizing things, a skill we'll desperately need as events and schedules get more complicated. I'm gonna get you started on the grunt work. Come with me."

She turned as they left the kitchen, down a hallway.

He explained as they walked. "In the study down here, staffers are putting together mailers for fund-raising. That should be enough for—"

"Alex!"

Running up to them was a blond girl holding a phone out to Alex as she approached. "It's ABC, and Stephen isn't around. Who handles the media when he's not around?"

"Eliza, I think." Alex took the phone from her.

"Not sure. Hey, Erica, you can head down to the room on the right, at the end of the hall. I'll catch up with you in a bit."

"Okay." Erica watched him rush off with the girl before she turned and headed for the hall.

"So you showed up."

Erica stopped at the sound of the slurred voice. She turned to her left to see Juliet Nolan standing in the doorway to what looked like a guest bath. Juliet was held together very well for a woman in her fifties who, Erica got the impression, had been drinking a lot for a long time. That was what money could do for you.

She was drab, but in a blue-blooded sort of way that still had an appeal. Her blue eyes were a little glassy and she wore practically no makeup. She had her blond hair in an updo; her pink button-down shirt was tucked tightly into white jeans. The only thing sparkling about her was the expensive pearl earrings and necklace she wore.

Erica had never had a good encounter with this woman. She could tell from the way Juliet was looking at her now, and the glass of wine she held in her hand, that this would be no different.

Jonah had told her from the beginning that Juliet knew about Erica being his daughter. He'd trusted her and told her. According to Jonah, she was the only person he'd ever told. She encouraged him to keep this a secret for his career. According to Jonah, it was cloaked in a play at concern for Erica's best interest. Erica could just imagine this woman pretending to care that going public would be hard on her. She didn't give a damn about Erica. The truth was, she didn't want her perfect family soiled and her chances to get into the White House compromised by his black love child.

In the past, Juliet had pretty much ignored Erica, except for the occasional chance to give her the evil eye. Erica had hoped that trend could continue.

"Do you even care how dangerous it is that you're here?" Juliet asked. The one hand that wasn't holding her wineglass was placed on her trim hip.

"I think you need to discuss that with Jonah" was all Erica said.

"I've tried to," Juliet countered. "But you've convinced him to keep you around."

"I've convinced him?" Erica had to laugh. "Is that what he's told you, or is that what you've decided to believe?"

Juliet leaned toward Erica, her face only inches from hers. "Just know that I don't want you here. I've worked my ass off for this chance, and I'm not letting you mess it up for me."

Erica didn't move or blink. The scent of superiority emanating from this woman was only overpowered by the alcohol on her breath. Did she actually think she was intimidating her? Did she have any idea where Erica came from? She'd faced five-year-olds tougher than this prissy lush.

"Juliet."

Juliet seemed startled when Jonah showed up in the hallway. Erica observed her as she seemed to try and pull herself together as he joined them. She was nervous, Erica could tell. She'd probably promised to behave; but after a couple of glasses of Pinot Grigio, she wasn't as in control as she'd thought.

"What are you doing?" Jonah asked her accusingly.

Erica watched as his eyes seared into Juliet's, not hiding his anger. She looked away and cleared her throat.

Then she turned back to him with something resembling puppy dog eyes.

"It's nothing, dear," she said sweetly.

"It didn't sound like *nothing,*" Jonah complained.

"I knew you'd take her side," Juliet curtly snapped. "She's going to ruin everything."

Looking as if she was about to get hysterical, Juliet turned and ran toward the kitchen. Jonah looked at Erica. She could see a sort of apology in his eyes, but also a look of helplessness. In that one look, Erica knew what their entire marriage was made of. It was kind of sad, and she felt sorry for him, even though he was an unabashed cheater.

"We'll talk later," he said, before turning to rush after his wife.

"That's a mess," Erica whispered to herself as she watched him quickly walk away.

He was only a few feet away when Alex appeared again in the hallway. He didn't look at Jonah walk past him. He was just looking at Erica and she knew why. He'd seen the whole thing. But what did he hear?

"What was that about?" he asked as he approached.

Erica shrugged. "I think she's a little tipsy. I stay out of things that aren't my business."

"Just make sure you stay away from her," Alex said. "I know I do."

"You do?" she asked. "Why?"

"I don't know her that well," Alex said. "She never came by Emma's house when Jonah did. But my mom didn't like her. She said she wasn't a nice person and I should keep my distance."

"I'm not afraid of her," Erica said.

"Afraid?" Alex looked confused. "Why would you

say that? Look, we'll both keep an eye out and give each other a heads-up whenever she's coming around. Deal?"

"Deal." She smiled as they bumped fists.

Sherise was having an unusually slow start this morning. After last night's argument with Justin, he'd come home and slept in the guest room. He was gone by the time she'd gotten up that morning and it was making her heart ache. This was all her fault. As usual, she had gotten a hot head. Instead of just telling him what had upset her, she attacked him. They'd gone over this in therapy, but Sherise obviously couldn't learn her lesson. She had to figure some way to apologize to him and fix this, and she had to figure out how to get Elena's ass away from her husband.

However, she couldn't do that without her morning coffee. As Sherise headed to the kitchen area of the office, her nosy nature stopped her. A man, looking shady as hell, in her opinion, was following LaKeisha into her office just a few doors down. He was white, rotund, with balding white hair, wearing jeans and a leather jacket.

After LaKeisha closed the door behind them, Sherise rushed over to Amy Griffin, who was LaKeisha's assistant. Amy sat at the desk closest to LaKeisha's office.

"Who is that?" Sherise asked.

She felt it was better just to come out with what she wanted to know. It usually held more weight than beating around the bush. She wasn't a consultant anymore. She was in a power position now and was going to use that if she needed.

"I'm told he's no one," Amy responded, with a rolling of her eyes.

Amy Griffin was a mousy, ponytailed twentysome-
thing, with a face that looked like she'd just tasted a
lemon.

"Well, then," Sherise said, "who is 'no one'? He
looks shady."

"He is shady," Amy responded. "All PI types are."

"He's a private investigator?" Sherise asked, her
antenna lighting up.

Amy nodded. "I didn't tell you anything, but
LaKeisha hired him to get some dirt on Jonah Nolan."

"What's his name?"

"His name is Jonathan T. No last name, just T.
That's your first clue."

"Who does he work for?"

"Apparently, himself," Amy answered. "I asked for
some paperwork to send to Livia, you know, to pay him
like we do all consultants, but LaKeisha was, like, no,
she would pay him."

"All our funds have to be accounted for," Sherise
said. "She doesn't want any paper trails leading back to
him."

"Or us," Amy added. "And you can't tell Northman. He's not supposed to know about this. Whatever
this guy does, I get the feeling that he doesn't always
follow the law. LaKeisha said Northman can't ever
know about him."

"That's not smart," Sherise said. "She should have
met him somewhere remote. He's been brought to our
offices now. Northman officially knows him."

Sherise was disappointed in LaKeisha's rookie
move, but she was more concerned about this PI. He
was looking for dirt. He was looking for her. Sherise
had to find out what Erica had learned so far. First,

though, she had to find out everything she could about Jonathan T. Would these new problems ever stop coming?

Billie's second date with Michael was going great so far. It was a Thursday-night movie outdoors at Capitol Riverfront, an area in Southeast D.C., between Capitol Hill and the Anacostia River. Every Thursday night, starting in May through August, the site was host to a movie on a large screen in front of a large park sitting area. It was a growing, developing area near the Washington Nationals baseball stadium, which looked very different now than it did when Billie was a young girl growing up nearby.

Michael had been prepared with a blanket and a basket filled with food, including two wine glasses and a bottle of Pinot to share during a viewing of *Raiders of the Lost Ark*. It wasn't the most romantic movie, Billie thought, but Michael more than made up for that with a spread of roasted chicken, dill potato salad, bacon-wrapped asparagus, and bread. He didn't try for a second to fake it, admitting right away that he'd picked up the whole set, including the tote it came in, at a catering company before arriving at her doorstep.

There was less talking than on the first date, just some whispering about the movie and chitchat. Although she had already done so, she thanked him again for the small painting he'd sent her.

They began the evening sitting up, but soon were lying down on the blanket. There had been a foot or so of distance between them during most of the movie as their food was placed there. After they'd eaten, Michael removed the plates and uneaten food back to the black-

and-blue argyle tote bag. At some point during the evening, that gap got smaller and smaller.

Billie wasn't sure how it happened—whether it was she or Michael who had moved—but at the point when Indiana Jones was warning the Nazis not to open the Ark, their shoulders touched. Her gaze left the large screen in front of them and went down to the blanket. She felt a definite spark, despite the tenderness of the connection. Billie let herself smile in a way he could clearly see, even though she wasn't so sure that was something she should give away so quickly. There was a moment of silence, which seemed painstakingly long to Billie, before Michael whispered to her.

"Sorry" was all he said as he pulled away a little.

The sound of his voice, deep and low, sent a tingling sensation through her. It took her a moment to gather the nerve to look at him. She was scared she'd give away how much she wanted his shoulder touching hers again, how much she wanted to hear him speak in that deep, Southern voice.

When she did turn her head slowly to him, he was looking at her with a very serious look on his face. Was it the dimly lit night, or was this man getting more handsome every time she looked at him? Billie felt her breath catch a little. She swallowed hard before managing a polite smile.

"It's okay," she said, speaking in a voice pitched higher than she'd hoped.

To Billie's disappointment, the movie only lasted another half hour. She wanted at least another hour of not-so-accidental shoulder brushes and nervous laughs at scenes that weren't actually intended to be funny.

When the credits began to run, everyone around

them—the people Billie had forgotten were even there—
began to get up. Chatter lifted and it was suddenly very
loud.

"I guess it's time to head on out," Michael said, his
voice showing a hint of reluctance, much to Billie's
pleasure.

"Yeah," Billie said as she started to get up. "We
should probably get . . ."

Maybe it was lying in one position for so long that
made her legs weak, having a couple of glasses of wine,
or just plain clumsiness, but Billie stumbled before she
was even halfway up and went flying toward the ground.

"Whoa!" Michael said as he reached out for her.

Humiliated, Billie banged right into him, landing in
his arms, which he used to grasp her and keep her from
doing more damage. She felt her whole body flush with
the heat of embarrassment. As soon as she turned to him
with the intent of apologizing, that heat changed to
something else entirely.

His eyes lowered to her lips as his opened just a
bit. Billie felt a pull in her stomach, which was notice-
able desire, as she lifted her mouth to his. When his
lips came down on hers, she let out a little whimper. It
was soft and tender, slowly deepening with intensity as
her body began heating up like an inferno.

She felt shivers as his hand came around and began
to caress her bare arm. Then he grabbed her more
firmly and pulled her closer to him.

Billie brought her hand to his chin as she cupped it
and immersed herself in the mastery of his lips. His
lips were soft and he worked them seductively, making
her feel this kiss throughout her entire body.

It wasn't until she heard some whistling from the

exiting crowd around them that Billie realized that they were full-on making out in public. She lightly made distance between them and leaned away. Their eyes caught in that moment and he seemed to realize the same, just a little later than she had.

"It's my turn to apologize," she said.

"Why would you?" he asked, letting her go. "That was great. Or maybe I'm speaking too soon."

"That kiss?" She smiled as she sat up. "Yes, that was, um . . . fantastic, but I meant for falling for you. No, I mean *on you* . . . for falling on you . . . again."

He sat up and faced her. "You're tiny, Billie. I barely felt anything. Well, I wouldn't say that I didn't feel anything, but it certainly wasn't pain."

She laughed and slapped him on the arm; that was the only thing she could think of to deal with the discomfort of her attraction to him and tripping over her own words. Billie thought it was a stupid move and imagined he was probably already regretting kissing a high-school girl who couldn't complete a full sentence.

"So you're okay with what just happened?" he asked, his eyes holding a little uncertainty.

"Haven't been that okay with something in a long time," Billie answered, feeling refreshed at not feeling the need to cover up anything.

He smiled in a very satisfied way. "Good, because I've been wanting to do that since that first time we met on the train. I thought at that moment, when I caught you, 'Man, I want to kiss this girl.' But I figured you'd slap me and have me arrested."

An open, kind smile formed at her lips. "Probably would have been a bit soon for that move."

He nodded, slowly standing up. "Which is why I

didn't do it. But I wanted to, and I'm glad I finally got to."

He held his hand down to her. Billie reached up and took it, hoping this time she could manage to stand up like an adult and not create another disaster. When she was finally on her feet, she looked up at him. His hand was still holding hers.

"I really had a great time, Michael. I—"

Her breath caught as his hand squeezed hers only slightly and he leaned forward. "I really want to see you again, Billie. Soon."

The intensity in his eyes turned her on even more than the kiss had. What was happening to her? Billie hadn't felt this attracted to a man physically since . . .

"Michael," she whispered to him, "I've had a lot of bad luck with men recently or since . . . forever. I hope you understand if I want to be cautious."

"I've had the same." He let her hand go and took one step back. "Romance has taken a backseat to my career because it just didn't seem like it was happening for me. Whenever I gave someone a chance, I ended up regretting it. I got tired of endless setups with nothing to show for it."

"So you do understand?" she asked.

He shook his head. "No, Billie. I don't think we should be cautious at all. I'm very attracted to you and I think you feel the same. There's something here and it excites me too much to be cautious. I think it's about time for both of our lucks to change. Don't you?"

"Then what?" Erica asked.

She was taking a break in a private room at Nolan

headquarters downtown and talking to Billie on the phone about her date with Michael last night. Not only was she happy to hear that flirtatious excitement in Billie's voice, which she hadn't heard in a very long time, but she was also grateful for the distraction from the monotony of labeling brochures.

"Did you agree with him?"

"I didn't know how to respond," Billie answered.

She was sitting at her desk, having spent most of the morning reliving the events of last night until the last moment. Billie had to share with her girls, but she knew Sherise had her plate full, so she decided to call Erica.

"I said, 'We'll see,' and left it at that. Then he drove me home."

"Is that it?" Erica asked. "You didn't kiss him again?"

"Of course I kissed him again."

"And?"

"Nothing happened," Billie said. "I mean, nothing happened after the kiss. A lot happened during the kiss."

"Sounds like he's a good kisser," Erica said. "God knows nothing is better than a good kisser."

"Just perfect," Billie said. "Perfect mouth mastery and pressure. You know, just the right amount to feel just overpowered enough to be turned on like crazy."

"But not crazy enough if you say nothing happened after."

"That's the thing," Billie said. "Enough happened for me to know I better not invite him in, or panties would have dropped."

"Didn't trust yourself, huh?" Erica laughed.

Billie laughed too. "So we're going out again this weekend."

"Look at you moving fast, Billie. That's not like you. I'm impressed. So date number three. That means—"

"Not moving *that fast,*" Billie insisted. "Well, at least I don't plan to."

"Sherise will be mad at you for sleeping with a guy before she's vetted him."

Billie made a smacking sound with her lips. "I don't need Sherise's vetting."

"You Googled him yourself, huh?"

"Of course I did, but he doesn't run in Sherise's circles. He's not a social climber. He's focused on real community work. Rolling-your-sleeves-up community service, not writing a check and clinking champagne glasses at a fund-raiser."

"Sounds like your kind of guy," Erica said.

There was a knock on the door and Erica could hear Alex call her name.

"I have to go," Erica said. "But we're getting to-gether this weekend, right? Even Sherise?"

"She says she'll be there," Billie said.

"Can't wait, bye."

Erica got off the phone and rushed to the door of the tiny space. Opening it, she saw Alex standing out-side with a look of concern on his face.

"You okay?" he asked.

"Of course," she answered. "Why?"

"Nothing." He shook his head. "It just seemed like you rushed out when you got a call. Just wanted to make sure everything was okay."

"Thanks for worrying." She gently placed her hand on his shoulder and incidentally felt his muscles. He didn't look that muscular on the outside, but rather more trim and fit. "I'm good. Just taking a break."

"Ready for your first trip?" he asked.

"I thought I wasn't high enough up to make a trip."

"Jonah wants you there," Alex said.

Erica wasn't sure what to think about that. She smiled a little nervously, wondering if Alex thought this was weird. He knew she'd worked closely with Jonah when she was at the Pentagon, but didn't it seem weird he would ask a low-level staffer to take a trip?

"Don't worry," he added. "Juliet won't be there."

"Good," Erica said, genuinely relieved. "So, where and when?"

"Iowa," he said. "I know, sexy, right? But all roads to the White House begin in Iowa. It's just for the day. You have two hours to pack."

"Now?"

Alex smiled. "Um, yeah. That's how these things work, kid."

"Kid?" She pressed her lips together and squinted her eyes at him. "Watch it. I'm four years older than you."

"But I'm the boss." He pointed at her playfully.

"So you think." She swatted at his hand. "Two hours isn't a lot, Alex."

"Don't be such a girl," he teased. "It's just a day. I'll make you a deal. Run to your place and get your things. You get back here by noon and I'll have some Korean tacos from that food truck you love so much waiting here for you. We'll have lunch together. Then we'll head to Iowa."

"Deal," Erica said.

She liked that idea a lot, maybe more than she was willing to admit to herself.

"But wait," she said. "The airport is a hassle. Won't it take longer than that?"

"We're taking a private jet. We get to bypass the bull-shit."

"Provided by a generous supporter, no doubt," Erica said.

"You're learning the lingo," he said. "Don't worry. I'll be there. We'll both make sure neither of us lets it get to our heads."

Erica could tell she had an ally in Alex and was probably going to need him to get through this.

8

High tea in the D.C. area was a social tradition that most of the area's residents weren't even aware of. Although it was available many days during the week, women who were considered "in the know" took part in it on Saturdays or Sundays at select hotels downtown.

It usually happened between three and five in the afternoon and early evening. Tea was served from individual pots, alongside finger sandwiches, such as smoked salmon and crab salad, presented on a silver tray. For around $45 or $50, women relaxed in comfortable chairs in luxurious settings and caught up.

Probably, the most elegant of high teas took place at the storied Mayflower Hotel's Café Promenade. However, for the last three years, the girls preferred high tea at the Empress Lounge of the Mandarin Oriental, where they were this Saturday afternoon. They preferred it because it was a younger crowd, less stuffy, and the food selections were more dessert oriented, with cakes and cookies. They used to do high tea at least once every few months. Lately, though, with their schedules and lives, it was turning into a twice-a-year event.

Although they usually enjoyed a glass of champagne before tea, in deference to Sherise's condition, they all stuck with tea, a selection of white lotus and rose petal, as they listened to Sherise share her concerns about Elena.

"You think I'm overblowing this," Sherise said, sensing the lack of urgency in their attention. "And don't you dare say I'm being hormonal. I'm a conniving, manipulative woman—and I know one when I see one."

Erica almost spit out some of her cupcake as she laughed. She gave it to Sherise—she wasn't blind to what she was.

"I'm not saying you're wrong," Erica said. "I'm just saying you don't have enough to go on to come to the conclusion that this woman is after your husband. You talked to your sources at the firm. She's a known flirt at the office. No one seems to think she's particularly interested in Justin. She just works for him."

"Do I need to repeat the phone incident to you?" Sherise asked, taking a bite of a fruit tart. She was ravenous—this being the first day in a while when she didn't want to throw up at the sight of food.

"Sorry, Erica," Billie chimed in, "but trust me. You know I'm an expert at this. Answering a married male coworker's private cell phone is a sign of danger. Think about it. Would you ever do that? Especially if you saw the name on the phone was his wife's?"

Erica couldn't deny that it sounded a little weird. "It's just that your marriage has enough problems without injecting jealousy in."

"I'm not jealous," Sherise insisted. "It's not about that. I just don't trust him. . . . I mean *her.*"

Erica pointed at her. "You slipped up there."

"I meant *her,*" Sherise insisted, frustrated.

"No, you didn't," Erica countered. "You don't trust him, and that's the problem. Justin has worked with beautiful women before."

Sherise sighed, placing her cup of tea on the table. "I should be willing to trust him again. I know that Jennifer targeted him. He would have never slept with her otherwise."

"She didn't force him down on the bed," Billie said. "You know how I tried to blame it all on Claire when I found out about her and Porter. Saying this little blond bitch seduced my husband, but Porter made his choices. Claire didn't force him to do anything. Justin made a choice to give in to whatever temptation Jennifer was throwing his way, and you're afraid he's gonna do the same with Elena."

"I don't trust him," Sherise admitted. "Now that Justin knows about Ryan, I just feel like . . . I don't know. That maybe I'm not worth being faithful to anymore."

"From everything that's been going on," Billie said, "it sounds to me like he wanted this to work as much as you did."

"You need to go back to regular therapy," Erica said. "Like you were, in the beginning."

Sherise's hands formed into fists. "I don't want to do that."

"Calm down," Billie warned.

"I'm just pissed," Sherise said loudly. "Why is this happening now? Just when I thought we were getting somewhere good again. We were sharing again, you know, really talking to each other. This job with Northman I can handle, but now Elena and this baby . . . I just don't know."

"The baby is a blessing," Erica said. "You can't think of it as anything but that, even if you didn't plan it."

"That's the thing." Sherise's brows narrowed as feelings of guilt took her over. "I think this is what hurts the most. I'm feeling resentment toward this baby. Like it's the baby's fault that Justin thinks I got pregnant to trap him. I blame it for making me get fat, just as another, younger, thinner woman has her eyes on my husband."

"That's not good, honey." Billie scooted over on the settee they were sitting on and wrapped her arms around Sherise.

Sherise leaned in and laid her head on Billie's shoulder. "I hate myself for feeling this way toward an innocent, little baby. It needs my complete love and devotion, and I'm being the worst mother."

"You're stressed out and hurting," Billie said. "You're worried about Jonah, Elena, Justin, and the job. It's too much."

"We're going to help you through this," Erica said.

"I know you will." Sherise looked at her.

"Erica is working on the Jonah issue." Billie nodded in Erica's direction as a hint for her to say something more.

"I haven't found anything out yet," Erica lamented. "I'm folding brochures and stuff. Even in Iowa, I was just following Alex around taking down names of potential donors. I barely even spoke to Jonah."

"LaKeisha has hired a PI," Sherise said. "His name is Jonathan T or something. I'm scared to death. He's so exclusive that even I couldn't find anything on him. Honestly, I've been trying to discreetly track down info on this guy for the past three days. In D.C., when a PI is invisible, that means he works for the most powerful and can get access that the average PI can't. You have to let Jonah know."

"How?" Erica asked. "You don't even know anything. Besides, he'll know I'm getting this from you."

"Sherise." Billie used her calming teacher's voice. "Jonah knows that the top people are looking into him. He'll be prepared for this Jonathan T. Hell, he's probably hired him before."

Sherise nodded. She wanted to believe that so bad. "Someone as underhanded as Jonah should know more, and, yes, it makes sense that he is prepared, but I swear I won't get any sleep until I find out what Jonah plans on doing. What about this boy Alex you keep talking about?"

"I don't talk about him," Erica said defensively.

"Yes, you do." Billie smiled. "You talk about him a lot. You had a lot of fun in Iowa with him, remember? You told me on the phone last night that—"

"Whatever," Erica said nervously. "He's my boss."

"But he's closer to Jonah," Sherise said. "He's probably in meetings with him."

"I don't want to take advantage of Alex," Erica said. "He's my only friend there. I would never use him."

Billie leaned away from Sherise and toward Erica, noticing that little gleam in her eye. "You like him, don't you?"

"He's the only person there I do like," Erica answered.

"That's not what she means," Sherise said judgingly. "She means you want to fuck him. Have you?"

Erica gasped. "Hell no. I'm not thinking about him like that. No way. We're friends. Can't I have a male friend I want to be loyal to and not use?"

"No," Sherise said. "Not when your loyalty to him interferes with your loyalty to me. If he was your man, that would be one thing, but he's not. He's not, right?"

"Stop it," Billie said to Sherise.

"No," Sherise said. "I'm glad that you like some- one who is actually worthy of you, instead of the thugs you're used to dating, but —"

"You really want to go there?" Erica asked. "Just when I was trying to comfort you."

"I don't need comfort." Sherise sat up straight. "I need answers. You're my sister, not Alex's. Or maybe it's not your loyalty to Alex that's the conflict."

"Here we go." Erica threw her hands in the air.

"You want to be daddy's little girl, still," Sherise continued. "But it's not gonna happen. Jonah isn't ca- pable of real love. You'll always be kept at arm's length. Don't let hanging out in that McMansion or flying in private jets to Iowa fool you. Jonah will never be the father you want."

Erica was indignant in the face of Sherise's repeated accusations. "I'm not . . . You know what, Sherise. Fuck you."

"Erica." Billie gestured for calm. Sherise was being a bitch, but she didn't need to be upset anymore.

"No," Erica said. "You put yourself in this situa- tion, but you keep attacking me as if that's gonna make me want to help you more. I'm sick of it. You say one more word to me about me wanting to be Jonah's pre- cious, little daughter, and I'm not gonna do one more thing for you."

"You're not doing anything for me now," Sherise protested. "My entire life is hanging in the balance and you won't even help me warn Jonah about a real threat to him."

"Just keep your mouth shut!" Erica yelled, loud enough to garner looks from ladies nearby.

Sherise's head went back and her eyes widened. "What do you mean by that?"

"I mean," Erica continued, "you're the threat to Jonah. He's going to cover his own ass, and as long as you keep your mouth shut, you won't have a problem. So just shut the fuck up!"

Erica hadn't really realized the impact of what she'd said until both Billie and Sherise stared at her blankly. In that second, she felt awful.

"Oh, my God." Sherise was smacked with the reality of what Erica was suggesting—what she was sure she was suggesting.

"What are you insinuating, Erica?" Billie asked.

"Nothing." Erica let out a groan and fell back on the settee. "I'm not suggesting anything. It's just . . . . That's just what Jonah told me. When I mentioned that Sherise was nervous about all this—"

"Wait a second," Sherise interrupted. "You're telling him about these conversations? You're telling him—"

"Of course not," Erica insisted. "I just mentioned it in general. He seemed to . . . Well, he seemed to say as long as you didn't say anything to anyone, that—"

"And if I did?" Sherise asked, her hand unknowingly going to her stomach.

"He didn't threaten you," Erica said.

"That sounds innocent coming from anyone but

Jonah," Billie said. "You know him, Erica. A man like that saying such a thing could mean more than just the words convey."

"He wouldn't hurt her," Erica said. "He wouldn't do that to me. He knows I would never forgive him. I would never let him get away with it."

"That's your problem, Erica." Sherise stood up. "You live in your little fantasy world where he's concerned. You say that like he'd even let you be around to forgive him or let him get away with it. Do you think for one second, if you posed a threat to him, you'd still be around?"

"He wouldn't hurt me!" Erica cried out.

"What are you doing?" Billie asked Sherise.

"I'm going home." Sherise reached for her jacket on the hook next to their table. "My life has just been threatened. I'm not in the mood for tea."

"Oh, for . . ." Erica couldn't believe this. "No one is threatening you, Sherise. Sit down."

"Sherise . . . ," Billie began to implore as she stood up.

"No." Sherise held up a hand to stop her. "Don't try to talk to me. I can't really take any more of either of you."

"What did I do?" Billie asked. "I'm trying to—"

"Stop!" Sherise was waving her hands frantically. "I can't take this anymore. I need to go home, where I feel safe."

"Sherise!" Erica called after her as Billie sat back down.

Billie's phone, resting on the table, made a *ping* sound as a text message came across. Billie reached for it, looking at Erica.

"You shouldn't have said that, Erica."

"It slipped out. She's not in danger. He just meant if she kept her mouth shut, nothing could be confirmed."

"You know it could mean anything with Jonah." She noted the message from Michael about their date later that night.

"I regretted it right away." Erica noticed Billie's expression. "Who is that from? Michael?"

Billie nodded, smiling. "We're going out tonight. Dinner at Komi."

Erica was impressed. "Wish I was dating someone that had the money to take me there. You really like him, don't you?"

"He's amazing. I can't stop looking at that painting he got me. It's so sweet. It's so not what I'm used to."

"You know we have to meet him," Erica said. "No point in your going much further until we've met him. He has to meet our approval."

"He will," Billie said. "You'll like him. I don't know about Sherise."

"He's got a good education and a lot of money?" Erica asked. "She'll like him. Besides, she'll be happy that you just have someone to make Porter jealous as hell when he finds out."

"He already kind of has." Billie recalled the situation when Porter asked about the gift brought to her office. "He was an ass, as usual."

"But this is your chance to be an ass right back," Erica said.

"You sound like Sherise."

Billie knew what she had the power to do, but Tara was always in the back of her mind. She needed Porter if she was ever gonna get Tara back in her life again.

Erica reached for her dessert, but she changed her mind. She couldn't really eat another bite. She only had Sherise on her mind.

"What am I going to do about her?" she asked. "I've really fucked up making her scared now. I just added to her worries. I have to call her."

"Give her some time," Billie said. "No matter what she said, it is hormones. But from now on, don't say anything to her unless it's good news. She can't really take it right now."

If you want something done right, do it yourself, Sherise decided. This oft-repeated phrase never rang more true for her than it did now. After realizing that she wasn't going to get any help from Erica in stopping Jonathan T from finding out about her and Jonah's affair, Sherise was going to take on yet another task . . . and would do it herself.

First thing that morning, she checked LaKeisha's phone for her private schedule after LaKeisha stepped out to the ladies' room. She got lucky right away. There was a blocked-out section between two to three in the afternoon. No names, no locations, no subject, just a block out. She kept an eye on LaKeisha; and, as expected, at a quarter to two, she headed out. Sherise followed. Fortunately for her, LaKeisha was walking to her destination, so no cabbies to try and explain her stalking to.

LaKeisha walked into a local dive called Ed's Bar and took a seat in a back booth. She sat down alone, so Sherise knew this was her time, before the other party arrived.

The look on LaKeisha's face as Sherise slid into the booth right next to her was surprise. For once, LaKeisha was speechless.

"You need to be better than this," Sherise said.

LaKeisha slid a little farther down the booth. "What are you doing here?"

"I followed you," Sherise said. "You're at too high a level in this game to be pulling these stunts, LaKeisha. You know better."

"What stunts?"

"You're meeting the PI, right?" Sherise could see from the expression on her face that she was right. "Jonathan whatever?"

"This doesn't have anything to do with you." LaKeisha fiddled with the silverware on the table. "He's the best PI on the East Coast. He's taken down the most powerful . . . How dare you follow me?"

"I know you're mad at me," Sherise said, "but hear me out. He should have never come to the office."

"I'm protecting Northman," she said. "You don't have to worry about that."

"You've already exposed him. He's been spotted at headquarters. He's tied to Northman now."

LaKeisha looked as if she regretted her choice, but then she suddenly shrugged. "Well, I can't change that. I'm meeting him outside of the office from now on. You should leave."

"This is a messy move too," Sherise added, setting her purse down to let LaKeisha know she wasn't going anywhere. "This is too close to HQ. I was able to follow you, just on a hunch. You don't think the Matthews people have a person outside our office looking for someone to follow?"

LaKeisha just made a little groaning sound. She

didn't like her mistakes being pointed out, especially if she couldn't refute them.

"What is he looking for?" Sherise asked. "Sex? Of course that's what he's looking for. Bad move, LaKeisha."

"How so?" LaKeisha asked, annoyed.

"No one cares about that anymore," Sherise lied. "Yes, it's titillating and all that, but it doesn't stick. After Clinton, no one thinks it can keep a man from governing well. It only matters when it can be targeted as hypocrisy, and Jonah has never been one to preach family values."

"It'll put a chink in his armor," LaKeisha said. "We need that."

"He's a VP candidate," Sherise said. "Sexual chinks in his armor won't be relevant. No one believes he'll be running the country for at least another eight years. That stuff fades after weeks."

"Well, I think—"

"You're not thinking," Sherise interrupted. "The key to bring Jonah down in a way that will hurt Matthews is to find something illegal or at least so professionally un-ethical that it compromised security. Stay away from the personal stuff. Make him dangerous to America, not just to his wife."

Sherise could see that what she was saying was sink-ing in a little bit.

Just then, the man earlier identified as Jonathan T showed up at the booth. Both women turned to him. He saw Sherise and his weathered face held a disappointed frown.

"I'm out," he said.

"Wait!" LaKeisha called after him just as he turned away. "It's okay."

He turned back, looking at LaKeisha with uncer-tainty. "You said I'm only dealing with you from beginning to end. If anyone else says otherwise, then it's a trap."

"I know." LaKeisha gestured for him to sit down. "This is Sherise. She works with me. She has some good ideas."

He eyed Sherise as he slowly sat in the booth across from them. She eyed him right back, not showing a hint of concern as her gaze never left his.

"Sherise," LaKeisha began, "this is Jonathan—"

"Jonathan is enough," he said quickly. "You know how I feel about meeting new people. I thought I was clear at our last meeting."

"Fine," Sherise said. "We can skip the niceties. What are we here for?"

The PI looked at LaKeisha, who gave him a nod. He sat back in the booth, looking around the restaurant.

"Don't worry," LaKeisha said. "I've told the waiter not to bother us until I ask for him."

"Like I told you the other day," he stated, "I have a source that gets me access to legal records that are not, I guess, public."

"How not public?" Sherise asked.

"Like they haven't officially been filed yet."

Sherise found that impressive, but also alarming. "How could you possibly get those without getting access to—"

"I was told I wouldn't be questioned," he said, sounding frustrated.

"Sorry," Sherise said. "Go on."

"I found something interesting," he said. "Mrs. Nolan wrote up papers for divorce, with Shali and Miller, divorce lawyers to the rich, citing 'infidelity.' "

Sherise swallowed, gripping at her knees under the table. "Did she name a . . . a third party?"

"No," he answered.

"I find it hard to believe she cited 'infidelity,' " LaKeisha said. "Everyone cites 'irreconcilable differences.' "

"They do now," Jonathan answered, "but this was twenty-five years ago."

Sherise felt herself breathe again.

LaKeisha made an annoyed smacking sound with her lips. "Who gives a shit about twenty-five years ago?"

Sherise pulled herself together, able to focus now that this information didn't involve her. "LaKeisha and I were just discussing that the focus shouldn't be on his dalliances past or present, but rather—"

"She's changing the mission now?" Jonathan asked.

"No." LaKeisha put her hand on Sherise's over the table in a gesture telling her to back off. "We're considering new ideas, but we aren't abandoning this. I just want something more recent. Unless it produced an illegitimate child, twenty-five years ago doesn't bother me."

Sherise didn't like the direction this was going. She thought of Erica and what could happen to her if Nolan's affair with her mother came out. She'd been so busy thinking of herself that she kept forgetting how vulnerable Erica was.

"He's had several affairs," Jonathan said. "There's no question about that. The secretary of state's wife, the daughter of the minority whip in Congress, and the French ambassador's ex-wife—"

"Those are rumors," Sherise said. "We can't dabble in rumors. It'll only reflect badly on our side."

"I don't do rumors," he said angrily. "My sources are concrete and I always find the evidence I need."

"So, recently then," LaKeisha said, "what do you have?"

Sherise wanted this to stop immediately, but she also wanted to hear what he knew.

"He had an affair with someone about eighteen to twenty months ago," Jonathan said. "I think it was someone in government or connected to government."

"That sounds good," LaKeisha said. "I hope it was a powerful woman."

He shook his head. "Don't think so, but I was able to get hold of a private schedule."

"How?" Sherise asked.

"He keeps it on his phone," Jonathan answered. "Those phones link to transmitters, and the phone companies keep records of what those phones store."

Sherise removed her hand from under LaKeisha because she didn't want her to sense it shaking.

"What else have you found?" LaKeisha asked.

"I also have my contacts at local hotels who give me access to cameras." He looked around before leaning in. "You think they get rid of those tapes or tape over them? They do for the most part, but in D.C., no, they don't. They keep everything on D.C. hotel cameras. Nature of the location."

Sherise thought of the times she had met Jonah at the hotel. She'd been sure to cover up in a hat and glasses, never looking up, so a camera couldn't get her face. Was that enough?

"I got my valets who know exactly who and what is on those tapes and just hold on to it for the right payday."

"So get it," LaKeisha said. She looked at Sherise's disapproving stare. "Then we'll talk about that other stuff."

"We have to be careful," he warned. "Jonah Nolan is a ruthless man."

"This is true," Sherise said. "And *that* is what we need to be focused on. How he deals with people, destroys lives, and—"

"Later," LaKeisha insisted. "Just get me definitive proof right away. We need to hit while he's still got the media's main attention."

"I promise you," Jonathan said, "I've got plenty."

Sherise knew she had to get rid of Jonathan, but she wasn't going to do it on her own. Jonah had to find out about him; and if Erica wasn't going to do that for her, she'd have to let him know herself.

The trick was not letting it get back to her. She had to get LaKeisha to tell her who else knew about Jonathan. So if it came to it, she could pass the blame. And then, she had to find out who Jonathan really was, so she could get something substantive to Jonah.

She hated Jonah with a passion, but he didn't fuck around. Jonathan would be dealt with. How, she didn't know, and that wasn't her problem. Could he just be replaced with another Jonathan? Possibly, but Sherise would cross that bridge when she came to it.

Billie let the praise and accolades sink in as she sat at the table in the conference room. She was in the room with Gil, Lane, and two other company lawyers. On the phone, conferencing with them, was Porter, another associate at the firm, and the partner in charge.

She had just told them all that she'd been able to get an extension to review the complaint and request, which they had all—especially Porter—thought was impossible. Billie imagined the look on his face and wished they had Skyped this meeting just so she could see it.

"Okay," she finally said. "Thanks, but getting back on track, I think we need to focus on framing our argument based on *Seton* versus *Wilson* because . . ."

She stopped when she heard some whispering on the other line. It was faint, but she'd recognize Porter's deep voice anywhere. Just moments after her silence, the whispering stopped. She looked at Gil, who frowned, and then back at the phone.

"I'm sorry," she said, "was someone speaking?"

"No," the partner said quickly. "Go ahead."

"Sounded like someone was talking," Billie insisted. She should let it go—and if it had been anyone else's voice except Porter's, she probably would have. "What did you have to say, Porter?"

"Me?" Porter asked. There was a pause. "No, I . . . I was just—"

"Just what?" Billie asked as she sat back in her chair. "Go ahead."

Porter laughed and Billie could tell it was his nervous laugh. He rarely used it; but when he did, it meant he was uncomfortable.

"I was just saying," Porter said, clearing his throat, "that there's gonna be a price to pay for that later down the line."

"A price to pay for getting that extension?" Billie asked.

"He didn't mean that exactly," the partner interjected.

"No," Porter offered. "I just . . . I mean, I've never heard of anyone getting a big favor like that from the FTC and not having to give up something big or have it come back to haunt them down the line. I've never been able to."

"Well," Billie said, slowly and calmly, "I guess I'm just better at this than anyone else . . . or you."

Sitting in the chair next to her, Gil leaned over nervously into the phone. He laughed before adding, "And that's why we're so happy to have her. So, can you guys just do your work on *Seton* versus *Wilson* and get back to us by the end of the week?"

"Of course," the partner said, his voice sounding a little uncertain.

"Thanks guys! Talk to you later," Billie said before reaching down and pressing the END button.

She looked up at Gil, noting the awkwardness of his expression.

"Don't worry," she said, trying her best to seem unfazed. "Porter and I joke with each other like that all the time."

He seemed relieved because he sighed and smiled a little bit before getting up. "Well, let's hope they do their job."

"I'm sure they will," Billie said. "You guys go ahead, I'm gonna read through my notes a bit."

As the others left the room, Billie waited for the last person to close the door behind her. *Something is weird,* she thought. The way she felt right now. She felt powerful. She felt aligned. Things were going so well with Michael and her career was back on track. Everything was working in her favor, except Porter, who still wanted to be the thorn in her side. However, she shot him down, and it felt great. It felt right. She was in control of her life again. The sooner Porter figured that out, the better.

Erica was grateful for the privacy of an office. So far, she'd been shoved in rooms or out in the open area of Nolan headquarters with several other aides and random campaign staff, most of them volunteers. She was asked to complete the graphics on the e-vite for the big fund-raiser that was next week. All of the important donors, of course, got a formal invitation in the mail. Everyone else, the small donors and courtesy invites, would get what she was just completing.

She was just about to finish everything when there was a knock on the door. She realized that right away she was hoping it was Alex. She hadn't seen him since that morning. He'd told her he had a busy day, so they couldn't do lunch together like they usually did. It bothered her that she was so eager to see him again, especially after last Saturday when the girls teased her about him.

Without waiting for her permission, the door opened and Jonah stood in the doorway. He looked fresh, even though she'd known he'd been in television interviews all day long after the latest Gallup Poll announced that his joining the ticket was the main reason for Matthews's rise of four points among voters.

"Hi, Jonah." She smiled at him for a second before turning back to the computer.

"What are you working on?" he asked.

"I'm just doing the . . ." This time, when she looked up, Jonah was all the way inside the office and he wasn't alone.

He was standing beside a tall, lanky African-American man, who looked to be in his late twenties. He was dressed in a black suit, white shirt, and black tie. He had small, soft features for a man and curly, wavy hair, which went out about an inch from his head.

"I'm working on the fund-raising e-vite." She smiled at his companion. "Hello."

"Hi." He waved to her awkwardly, staying beside Jonah.

"Well, it's time for a break." Jonah gestured for the young man to step forward, which he promptly did. "I want you to meet someone."

Those words put a brick in Erica's stomach, but she tried her best not to show it for the other guy's sake.

"This is Malcolm Sweeney," Jonah introduced. "He's a vice president at Foresight Communications."

"Hi, Malcolm." She smiled nicely at the man, who seemed a little young to be a vice president anywhere.

"It's nice to meet you, Erica." His voice was hoarse, like a boy who was going through puberty.

Erica looked at Jonah, making sure her eyes caught his. She glared at him, but he didn't even flinch.

"Malcolm's father is Phillip Sweeney." Jonah slapped him on the back like that was quite an accomplishment.

Malcolm winced as he went forward a bit and tried to cover it up by laughing.

"Phillip Sweeney is the host of the fund-raiser next week," Jonah continued.

"Of course," Erica said. "That's why I recognized the name. I'm working on the invitation."

It all made sense now. Phillip Sweeney was one of Matthews's, and now Nolan's, biggest supporters. He was a rich political consultant and CEO of Foresight Communications.

"I thought you two should meet," Jonah said. "Since you'll be seeing each other at the fund—"

"I don't think I'm gonna be going," Erica said, deciding to give him a hard time. He knew he was breaking the rules, and she wasn't going to let him get away with it.

Jonah frowned. "Of course you are. All the staff is coming."

"I don't know." She leaned back in her chair and began to move from side to side. "I haven't finalized my weekend yet."

"You're very funny," Jonah said flatly. "I didn't mention that to you, did I, Malcolm?"

"I don't think so," he answered nervously. "You said she was 'nice and pretty.' I don't remember 'funny.' "

"Well, she's *quite* a comedienne," Jonah emphasized. "We'll let you get back to your work, Erica."

"Thank you." Erica was satisfied that Jonah had gotten the message. She was going to make this difficult, so he had decided to cut it short. "It was nice meeting you, Malcolm."

"Nice meeting you as well," he said, almost with a nod, which confused her. He turned to Jonah. "I guess I'll get going."

"Yeah." Jonah gestured out of the office. "Someone will show you out."

Once Malcolm was gone, Erica returned her attention to the computer, even though she knew Jonah was still standing there.

"You could have been nicer," he said.

"And you could have followed the rules," she answered back.

He laughed a little bit, making her look up at him. She could see the look on his face was . . . Yes, it was pride. It made her smile, despite not wanting to. He was clearly pleased by this, and he promptly turned and walked out of the office.

Erica wasn't sure what had just happened, but she continued to smile for a little while longer.

9

Sherise was pleased with her day, to some extent. Even though the earlier meeting with Jonathan had upset her, she felt she was able to get enough information from LaKeisha to stop him in his tracks. Now she just had to figure out how to get this to Nolan without letting it come back at her. She had an idea, but she would have to stay later than usual at the office before she could make it happen. She felt a little guilty about it, but sacrifices had to be made.

When she called Justin to tell him she'd be late and he would have to pick Cady up from day care, he surprisingly gave her no argument. She was taken aback a bit. It had seemed like every discussion related to work these days only ended in an argument.

"Anything else?" he asked.

She realized that his acquiescence was just to make this short so he could get her off the phone.

"I'm sorry," she said, "Am I keeping you from something . . . or someone?"

There was complete silence on the other end of the phone. He wasn't going to take her bait; it angered her.

"I can pick her up today," Justin said, "but I can't drop her off tomorrow morning. I have to be on the Hill for the hearing at eight sharp."

"Fine," Sherise answered back, feeling sad about the emptiness of their conversation.

"If that's all," he said, "I have to get back to work."

"Is this what we're reduced to?" she asked. "Scheduling updates? We're married, Justin."

"I just don't want to fight with you, Sherise. These days, the only way to avoid that is to keep our conversations short."

"I'm not happy," she said. "You're not happy. We're supposed to be happy. We're having another baby, Justin. We got through some really ugly times, but—"

"Everything will be fine," he said.

The lack of conviction in his voice really upset her.

"It won't," she said, feeling herself choking up. "Not if we keep things going this way. We should go back to Dr. Gray. She was helping us communicate. I think we abandoned counseling too early."

"You were the one who said we didn't need it anymore."

"I know, and I was wrong. If I make an appointment, will you come with me, baby?"

"Of course I will," Justin said.

She smiled, so grateful he didn't hesitate in his response. "I know things are hard, but I love you."

"I love you too."

Erica could hear a ruckus outside the office and decided that the daily meeting was done. All the top people were done for the day, which meant everyone could go home. It was a long day and she was eager for it to be over. She was getting her things together just as there was a knock on her door.

"Come in," she said.

When Alex stuck his head in, Erica smiled and waved him in farther.

"Hey, stranger," he said as he entered, leaving her office door open.

"I know, right?" She got up and walked around her desk, stuffing her purse inside the large bag she carried with her everywhere. "Long time, no see. You're very important here, so I can't expect to have you all to myself."

"It's weird," he said, reaching for her jacket off the door hook. "We hang out so much now, I was starting to miss you. I've texted you more today than anyone else."

"You're such a stalker," she teased, reaching out for her jacket.

"No, I'll put it on," he said. "We'll be having lunch tomorrow, right?"

"Sure." Erica turned around and placed her arms out. "But it has to be better than a sandwich this time. I want a hot meal out of you."

"Well, you're paying, so I'm good either way."

They both laughed as he placed her jacket on. After he was finished, she turned around to face him with the intent of thanking him. But as their eyes met—their bodies still close—both of them stopped laughing. Erica felt a little twitter in her belly; things were suddenly, intensely serious—and, at least for Erica, a little frightening.

She wasn't sure how long this lasted, but Jonah appearing in the doorway, and loudly clearing his throat, certainly put an end to it. They both jumped a little and separated, turning to face him. He didn't look angry, just very annoyed.

"Alex," he said in almost a scolding, fatherly tone. "I think Linda Fletcher is looking for you. You should go find her before she leaves."

"Um." Alex stepped forward, then looked back at Erica as if he felt he should say something, but then he decided against it. He just waved to her and added, "Okay."

"Really?" was what Jonah asked Erica after Alex had gone.

"What?" She reached for her bag, trying to ignore what she'd just been feeling.

"Is there something going on between you two?"

"Nope." She leaned against the door, looking uninvolved and uninterested in this conversation. She just wanted him to go away so she could process what had just happened.

"Because it's not a good idea," Jonah said. "You work together here. Campaigns can get emotional enough, Erica. No need to add sex to the mix."

"Yes," Erica agreed, offering the most sarcastic tone she could manage. "That would be an inappropriate sexual relationship. Thank you for your wise advice on the topic."

Jonah stepped farther into the office and stared her down. "You know, Erica, I'm not proud of all the mistakes I've made, but   "

"So you are proud of some of them?" she asked.

"I'm still your father."

She swallowed hard, unable to hide that he made her nervous when he got that serious look on his face that radiated, *Don't fuck with me.*

"There's nothing going on," she said. "We're just friends. Mind your own business."

With that, she pushed past him and went out of the office.

"Damn!" was all Billie could say when her door-bell rang.

She looked up at the kitchen clock and knew it was all her fault. It was 7:20 P.M. Michael wasn't early at all. She was running late. Not a good impression when inviting a man to your home for dinner for the first time.

Tonight was supposed to be perfect. She had planned to leave work early. Well, she was going to leave at five, which wasn't technically early. She needed the time to prepare for dinner at seven-thirty. She was making a romaine and artichoke salad, with fennel and saffron chicken. She was placing the salad in the refrigerator and the chicken still had about fifteen minutes to cook.

She ripped the apron off her, tossing it in the pantry and shutting the door. She rushed to the mirror that was next to her front door and quickly checked herself, liking what she saw.

She opened the door—a welcoming, sexy smile on her face, which she had been practicing for the last hour—only to feel life slap her in the face at what she saw.

"Go!" She pointed. "Just go, Porter! You can't be here."

He ignored her, going right into his tirade. "How dare you try and humiliate me like that today? Who the fuck do you think you are, Billie? Do you have any idea who you're messing with?"

"You started it," Billie said. "I'm not gonna discuss this with you. You have to leave. You're not welcome at my house anymore."

"It's a fucking apartment and you rent it," he said.

"So what?" she said. "It's the apartment of your client, who you are harassing. How well will that look to your firm when I report you?"

He looked shocked that she would even consider such a thing. "Billie, I was trying to help you."

She laughed out loud. "Bullshit! You were snickering behind your clients' backs while on a conference call with them. Any lawyer deserves to get called out for that, and you know it."

"You did it to humiliate me," he insisted. "I looked like a fool."

"You are a fool, Porter." She loved the look of astonishment on his face. "Especially if you think you're going to show me up professionally. Every time you try, I'll make you pay for it. So it's in your best interest to stop."

He was shaking his head as if amazed at what he was seeing and hearing. "You've changed, Billie."

"I haven't changed," she said confidently. "I'm just fed up. Now I want you to leave and never, ever come back here again."

"I'm not done with—"

"The woman told you to leave."

Porter turned to his left and Billie stuck her head out the door to see Michael approach. He was dressed in a gray suit, with a striking red tie, and was carrying a bottle of red wine. He came to within a couple of feet of Porter and was looking into his eyes with a stoic stare.

"Who the fuck are you?" Porter asked.

"He's my date," Billie said. "So you need to leave."

"You heard her," Michael said.

Porter held up his hand. "Look, man——"

"In that case," Billie said, "I think I'll just call the police and have you arrested. I'll press charges for harassment. Tomorrow I'll call your bosses and then drop a note to the D.C. Bar. Good luck on that promotion meeting coming up in a couple of months."

He looked at her with complete disgust. Billie knew that some time ago, that would have upset her, but it didn't now. She didn't give a damn. So she smiled at him as he rolled his eyes and turned to walk away. He ignored Michael, who kept a watchful eye on him, as he walked by.

"Come in, Michael," Billie said. "I'm sorry you had to see that. He has the worst timing."

"That had to be Porter, the ex," he said as he entered.

He leaned down to kiss her gently, but Billie didn't want a gentle kiss. She grabbed him by his tie and pulled him down to her. She pressed her lips hard against his, aggressively and demanding. She claimed his mouth with hers for a long, greedy kiss before letting him go.

"Wow," he said, looking genuinely floored and sounding a little breathless. "Where did that come from?"

"Victory," she said. "It's kind of a turn-on. And, yes, that was Porter."

"I'm not sure if I'm happy that an interaction with your ex-husband has you turned on."

He offered her the bottle of Merlot.

"No, silly. Putting him in his place is what turns me on." She took his hand and led him to her dining room. Fortunately, she had already set the table. "You have no idea what that man has put me through. Revenge is sweet."

"I hope his visit won't ruin our evening," he said. "I've been looking forward to this all week."

She looked him in the eyes as she felt him squeeze her hand more tightly. If everything went according to plan, this was going to be a monumental night for the two of them.

"Nothing could ruin this," she said. "I promise."

Everyone was gone and Sherise was almost finished. Sitting outside of LaKeisha's office, she was nervous as hell, wondering if someone would come back for the phone they forgot and would spot her. She worked fast, getting the information she needed quickly.

The thing about computers was that many people didn't turn theirs off at the end of the day, even though they were told to do so. They left them on and waited for them to turn themselves off due to being out of use. But any little use, even the casual swiping of the mouse pad as you walked by, unnoticed, would keep the computer alive for another fifteen minutes.

Sherise had to do this three times before everyone left prior to being able to actually access the computer. From that point, the cookies that saved and remembered passwords did all of the work for her.

As she got up from the desk, Sherise froze in place. She swore she heard something down the left hallway. She stayed in place for a few seconds more and heard nothing. She took two steps toward her office before she heard it again.

"Shit," she whispered. Someone was definitely there. She had to get out. While the office space was carpeted, the walkways were hardwood, so she took off her heels and slowly headed for her office, which was down the other end of the hallway.

The giggling got louder and then she heard a click. A door was opening. She was in the middle of the hallway. Panicking, Sherise leapt for the bathroom closest to her, the men's room. She grabbed the door, so it wouldn't shut closed. Once inside, she could hear the voices. There was a man and a woman, or a girl. Heels were tapping the walkway.

Sherise was a mess as she listened to the man and woman walk around the office, stopping occasionally to make out. She didn't know who it was and didn't care about office romances. She would be done for, if anyone saw her here tonight.

She could hear some whispering, but not much. She wondered if either of them would bother to look at the computer she had just left. It was still lit up, while all the others had long since gone dark. Would they be suspicious and come looking for her? How would she explain being in the men's bathroom?

She was in the bathroom for almost twenty minutes before all the sounds stopped. She had moved to one of the stalls, just in case someone decided to peek in.

Her phone vibrated, which made her nervous for a moment. She fumbled to get it out of her pant's pocket and read it. It was from Justin, telling her to get home quickly. Thinking of Cady, she quietly typed back for an explanation. Justin's only response was Get home now!!!!!!

Great, she thought, *another problem.*

* * *

The last drop fell out of the wine bottle and into Billie's glass before Michael placed it on the table.

"I think that's it," he said.

"I have others," she offered, taking a few more sips.

After a successful dinner of flirtation and teasing gazes, they made it all the way through the chocolate cream pie, which Billie admitted she didn't actually make, but rather had picked up from the German bakery three blocks away.

As far as Billie was concerned, things were going great—although she had a feeling that she'd had a lot more wine than he had. After all, this was her third glass, and it was only one bottle. She hadn't kept track. She was just enjoying herself too much.

She'd spent a lot of time talking about work, but Michael shared more of himself with her. He talked about growing up poor in Atlanta and the struggles he had staying out of trouble. He reminded her a lot of herself and the girls, only they'd had each other. Michael was alone in his fight to get out of the projects unscathed. He'd had no friends because he wasn't "down," as he phrased it. The more she found out about him, the more she admired him.

Michael looked prepared to respond to her offer of more wine, when Billie's phone, over on the kitchen counter, suddenly rang.

He looked toward it before turning back to her. "It's been ringing a lot."

"Ignore it." She waved her hand dismissively. "It's probably just Porter. He's such a sore loser."

"So you've said." He placed the napkin from his lap onto the table.

Michael looked down and Billie thought she'd heard him whisper something under his breath, but he smiled when he looked back up at her.

"You should have seen me, Michael." She slid her chair closer to his at the dining-room table. "I didn't stutter or hesitate. I usually do with him, because I let him irk me so much, but this morning—"

"You went right back at him," Michael said. "You've told me . . . a few times."

She realized from the expression on his face that he wasn't pleased. It took her only a second to understand why.

"Oh, my God," she said in a gasp. "Have I been talking about my ex too much?"

"You've certainly had a lot to say about him tonight." Michael wiped at his lap, a gesture that conveyed his discomfort with the topic. "I think I've had my fill of Porter talk, if you don't mind."

"I'm sorry." Billie felt awful. She hadn't been paying attention at all. "What do you want to talk about?"

"I want to talk about you."

"Aside from being very rude to my date," she said, standing up from her chair, "there isn't much I haven't told you."

She leaned down and kissed him on the forehead, reaching out and taking his hand. She pulled at him, heading for the living room. Slowly he smiled and stood, allowing her to lead him to the sofa.

"This is certainly more like it," he said.

Billie pointed to the sofa. "Sit."

"You're pretty bossy." He did as he was told. "I like it."

"I'm kind of liking it too." She sat next to him, leaning against him.

He wrapped his arm around her. "What are you planning to order me to do next?"

She didn't hesitate to show him.

Leaning in closer, her lips pressed against his softly as she waited for his response. She didn't have to wait long. She felt his lips push against hers and his arms quickly wrap around her. She felt an intense flare of desire as the kiss deepened and his grip tightened. She arched her back in response to his hold on her and their chests pressed against each other.

Her pulse was pounding so hard—it felt like a jet engine was inside her as she felt the tip of his tongue. She responded, opening her mouth just a little. The touch of his tongue against hers was electrifying and sent blood surging through her entire body. Her arms reached out to him and gripped the back of his head, pulling him to her because she wanted him closer.

They fell back on the sofa. His kiss deepened. As their tongues explored each other, their hands did the same. Billie felt every place that he touched go on fire. When his hand slid up her blouse and pressed against her belly, she felt a scorching heat that reached so deep within her that she let out a quiet moan.

Then suddenly Billie felt his hand leave her and he pulled away. His lips left hers and his arms released her.

"What's wrong?" she asked, completely out of breath.

He was looking down at her, his eyes smoky and full of desire. He frowned, seeming tortured, making her reach out to touch his cheek.

"It's okay," she whispered. "I want you."

He shook his head, lifting up until he was sitting

down. Awkwardly and embarrassed, Billie sat up too, looking at him. She placed her hands on his thigh, still aching to feel him.

"I think we should call it a night," he said, his tone filled with uncertainty.

"Why?" she asked.

She could tell from his voice that he didn't want to leave her. So, why was he saying that? He looked at her and she could see the regret in his eyes. He wanted her—that was clear. What was going on?

"I want you too." He shook his head. "More than you can know, but I feel like there's something . . . no, someone between us."

"What do you mean?" she asked.

"The man you've spent more than half this evening talking about."

Had she really talked about him that much? Why would she do that? She had this incredible guy she wanted more than she'd wanted a man since she could remember and she completely turned him off with ex-drama.

"I'm sorry," she said. "I didn't do it on purpose."

"I don't think you even noticed," he said. "The look in your eyes when you went over that conference call, all three times, and then telling me how you felt watching him walk away from your front door earlier, looking so defeated. Your eyes lit up."

She was shaking her head. "It's complicated, Michael. I've been on the receiving end for so long, it just . . . Look, Porter is gone. He's not in this room now. It's just me and you."

Michael smiled at her as he stood up. "Nah, Billie. He's been here all night and he's still here. At least for me, he is."

She got up from the sofa; her head was still feeling a little dizzy. "I've offended you and I'm sorry."

"You haven't offended me." He sighed. "I know you didn't do it on purpose. I get it. Working with your ex can't be easy, but you've got to let him go when you leave the office. At the least, you've got to let him go when you're with me."

Damn Porter, finding a way to ruin things for me, no matter what. Billie felt her anger at him rising. *I'm going to make him pay for this,* she thought. He had to know he wasn't allowed anywhere near her home.

Michael reached down and placed his fingers gently at her chin, lifting her face to his. He smiled at her before leaning down and kissing her lips gently.

"Billie," he whispered, his face still inches from hers, "I'm not mad at you. I don't think I could be mad at this beautiful face, even if I wanted to be."

"But I ruined everything," she said, pouting.

"Aside from all the talk about Porter, the night was great." He lowered his hand, but his eyes still held hers. "You're an amazing woman and the way you look tonight . . . The truth is, I've wanted to make love to you since—damn, girl—since I met you, if I'm being honest. I just need to know I'm the only man on your mind when I do."

Even though she'd come close to getting caught, Sherise was feeling good after getting away with what she'd done tonight. It put her plan in action. It was risky as hell, but she thrived off that. She was feeling like her old self. Being vulnerable was for losers.

However, when she arrived home at Justin's frantic request, all sense of power and rejuvenation evaporated. Even before she saw Justin, Sherise got a very, very bad feeling. The second she opened the door, the house was very dimly lit and quiet.

Justin was sitting on the living-room sofa. His head had been in his hands. When she entered, he looked up at her. He looked awful, like he'd just lost someone he loved.

"Where's my baby?" she asked, unable to think of anything before making sure her baby was okay.

"She's upstairs, sleeping."

Sherise jumped, not realizing there was another person in the room. She turned around to find Jacob Swift, Justin's law school friend and his lawyer, standing at the stairwell, looking very somber. He was a tall, large man in his midthirties, with unruly dark curls, a beard, and a thoughtful, intelligent face.

"Jacob?" Sherise looked back at Justin, who fell back on the sofa, looking exhausted. "What is he . . . What are you doing here?"

"This," Jacob said, handing her a piece of paper, which looked very official. "It's from human resources at the firm."

Sherise cautiously took a few steps toward Jacob and accepted the paper. She looked at it for a second, but she didn't understand anything. She turned to Justin, who was looking at her with the look of a pitiful dog.

"It's Elena," Justin said. "She's filed a claim of sexual harassment."

Sherise took a quick, sharp breath. Her head felt like it was decompressing and she was feeling dizzy. She grabbed the edge of the closest chair and sat down. She thought she heard Jacob say something, but she couldn't decipher it. She looked down at the paper in

front of her and it could have been written in Russian.
It made no difference to her. She looked back at Justin.

"Wait. . . . What?"

"She's threatening to sue me and the firm," Justin
clarified. "That bitch is saying I sexually harassed her!"

"What did you—"

"What?" Justin shot up from his seat. "Were you
about to ask me, what did I do?"

"No," she assured him, shaking her head vigor-
ously now. "No, I just . . . I wanted to know."

"I didn't do this, Sherise!" Justin proclaimed
loudly. "Jesus Christ, I can't believe you would—"

"I believe you," she pleaded. "Please, Justin . . .
I do."

He looked down at her, disappointment and hurt
on his face. "For a second, you seemed like you didn't.
Damn it, Sherise, do you think I would ever do something like that?"

"No," she said. "Of course not. You're too professional to make this type of—"

" 'Too professional'?" Justin looked completely
astonished. "How about I'm not the kind of person to
do this under any circumstance, professional or not?"

Sherise didn't know what to say. He was confused,
scared, and angry. She could tell that she wasn't going
to be able to make him feel better right now. She turned
to Jacob, who remained where he'd been standing.

"Can she do this?" she asked.

Jacob nodded. "She's claiming several instances in
the last three months where Justin said or did something in a sexual manner, despite her asking him not to,
or in order to make her feel uncomfortable. She claims
to have a witness, and—"

"A witness?" Sherise asked.

"Fucking Dennis Stevens," Justin said. "She says he'll say that he saw me grab her ass and her looking very upset about it. He's gonna claim that he talked to me about it, like a month ago, so it seems like I got a warning and didn't heed it."

"It's no-good," Sherise said. "Dennis was passed over by Justin for the promotion to principal almost two years ago, right?"

Justin nodded. "He was pissed that I was given the Okun Industries project."

"What was that about?" Jacob asked.

"Okun was a client and we were lobbying the finance committee to introduce a bill that . . . Look, that part is boring. What matters is Dennis started the project, but he got in trouble over his drinking problems, so it was handed to me."

"See," Sherise argued. "He's bitter. He's not reliable."

"Don't worry about that," Jacob said, retrieving the paper from Sherise. "I'll do my job. He's a horrible witness for several reasons."

"We'll bring them all up," Justin said.

"I'm gonna leave," Jacob said. "I need to get to work on getting this claim shot down immediately. Justin, you and Sherise need to discuss the . . . immediate consequences."

"What 'immediate consequences'?" Sherise asked. "Is this public? Are people going to know about this?"

"You mean Northman?" Justin asked sarcastically.

"No," she said, realizing what he was insinuating. She honestly hadn't thought of her job, just her family's reputation in general. "Not for me, but for all of us. D.C. is a rumor mill and these types of things can—"

"Sherise." Justin stopped her. "That's not my concern right now. The immediate consequence that Jacob is talking about is my job. They've asked me to take a leave of absence until this gets resolved."

"They can't do that!" Sherise shot up from her chair. "It's just a complaint. That's not the protocol. They can't punish you without any proof. Jacob, this isn't legal, is it?"

"I will fight this." Jacob was already heading for the front door. "They can't demand he take a leave, based solely on an uninvestigated claim, but they can ask for propriety's sake. I'll call you by noon tomorrow with my progress."

"Thanks, Jacob." Justin waved to him before turning and heading to the window that overlooked the dimly lit Georgetown streets.

"I'll see myself out," Jacob said.

Sherise turned to Justin, walking over to him. She placed her hand on his shoulder and caressed him.

"Baby," she said, "Jacob will make this go away, won't he?"

Justin didn't answer and it ached her.

"If we can prove it's empty," she said. "Not only will he get rid of it, but we'll be able to sue her for defamation of character. She won't get a job—"

" 'If'?" He swung around to face her. "There you go again, using words of doubt."

"I'm sorry." She threw her hands in the air. "I don't know the right words. That's not the point."

"From someone whose career it is to say the right words?" He moved away from her, walking to the center of the living room.

"I'm not the bad guy here," Sherise said.

"But you're not sure I'm not either," Justin said back.

"What I am sure of," Sherise said, "is that I knew this bitch was trouble from the first day I saw her. Lying for a payday is something a woman like her would do without a second thought. That's what this is, baby. Jacob will show that."

"He has to." Justin's voice held a sense of despair. "I've worked so hard to make my name in this industry. She can't ruin everything over a lie. She can't!"

Sherise rushed over to him and wrapped her arms around him. This time, he responded and held her back, burying his face in her shoulder. She could feel his heavy sighs and she held him even more tightly.

"She won't," Sherise said. "I won't let her."

10

On her way out of campaign headquarters, Erica was trying to calm Sherise down over the phone. She was extremely upset and not thinking rationally. She had called Erica in a fit, yelling about Elena filing a harassment claim against Justin at the firm. Sherise had gotten an epiphany that somehow Elena was a plant from Jonah.

"You're not thinking clearly," Erica said. "Jonah would have no reason to do this to Justin or to you. It makes no sense."

"Jonah will do whatever he wants," Sherise insisted. "He could have created this situation to distract me from my work with Northman—to get me out of the way."

"You're his communications chief, Sherise. You're not a strategist for them."

"But I know his secrets," she answered back.

Erica sighed. "His secrets are your secrets. Don't you get that? He knows you won't tell. Because even though he could lose his chance at the White House, you would lose your reputation and your family. He's not afraid of you."

"Then why?" Sherise asked.

"That's my point," Erica said as calmly as she could. "There's no reason why. Whatever Elena is up to, whatever she is about, and wherever she came from, it's not connected to . . ."

Just as the elevator door opened, Erica came face-to-face with the man of the hour. Jonah was standing in the middle of the elevator, with one of his Secret Service guards flanking his left side. Jonah had his head down, busy talking on his phone, but he looked up as the door opened.

"Get in," he said, a smile coming to his face.

"I can, uh . . ." She wasn't sure what to say. "I can take the next—"

"Get in," Jonah ordered, "before it closes."

Upon that note, the guard reached out and placed his hands at the elevator door to keep it from closing. Erica didn't have much choice.

"I'll call you back," she said into the phone before shutting it off and stuffing it into her pocket.

"By tonight," Jonah whispered into the phone.

Erica nervously turned her back to him. Even without having just been talking about him to Sherise, this was awkward and weird. When would it ever not be with this man? Especially not when his mute, burly guards, with spiral wires coming out of their ears, were around.

"I don't care about the delicacies," Jonah said. "He goes down tonight. Period."

Erica felt a bit of a shiver down her spine at the thought of whoever it was that Jonah was talking about.

The way in which he yielded his power was both disgusting and fascinating to her.

"I will see you tomorrow night," he suddenly said in a much lighter, jovial tone.

Erica turned to face him. The look on his face made it very clear this was an order and not meant in the way normal people, who didn't think everyone had to do what they said, would mean.

"Yes," she answered dutifully. "And I'll be bringing my date. You'll love him. Only three stints in jail. Never been to prison even once."

He wasn't impressed. "You don't have a date."

"You don't know that," she said, forgetting for a second to whom she was speaking. He knew everything.

"Everyone has to pass security," Jonah said. "Even dates. But nice try."

"I'll try harder next time," she said smartly.

"I wish you wouldn't," he responded flatly.

The elevator door opened onto the first floor of the building and Erica turned to step out. Jonah was right behind her as she walked toward the lobby.

"Let's make a deal," Erica said. "I won't try to piss you off, if you don't try to set me up."

"Malcolm has an incredible amount of promise," he responded.

"You mean the kind of promise that a silver spoon offers."

"A silver spoon didn't get him a 4.0 GPA at Harvard Business School."

"But it probably got him into Harvard Business School in the first—"

"Jonah!"

Erica looked toward the center of the lobby, where

there were a few people standing around. One of them was Jonah's other security detail, who joined them immediately. But also coming toward them was Alex, with a reluctant Mexican woman, who looked to be in her fifties, following behind.

"I'm glad I caught you," Alex said as they approached. He looked at Erica. "Hey, Erica."

"Hey," she said. "I was just on my way home, so I'll leave you two—"

"No." Alex took her arm to hold her there. "I want you to meet someone. Jonah, you remember my mom, Leeza."

"Of course I do," Jonah said cordially. "It's nice to see you again, Leeza. It's been a very long time."

"Yes, it has," she agreed, her accent softly detected. "Always nice to see you, Mr. Nolan."

"Mr. Nolan?" Alex laughed. "Mom, you know you can call him 'Jonah.' "

"I'd really prefer you to," Jonah said, seeming a bit annoyed.

Her expression was stoic as she offered, "Old habits die hard. Jonah."

"Well, I have to get going," Jonah said. "You all have a good evening. Erica and Alex, I'll see you tomorrow night."

"Of course, sir," Alex called after him as Jonah abruptly turned and walked away with his security.

For a second, Erica noticed a look of derision on Leeza's face as she watched Jonah walk away. It was only for a second. If Erica had blinked, she would have missed it. Leeza quickly replaced it with a kind smile and turned her attention to Erica.

"So you're Erica," she said, holding out her hand. "My son has told me a lot about you."

Erica shook her hand firmly. "That I mostly annoy him, I'm sure."

"Not at all." Alex laughed a little nervously as if he didn't want his mother saying he'd been talking about her. "I've only had great things to say about you. As a matter of fact, I told my mom you would back me up on a disagreement."

"I don't want to get between you and your mom," Erica said.

"It's a waste of time," Leeza said. "He wants me to come to that fund-raiser thing with him and I won't."

"She's supposed to be my date." Alex pouted. "But she's not a big fan of Jonah's."

"Why not?" Erica asked, even though it wasn't any of her business.

Leeza shrugged, seeming annoyed with Alex for even bringing it up. "I'm a Northman fan. That's all I'll say."

Alex rolled his eyes. "You could stomach it for me."

"I'm busy." Leeza crossed her arms over her chest and tilted her head away.

Erica laughed, seeing how much it annoyed Alex.

"You see how the love of my life treats me?" Alex asked. He leaned over and kissed his mother on the cheek.

"Aw," Erica said. "So sweet."

"I know," Leeza said, pointing at Erica. "You take Erica!"

"Um . . ." Alex looked embarrassed.

At that moment, Erica remembered the last awkward moment between them when he'd helped her put her jacket on in the office. Jonah had interrupted them, probably the only time she'd been grateful to see him.

"Do you have a date?" Leeza asked.

"Mom . . . stop," Alex pleaded under his breath.

"No, I don't," Erica answered.

"You don't?" Alex's eyes widened. "Oh, I . . . Well . . ."

"Then you'll go together," Leeza said, clapping her hands together and rubbing them as if she'd solved the puzzle of the century.

"Enough, Mom," Alex pleadingly warned.

"Why don't we agree to meet there and walk in together," Erica suggested, hoping to at least end some of Alex's clear suffering.

He pointed at her with a satisfied smile. "There you go. Sounds good. Genius. Happy, Mom?"

"That's a solution?" she asked, rolling her eyes. "You kids these days and your dating rituals. Do what you want. What do I care?"

Erica laughed, already knowing she was going to like this woman.

When Michael opened the front door to his West End apartment, Billie could see the look of amazement on his face. She didn't waste the advantage the element of surprise offered her. She brushed past him quickly and entered the apartment. When she turned around to face him, he was just standing there, with his mouth open.

"Billie—"

She held up her hand. "Before you start, I need to say something."

As he shut the door behind him, Billie turned to him. She'd been so focused on getting her frustrations out that she hadn't even realized until now that he was shirtless. He was wearing a pair of sweatpants and his feet were bare. His chest was dark and his skin smooth and muscled. It gave her pause, just taking it in.

"I'm extremely angry with you," she said, her voice cracking throughout. She was very warm.

"Me?" He laughed. "What did I do?"

"I haven't been able to sleep since you left my apartment the other night." Billie really doubted her resolve in the face of his chest.

She placed her purse on a console table in the hallway as an excuse to look away. His apartment was nicely designed in a modernist, bachelor style. Not a lot of details, but large pieces of furniture and art, which took up space and gave the place a masculine look.

"You know why I left," he said.

"You didn't give me a chance to explain the situation to you," she emphasized. "Basically, Porter has haunted me since I left him."

Michael shook his head in disbelief. "You came over here to talk about him?"

"Ugh!" She raised her hands in fists in the air. "You are so damn frustrating. I'm trying to tell you that you're right. You were right to leave, and you were right to call me out."

"I wasn't trying to be right," Michael said. "I was just—"

"Can you put on a shirt?" Billie asked.

"What?" Michael looked thoroughly confused.

"You're making this impossible, standing there, looking like"—she pointed to his chest—"that."

He laughed for a second, but then he frowned. "You're serious?"

"Yes," she maintained. "I want to have a serious conversation with you about how I want to move on from Porter and let him go."

Michael shook his head. "You're an odd bird, Billie."

He started down the hallway and Billie followed. The hallway led to an open area, with consistently masculine design and dark colors set up with a living room, center stage.

"I understand why you were avoiding me," she said.

He reached down on the sofa and grabbed a T-shirt with one hand, while reaching with the other for the remote and putting the baseball game playing on the fifty-inch HD television on mute.

"I wasn't avoiding you," he said. "I was giving you space to figure shit out. Looks like that was a good idea."

"I came over here to tell you," she continued to say as he put on his Morehouse T-shirt, "that I'm doing just that. I mean, I'm ready to. But I'm not doing it because you told me to. I'm doing it because not being able to sleep at night gives a person time to think."

"And what did you think about?" he asked, walking toward her.

He stopped about a foot from her, with an engaging, amused look on his face. With him standing this close, having the shirt on didn't seem to be doing much to help the situation.

"I'm being serious," she warned, pointing her finger at him. "You said you wanted to be the only man on my mind that night if we made love. Well, you've been the only man on my mind ever since then."

"Good," he said.

"You're damn right it's good," she asserted. "I don't deserve to be hung up on the past. I deserve a future—a better, bigger future. I asked myself, what do I want more? To battle in a boardroom with Porter or in a bedroom with you."

"Battle?" he asked. "Is that what you're into?"

"Battle, celebrate, whatever it is." She reached out and clutched at his hand. "I want to do it with you, and only you. And I won't take no for an answer!"

"You won't have to." Michael grabbed her by the waist and pulled her to him.

When his lips possessively took hers, Billie gave herself to it freely and swooned into him. His arms held her tightly as hers went up and around his neck. Immediately a flame traveled from her lips through her chest and the rest of her body. She wanted him so bad.

Billie looked him in his eyes, her voice giving away its eagerness as she asked, "You're not going to get me all heated up and call it a night again, are you?"

"I'm not that good of a tease," he answered. "Tonight, ain't nobody going anywhere."

He took her by the hand and led her to the sofa and they both sat down. Not wasting any time, his lips were on hers again, even more demanding this time. Billie let out a gasp as his mouth swiftly moved from a soft, moist kiss on her chin to her neck. His mouth was softly leaving molten lava wherever it touched.

Billie reached out for his T-shirt and began pulling at it. He separated from her for just a brief moment, although it seemed like forever, to let her pull it off him and toss it aside. Her hands explored his hard chest as his mouth claimed her again. She could hear him groan in response to her caress and it made her crazy.

As his hands left her waist and began unbuttoning

her silk blouse, Billie began to lean back. But as she did, she felt something push against her, and her reflexes sprang into action as she quickly lifted up.

"What is it?" he asked, looking just a second from being lost in the passion.

"It's . . . um . . ." Billie twisted around to see what was impeding her downward movement.

She was touched by what she saw. It was a pair of pink boxing gloves. She picked them up and showed them to Michael.

"What are these for?" she asked. "New and pretty boxing gloves."

Michael grinned proudly. "A gift for a next date. You and I are going boxing."

"When?" she asked, placing the gloves out of the way.

He pulled her back to him and said, "Next week, we box. Tonight, we burn calories another way."

He quickly led her to his bedroom and got back to the business at hand. Billie found her body sent into spasms of desire and pleasure as he masterfully stroked, massaged, rubbed, and caressed her every inch. A storm set off inside her as he manipulated her body for his pleasure. Every whisper, kiss, rub, and touch sent her deeper into sexual bliss.

She responded with demands of her own. She was ravenous and he fed her everything she wanted, and more. She wanted to be taken, to have an intense, erotic experience; he delivered tenfold. After his lips left scalding kisses over her entire body, he thrilled her with his mouth until she exploded in sweet abandon.

The intensity reached a level of mania when he finally entered her. She melted at the sweet pain and pleasure as he moved in and out of her. His face was buried in her neck, and he was kissing her madly. Their bodies moved together like a current in the water, in unison, sharing immense ecstasy.

As his control began to slip, Billie felt the hysteria in both of them building up. Their bodies were frantic; their groans and moans got louder and louder until they exploded in each other's arms.

When Sherise and Justin sat down in Jacob Swift's DuPont Circle–area office, their hands entwined in each other's, they knew they weren't going to get good news. After all, they were there for an update on Elena's claim, hoping that it would get refused as not being sufficient.

"The firm wants to give her money," Jacob said, sitting behind his desk.

"What?" Justin shot forward in his chair, in complete shock.

"No," Sherise said. "They can't do that. She just filed. There's a grievance process that the firm has to follow. I read it in Justin's papers. What kind of bullshit is this?"

Jacob was shaking his head. "This is ridiculous, I know. I've never heard of a firm doing this, except—"

"Except when?" Justin asked.

"When the firm has just emerged from some serious legal issues and can't afford any more so soon after."

"Legal issues?" Justin asked.

Jacob nodded. "She's saying that if she isn't happy with the firm's response, she's going to the EEOC to see if she qualifies for a lawsuit."

Sherise was shaking her head. She couldn't believe

what she was hearing about the Equal Employment Opportunity Commission. "What are they talking about, legal issues?"

"They just don't want a show," Jacob said. "They don't want this to spread in the firm and especially outside of it."

Justin turned to Sherise. "Last year, there was a sexual harassment issue on the legal side of the firm. I told you about it. A partner was having an affair with one of his associates."

"But that never went public," Sherise said. "Didn't they handle that in-house?"

"Yes," Jacob said, "but if this goes public, last year's mess will certainly come out. She already plans to use it as evidence of a sexually hostile environment."

"That bitch," Sherise mumbled under her breath.

"And there was also an incident last year." Jacob looked down at the papers in front of him. "She didn't bring this up—so for now, she doesn't know about it. But if the court requires the firm to give reasons for all disciplinary actions in the last year, the firm said they would have to disclose an inappropriate sexual relationship with a client. They'd like to keep that secret as well."

"Oh, for fuck sake," Sherise said.

She knew right away what he was talking about: Billie and her pro bono client, Ricky. She looked at Justin, who also knew. Of course she hadn't told him, but he'd heard the rumors at the firm. After Billie resigned, Justin put two and two together on his own.

"There are a lot of vulnerabilities here," Jacob said. "They are justifiably nervous, but I think they're moving too soon."

"When do I get a formal hearing?" Justin asked.

Justin told Sherise he'd been given only a few minutes to deny the claims to his boss and the heads of the firm before they asked him to take a leave of absence. He chose then not to say another word until he had Jacob with him.

"I'm setting that up for Monday," Jacob said. "If they're not happy, they'll be more likely to give her money so she doesn't make a fuss."

"Is Justin going to have to sue the firm to keep his job?" Sherise asked.

"I don't want to do that," Justin said. "I don't want it to come to that. I've put too much into the relationships there."

"Look what good it's done you," she postured. "The second some bitch accuses you of something, they turn on you."

"They're just afraid because of all the stuff we just talked about," Justin assured her. "When I go in on Monday—"

"I want to come," Sherise said.

"You need to," Jacob said. "You can't sit in on the conversation, but you need to come to show your support and that you believe him."

Justin squeezed Sherise's hand more tightly and she smiled at him.

"They want to avoid a mess," Jacob said. "Even if she'd likely get turned down for a suit."

"But that's my reputation on the line," Justin said.

"We need more time," Sherise said. "We have to convince them of that. We have to fight her. We'll hire a private investigator to dig up all her dirt. I'll ask around and find out—"

"I've taken care of that," Jacob interrupted. "We're looking into her past, but we have to be careful. We can't make it seem like we're trying to make the truth look like a lie through distraction. And we certainly can't have what looks like a jealous wife pursuing her."

"Not jealous," Sherise insisted. "Pissed off, pregnant, and ready to scorch the earth to protect her husband and everything he's worked for."

Sherise looked over at Justin and could see how proud he was of her. He hadn't looked at her that way in . . . She couldn't even remember when. Yes, this was a disaster, but Sherise was better than any obstacle that had come her way. She would conquer this problem, and their marriage and their lives would be better for it.

Jacob's cell phone rang and he quickly picked it up. "It's the firm. Let me take this. I'll be right back."

"Tell them to wait," Justin demanded as Jacob hurriedly rushed out of the office.

Once alone, Justin turned to Sherise.

"You know," he said, "if we do get them to wait and she goes public, it will reach Northman's people. You have to tell them."

"I'm not worried about them," Sherise said. "If they make a stink about it, I'll handle it."

"You could quit, if it's too much for you." He reached over and pressed his hand on her belly. "That's all I care about."

Sherise placed her hand over his. "If that's the only thing that can protect you, I'll do that. I'll do anything. Justin, I'll walk through fire for you . . . for our family."

Considering all the battles she was facing, Sherise was afraid she'd have to do just that.

11

The second Billie entered the conference room, where the others were waiting, she made eye contact with Porter. Everyone was sitting down, waiting for her and Gil, who had walked in with her. She almost laughed out loud at how quickly Porter's expression changed from when he greeted Gil to when he greeted her. She was kind and polite, despite his grumbling niceties. Yes, he was still pissed off from her putting him in his place last week, but he had no idea what was coming.

Despite what she'd told Michael, Billie had spent quite some time trying to figure out how to make Porter pay for ruining her evening with Michael. She hadn't lied to Michael—she was never going to bring Porter up around him again, ever—but there was no way Porter would get away with what he'd done.

The meeting started off on a bad foot, considering Gil called it in response to the firm's work. He felt it was weak and too brief. It didn't touch on some of the points Gil clearly shared with the partner regarding his wishes, and it didn't rely enough on the case they'd discussed, which they'd agreed was the best case to cite in this particular court district.

Billie hadn't said a word yet. She was waiting her turn. She ignored Porter's searing eyes and kept focused on Gil, nodding in agreement with his points to show her support. By the time he was finished, everyone was already uncomfortable—everyone except Billie.

"Gil," the partner spoke up first after Gil finished. "Let me respond first by saying—"

"Wait." Gil held up his hand. "I was going to ask Billie if she had anything to add first. I believe in getting it all out."

Everyone turned to her. Billie looked down at her notes as if she wasn't sure what to say, even though she absolutely was. She was going to attack an argument that she knew to be Porter's, because it was a case that he litigated.

"I can't think . . . ," she started, before pulling out a piece of paper. "Oh yes, I do have something. There was a reference to *Gregson* versus *Peyton* in terms of alternative clauses in the contract revision that would remove vertical question. I was confused. You're arguing Gregson's point, but that's a losing point."

While Billie looked up at Anthony he turned to look at Porter.

"The district court found in favor of Gregson," Porter said through gritted teeth. "Point payment revision is a strong argument, and the defendant—"

"Yes," Billie interrupted, "but the appeals court overturned it, saying that there was nothing in place to guarantee that revision wouldn't just be excluded in an addendum. I really don't think we need to be arguing points that have been overturned. That's just not good law."

"It's fine," Porter said. "The ruling was based on a lack of a binding addendum, which doesn't exist in this case."

"Still," Billie said, trying to sound uncertain enough of her own words that she didn't come across as biting, "I'm concerned that—"

"Still nothing," Porter spat out. "The appeals court clearly stated that if a binding addendum had been in place, which is the situation in this case, it would've agreed with the lower court."

Billie nodded quickly, seeming to want to appease Porter, knowing that it would only make him angrier. "I know, but let's face it—judges look at the highest-court ruling and see that as the final vindication. The appeals court addressed this particular aspect of the case in its ruling in favor of Peyton, and—"

"That's ridiculous," Porter scoffed. "I clearly state in the brief that—"

"Porter." Anthony's tone admonished him sharply.

Everyone in the room froze in response as an awkward moment of silence settled in. Porter turned to his phone, pretending to be more interested in something that was on there than anything happening in the room.

"I'm sorry." Billie was working hard to conceal her delight. "I didn't mean to—"

"It's all right," Anthony assured her. "You were right. Porter just gets passionate about his cases. Look, Gil, we've taken copious notes. I think we're finally on the same page here."

"My comments," Gil said, "are all on the brief in track changes. It should have been e-mailed to all of you."

"I can commit to working on this nonstop," the partner said. "You and I need to set up a conference call tomorrow to go into further detail over the changes, but I'm certain we can handle this."

"I know you can," Gil said confidently. "This is a first draft. We've all had them. I just want to make clear the direction we'd prefer before we go into further drafts."

Porter was up and out of the room in a flash, before the others had even left their seats. Billie acted unaware as she focused on giving Evelyn some instructions for closing out the presentation.

After everyone from the firm had left, Gil walked over to her.

"What was that about?" he asked. "Porter?"

Billie shrugged. "I have no idea. I thought it was a professional and civil conversation, but—"

"You were perfectly professional," Gil said. "He was way out of line. Not only are you a client, but you had a perfectly valid point."

"He certainly didn't think so," Billie said.

"I don't think it was about your point at all," Gil said. "Maybe it's too difficult for him to work for you. I overestimated his professionalism."

"His expertise in this area is unquestioned," Billie said. "Which is what made the mistake all the more curious."

"He might be off his game," Gil said, nodding as if he'd figured it out. "We can't afford that. I'll have to do something about it."

Billie watched as Gil walked out of the office, deep in thought. She was getting very good at this and liking it. She thought for a second that might not be a good thing, but then she dismissed it from her mind. This was a long time coming.

The Sweeney home was located in one of the toniest neighborhoods of Bethesda, Maryland. It was newly designed and almost eleven thousand square feet. The Georgia-stone-and-wood-style house had five bedrooms, an Olympic-sized pool, a media room, a mini-gym, and a kitchen that was the size of most one-bedroom apartments.

Erica felt somewhat guilty for accepting the driven car that Jonah had sent for her. It seemed wrong to her at first. However, once she realized how far the place was from any Metro stop, and considering she was dressed semiformal, it was really the best solution. So she accepted, wondering all the way there how nice she was going to have to be to Jonah in order to show her appreciation.

Once she arrived at the home, after picking her mouth off the floor at the sight of all its tasteful art and expensive furnishings, Erica's first thought was how happy she was to see other people dressed in semiformal wear. For some reason, despite knowing the dress code, she imagined herself walking into a home filled with women in formal gowns; they'd take one look at her and ask her to get them a drink.

However, any insecurity she had about her looks immediately disappeared the second Alex showed up in the foyer. Erica couldn't describe it perfectly, but the way he looked at her, although brief, made her feel beautiful. He looked for just a second as if his breath was taken away, stopping in the archway to take her in. He gathered himself, smiling and heading toward her.

"You look amazing," he said, reaching her.

"You think so?" she asked. "You've been in the main room. Will I fit in?"

"No," he said. "You'll stand out, but in the best kind of way."

"Stop it."

"Seriously, though," he said, reaching out and placing his hand on her shoulder. "You wear way too much clothing most days."

Erica tried to hide how flattered she was and how aware she was of his touch. "You think I should be showing more skin in the workplace?"

He laughed. "Not exactly, just less . . . Let me stop while I'm ahead. You look great."

"Thank you," she said gratefully.

Their eyes met and Erica knew this was trouble. What was she doing? Was she trying to make this a thing? Was this what Alex was trying to do, or was she misreading his kindness?

"I can't believe the way my mom acted the other day," Alex said, breaking the silence.

"I thought she was great," Erica said.

"Exactly," he said. "Whenever she gets the hint that I like someone, she immediately assumes she's no-good. You're a tramp until proven a nun."

"She wants you to be with a nun?" Erica asked, trying hard to ignore that he basically just admitted to liking her.

"She's old-school Catholic," Alex said, "so, pretty much, yeah."

"I'm not her girl then," Erica announced.

"That's just it," he said. "She liked you right away. She talked about you a lot after meeting you. She wanted to know all about you."

"What did you tell her?"

"That you're all right, but you have an attitude problem." He laughed.

"Erica!"

They both turned to see Malcolm striding toward them, with Jonah right behind. Erica felt that familiar dread as she looked at Jonah, hoping to convey her anger at his refusal to abide by their deal, but Jonah wasn't focused on her. He was looking at Alex and he wasn't happy.

"Hi, Malcolm," she said as soon as he reached them.

Alex stepped over and stood beside Erica. "Hey, Malcolm."

Malcolm looked at him with a confused frown on his face. "I know you, right?"

"Alex Gonzales," he said, annoyed. "We met at headquarters last week. We talked . . . twice."

"Oh yeah." Malcolm adjusted his glasses and laughed. "Hi, Alex. Um . . . Erica, how are you?"

"Fine," she said, feeling more uncomfortable now that Jonah was there.

How did he have a way of making her feel guilty? She wasn't doing anything wrong.

"Alex," Jonah's voice was curt, sounding as if he was about to give a military order. "Can you please make sure that the raffle tables are being manned? Someone mentioned they weren't earlier."

"I . . ." Seeming to figure out what was going on, Alex didn't seem at all happy. But he knew there was nothing he could do about it. If Jonah wanted him gone, he was gone. "Yeah, I guess."

He turned to Erica. "I'll see you in a bit."

"Count on it." Erica felt horrible for him, because of how uncomfortable he suddenly seemed.

She detected a hint of jealousy in his eyes when he looked at Malcolm one last time before heading off. That was silly. They weren't the closest of friends, but he should have known enough of her by now to know that a bow tie–wearing, entitled trust fund baby wasn't her type at all.

"Malcolm," Jonah said, his tone suddenly light and warm, "why don't you get Erica a drink and show her around your house?"

"Sounds great," Malcolm said, turning to Erica. "Do you want to start upstairs or downstairs?"

"Wherever you think is best," she said, trying to sound as polite as possible, even though she wanted to strangle Jonah.

After all, it wasn't Malcolm's fault. He was just being a nice guy, so Erica was going to try her best to be a nice girl. She would bide her time. Jonah would have to get busier as the evening progressed and she would fall down the priority list. Then she could focus on what she really wanted, which was hanging out with Alex.

When Sherise showed up for work on Monday morning, she noticed something was wrong right away. She was getting stares from everyone. That wasn't unusual. She always got stares from men and women when she walked into a room. Only these stares lasted a little too long and were directed right at her face, not at her body, her clothes, or her shoes.

It was clear to her now. The firm had acquiesced to

their request to hold off on giving Elena money, which gave them a chance to fight her accusations. However, once this information got back to Elena's lawyers, it was only a matter of time. They were supposed to give them until Wednesday, but Sherise knew that was bullshit.

"Sherise?" LaKeisha met her in the hallway near her office. The uncomfortable look on her face wasn't a good sign. "Can you come with me to Northman's office?"

"Fine," Sherise said, not bothering to pretend she didn't know what this was about.

Once inside Northman's office, after everyone else had left the adjacent area, both Sherise and LaKeisha sat across from him at his desk. Northman explained to her that news of her husband being at the center of a scandal at one of D.C.'s top lobbying firms had reached the campaign. From back when he was a senator, Northman had remained a close friend with the head of the practice at the firm.

As soon as she had to a chance to speak and explain her side, Northman stopped her in her tracks.

"Honestly, Sherise." He sighed, seeming exhausted just from this conversation. "I'm sure you'll say he's innocent, and I'm inclined to believe you. Most of these harassment claims are bullshit. I would think the best move would be for you to take a leave of absence until you can get this accusation thrown out of court, but . . ."

Sherise noticed him glance at LaKeisha. When she turned to her, Sherise could tell that LaKeisha was embarrassed about something that had nothing to do with her.

"Honestly," Northman continued, "with all the mistakes being made around here, I can't afford to lose you too."

Sherise's curiosity was piqued. "What's going on?"

"Jonathan was arrested two nights ago," LaKeisha said.

Sherise didn't have to feign surprise; it was genuine. With all the mess Elena had brought into her life, she'd temporarily forgotten about Jonathan and what might happen to him once Jonah's camp found out.

"I thought . . . ," she started to say, ". . . I thought we agreed that Northman shouldn't know about him."

"It's too late for that," Northman said.

"Arrested for what?" Sherise asked.

"DUI," LaKeisha said. "He ran up on a curb in Friendship Heights. Someone called the cops. Supposedly, he was high and drunk and had some drugs in his possession."

"Oh no," Sherise said.

"I talked to him yesterday morning," she said. "He thinks he was drugged while hanging out at a bar earlier. He says he's never done drugs in his life."

"He's saying he was set up?" Sherise asked.

Wow, she thought, *Jonah acts faster than I ever expected.* She wasn't sure how happy she could be about this until she learned more.

"It had to be Nolan's people," Northman added. "I've seen this shit before. Nolan found out about him and made sure he wasn't a threat anymore."

"Was there any connection to the campaign found in his car?" Sherise asked.

"There's no way to know," LaKeisha said. "His car was wiped clean. Not only that, but when he finally made bail and went home yesterday, his place was ransacked."

"That's why she had to tell me," Northman said. "This was definitely a setup and search."

"We did a search of the office," LaKeisha said.

Sherise held her breath.

"Looks like Amy Griffin sent Nolan an e-mail from her personal e-mail account." LaKeisha shook her head.

Sherise let her breath out and relaxed a little. Just as she had planned.

"She's my assistant," LaKeisha continued, "so I know it's my fault, but I honestly believed I could trust her. She was so passionate about the campaign."

"Obviously, she was getting paid by the Nolan people," Northman said.

"What did she have to say for herself?" Sherise asked.

Yes, part of her felt bad for setting the girl up, but she was fighting for her life and her family. There would be collateral damage that was regrettable.

"She denied it," LaKeisha said. "She even denied being in the office at the time. She said she'd left almost an hour before."

"But she was there," Northman said. "A couple of staffers who came back from dinner that night, around the time it was sent, reported to security that they thought they'd heard someone. Also, one of them remembers seeing her computer as being the only one in the entire area that was lit up. If she'd been gone almost an hour, it would have powered down by then."

Funny, Sherise thought. *Who would have thought having random staffers would only bolster my plan?*

She desperately wanted to smile, so she did—only on the inside, though. On the outside, she maintained a look of utter seriousness and surprise.

LaKeisha shook her head. "She couldn't explain how someone could know her password, though. Only the IT guys know it and none of them were there. They were all at the governor's mansion, setting up security stuff that afternoon and evening."

Sherise realized this could be better than she expected. LaKeisha was suffering the brunt of what her assistant had done. Northman himself said that he needed Sherise because of LaKeisha's downgrade in his eyes at the moment. This was more power for her. Considering how things were going elsewhere, she thought it was capital she might really need down the line.

"You don't have to worry about me," Sherise said. "Justin and I have gotten this under control. It's not going to even make it through the investigations process. We're not gonna let the firm pay her off, so people can still speculate that he was guilty. These false accusations will be brought to light, and in a way that completely erases any doubt that Justin is innocent."

"See to it that you do," Northman said. "Because if you can't, Sherise, you know the result."

The result would be that the campaign couldn't be associated with this. There was no way that the top spokesperson for a presidential candidate could have a spouse publicly disgraced from a sex scandal.

Sherise wasn't going to let that happen. She had solved one problem, but there were just a million more there to take its place. She had a lot of work to do.

12

Erica was on the phone talking to a donor about contribution options when Jonah rushed into the large room set aside for making phone calls.

He didn't seem to care that there was a room full of volunteers and young staffers, who all stopped in their tracks as he walked in. He was heading for Erica; the look on his face made her wonder if she should run for her life. He was flaming angry and everyone could tell.

"I . . . um . . ." Erica suddenly remembered that she had stopped in the middle of a sentence and was trying desperately to get back on track. Her mind was blank as he approached.

Without a moment's hesitation, Jonah grabbed the phone from her hand and hung it up.

"Come with me," he ordered harshly.

"I was talking to a donor," she protested. "You just hung—"

"Now!"

Everyone went silent.

Erica was embarrassed as she stood up and came

around the table. Jonah was already walking out, assuming that she was following. She picked up speed to keep up with him, but she also hurried just to get out of the room, where everyone was looking at her.

Her mind was racing a mile a minute. Jonah hadn't been happy that she'd spent a lot of time at the fundraiser with Alex. She could tell from the glances he sent her. She ignored him and he seemed to give it up by the end of the evening. Malcolm had asked her to dinner; and although Erica told him she found him to be very nice, she didn't think it was a good idea. Maybe Malcolm had told Jonah that she'd turned him down?

No, that couldn't be it. The anger in Jonah's eyes told her it was something much more important. For some reason, she suspected it had to do with Sherise.

He didn't lead her to his office. Instead, he stopped at a private room in the hallway and went inside. She quickly followed him in and closed the door behind them.

"What the fuck is this?" Jonah asked, shoving a letter at her.

Erica took it, keeping her eye on him as she opened it.

"That was on my desk this morning," he said. "Delivered to the fucking building."

It was inside a regular-sized white envelope, no return address. The letter was on colored paper, a very light, almost baby blue sheet of stationery, with hunter green ribbons at the top and bottom. It looked familiar to Erica; but before she could think further on that, she read the words that had been typed: *You don't deserve this. You ruin lives. You cheat. I can prove it. Drop out or else.*

It wasn't signed by anyone.

"I didn't send it to you," she said.

"You know who did?" he asked. "Sherise! That's who."

Erica handed the letter back to him. "Think about what you're saying. She has just as much to lose as you do if this came to light."

Jonah laughed. "Just as much? Hell no. She'll just go back to being a nobody. I'd lose my chance to be the most powerful man in the world. They can hardly compare."

"Unlike you," Erica said, "losing her family is more important than running the world. Your wife would just down a few more shots of vodka and pretend like nothing happened. Justin would actually give a shit. She wouldn't do this."

"She wants me to drop out of this race," Jonah said. "If you notice, there's no threat to go to the press. That's because the person who sent this doesn't want it in the press. They just want me to go away, so it never gets a chance to get into the press. That's her."

"Of course her life would be much easier if you didn't run," Erica said, "but this isn't her style. Sending a cryptic letter. That's amateurish, hustler stuff that Sherise wouldn't be caught dead . . ."

Erica snatched the paper back from Jonah, feeling a sudden shock at what leapt into her mind. She looked at the stationery again and it hit her. It was familiar to her!

"Holy shit," was all she could say.

"What?" Jonah asked.

She looked at him, seeing the anger in his eyes. Jonah was not a man to threaten. This wasn't going to end well at all.

"Tell me," he demanded.

She shook her head. "It's not Sherise. This is beneath her, and you know it. Just stay away from her."

"Fuck that," Jonah said. "Whoever this is has just declared war on me and . . ."

Jonah was studying her face. Erica could see he was working something out, and she wanted desperately to turn away from him. But she couldn't. He was going to figure it out.

"You recognize this paper," he said. "You know who this is."

"Jonah—"

"That piece of shit." Jonah seized the paper back from her and crumpled it up before throwing it against the wall. "I will kill that little shit."

"Don't say that!" Erica yelled.

"Keep your voice down," he ordered.

"I won't! Not if you keep threatening Terrell!"

"Shut up." He grabbed her arms to get her under control.

Erica broke free of his grasp and backed away. "Take that back. You won't kill him."

"You can't possibly still give a shit about him," Jonah said. "How many times has he let you down?"

"Almost as many as you have," Erica said. "And, yes, I'll always give a shit about him. I loved him once. We were engaged."

"That wasn't real," Jonah said dismissively.

Erica knew she shouldn't let Jonah's words hurt her, but that stung. He didn't really know anything about her and Terrell. Still, it made her insanely angry to hear him dismiss their love like that.

"You are such an asshole," she said.

"I'm worse than that," he warned, seething with danger. "Much worse, and that little thug is about to find out."

"No," Erica said. "You promised you wouldn't touch him."

"That deal I made with you pertained to another matter," he said. "You agreed to stay away from him, then so would I. This is different. He's a threat to my plan, to what I've worked my life for."

"I don't care," Erica said, summoning a level of courage she didn't even know she had. She stared up at him, resolute and unwavering. "You won't hurt him. I won't let you."

"You can't stop me," he said.

"Well, then," she answered back, "I won't let you get away with it."

They stared each other down for several seconds. Erica felt her knees begin to weaken and she could barely breathe. Was it showing? Probably, but she couldn't back down. Terrell's life depended on her staying strong. No, she didn't love him anymore, want him anymore. But Erica couldn't live with herself if she let Jonah do something to him—even if Terrell deserved it for getting into a fight he couldn't possibly win, over and over again.

Jonah blinked first. He sighed, then looked past her for a second, as if deciding this wasn't worth it. When he looked at Erica again, his expression was softer than before, but still very serious.

"I'd get away with it, Erica. I think you know that."

She was visibly upset and that seemed to bother him a little.

"I wouldn't hurt you," he said, "but I wouldn't let you hurt me either."

"I'd try my hardest," she said, feeling herself shaking all over, and hoping it didn't show.

He smiled at her, seeming impressed. Erica realized that this was the kind of thing Jonah admired. It made her think he might be crazy. Or maybe she was crazy for basically threatening him to his face. Either way, she might have won this battle for now.

"Give me a chance to find him," she said. "I don't know exactly what he's doing now, but I can find out from my brother—"

"He's washing cars in Columbia Heights," Jonah said. "He's been there since he was fired from Destin, five months ago."

"Of course you'd know," Erica said.

"I make it a practice to keep track of anyone who threatened me," Jonah said.

"I guess I just added myself to that list, huh?" Erica asked.

"I don't need to keep track of you, Erica." He smiled softly. "You're right next to me."

"I'll handle this," she said.

His smile faded, seeming annoyed at having to return to the topic at hand.

"I'll give you some time," he said flatly. "If I don't hear something from you in the next few days that makes me feel better about this, your boy is history."

He walked to the door; but before opening it, he turned back to her. "Just in case, you might want to say your good-byes to him either way."

After he left, Erica grabbed her phone out of her pocket and started texting both of her girls immediately. At the last minute, she thought about it and only texted Billie. The last thing she needed was another Sherise freak-out session. She wanted to be the only one freaking out right now.

Billie felt greedy and she loved it. It had been a long, long time since she'd had sex with no guilt, shame, or secrecy attached to it. It was liberating and totally arousing.

After freshening up in her bathroom after an hour-long lovemaking session with Michael, she returned to her bedroom with the full intention of a second round. However, the look on Michael's face when he turned to her told her that wasn't going to happen.

"What's wrong?" she asked.

As Billie reached the bed, he held up what was in his hand. It was her phone. She snatched it away from him.

"What are you doing looking at my phone?" she asked, angry.

"I wasn't," he said. "It made a sound and I was going to call you to tell you, but I noticed the text."

"You noticed?" she asked.

Looking down at the screen, she saw it was a log of a few texts she and Erica had traded before she headed to the bathroom.

"You're mad because I texted in bed after sex?"

"You know that's not it," he said, crossing his arms over his chest.

Billie rolled her eyes. "Because I was texting about Porter? You really shouldn't have read that."

After mentioning Erica's dilemma with Terrell,

Billie briefly mentioned her victory over Porter at her apartment and later at the conference. It was harmless. As far as Billie was concerned, there was no reason for Michael to be upset.

"I shouldn't have," he said, seeming somewhat remorseful, "but I did, and I can't believe you're talking about your ex right after having sex with me. We discussed this, didn't we?"

"We discussed that I wouldn't talk to you about Porter." She placed the phone on the nightstand, standing at the edge of the bed. "And I haven't. You can't possibly have meant that I don't talk about him to anyone."

"No, of course I didn't." He was clearly still unsatisfied.

"My conversations with my girlfriends aren't any of your business." She walked to the end of the bed and reached for her bathrobe, not really in the mood anymore. "Stay away from my phone."

"You're right," he said. "But you can't expect me not to be upset. We just had what I thought was amazing sex, but the first thing you do once it's over is text your girlfriend about our interaction with your ex."

She put her robe on and sat down on the edge of the bed. "It's out of context, Michael. She was trying to come up with ideas on how to handle her ex."

"I wasn't asking for an explanation," he said.

"You don't deserve one!" she exclaimed. "But since you seem to misunderstand everything that has to do with him, I thought I'd tell you."

He looked at her crisply. "Fine. Then, since you're explaining, why? Why did you feel the need to humiliate him again?"

"Honestly," she said, standing up again. "He humiliated himself. But my motive was revenge for ruining our night together last week. I wanted him to know, once and for all, I wasn't one to fuck with."

Michael laughed, shaking his head, and it infuriated Billie.

"This is funny to you now?" she asked. "At first, you're upset. Now you think it's a joke? I don't get it with you, Michael."

"You don't get it at all," he said. "Porter didn't ruin our night, Billie. You did. You just want to blame it on him so you can excuse your little obsession with him."

"Obsession?" Billie laughed incredulously. "You're way out of line."

"Revenge never goes the way you want it to, unless you're evil enough to risk everything. You're not evil, Billie. You're just angry. For someone like you, revenge will only end up hurting you more."

Billie glared at him with burning anger. "You're just like him."

His eyes widened in shock. "I'm what?"

"You're just like him," she repeated. "You think I'm weak. You think you know me, like you have my number. I'm not strong enough to follow through on my threats, to win a fight."

"Billie." Michael got up from the bed and turned to face her. "You took that wrong. Maybe I said it wrong. I don't think of you that way. I was just saying—"

"That I'm not strong enough to win this battle!"

"What battle?" he asked.

"This battle we've been waging since I left him! You think I'm too delicate to win it, so I should just get out. That's what he thought, and he was right, at first.

That's why I always ended up getting the short end of every fucking stick!"

"Billie." Michael started walking toward her. "You need to calm down. You're getting too emotional."

"I haven't seen my daughter in eight months!" she yelled. "So fuck him, and fuck you, Michael. I'm not backing down."

"Billie, I'm sorry," he said with a sigh. "I was just saying—"

"You need to leave."

Billie darted for the door to her bedroom. She opened it wide, refusing to look at him.

"Billie, please."

"Leave!" she yelled. "I want you out of my house, now!"

Erica was feeling some panic setting in. At the time, when she'd promised Jonah she could handle Terrell yesterday, she'd felt confident she could do it. But as every hour ticked by, she was less so. She needed to talk to her girls, and she was going to get that chance later tonight when they met.

Still, she was going crazy at work and needed something to help her calm down. All she could think of was Alex. If she hung out with him for a bit, she could unwind like she usually did. He'd been in meetings all morning, but she heard that meeting was over, so she headed over to his office. He wasn't there, so she assumed he was still in the conference room and headed there.

When she reached the main conference room, it was empty. She was about to turn and leave, when the door on the other side of the room opened. In walked

Juliet Nolan. She looked like the perfect political wife—
this time dressed in a smart blue skirt suit, with flowers
at the edges of the jacket. Her hair was down, making
her look a little younger than usual. With makeup on,
hiding the aging that drinking had done to her, she
looked much younger, but still unhappy.

"Well," Juliet said, with a sly smile on her face, "if
it isn't little Erica."

Erica sighed, deciding to turn and leave instead of
putting up with this bitch. She didn't need this.

"What are you afraid of?" Juliet called after her.

Erica had the door halfway open and she wanted to
listen to the voice that told her just to keep going. She
really wanted to.

"I'm not afraid of you," she said, turning back to
her. "And I'm not 'little.' "

Juliet looked her up and down, with a nod, which
made Erica want to walk across the room and punch
her in the face.

"Are you sober?" Erica asked with as fake a smile
as she could imagine.

"For now," Juliet said, not seeming fazed by the
comment. "But I'm looking for my husband, so I probably won't be a couple of hours from now."

"That's more information than I needed," Erica
said. "I'm gonna leave you to—"

"I don't blame you," Juliet said.

"That's good," Erica responded. "Because I didn't
do anything."

"I do blame your mother, though."

Erica quickly became infuriated at the mention of
her mother, a hot button in any situation, but especially
as an accusation from this woman.

"My mother didn't do anything to you," Erica said. "Just don't mention her, Juliet. She's not for you to mention."

Juliet laughed. "Didn't do anything to me? She slept with my husband. I would suggest that qualifies as 'doing something' to me and gives me the right to mention her."

"She didn't sleep with your husband." Erica walked over to her, close enough to point her finger in her face. "Don't you talk about my mother like that! She would never be someone's mistress. He wasn't your husband."

"He was!" Juliet screamed.

"You're a fucking liar!" Erica yelled. "He hadn't even met you when they were together."

"Don't try and bullshit me," Juliet said. "I don't know what your mom or Jonah told you, and I really don't give a shit. I know he slept with her right after we got married. I almost divorced him over it."

"No!" Erica was trying desperately to control her outrage, but she was losing that battle. "You're not gonna get away with that. She would have never, ever—"

"Erica!"

She swung around to see Alex, who was standing at the door, rushing toward her. He grabbed her by the arm, pulling her back. She was consumed with rage; her instinct was making her try to break free of his grasp.

"Let me go!"

"No!" Alex tightened his grip. "What are you doing?"

Erica turned to Juliet, who had an evil smile on her face.

"You know it's true." Juliet turned around and left out the door she had come in.

"That bitch is a liar," Erica said.

"What is she talking about?" Alex asked, still gripping her tightly. "Why are you so crazed? That's Jonah's wife, for Christ's sake."

"I don't care," Erica said. "She's lying!"

"About what?" Alex asked.

Erica was just about to tell him everything, but then she caught herself. What was she doing? She couldn't do this.

"What did you hear?" she asked, trying to calm down.

"I heard yelling," he said. "When I opened the door, you told her she wasn't going to talk about someone like that. Who are you talking about?"

"I can't tell you." Erica finally broke free of him, but she was still shaking all over.

"Look at you," he said. "You're falling apart. You have to tell me what's going on."

"I can't." Erica started to cry. "I can't. It's too fucked up. I just gotta get out of here."

"Stop."

Alex grabbed her as she tried to pass him. She pushed away, but he pulled her close. He wrapped his arms around her and held her tightly. Although she was feeling like such a fool for crying, she felt better in his arms.

"I can't tell you," she whispered. "I'm sorry."

"Then don't tell me." His voice was tender and compassionate. "Just let me help you."

"Sherise, you need to listen to your lawyer," Billie argued.

The women were together, meeting briefly at an outdoor café to discuss their latest emergencies. Billie could tell that Erica was nervous about bringing up the topic of Terrell and wasn't really paying attention to Sherise's complaints about Elena's harassment claim. Sherise was acting reckless, though, having hired a private investigator to look into Elena's background and was now threatening to stalk the girl herself.

"You'll only make things worse for Justin," Billie added. "This is his career. He's worked forever to get here. Don't ruin it for him by being impatient. Your marriage is already in a tense state."

"That's just the thing," Sherise said. "This thing— this horrible thing that this bitch has brought into our lives—is our chance to fix everything. We have trust issues. That's what's holding us back. But by me leading the fight against this woman, I'm proving to Justin that I believe him. I can see he's trusting me again too."

Billie shrugged her agreement. "They say things like this can either break or seal a marriage."

"We had sex for the first time since finding out I was pregnant," Sherise said proudly. "It wasn't just good sex either. It was great, passionate sex. Feeling like it's us against the world has brought us together."

"That's good," Billie said, "but trust me as a lawyer, not just your friend. If you get caught stalking this girl, things will get worse for you. It's not the answer."

Sherise rolled her eyes. "If I could count on a PI to do all the work, I would. But I'm on a deadline here. They've already leaked it to the campaign. It's gonna be public on Capitol Hill any day now. I have to make sure that they don't pay her off. I want Justin one hundred percent exonerated."

"I hope it works," Billie said. "We all do, don't we?"

Billie kicked Erica under the table. Since her confrontation with Juliet, she hadn't been able to think of much else, even though she had a lot to do.

Coming out of her trance, Erica jumped a little in her seat.

"What?" she asked. "What did I miss?"

"You've been worthless to me so far," Sherise reminded her. "You haven't helped me find out where I stand with Jonah. I had to handle Jonathan myself. You're not listening to anything I've had to say about—"

"It's all about you, isn't it?" Erica asked.

"Hell yes, it is," Sherise answered. "I'm the one whose world is falling apart, so, yes, right now it's about me."

"It's not, you know," Erica corrected. "Billie had a fight with Michael, but you don't give a shit. Instead of us helping her out, we have to talk about you, you, and more you."

"It's okay," Billie said. "It's not a big deal."

"But it is," Erica argued. "We're supposed to talk about everyone's problems, so we can help each other out. All we seem to do now is talk about the shit Sherise has gotten herself caught up in."

"To be fair," Billie said, "Sherise didn't start this one. And don't worry about Michael. He's already called me and wants to see me again."

"Fine," Sherise fumed. "Just to prove you wrong, let's talk about Billie and Michael, even though a little fight doesn't even remotely compare to what I'm going through."

"You're going to see him again, aren't you?" Erica asked, ignoring Sherise.

"It depends." Billie shrugged. "I like him a lot."

"I think it's more than a lot," Erica said, "from the way you talk about him."

"Why haven't we met him yet?" Sherise asked.

"I don't know if you will," Billie said. "He needs to get with the program. He can't be telling me who I can and can't talk to about Porter."

"Porter isn't worth losing him over," Erica said.

"Porter ain't worth shit," Sherise added.

"That's not true," Billie said. "He's worth access to my daughter."

"Billie." Erica placed her hand on Billie's shoulder. "We've been through this. She's not your daughter."

Billie shirked away. "She is in every way that matters, and Porter is gonna give me access to her again or he'll be sorry."

Sherise studied Billie. "I think I'm liking this new Billie. As long as you're giving Porter some of the hell back he gave you, I support it."

"I think Michael is right," Erica said. "Don't get me wrong. He had no right to look at your phone and comment on our conversation. It's just that revenge doesn't suit you, Billie."

Billie shot up from her seat. "If one more person tells me that, I'm gonna crack their—"

"Easy," Erica said. "Jesus, calm down. I'm just telling you the truth as I see it."

"At least I'm willing to stand up to my ex," Billie said. "You're so afraid of confronting Terrell that you can't even talk about him."

"What about Terrell?" Sherise asked.

Erica eyed Billie with daggers, wanting to choke her for that.

Billie didn't seem to care. She sat back down and grabbed her drink, chugging it down like it was a reward.

"Why are you even talking to that asshole thug again?" Sherise asked. "You know better."

"I'm not," Erica said. "I don't want to. And I'm not afraid, Billie. You're such a bitch for bringing it up like that, when you're the one that said not to give Sherise any bad news."

"It had to get out there," Billie said. "Sherise needs to know."

"You just wanted to take the attention off you," Erica argued.

"You're the one so eager to share everyone's—"

"Wait!" Sherise stopped Billie midsentence. "Why would I want to know? What the fuck is going on?"

Erica sighed before proceeding to tell Sherise about the letter sent to Jonah and his threats about Terrell. Before she could even finish, Sherise commenced to freak out just as she expected.

"Honestly," Erica said. "I would remind you that losing your shit is not good for the baby, but I think that's been done, and done."

"Why didn't you tell me about this before now?" Sherise asked.

"Because it happened yesterday," Erica said. "Besides, I've had other things . . . I mean, for fuck sake, you guys don't know what I'm dealing with."

"What else could be more important than this?" Sherise felt like her heart was going to leap out of her chest.

She was trying to pace her breathing, but she couldn't. It was bad enough that Jonah could ruin her life. There was no way this piece-of-shit thug was going to bring her down.

"Juliet was talking all kinds of shit to me about Jonah and my mother," Erica said, feeling her blood boil as she recalled the confrontation. "She's saying that their affair continued after he was married."

"Impossible," Billie said. "Your mom would never—"

"I know!" Erica exclaimed. "That's what I said, but she's saying she had evidence—enough so that she almost filed for divorce before he put an end to it. I wanted to punch her in the face. If Alex hadn't been there, I think I would have."

Sherise recalled her meeting with Jonathan, who mentioned the divorce papers, but she decided to keep it to herself. She didn't want Erica focusing on this side issue. That could be dealt with later. She needed to remain focused on Terrell.

"So, what are you going to do about Terrell?" Sherise asked.

"Wait a second," Billie said. "Alex stopped you? He heard you? He knows now?"

Erica shook her head. "He doesn't know, and, thank God, he didn't push me for an answer. He's just the best. He was there for me and kept me from losing my mind, but he didn't push me when I shut him down on my secret."

"It's Jonah's secret," Billie said. "Not yours."

Erica nodded, smiling at Billie's attempt to comfort her. She was still mad at her, though. "I don't know how long I can keep it from him, considering he's helping me with Terrell."

"No," Sherise said. "You can't tell him about Terrell. If you do, then you'll have to tell him about me. I can't have any more people knowing."

"I wouldn't have to name you," Erica said. "Besides, I haven't told him anything. He knows that I have to confront my ex tomorrow, and he wants to be there with me when I do it."

"It should be us," Sherise said. "We should be there with you. Not an outsider."

"He's not an outsider to me," Erica said. "Not anymore."

"How much time do you have?" Billie asked. "I mean, before Jonah decides to take it into his own hands."

"Yes!" Sherise slapped her hand on the table. "You should let Jonah take care of it. It's about time Terrell suffers the consequences of biting off more than he could chew. He never learned his lesson, and this just shows he never will."

"I'm too afraid of what Jonah will do to him," Erica said.

"Fuck him," Sherise responded. "He's a danger to us all."

"Not me," Billie said. "And I agree with Erica. There is no telling what Jonah will do to him. If she has a chance to save him from that, she should take it. I do think we should go with you, though."

"No," Erica said. "I have to do this alone."

"But you just said you're bringing this boy with you," Sherise reminded her.

"He's bringing me," Erica said. "I've already told him he can't be a part of the conversation. I have to see Terrell alone. This is what Terrell wants. I really think if I can just see him, he'll be satisfied. If I bring you two or someone else in with me, he'll just get angry."

"Well, you know him best," Billie said. "I'm still afraid. I don't like the way he acted when you broke up with him."

"I can handle Terrell," Erica said. "At least I used to be able to."

"Well, you better handle him," Sherise said. "Or Jonah will."

13

Sherise was being as careful as she could under the circumstances. She was dressed in workout clothes, which weren't too attention grabbing. She tried to blend in, not an easy thing to do for her. She was at the health club for a reason, a purpose, and a mission. Part of that meant not drawing the usual attention to herself.

Elena had been working out midmorning. She was no longer working at the firm, having quit once she was informed that they would not pay her off immediately.

Sherise had been watching all week and was correct in thinking today Elena would show up at ten. Sherise arrived at nine in the morning, claiming to be interested in the club. She was given a tour, which lasted almost forty-five minutes, and then was left to discover the equipment on her own. She'd waited in the locker room after that, and Elena showed up a few minutes after ten.

She picked a locker in the middle of the row, which was not good. Sherise had hoped she'd choose one on the end, making it easier to escape if she got caught inspecting. It didn't matter. After she'd left, Sherise checked her lock and it was solid.

She didn't want to risk being seen out and about. This was a pretty high-end club and she would certainly run into someone she knew. If her cover was blown, there might be hell to pay. Of course, she could always play it off as an incredible coincidence, which was why she laid the groundwork with the tour, but Sherise didn't want to have to deal with that. It would upset Justin—and as good as things were going with them now, that was the last thing she wanted to do.

So she waited and it paid off.

Forty-five minutes later, Elena showed up briefly, grabbed her soap and loofah, and disappeared. Within minutes, having showered, she was back, and in a towel. She dragged her bag out of the locker and placed it on the bench in the middle of the row. The locker room wasn't very active at the moment, so Sherise was able to spy easily. As she suspected, Elena dressed quickly and grabbed her towels with the intent of placing them in the dirty-laundry baskets, which were against the walls several feet away.

This was her chance.

Not bothering to lock her bag up for a short trip, Elena just headed over. No one was in the aisle. Sherise rushed over to her bag and started searching frantically. She reached for the phone and looked at the text messages. Scrolling down, she found what she was looking for. The witness, the biggest threat in her case against Justin: Bartholdi Park. Wed. 3! - Dennis.

Dennis Stevens must be getting nervous, she thought. *Good.* He was going to have to recant everything if Justin was going to be exonerated fully.

Sherise knew she was out of time. She only had a

few seconds. She tossed the phone back into the bag and turned to leave. Just then, she noticed something. She turned back to examine it. On the bag was a button.

It was a picture of Elena as a young girl with another girl, who looked a lot like her, inside a heart frame. She looked almost exactly like her. They had to be siblings. But hadn't their PI told them that Elena was an only child?

When Sherise realized she was wasting more time, she leaned up to leave. Elena was walking right toward her!

Sherise froze; then she realized that Elena hadn't seen her yet because she was looking at something on her hand. But it didn't matter. She was less than twenty feet away; and even if she didn't look up from her hand, the second Sherise moved, Elena would notice. Sherise was caught.

There was nothing she could do. Was she going to have to fight this girl? She was pregnant, still in her first trimester. She couldn't get into a fight, no matter how appealing the idea of tearing out some of this girl's hair might seem.

"Elena!"

Sherise jumped at the same time Elena jumped. Someone was calling her name. Sherise was immensely grateful, as it caused Elena to swing around and look toward the call, giving Sherise the two seconds she needed to jump around the corner of the lockers.

"Elena Brown!" the high-pitched voice called.

"Brown?" Sherise whispered.

Sherise could hear Elena rustling up her bag and slamming her locker shut. She was too curious not to look. Peeking around the corner, Sherise caught a view of Elena and could see that the girl was nervous as hell. Elena wanted to get away from there.

A dark-haired, pale beauty in her thirties, wearing a bloodred workout combo, came into the row, looking confused as to why she'd been ignored.

"Elena," she said, "didn't you hear me?"

Elena quickly swung the bag over her shoulder, turning to the woman. Her back was to Sherise now, so Sherise felt safer, observing them, and leaned farther in. She could read Elena's body language. She was not happy.

"Laura!" Elena said, and laughed. "Was that you? Sorry, I've just got so much on my mind."

"What are you doing in D.C.?" Laura asked.

Sherise detected a distinct Southern accent, more like a Texas twang.

"I'm . . . I'm visiting a friend," Elena said. "She gave me a pass to her club."

Wait a second! Sherise wasn't sure, but she thought she suddenly detected that same twang in Elena's voice. *What is going on?*

"Who are you visiting?" she asked. "Do I know her?"

"Um . . . no, I just met her last year at a conference." Elena slammed the locker shut. "She's not from home."

The woman looked confused, but she persisted. "We should have lunch. How long are you gonna be in—"

"I'm leaving today," Elena said quickly. She brushed past Laura without bothering to look back. "It was nice seeing you, Laura. Bye!"

"Um . . ." Laura looked thoroughly perplexed. "Bye?"

Sherise didn't hesitate. She walked around the corner into the row and made eye contact with Laura.

"Did Elena come back yet?" she asked. "I thought I just heard her?"

Laura pointed toward the door. "She left, I guess. That was weird."

"She left?" Sherise asked, looking utterly confused. "We're supposed to be going to lunch before she heads back home today. Maybe she's coming back."

"You're the friend she's staying with?" Laura asked.

Sherise nodded. "Yes, I'm Kelly. She came here to visit me, but she's been acting so weird. I guess I'll go look for her."

"I'm Laura." She shook Sherise's hand. "That was the weirdest encounter I've ever had with her, and that's saying something for Elena. We grew up together in Denton."

Denton. Sherise caught that red flag right away. *Cleveland, my ass.*

"What do you think it is?" Sherise asked. "I mean, she called me up and said she just had to get away and could she stay with me for a bit. I didn't ask questions."

"It's probably about Rose." Laura was shaking her head, seeming sad. "It's been over a year, but she's still having a hard time getting over her death."

"Must be," Sherise said. "And what exactly—"

"Oh, my God, is that the time?" Laura asked, glancing down at her watch. "I'm going to be late for Zumba! It was nice meeting you, Kelly. Bye!"

"But . . . ," Sherise called after her, but Laura was gone.

Sherise contemplated waiting again, but she couldn't pull it off. It would be weird to find her still in the locker room an hour later. Laura would get suspicious. Also, she had to get to work. The doctor's appointment she claimed to be on could only last so long.

She would have to work with what she had, and it just might be enough. Elena Brown was up to something as Elena Nichols—and she didn't want anyone who knew Elena Brown to know about it. Maybe she had an agenda that went beyond getting a few bucks out of the firm at Justin's expense. There was a lot to do, and very little time to do it.

As she waited outside Porter's building, Billie reflected that she probably shouldn't have drunk that Red Bull before coming over. She was a tiny dynamo at the moment, having a hard time focusing. But this shouldn't be difficult. She just needed a little help with her nerve.

She was actually very excited. Things were about to change for her. When she'd mentioned to the girls the other day about getting Porter to let her see Tara again, it hadn't really occurred to her before that moment. Now it was all she could think about.

She did everything she could to keep her thoughts from Michael, not wanting it to interfere. Things were going so well with him in the last week. After their argument, they'd met for dinner and he said his apologies. He admitted to being wrong for reading her phone and said he wanted to understand, but he just didn't want to invest his heart in someone who was obsessed with her ex.

For her part, realizing how much she missed him in just that short span of being apart, Billie made promises to let her issues with Porter go. It wasn't a lie.

Now that she was confident she'd get to see Tara, she truly intended to keep her promise to Michael and Porter. She was going to let it go. After all, she could really see herself falling in love with Michael. If she could have Michael and Tara, then Porter would lose all significance in her life.

She and Michael had spent almost every evening together. It was hard not bringing the topic up. She loved Tara and missed her so much; Billie wanted to share that with him, but she knew it wasn't the right time. Of all the pain she'd felt in the last year, losing her connection to Tara was the worst.

It was remembering this truth that gave her the courage the second she saw Porter step out of the building. He turned right to head down the street and that was where Billie intercepted him.

He stopped in his tracks, taking a moment to register what was happening.

"What the fuck do you want?" he asked.

"I'll be quick," she said. "I'm meeting my boyfriend for dinner."

"Great," he said. "Be on your way to your next failed relationship."

"I was on my way up to your offices." She placed both hands casually on her hips and looked up at him with a teasing gaze. "I was going to tell your bosses how disappointed I am in your work."

"I got to hand it to you, Billie. You got me last time. You played that well."

"I learned that trick from you," she said. "Making someone else look foolish, while you seem so innocent and not intentional. I did a great job, if I say so myself."

"It worked once," he said, a look of disdain on his face, "but it won't work again. I'm onto you now. You're not gonna get away with that shit."

"I don't need to," Billie said, feigning sympathy. "You see, Gil caught the bait too. He's actually worried you're not up to working for me, for us. I'm inclined to agree with him, especially after that last outburst."

Porter sighed heavily, his entire body lifting and lowering in defeat. He tilted his head to the side and looked at her with no sign of emotion on his face.

"You've won," he said. "Whatever it was you wanted to win, you got it. So, why not just stop before it gets out of hand?"

"Funny," Billie said, placing her index finger on her chin and looking up, "I recall saying that same thing to you during our divorce proceedings when you blindsided me and took everything. I think I also said it, after you paid a paralegal at my firm to spy on me so you could get me in trouble. And what about that time—"

"I get it," Porter said. "I don't have time for this, Billie. What do you want?"

"I want my daughter," she said plainly.

Porter's jaw clenched; his eyes narrowed. "She is not your daughter. She was—notice the word 'was'—your stepdaughter. She's not anymore."

"Leave it to someone like you to think that titles are what matter," Billie said. "I want to see her."

"I'm surprised at you, Billie," he said, seeming disappointed. "I never thought you'd use her in all of this."

Billie laughed. "Your hypocrisy is disgusting. You used her so many times to hurt me or to pull me closer to you. You sent her away to hurt me for turning you down again."

"I love my daughter," he said. "More than you ever could, and I—"

"Save it," Billie said, determined to get this straight. "Besides, I'm not using Tara to get to you. I'm using you to get to Tara. I want to see her."

"So you can fill her head with poison against me?" he asked.

"I've never done that!" Billie yelled, losing her cool for the first time in this encounter. "Even after everything you've done to me, I never tried to turn her against you. You would have deserved it, but I never did that."

"Then for what?"

Billie shook her head in disbelief. He could never understand. That was how void of real feelings he was. It was pitiful and maddening at the same time.

"I love her, Porter. I want to see her, hug her, and talk to her about her life. I want to remind her that I still think about her, miss her, and pray for her."

Porter lifted his head up, leaning away to gain his own composure. For a second, Billie thought she saw some real feeling, some weakness in his eyes, but only for a moment. Within seconds, that cold stare came back. That wall was never going to fall, but Billie had passed the point of caring.

"Not only will I stop . . . this," she said. "But I'll give you a glowing review to your bosses. I'm sure that'll smooth things over when your promotion comes up in a few months."

Porter contemplated her words for a moment, before asking, "What about Gil?"

"I'll get him to do the same," she agreed. "Don't worry about how. He's my boss and he likes me. If I want him to give you great marks, I'll figure out how to get it."

"Because his praise is what matters," Porter said. "Not yours."

"Don't push me, Porter," she warned. "Make it happen."

Without another word, she turned and left.

When Erica showed up at Distinctive Car Wash in Columbia Heights, she immediately spotted Terrell. Her stomach tightened at the sight of him. He'd changed since the last time she'd seen him, about five months ago. After they'd broken up, he started to deteriorate. He looked worse every time she'd seen him in his hopeless attempts to get her back. Eventually he'd given up.

Erica was grateful. She wasn't afraid she'd take him back. That would never happen after he'd gotten Nate involved with drug dealers. There was no going back from that. It was just as long as he tried to win her back, he would be on her mind. She needed him to stop believing they could get back together, so she could move on with her life.

Erica had. Even though she hadn't started dating yet, she was going very long periods of time without even thinking about Terrell. Now, looking at him as he sprayed a white SUV down with the hose, he'd gained weight and let his hair grow into cornrows. He had a cigarette in his mouth, and he'd never smoked a day that she'd known him. At least she hoped it was a cigarette.

There were two other men with him. One was wiping the car with soap, while the other was inside the car, cleaning off the dashboard. Both of them saw her before Terrell did. Their stares are what made him turn to look. When he did, his mouth opened just enough for the cigarette to fall out. The hose nozzle fell to his side with only a drip. He stared at her for a few seconds more before dropping the hose and walking over to her.

"Erica," he said softly.

He was standing a couple of feet from her now, looking as if he wasn't sure she was really there.

"Erica," he repeated.

"Hi, Terrell," she responded. "Can we talk?"

"What are you doing here?" he asked.

"You know why I'm here," she answered.

His dumbfounded expression changed as reality seemed to set in. He sighed, lowering his head for a bit before looking at her again.

"Yeah, I guess I do." He nodded for her to follow him as he walked toward the side of the building.

Erica followed him; and just before turning to head down the alley next to the building, she looked back at the green BMW parked on the street. Alex looked back at her from the driver's side. She gave him a thumbs-up to let him know it was okay and disappeared around the corner.

"This private enough for you?" he asked.

She nodded. "I just want—"

"I miss you," he said. "I feel like . . . I don't know, Erica. Seeing you . . . I just miss you."

The way he was looking at her, as if about to break down and bare his soul to her, made Erica uncomfortable.

"Jonah knows it's you," she said. "You sent that letter. It was stupid, Terrell."

Terrell shook his head. "You haven't seen me in five months and all you can do is put me down?"

"I'm sorry," she said, "but this is serious and you need to understand that. You're playing with fire."

"Blah, blah, blah," he said, gesturing his annoyance with her warning. "I've heard it all before. I don't give a shit."

"You have to give a shit," Erica warned, "because Jonah does. And when he gives a shit, it is on."

"I saw you," he said, running his hand over his cornrows. "I went over there, waiting for him to show up. I just wanted him to see me to get a little nervous."

"That's just it," Erica said. "Terrell, men like Jonah don't get nervous. They get mad."

"But I saw you," he continued, ignoring her words. "I saw you walk in that building and I knew that he'd gotten you."

Now it was time for Erica to lower her head. She felt ashamed, remembering all of those times she'd promised Terrell she would keep Jonah at arm's length.

"It's not what you think," she explained. "I'm just working for him. It's a job. It's a paycheck. We're not close or anything."

"Then why are you here?" he asked. "He sent you, didn't he?"

"I'm not here for him," Erica said. "I'm here *for you*. He didn't send me, Terrell. He was just gonna handle it. I'm here to warn you."

"So you do care about me?" He shoved his hands into his pockets.

Erica took a step back from him. "Don't read this wrong. Please don't do that. I'm here to save you from harm, possibly even save your life."

"You were my life," Terrell said. "That's why when I saw you walk in there, I was like 'fuck it.' Then I left the note, because I'm not afraid of him anymore. And I've lost you."

"You don't have to lose everything else," she said.

Terrell laughed. "Have you taken a look at my life, girl?"

"Jonah is the only reason you aren't in jail now," Erica said. "When that bust happened last year, your name was left out because of him."

Terrell smirked. "I don't owe him shit. He ruined my life."

"You ruined your life," Erica said. "You used to be man enough to know that. You didn't used to blame other people."

"And I won't anymore," he said, smiling. "Whatever happens, happens."

"If you think knowing the streets is gonna keep you safe, you're—"

"I'm gonna talk," he said. "I'll call the news and the blogs and all that shit. He's the VP candidate. They'll want to hear from me. I'll get famous, and he can't do shit."

"He'll get to you before you get to them," she said. "Or, he'll get to them before they can report what you told them."

"I have another solution."

Erica swung around in astonishment to see Alex walk toward them.

"Who the fuck are you?" Terrell asked, looking around nervously.

"What are you doing?" Erica asked. "I told you not to—"

"He's with you?" Terrell asked.

"No." Alex passed Erica, giving her a regretful glance. "I'm with Jonah Nolan, Terrell. I work for him."

Terrell got into a fighting stance. "Bring it."

"I don't want to fight you," he said. "I just want to make you an offer."

"Alex!" Erica wasn't sure what was going on, but she knew it wasn't good. "What are you doing?"

Alex held his hand up to her in a gesture to hold on. "I have this under control, Erica. I'm on direct orders from Jonah."

"What do you want?" Terrell asked.

"One hundred and fifty thousand dollars," Alex said. "Have you ever seen that much money, Terrell?"

"Don't talk down to me," Terrell warned him.

"Sorry." Alex nodded apologetically. "But it's a lot of money, and I think it would be enough to guarantee you'll let this go . . . forever."

"Oh, my God," Erica said, disgusted. "Alex, he doesn't care—"

"How fast?" Terrell asked.

Erica's eyes widened as she saw Terrell. He had an eager expression on his face as he looked at Alex.

"Twenty-four hours," Alex said. "But you have to understand that—"

"Wait a second." Erica stepped in between them, looking at Terrell. "Is this what it's about? Money? You just want money?"

Terrell wouldn't look her in the eye, his gaze averted to the left. He looked ashamed, but resigned to his choice.

"I got nothing left, Erica. I'm not getting you back. I'm not getting back on track without you. Like you said, I can't fight Jonah. I need to get mine. I need to get something out of this. I've gotten shit and I've lost everything."

Erica just let out a breathless whimper to signify her complete disappointment. She turned away from him, to Alex.

"Jonah told you to do this?" she asked.

Alex nodded, before turning back to Terrell. "But you understand that this is forever. If you say anything, or if you come back asking for more . . . Just don't do that. For your own sake, buddy."

"I'm not your *buddy*," Terrell said. "You work for that piece of shit. That makes you even lower than a piece of shit."

Alex frowned, clearly offended by Terrell's words. Erica could tell Alex didn't want to do this. He was very uncomfortable.

"Don't," she said, taking hold of Alex's elbow and turning him to her. "Don't let him turn you into this."

Alex looked at her as if he wanted to explain, but he simply couldn't. He'd made his choice, his eyes told her. He moved his arm away from her grip and she let go.

"You're all the same, aren't you?" she asked, shaking her head as she backed away. "Everything is a fucking game and it all comes down to money. Well, all of you can go to hell."

Feeling herself about to cry, but not willing to let either of them see her do it, Erica couldn't get out of there fast enough. So she left Alex and Terrell to finish their business in the alley and was fine never seeing either of them ever again.

"Justin," she whispered. "Justin."

Sherise felt his tongue against her neck as she wrapped her legs around him, waiting for him to enter her. But he never did.

He only sighed, lifting up; and when she unwrapped her legs from him, he slid off and positioned himself to the left of her on their bed. Sherise thought he was feeling awkward about her pregnancy, but she wasn't showing enough to make sex uncomfortable yet.

"What's wrong?" she asked.

"I'm sorry," he said. "I don't think it's happening."

"Is it me?" she asked.

Her being pregnant had never hindered his attraction to her during her first pregnancy, and it hadn't bothered him the last couple of weeks when they'd been having sex—very good sex—regularly.

It was something else.

"The firm will be begging you to hurry back as soon as this is over." She reached down for the covers to pull up over her.

He looked at her and managed a tepid smile. "The final hearing on major legislation was today on Capitol Hill. I missed it. You know how long I've been working on . . ."

He shook his head.

"What happened?"

"We lost by two votes in committee," he said. "The two representatives I was supposed to spend the last two weeks convincing to take our side. But I wasn't there and it failed."

Sherise turned to her side to face him. "That's good, Justin."

"How is that good?" he asked. "We've been working on getting that bill to Congress for a vote for almost a year now. It would have had serious ramifications in the industry."

"And your firm failed because they pushed you away," she said. "They chose to side with that lying bitch over you and paid the price."

"They didn't side with her," he said. "She's threatening to expose them."

"They should have stuck by you," she said. "By asking you to take a leave of absence, they've admitted that she could be right."

"If it weren't for Dennis," he said, "I don't think they would have done it. I don't think they would have taken just her word over mine."

"We'll deal with him too," she mumbled.

Justin looked at her with a confused frown, but Sherise just shrugged. She hadn't told him about her spying session, but she had told the private investigator she'd hired. She was hopeful something great could come from this, and she would be the one to tell Justin about it. He had to hear it from her.

"Is there something you want to tell me?" he asked.

"That I love you." She smiled, reaching out and touching his nose with her finger. "I can't wait until this is all over so we can get back to normal and focus on preparing for our baby."

He turned to her and pressed his hand against her stomach over the sheets. As he looked at her, his smile turned to a regretful grin. "I'm so sorry, baby."

"Don't," she said. "We don't need any more apologies."

He shook his head in disagreement. "No, I owe you. When I found out you were pregnant, I should have been a man about it."

"At times, we've both failed to be the spouse we should have been," she said. "And, baby, we're gonna fail again. We're just human and we have fifty or more years of this."

He laughed. "If we're lucky."

"We will be," she said, pausing before adding, "again."

"I know I pushed you away at first," he said, "but I know now that I couldn't even begin to get through this without you. You're my rock, Sherise. You drive me crazy, but I need you more than anything in this world."

Her heart warmed at not just his words—after all, they were only words. No, it was also the look on his face, the slight crack of emotion in his voice—which told her he meant those words—that reached inside her. She hadn't been a great wife. At times, she'd been a horrible one, but that didn't matter now. Nothing mattered now but the three of them and the new baby, who was joining their family. She would die before letting some greedy slut with an eye for dollar signs mess with that.

"No matter what happens," he said, "we'll survive this together."

"What's going to happen is you're gonna be exonerated," Sherise said, "and she'll pay the price for trying to ruin your life for a few bucks."

"If you're talking about a defamation suit again, I don't know if—"

"She wanted to ruin your life," Sherise said. "She can't get away with that."

"Whatever the case," he said, "when the truth comes out, she'll get hers. How much more I want to be involved in that, I haven't decided yet. First things first."

"Fine," Sherise acquiesced. "What happens after that, we can decide together, but we'll have to do it soon. I have a feeling things are about to turn our way."

He studied her for a while. "Sherise, we can't risk—"

"Can't a woman just have an intuition?" she asked, not wanting him to ask a question that she would feel compelled to answer.

His doubt faded and his smile returned. "So you don't think I'll have to get used to being a stay-at-home dad? Although I love spending the day with Cady."

"Stay-at-home dad, with me the moneymaker?" Sherise frowned. "I think that setup is a bit too modern for my taste. Does that make me bad?"

"You're already bad," he said.

14

Standing in the kitchen, making breakfast for two, Billie looked over at Michael as he lay back on her sofa, watching cable news. Everything had gone great, as it had all week. Michael brought up the idea of a weekend in the Virginia country in their near future, and even the sex was getting better. Billie found herself lost in him, feeling her body and mind become one in their desire for him. She wanted to make something with Michael, and she wanted it bad.

He looked away from the television and caught her staring at him. He smiled in a way that made Billie's knees weak.

"You checking me out?" he asked.

"Mmm-hmm," she answered. "Sorry, but these eggs might be a little burnt. The cook was distracted."

"I'll find something else to eat then," he said, winking at her as he licked his lips.

"You so nasty," she said, laughing.

Just as she placed the eggs on both plates, her phone, sitting on the kitchen counter, rang. She knew it was

Porter right away from the ringtone. The question was, did Michael know that as well? He'd been there that night when Porter kept calling, but there wasn't really enough reason for him to believe this wasn't her regular ringtone was there? Usually, when she was with him, she had it on vibrate, anyway.

She reached for the phone, trying to seem as nonchalant as possible.

"Hello?" She looked at Michael and met his smile with one of her own. "Oh yeah, girl! Hold on a second."

"It's Sherise," she said, not skipping a beat. "It'll just be a second."

Michael nodded, but his eyes still held curiosity, which wasn't a good thing. Billie didn't have time to worry about that now. She would give Porter a few seconds to give her the news, and that would be it.

She rushed a few feet down the hallway from the kitchen to her bedroom, closing the door behind her.

"I'm busy," she said. "Be quick."

"You think I want to have a conversation with you?" Porter asked. "Let's talk about the weather. I'd rather you'd just go fuck yourself more than—"

"Porter, get yourself under control," she whispered.

There was a short pause. She really didn't have time for this.

"Tara will be coming for a week, starting Wednesday," he finally said in a flat tone.

"What time Wednesday?" she asked. "I'd like to have dinner with her Wednesday night."

"She's getting in Wednesday night. I'd like to spend some time with my own daughter first. I haven't seen her in three months."

"It's been much longer for me," Billie said. "I want to have dinner with her Thursday."

"Fine," he said, sighing. "You can have dinner with her Thursday night. Are you happy now?"

"For starters," she said. "She's here a week. I want more than one night."

"Fine!"

"And, yes, I'm very happy," she said. "I didn't expect you to comply so quickly, but I'm grateful that you have."

"You're not grateful for shit," he said.

"I am, Porter. I can understand how gratitude might be hard for you to detect, since you've never felt it, but it's time you start acquiring that ability."

"Is this where I'm supposed to be grateful to you?" he asked.

"Aren't you?" she asked back. "After all, your career, everything you've worked for, is in my hands."

"But not anymore," he said. "I'm letting you see Tara. That was the deal, right?"

Billie sighed, almost feeling sorry for him. "Yes, Porter. As long as you don't fuck this up, you won't have to worry about me. But remember, I can ruin everything for you, and I'd gladly do it."

"I'll call you Thursday," Porter said, and then hung up.

Billie was grinning a satisfied smile as she turned to head back out of the room, but she was stopped in her tracks by the sight of Michael standing in the doorway.

"You didn't close the door all the way," he said.

"Were you listening in on me?" she asked.

"Is that the strategy again?" he asked. "To make me the asshole?"

"Were you listening in on me?" she repeated.

"I was bringing the plates to the table, but I dropped one and it shattered. I was just coming to tell you."

"How convenient," she said.

"Since when did you start calling Sherise, 'Porter'?" he asked.

Billie sighed, not wanting to go through this again. "This doesn't count, Michael."

"It doesn't count?" he asked, laughing. "That you lied to me? That doesn't count."

"No, I know that was wrong, b-but I mean . . ." She stammered for the words. "I—I mean, talking to Porter doesn't count. We're talking about Tara. You can't expect me not to—"

"I know you care about your stepdaughter," he said. "Your ex-stepdaughter. But what I heard wasn't about that. What I heard were threats."

"That's the only way to deal with Porter," she said. "You don't know him."

"You're right," he agreed. "But I don't know you either, Billie, and I'm tired of trying to."

He turned to leave and she went after him.

"Wait!" she called out. "Michael, I swear this was the last time. I just needed to make sure he'd let me see her."

"I heard your words and the tone of your voice," Michael said, continuing into the living area, grabbing his sweater off the living-room chair. "This is far from over. You were enjoying your threats too much. You're still focused on hurting him."

"What are you doing?" she asked as he reached the door. "Are you leaving?"

"You don't have to kick me out this time," he said. "I'll leave on my own."

"I wasn't going to kick you out." She reached him, grabbing his arm and turning him back to her. "Michael, I don't want you to leave. I want you to believe me when I tell you that this is it. This is what I wanted. Access to Tara. Now that I'll get it—"

"Then what?" he asked, freeing himself from her grip. "You don't even see yourself, Billie. You're on a terror mission. It won't be enough, at least not for you. For me, I've definitely had enough."

"Michael!" she called one last time before he walked out.

She didn't go after him. One, she was in her bathrobe, but she also knew that there was no saving this. She'd lied to him and he was pissed. All the sweet nothings over eggs and sausage weren't going to take that bad taste out of his mouth. She shouldn't have said it was Sherise. That was wrong, but he gave her no choice. She was on pins and needles around him when it came to Porter.

She turned behind her to attend to the broken plate on the floor in the dining room. Maybe he was telling the truth, but she still suspected he was spying on her.

She couldn't lie to herself like last time they argued and say it didn't matter. They had crossed a bridge in their relationship and she cared for him too much to believe that. But she believed he'd be back. She'd give him a day and then call him. It really was over between her and Porter. She could make Michael understand that. Now that she had Tara, it was really over. Everything was going to be fine from here on.

* * *

The second Erica opened her front door and saw Alex standing on the other side, she slammed it shut. *I have to remember to look through the peephole,* she told herself as she turned and headed back to her bedroom.

The doorbell rang again.

"Erica!" Alex yelled from the other side. "You have to talk to me eventually."

She'd avoided going to work that day just so she wouldn't have to face him. After the entire scene at the car wash, she went home and took a shower, emotionally washing herself of all the men in her life. She couldn't trust one of them. She was hurt by Alex's joining the dark side, but she was still plenty angry too. She had ignored his calls and deleted his texts.

She stopped, but she still didn't turn around. "Go away!"

"It's better to do it here than at work!" he yelled.

She turned to the door. "Maybe I'm not coming into work anymore!"

"Bullshit!" he yelled back. "Stop acting like a baby, Erica. We have to talk about this, and I'd rather not share this with your neighbors."

She walked to the door. "Be quiet and go away!"

"That's two orders," he said. "'Be quiet' or 'Go away.' Pick one."

"Do both!"

"Fine," he said. "If the only choice you give me is to talk through the door, I can. First of all, I want to apologize for keeping what Jonah told me away from—"

Erica swung the door open, delivering a seething glare.

"You think you're funny?" she asked. "Yelling Jonah's business down the hall?"

"Not funny." Alex bypassed her attempt to block him and stepped inside the apartment. "Just smart enough to know it would get you to open the door."

She closed the door behind her.

"I don't want to hear any of your explanations," she said. "Men. All of you make me sick. You're deceptive and greedy."

"Which are traits that no woman has ever exhibited," he said sarcastically. "It's just us men."

"Do you want to get into a gender argument with me?" she asked. "I'll blow you away."

"I don't doubt it." Alex sighed, walking closer to her. "Erica, I feel bad, but please just listen to me."

Erica knew this was probably a mistake, but he looked so earnest and she had a soft spot for him. After rolling her eyes to convey her annoyance with her own choice, she gestured for him to sit on the sofa.

"You have five minutes and then you have to leave," she said. "I'm serious, so skip the bullshit and excuses."

He sat down on one end and she joined him on the other.

"I know you're mad," he said, "and you have every right to be."

"It was really more disappointing than anything," she said. "Seeing you basically bribe someone. That's something Jonah would do, but I didn't think you'd do it."

"I didn't feel good about it," Alex said. "But Erica, Jonah told me that this Terrell guy, your ex, was a threat to you. He told me his background with drugs and all that. He said you were in danger."

"He lied." She couldn't deny she was touched by his concern. "What a surprise. He thinks he knows Terrell, but he doesn't. He knows information, but he doesn't know the man."

"He took the money," Alex said. "So Jonah seems to know him well enough."

"Terrell would never hurt me," she said. "At least not physically."

"I don't want him hurting you in any way," Alex responded. "You mean too much to me, Erica."

There was a short silence as they shared a glance.

"Do you really think he'd give some random guy all that money to protect anyone but himself?"

"I don't ask things that aren't my business of a man like Jonah."

"You ask them of me," Erica said.

"Well, I'm not afraid of you," he said, smiling. "Well, at least not that much."

Erica sighed, releasing any anger she'd felt toward him. "It's not your fault, Alex. Jonah does that to people. He makes you want to please him, do things for him—whether you want to or not."

Alex nodded. "I felt like . . . I felt honored to be able to do this. It wasn't until after I agreed to it that my stomach got all tight and I was nervous. At the time he was asking me, I felt like a soldier being given a special mission by my commander in chief."

"He uses your weaknesses to tie you in," she said. "With me it was my brother, Nate, or my friend Sherise."

"What does your friend have to do with it?" he asked.

"Oh, nothing." Erica looked away awkwardly. "It's just that he's a master manipulator."

"Why does he care so much?" Alex asked. "Things seem so personal with you."

"When I was working for him at the Pentagon," she said, her voice stuttering a bit, "he c-clashed with Terrell a few times."

She could see that Alex wasn't really buying this. Why would a man like Jonah even notice someone like Terrell, let alone consider him someone worthy of clashing with?

"He got very protective of me," Erica said.

"I get it," he said, nodding. "He's odd like that. Sometimes I think he's very protective of me too. Other times, I'm just a nameless staff member who means absolutely nothing."

"I think there's a part of him that's human," Erica said. "A small part, but it's there."

Erica laughed until she realized Alex wasn't laughing along.

"I think he's a great man," Alex said. "I really do."

"But he asked you to pay off someone."

Alex shrugged. "For a good reason. If someone is a danger to you, Erica, I consider that a problem worth paying money to get rid of."

"Jonah doesn't do anything for anyone but himself," Erica said.

"It's like you have some underlying agenda regarding him. What is it?"

"Ignore me," Erica advised. "I'm just mad at him right now. He shouldn't have done what he did. I could handle Terrell."

"I feel like you're mad at him because he was right," Alex said. "Why do you care so much?"

"I don't," she lied.

"I'm not buying it." Alex shook his head, with a confused frown on his face. "You seem to dislike him so much. And you clearly hate his wife, which is a story you're gonna have to tell me sooner or later. Why are you even working for him?"

Erica was getting visibly uncomfortable. "My job at the Pentagon sucked and he was paying me more to do less stressful work."

"Well," Alex said, "I believe in him. Besides, I'd do anything to keep you out of danger, Erica."

When their eyes met this time, it was more intense, not awkward at all. Erica felt a pull in the pit of her stomach, which drew her closer to him on the sofa. Without hesitating, he reached for her face, guiding it to his, and placed his mouth gently on hers. The kiss was soft and tender as their lips pressed against each other.

Having first come to him without a second thought, Erica suddenly realized what she was doing. She was kissing a man for the first time in forever and it felt . . . wrong.

She quickly pushed away and jumped up from the sofa.

"What?" Alex asked.

She turned her back to him, heading to her door. She couldn't exactly explain why, but she was embarrassed by her own behavior and couldn't look him in the face.

"I'm sorry." Alex quickly got up from the sofa and rushed over to her. "I thought . . . I misread you."

"It's not your fault," she offered.

Erica finally looked at him and felt awful at the expression on his face. He looked so guilty, like he'd done something terribly wrong.

"You didn't read me wrong," she assured him. "I promise you, Alex."

"Then what?" he pleaded.

"I just can't do this," she said. "I'm really emotional right now over Terrell and everything. There's just a lot going on."

"I didn't mean to add to your problems," he said.

"You don't," she said, wondering if there was anything she could say that wouldn't make him feel bad. "Honestly, Alex, you're like the only good thing in my life right now. Everything else is stress or worry or lies or secrets. I just don't think I want anything . . . romantic right now."

Alex's disappointment was evident, but only for a second. He quickly recovered, with a kind and understanding expression on his face.

"I just want to make sure you're not mad at me about that whole thing with Terrell," he said.

She shook her head. "Your heart was in the right place. You're a good guy, Alex. I worry about you being so close to Jonah."

"I may be a few years younger than you," he said, "but I'm not a kid. I can handle myself."

"So can I," she said. "So the next time Jonah asks you to do something for me, just say 'no.' "

"I promise." He placed his hand to his chest. "So you'll come to work tomorrow, yes?"

Erica nodded.

After he finally left, Erica was trying to examine her own feelings, but she couldn't figure it out. It had been a long time since she'd kissed Terrell, since she'd felt enough attraction to a guy to want to kiss him. So, why had that kiss upset her so much?

Was it just seeing Terrell the other day? Was it because Jonah disapproved of them together? Was it as simple as their working together made this a bad choice? Erica didn't know, but she needed to figure it out. A guy like Alex didn't come around often.

Sherise was on her way back to work, with her lunch in hand, her mind focused solely on Elena and what she'd been able to find out from her trip to the health club. She had a big speech to edit for Northman, who was speaking at the largest media convention in the country, so she had to try and let it go for now. There were so many eggs in her basket right now that it was overwhelming.

And then there was the most important egg of them all. As she saw a woman walking, with her hands guiding the stroller that held her new twin boys, Sherise's hand automatically went to her own belly. She was just approaching three months, and it would soon be okay to tell everyone, even though it really wasn't a secret to anyone.

She felt like such a bad mother for not spending enough time thinking about this baby and preparing for it. She'd been taking her vitamins and had gone to the doctor. She would be getting her first ultrasound soon; she hoped Justin was looking forward to it as much as she was.

She smiled at the thought of having a boy. She knew how much Justin treasured Cady. She was the jewel of his whole heart, but she felt like it would be just perfect to give him a son. She'd like a boy. After all, almost every mother who had both told her that boys were much easier to deal with than girls were at almost every age. Cady was such a little diva already; Sherise felt it was better to have just one diva to deal with.

She was thinking about all the new clothes she would need to buy, when her phone rang. She reached into her pocket and looked at the ID. It was Beth Martin, her favorite private investigator and the one she used most often. Everyone who was anyone in D.C. had a favorite PI. You had to know who it was that you were really dealing with around here, and everyone was a liar.

"Beth," she said upon answering. "What do you have for me?"

"I was there," she said. "Bartholdi Park."

"Elena met with Dennis?"

"I couldn't hear their conversation—where they met was too remote. There weren't any nearby benches or anyplace I could be without being suspicious."

Sherise was disappointed to hear that. What good was any of it without overhearing what they said? "Don't you have one of those devices to hear from far away?"

"Didn't work. They picked a bad time. There were a lot of people walking, running, talking, dogs barking, birds, all that."

"So, what did you get?"

"They kissed," Beth said.

Sherise stopped in the middle of the sidewalk; her mouth dropped open. "They kissed? Are you serious? A for-real kiss?"

"Yes. Well, it was clearly more earnest on his part than hers. She seemed to be annoyed and didn't want anyone seeing. He seemed a little desperate."

"So that's how she got him on her side." Sherise

made a smacking sound with her lips as she shook her head. *Men are easy.* "Dennis's wife left him over a year ago. He's hard up for anything. A pretty young thing like her comes around, and, of course—"

"I'll have to look more into that," Beth said.

"First, we figure out Denton," Sherise said.

"Denton is in Texas, like you thought. If you're right about her accent, then that's definitely where she's from. There are a lot of women around her age in that area named Elena Brown. Who would have thought it would be so popular?"

"But how many of them have a sister named Rose?" Sherise asked.

"Exactly," Beth said. "I'll have that information very soon. We'll know what's behind lying about Denton."

"I have a feeling that's the key to everything," Sherise said. "I don't know why she would target Justin. He has nothing to do with Texas or anyone from there, but my gut instinct tells me that when we find out who she is, and why she lied about where she's from, we'll get our answers."

"I'll get back to you as soon as I can, Sherise."

When Sherise hung up the phone, her hand was still on her belly and she started again for the office. *By the time this baby gets here, everything is going to be back to the way it was before. No, it will be better than it was before.*

What more could a mother ask for?

"You're not gonna finish?" Tara asked Billie, pointing to her plate.

Billie squinted her nose, shaking her head. She pushed away her plate, which contained a large waffle sandwich of tomato, mozzarella, and basil.

"It's just not calling my name," she said.

"Aw." Tara frowned. "Now I feel bad for picking this place."

Tara's choice for their second get-together that week was a waffle restaurant, which made both basic and elaborate sandwiches using waffles as the bread. Billie wasn't crazy about the idea, but their first meeting was dinner at a fancy restaurant and Tara wasn't very comfortable. She wanted her to pick where they'd meet from now on.

"It doesn't matter," Billie said, smiling. "I'm just happy to be with you. I don't care where we eat."

The almost sixteen-year old—with glowing, beautiful dark brown skin, her father's piercing eyes, and tiny features—looked annoyed. "You're not going to start crying and kiss me again, like you did Thursday night?"

"Was I that embarrassing?" Billie asked.

"Yes, you were," Tara insisted.

"But I missed my little girl," Billie said.

She'd been so happy to see Tara that she couldn't contain herself. She kissed her and hugged her, holding her tightly. The tears came immediately; and although Tara was happy to see Billie, the teen expressed complete embarrassment at her onetime stepmother's display of affection.

They spent dinner catching up. Billie was relieved to find out that Tara's life in Detroit hadn't been that bad. She was getting along with her grandmother and had made some friends at the private school she attended. She was still sad not to be "home" anymore. She missed her friends. She even missed Porter, even though she was still very mad at him for shipping her off.

It was all a great distraction for Billie, who was hurting over Michael. She'd expected him to call her; but after a couple of days, he hadn't. She'd been trying to reach him, but got his voice mail. An e-mail was not returned and her texts were ignored. As every day passed, she believed she'd really lost him.

But there was Tara, who made her heart warm and allowed her to smile and feel good for the short time they were able to spend together. This little girl was saving her life right now.

Billie's phone, resting on the table, vibrated. She quickly checked it, hoping it was Michael, but it was just work. She ignored it and tried to remove the disappointment from her mind.

"Stop calling me your 'little girl'!" Tara smiled as she said this, showing that she was actually touched despite what she was saying.

"I have to stop, don't I?" Billie responded. "You're not a little girl anymore. You've grown so much just since you left, and it hasn't even been a year."

Tara's smile faded as she looked away and a veil of sadness took over her face.

"Am I ever coming back?" she asked.

Billie was touched by the innocence in Tara's face as she asked that question. Her eyes widened and she looked afraid to be hopeful. *Poor child. This all has to be so confusing to her.*

"It's been hard on you," Billie said. "I'm sorry about that."

"No one will tell me what's going on," she said. "Daddy gets pissed at me and sends me away. He even won't let me be friends with you on Facebook!"

Billie was getting angry at the thought of this. It was all Porter's fault. *Doesn't he love his own daughter?*

"I think things are going to get clearer soon," she said.

"I mean," she continued, "it's weird, because all of a sudden he says he wants me to come visit him, so I come out here and he's just . . . He is just in a really bad mood and doesn't really want to do anything."

"For now," Billie said, "all that matters is that you're here. We'll work on making sense of all the stuff that's confusing."

It bothered Billie that Porter's mood was upsetting Tara, but was that her fault? He was reaping the seeds he'd sown. The fact that Tara was upset about it was his fault and only made Billie angrier with him.

"I don't know what I did," Tara said. "I just feel like—"

"No." Billie sat forward in her chair, looking intently into Tara's eyes. "You didn't do anything. Tara, don't let anyone tell you that you did."

"Obviously, I did," Tara said. "He sent me away because you told him about Greg wanting to . . . you know, do it with me, and now—"

"He sent you away because he was afraid of dealing with you as a father," Billie said. "It wasn't your fault. God, I was so afraid you'd think that. I can't believe this has been festering inside of you all this time. This is why I begged him to let me see you, because I knew you worried about—"

"Shhhh," Tara quickly said as she sat up, looking behind Erica.

"Are you ready?" was all Porter asked when he reached their table.

He ignored Billie, but she wasn't going to let him get away with this. He was doing irreversible damage to Tara and it was going to stop.

"We're not finished, are we?" Billie asked Tara.

Tara shrugged. "I'm done, I guess. I gotta go to the bathroom, though."

"Fine," Porter said shortly. "Hurry up, and we'll leave. I'll wait for you in the car."

Tara grabbed her purse out of the chair next to her and hopped up from the table. As Porter turned to leave, Billie called out to him.

"I'm just here to pick up my daughter," he said, turning back to her. "I don't have to talk to you."

"Yes, you do," she said, looking up at him. "You still have Tara believing it's her fault you sent her away."

"No," Porter argued. "I made it very clear to her that it was yours."

"This is all your fault, Porter, and you know it. You wanted to be with me again after dropping your mistress. I wouldn't agree and you retaliated by sending Tara away. It was all you had left to hurt me."

"I don't want my daughter around someone who wants to get her on the Pill so she can sleep around. As a father, I have that right."

"But you're confusing her," Billie urged. "You're making her feel punished, and it has to stop. It's doing damage that could be irreversible, even if you do come to your senses down the line."

"Look," Porter said, "you got to see her, Billie.

Twice. That's enough. Otherwise, you need to stay out of it."

Billie shook her head. "That's not enough."

"She's leaving in two days," Porter said. "I think I'm entitled to spend some actual time with her."

"Two meals is not enough for me," Billie insisted. "She needs to stay longer."

"She's leaving Tuesday," he said.

"She's on summer break," Billie countered. "It's not hard for you to manage. I want more time with her. I need more time with her."

Porter looked amazed at what he was hearing. "I knew you'd go back on your promise, you bitch."

"That was before," Billie said. "Someone has got to be here for her and let her know there was nothing wrong with her asking about birth control. She's confused about why you won't let her talk to me, and she's—"

"I don't care," Porter said. "Billie, we had a deal."

"We have a new one," she insisted. "At least a month. Make it happen, Porter."

"No," Porter said, standing his ground. "She's my daughter. She's the one thing in my life—"

"I'm the one thing in your life," Billie said as she hopped up from the chair to face him. She was still looking up at him, but she was feeling just as tall. "You need to think of it that way. I can ruin you, Porter. I can make it so that the closest you get to practicing law is critiquing it on television."

"Billie, please—"

"Don't say 'please' to me," she demanded. "Just *please me,* Porter. You do what I want or I'll destroy you. Or I'll make you wish you never met me."

"I already do," he said.

"What is going on?"

Neither Billie nor Porter had realized that Tara had returned from the bathroom. From the look on her face, she'd witnessed more of this scene than either of them wanted.

"Let's go!" Porter ordered.

Tara wasn't listening. With frustration, anger, and fear all mixed together on her face, she stormed straight to Billie.

"Why are you doing this?" she asked.

"What do you mean?" Billie asked, feeling awful that Tara saw that.

"Why are you saying those awful thing to my dad?" she asked. "Why would you threaten to ruin his life? Why are you telling him . . . Wait, you're the reason he's so unhappy. You're doing something to him."

"Sweetheart, you don't understand." Billie reached out to calm her.

Tara smacked Billie's hand away and Billie gasped.

"What is it?" Tara asked, looking from one to the other. "Is it about me? I know you're talking about me! What did I do to cause all of this?"

"Tara," Billie pleaded. "I've told you—"

"It's not you, baby girl," Porter said.

"Then why are you both doing this?" she asked, tears beginning to come down her cheeks. "Everything was getting better, and then I make one mistake and everything falls apart. Now this? Now you're calling her a bitch and she's threatening to ruin you! This is crazy!"

"You happy?" Porter asked Billie. His face was racked with hatred for her.

"Don't you dare!" Billie spat at him. "This is all your fault."

"Not this time," he said. "You're the one with the threats and—"

"Stop it!" Tara screamed so loud that everyone in the place stopped what they were doing and looked at them. At least everyone who hadn't *already* been looking at them turned around now.

"You're awful!" she yelled. "You're both just awful!"

"Tara!" Billie called after Tara as the teen turned and ran out of the restaurant.

She started to go after her, but Porter grabbed her by the arm and pulled her back.

"Get your hands off me!" she yelled.

"No!" He was fuming. "You stay away from her. Go ahead, Billie. Ruin my career if you want, but I'm not letting you hurt my daughter anymore!"

He let her arm go and rushed out of the restaurant after Tara.

Billie didn't know what to do. She felt panic swelling in her throat, and she couldn't get out of her mind the look on Tara's face. This was the worst possible outcome. Billie wanted to blame Porter, but she knew she couldn't. She was just as much—if not more—to blame this time around. She'd gone too far. All she wanted was to see her daughter, but she couldn't stop.

Just like Michael had said she wouldn't be able to do.

She felt an aching of regret throughout her entire body. Her first thought was to call Michael. She needed to talk to him. But when she dialed his number, she got the same thing she'd been getting all week, his voice mail. He wasn't talking to her.

She felt like crying now, thinking of the mess she'd made of her life. It was supposed to get better. It was looking up. The new job and the new, guilt-free boy-friend were what she'd been wanting. But she let a desire to get revenge on Porter ruin everything.

Michael was so right. Billie thought that God must have sent him to her at this point in her life to steer her in the right direction, but she ignored it. Now the man she was falling in love with wanted nothing to do with her, and she was ruining the life of the child she loved more than anything.

15

"You shouldn't have done that," Billie admonished as she stood over her kitchen counter, eating a frozen dinner.

"Did you hear anything I just said?" Sherise asked.

Standing in her dining room, with her baby cradled in her arm, Sherise had just told both Billie and Erica about what she'd found out from her PI.

"Yes, I heard," Billie responded. "And you shouldn't have done it."

"She really did yield some great information," Erica added, speaking loudly into the phone, which lay on her chest, as she sat back on her living-room sofa and ate ice cream out of the carton.

"Better than great," Sherise said. "This woman is a serious fraud! When I find out who she is, I'm going to shove it down her throat and choke her with it."

"That was pretty violent imagery," Billie said.

"She makes me feel violent," Sherise said. "She's threatening my family. She's threatening everything."

"Don't get into a confrontation with her," Erica

warned. "Even though you could probably take her, you have a baby."

"Trust me," Sherise said. "I would never put this baby in danger, no matter how much I'd love to slap her across that little lying face of hers. I'm speaking all metaphorically."

"Just let the private investigator do all the work from now on," Billie advised. "Legally, you're really crossing a line."

"Worth it," Sherise said. "Besides, no one can say I wasn't really trying out that club. D.C. is a small city. People in legal disputes come across each other all the time."

"Sherise, you're not taking me seriously!" Billie yelled.

There was an awkward silence for the moment it took Billie to realize that she'd yelled at her friend.

"Sorry," she said. "I'm just upset."

"Michael still isn't calling you back?" Erica asked.

"No." Billie put down her fork, never having had an appetite, anyway. "And Tara is gone. She's back in Detroit, where I can't reach her, and she hates me."

"She doesn't hate you," Sherise said. "From what happened, Porter came off looking as bad as you."

"I think she expected better from me," Billie said.

"That's not fair," Erica added.

"It's how it is," Billie answered back. "Porter is her dad. He's her parent. She has to forgive him. She needs his love and approval."

"She feels the same about you," Erica assured her. "She'll calm down. She's an emotional teenager. Everything that happens is the end of the world."

"But I won't be there when she calms down," Billie said. "Porter will, and he'll poison her against me."

"Forget Porter for now," Sherise said. "You need to figure out how to get Michael to respond to you. Go to his home."

"I can't do that," Billie said. "Can I?"

"That's a little desperate," Erica said. "They've only dated for about a month, right?"

Sherise sighed. "Frightened little girls never get what they want. You two are ridiculous. Fine, if you're too scared to go right to him, then you've got to run into him by accident, but on purpose."

"I tried that," Billie said. "I went to the CEO's office and basically bribed his admin to find out when Michael was going to be at the office again for any meetings. He rescheduled all his meetings to be at his office, not at the company."

"Wow," Erica said. "He's really avoiding you."

"Thanks," Billie said. "That makes me feel a lot better."

"So find out where he goes socially," Sherise offered. "Find out where he shops. Didn't you ever talk about the things he likes to do? Track him down there."

"What do I say?" Billie asked.

"Do you really want him?" Erica asked.

"Of course I do," she said. "Why do you think I'm going through this?"

"I mean, do you really, really want him?" Erica asked again. "Or do you just want him to get with the program?"

Billie knew what Erica meant. She'd placed too much blame on Michael for his inability to understand the dynamic between her and Porter. She'd wanted him to get behind her and support this ridiculous vendetta she had.

"I really want him," Billie said. "No more games. I get it now. I felt something really special with him. I was falling in love, and I know he was too. I want him more than I want anything else, including hurting Porter."

"Then you'll know what to say," Erica said, "as soon as you see him."

"This isn't a romance novel," Sherise observed. "You better prepare your shit, girl."

Billie found a way to laugh at Sherise being Sherise, making her feel a little better.

"I'll make it happen," she said, only hopeful she could.

"This will be great," Sherise said. "I'll deal with that bitch, Elena, and Justin and I will be back on track. You'll get back with Michael. And we can all focus on getting Erica laid."

"Leave me out of this," Erica said.

"What about Alex?" Billie asked. "You still mad at him for giving Terrell that money?"

"That was a good thing," Sherise said. "Don't hold it against him."

"You don't understand," Erica said.

"We know you like him," Sherise said, "so stop trying to front. Why aren't you moving faster with him?"

"I didn't tell you?" Erica asked, even though she knew she hadn't. She would have to get around to it at some point. "We kissed."

After hearing the gasps, Erica went on to tell the story of Alex's visit the other day, ending with her making him leave and agreeing to let go of the issue of him helping Jonah bribe Terrell.

"What was wrong?" Billie asked. "Was he a bad kisser?"

"No," Erica said. "The kiss itself was good, but—"

"But what?" Sherise asked.

"I don't think . . ." Erica sighed. "I don't know. I think I just let Jonah get into my head, and he's against Alex and me—"

"Who gives a shit what Jonah wants?" Sherise asked.

"Obviously, she does," Billie answered. "I think there's more to it, Erica. Are you not telling us, or do you just not know yourself?"

"I think its Jonah." Erica sat up on the sofa. "Between him, Terrell, and that damn Juliet accusing my mother of—"

"Let's not go there again," Sherise interjected.

"I can't get it out of my mind," Erica admitted.

"Then confront him about it," Billie said. "If this is blocking you, you need to deal with it. So you can move on with Alex."

"How would those two be related?" Sherise asked.

"I don't know that they are," Erica said. "I mean, I think this whole thing with Alex is completely different."

"Since we're all being so confrontational of late, literally and metaphorically," Billie said, "I say, you go face Alex and tell him how you feel."

"What if I don't know how I feel?" Erica asked. "What kind of lame shit is that?"

"That's exactly what he's going to say," Sherise said.

"Maybe he's experiencing the same thing," Billie said. "Maybe getting it out on the table will help you both figure it out."

"Is it even that serious?" Sherise asked. "He's just a boy. It's just a kiss. One kiss, right?"

"Yeah," Erica said, "but I have a feeling he wants another one."

"Do you?" Billie asked.

That was a question Erica couldn't answer. Why couldn't she? She wasn't sure, but something was blocking her. She felt like her subconscious knew what it was, but her conscious self couldn't grasp it.

Alex didn't deserve this. He was a good guy, who had done something he wasn't comfortable with for—what he thought—was her sake. He deserved her honesty.

Sitting on her bed, early on Friday morning, Sherise could barely contain herself. She was talking on the phone with Beth and had gotten a massive amount of information. Some of it made no sense, but she'd figure it out soon enough. What she could figure out was a gold mine, and she'd done it again.

"Is there anything else?" Sherise hopped up from her bed and walked over to her dresser.

"Isn't that enough?" Beth asked.

"You have no idea," Sherise said, almost sounding giddy. "Put this all in a report and send it to me. I want all the originals you have. I want pictures, everything."

"What about Dennis?"

"Dennis is unimportant at this point," Sherise said as she reached for the red panties-and-bra set. She was feeling red today and only hoped she could still fit into them. "We have everything we need to get rid of Elena Brown."

"I'll get that to you as soon as possible."

"Who are you talking to?"

Sherise swung around from the dresser to see Justin standing in the doorway to the bedroom. Why was he still here?

"I . . . I thought you left," was all she could muster to say.

"Who are you talking to?" he repeated, entering the room. There was a suspicious look on his face. "I heard you say 'Dennis and Elena.' What was that . . . 'Brown'?"

"I have to go," she said quickly into the phone before tossing it on the bed. "You were spying on me?"

"I forgot my tablet," he said, pointing to the device, which was sitting on the settee at the end of their bed. "Stop deflecting."

"I'm not deflecting," she said. "I was just surprised."

"Jacob warned us, Sherise!"

"I told you I was going to hire a private investigator," she said.

"And I told you not to," he answered back. "Jacob told you not to. His firm is doing this on their own."

"They suck at it." Sherise walked over to the settee and grabbed the tablet. Walking over to Justin, she handed it to him. "Here."

"Actually," Justin said, "Jacob just called to tell me that he's given the firm enough of a headache for them to want me back."

"Good," Sherise said. "It was unjustified. They overreacted because of problems they've had in the past."

She reached out to hug him, but he backed away.

"What were you talking about, Sherise?" he asked, sounding more forceful this time. "And don't lie to me. I don't want any of your sneaky shit."

"Okun Industries," she said. "That was the account Dennis had that you took over because he had to go to rehab, right?"

He nodded. "What does that have to do with this?"

"It's a toolmaking factory in Denton, Texas."

"So we're doing trivia?" he asked, annoyed. "You're pissing me off, Sherise."

"Baby," she pleaded. "If you give me one day, I promise you, I will—"

"No!" He halted her. "No secrets. Tell me what's going on."

Sherise knew he was right. She would always have her games, but she couldn't play any with him. He was her husband and the father of her children. There would be no more secrets. Well, no more from this day.

"We need to get Elena alone," she said.

"To do what?" he asked skeptically. "We can't harass her, Sherise."

"No, we need to get her somewhere neutral so we can meet her face-to-face."

"No." Justin was backing out of the room. "That's not going to happen. Not with me or with you. Get it out of your mind, now!"

"You said you trusted me!" she called after him. "Do you?"

He stopped, looking at her for a second before shaking his head. "What the fuck are you up to, Sherise?"

"Do you?" she asked again.

He looked her deep in the eyes, searching for something that Sherise hoped she could help him find. She didn't blink, letting him take his time. He had to agree to this if it was going to work.

"What do you need me to do?" he asked, sighing,

sounding as if he was resigned to his fate with this woman.

She rushed up to him and wrapped her arms around him. She kissed him hard on the lips and both cheeks. She leaned away, holding his face in her hands.

"Together, we're about to end this, baby," she said gleefully. "In a big, big way."

When Erica entered Jonah's office at the Pentagon, there were several people already there. A meeting had just completed and she was shuffled in before the rest of the team left. She recognized some of the people as having been part of his staff when she worked for Jonah. Seemed like ages, but really it wasn't that long ago.

Erica wasn't in the mood to be polite, so she sat down in the chair on the opposite side of the desk and just waited, not bothering to speak to anyone.

She had a lot on her mind. She'd been to work today, but she felt awkward around Alex after they had kissed. She said hello to him in passing, but she did her best to avoid him. It was childish, she knew, but she wasn't yet sure what to make of that kiss and what to do about it. Besides, she was distracted from thoughts of it because of her issues with Jonah—issues that were too many to count. But for now, Erica would concentrate on his injection of Alex into their conflict with Terrell, and his bitch of a wife accusing her mother of being a home wrecker.

Within a few minutes, everyone had left. Jonah stepped out to say a few words to his assistant; then he reentered the room, closing the door behind him.

"I know what this is about," he said, before even sitting down at his desk. "I know you're upset about me sending Alex to pay Terrell. Alex told me. Honestly, Erica, I could try and appease you, but the truth is—"

"The truth?" She laughed. "Do you even know what that word means?"

He sat down, giving her a stern glance. "The *truth* is, I don't care. I can't allow my future, that of my family, and the people who have supported me all these years to be affected by a car washer."

"You say that like he's not even worthy of mentioning," Erica said. "He's a human being."

"Just barely," he mumbled back.

Erica felt her blood boil. "The disregard with which you speak of some people is disgusting and borderline racist."

"Racist?" He seemed disappointed. "Trust me, I place value on people according to how they conduct themselves in their lives and their contribution to society. It has nothing to do with race."

"Just that some people are worth the respect of a human being and some aren't," Erica concluded for him.

"Those are your words," Jonah said.

"Look," Erica said, sighing, "this isn't even about Terrell—even though I'm pissed you didn't give me a chance to try and fix that myself. This is about Alex. How could you include him?"

He looked at her; his expression seemed to note that she really cared.

"He's a good guy," she continued. "You do things the way you do them. I get that."

"Do you?" he asked doubtfully.

"But Alex isn't like that."

"How well do you think you know him?" Jonah asked.

"We're friends, Jonah. I know him."

"Then you should know, he was eager to help me."

"He wasn't eager," she said. "He just made it seem that way because he didn't want you to think you couldn't count on him. He only did it because you lied to him about me being in danger."

Jonah shrugged. "Whatever the case, it's done."

"You really don't care who you trap in your web, do you?"

Jonah laughed. "You're being a bit dramatic. I don't need to trap anyone. Besides, you're the one who brought him into it, Erica. I told you to keep your distance from him, from a personal standpoint."

Erica rolled her eyes. "Are you on that again?"

"It's his closeness to you that allowed me to convince him so easily," Jonah said. "So, can you just blame me?"

"Yes, I can *just blame you*!" Erica couldn't believe what she was hearing.

"Are you involved with him or not?" Jonah asked, leaning forward on his desk.

"Not," she said, remembering their kiss and feeling uncomfortable. "We're just friends, I told you. But I'm surprised you don't want more. After all, the closer we get, the easier he'll be for you to manipulate."

"I don't need your help for that," he said. "But despite your concern, Alex will be fine. You just don't tell him anything he shouldn't know and he won't be compromised."

"I'm the one making all the compromises," she said. "But I guess it would be a waste to even *ask* you to. You never keep your end of any of our bargains."

"If this works, and it better work," he said, his face

transforming to grave seriousness, "there will be no need for him to be involved for one second more."

"What is that worth?" she asked.

He frowned, appearing offended for just one second. "Is that all, Erica? I'm very busy."

"No," she answered. "Did your wife tell you about our last interaction?"

"Why would you be interacting with her at all?" he asked.

"She was at campaign headquarters a couple of weeks ago. She was drunk, by the way."

"You don't have any proof of that." He leaned back in his chair.

"Really?" she asked, disbelieving his attitude. "I'm not the press, Jonah. Is that necessary?"

"It's best you keep your distance from her."

"I've tried to," Erica exclaimed, "but she accused my mom of carrying on an affair with you after you were married."

Jonah immediately sat up straight. At first, he seemed offended by the suggestion; but then, Jonah appeared as if trying to figure something out.

"Well?" Erica asked finally.

"Tell me what happened," he said. "That can't have been all."

Erica replayed the conversation for him; she was heating up with anger all the while.

"So, what are you going to do about it?" she asked. "I don't care if she is a drunk. She can't say things like that about my mom."

"Juliet is under a lot of stress right now," he said. "She's saying things she doesn't mean, and she's not a drunk."

"You said that you cared about my mother when you were together."

Jonah's face grew very still and more serious. "I cared about Achelle very much. And, of course, there wasn't anything between us after I left for the military."

"Well, you slept with someone," Erica said, "and she almost divorced you over it."

"That's none of your concern," Jonah said. "Now, if you'll let me get back to—"

"It is my concern!" Erica stood up from her chair. "My mother deserves more respect than that. You need to clear it up, *now*!"

"Don't give me orders," Jonah warned. "And sit down."

Erica stood where she was, folding her arms across her chest.

"I'm serious, Jonah. I don't care what that woman thinks of me, but I'm not having her think my mother was your mistress."

"You're right," he said, nodding. "I'll clear it up with her."

"How will I know you'll do it?" Erica asked. "You lie all the time."

"I don't lie all the time," he protested, "but all I can give you is my word. I respected your mother tremendously. And, even though you're acting like a brat, Achelle deserves to have her name cleared. I'll handle it."

"Good." Erica turned and headed for the door. When she reached it, she turned back to him. "And from now on, leave Alex out of your dirty dealings."

"Mind your own business," Jonah said. "I'll do what I want."

"Ugh!" She threw her hands in the air and left his office. He didn't deserve a good-bye in her opinion.

She was extremely frustrated just thinking about Juliet's accusations. But for some reason, she believed Jonah. It was crazy, but she had a feeling that whatever it was he had with her mother was real enough that she could count on him to at least clear her name with his wife. He was right. She deserved that.

Regarding Alex, Erica didn't know what to think, but she was afraid for him. Jonah could pull him in and then he'd stop being the great guy she had come to care about so much.

Sitting on a park bench after eating lunch, Billie was checking her face in her pocket mirror. She'd hoped to clean up before going back to the office, but she wasn't having much luck. Lately she'd been crying often. It wasn't just that the person she loved most in the world hated her, but it was that she deserved it. She deserved all of it.

She was blaming Porter for being an asshole or Michael for not understanding. She wasn't willing to face up to her own weaknesses and faults. She'd gotten a taste of power and felt like she could get justice for wrongs done to her in the past. For once in her life, she felt in control and thought she could do whatever she wanted. No, she thought she was *entitled* to do whatever she wanted.

With Michael ignoring her and Tara feeling worse than ever, Billie reached a low she hadn't felt in a long, long time. It was similar to how she'd felt when her marriage first fell apart and Tara begged her not to leave, but she had to. She'd felt like such a failure.

She watched as a couple sat down on the bench less than twenty feet from her. They had to be at least in their eighties. Still holding hands, they sat and looked around. The woman made eye contact with Billie and smiled softly. Billie smiled back, noting the look of happiness and contentment on the woman's face.

She wondered, how long had they been together? How many kids did they have? How many grandchildren? How many times had one of them hurt the other and thought it was over, only to figure out he or she couldn't be without the other? How many times had one failed and the other lifted the spouse up with love and support?

The man looked at the woman and said her name. She'd been looking at a pigeon on the grass, but she looked back at him. He winked at her and she giggled, squeezing his hand more tightly.

Billie felt her heart catch in her throat at that small gesture. She wanted to cry—but not the painful crying she'd been doing this last week. No, she wanted to cry from joy at seeing real, enduring love.

This was what she wanted—what she'd always wanted. She'd thought she'd had it with Porter, but it didn't happen. She had blamed him, claiming his affair ruined it all. It broke their marriage, but he didn't ruin it all by himself. She allowed herself to believe that the way he'd treated her ever since she left him was his fault alone. It wasn't, though. She'd let him in her bed. She'd let him tell her lies. She'd let his touch mean more to her than her self-esteem.

She was still so angry because that enduring love had been ripped from her, and she'd thought she knew who was to blame. But nothing was that simple, and

she was a big-enough girl to face up to that. Finally . . .
but probably too late.

Erica was nervous as hell as she knocked on the
door to Alex's office at campaign headquarters, but she
knew she had to face him. It was ridiculous for her to
continue bending over backward to avoid running into
him. She had ignored any texts or e-mails from him
that weren't strictly work-related. She'd made excuses
to avoid their usual lunch together, or she'd made sure
that she left for lunch while he was still in a meeting.

She didn't care what Jonah wanted. Yes, there was
a part of her that craved pleasing him, right alongside the part of her that wanted to tell him to go to hell
every time she came face-to-face with him. It was not
the father/daughter relationship she had in mind, and she
imagined it would never be what she'd wanted. But she
wasn't about to let him get in her head so much that
she couldn't move on with her life.

"Come in!" Alex yelled.

When she entered, he was talking on his cell phone,
but stopped the second he saw her. Erica sensed surprise and annoyance in his expression.

She closed the door behind her and walked over to
his desk as he quickly finished his phone call and
placed his phone on his desk.

"Long time, no see," she said with a cautious, almost questioning tone.

Alex nodded. "So you're not ignoring me anymore, or is this about work?"

She sighed, walking around the desk. She leaned
against it, trying to appear as humble as she felt.

"I know I've been a bitch about this, Alex. I'm sorry. I genuinely am."

"It was just a kiss," Alex said. "You acted as if we'd almost had sex."

"It was just unexpected."

"Was it really?" Alex asked, looking up at her. "I feel like this has been building between us for a while. Was it completely one-sided?"

"No," she assured him. "It wasn't. Obviously, we were growing . . . We were becoming good friends."

"Friends?" He laughed, leaning forward. "Wow, I guess I had this all wrong."

"This isn't easy for me, Alex. Please give me a chance."

He nodded, sitting back.

"I don't have a trusting nature," she said. "Growing up without a father and . . . Just where I was, I had to be on my toes all the time. It's a coping mechanism to believe I shouldn't trust someone, shouldn't get close to them."

"You've proven yourself to be someone I can trust," she continued. "Even though that whole scenario with Terrell threw me for a loop, I know you did it because you care about me."

"I do," Alex said, quickly getting up from his chair.

Erica was a little startled at the sudden action, but she didn't move. He was standing next to her, facing her, only a few inches from her.

"I don't want explanations," he said. "Erica, I want to know how you feel."

"I—"

The door to his office swung openly suddenly and Jonah entered, yelling Alex's name in a dangerous tone. They both turned to face him. The second he realized what the scene was, or what it appeared to be, the dark expression on his face grew even darker.

"What in the hell is going on here?" he asked, entering the room.

"Nothing." Erica quickly stepped away from Alex and walked around the desk.

"We discussed this, Erica." He eyed her sternly.

"Nothing was going on," she repeated.

"You both looked very close," he accused. "Is this what you're getting paid to do?"

"Sir," Alex began, "we're working very hard. You can be assured—"

"I can't be assured of anything with you," Jonah responded sharply.

Alex looked genuinely shocked and offended. It made Erica angry. Why was he so mad? What was going on?

"Jonah—"

"You're to blame for this too, Erica," he said.

"We were just talking!" she yelled.

Erica noticed that Alex looked surprised at her tone. He gave her a warning glance, as if to tell her to watch it. She imagined Alex must have thought she was crazy for yelling at Jonah.

"Not that," Jonah said, pointing to the place where they'd been standing when he entered. "I'm talking about DC Whisperings!"

"What is that?" Erica asked.

"It's a blog," Alex said. "It's a gossip blog, mostly about national politicians and society people in D.C. What happened?"

"The campaign got a call from the editor," Jonah said. "They posted a picture of me and my wife at a fund-raising dinner party. One of their commenters said they had undeniable proof that I've cheated on my wife—DNA proof!"

"DNA proof?" Erica asked, knowing exactly what that meant.

"Are we talking about some kind of little blue dress?" Alex asked, referring to the President Clinton sex scandal.

"Worse than that," Jonah said, looking at Erica.

Erica felt her stomach tighten as she realized what Terrell was planning to do. He wasn't just going to expose Jonah's relationship with Sherise. He was going to expose her own relationship with Jonah. Now that she made it clear that he was out of her life, he was going to try and hurt her as well!

"What is worse?" Alex asked, confused. He then looked at Erica, perplexed, but she only shrugged in response. Jonah was giving up way too much.

Jonah pointed accusingly at Alex. "You were supposed to pay Terrell, and he was supposed to leave town and stay out of this."

"I did exactly what you said," Alex said.

"You don't know it's him," Erica stated.

"I don't?" Jonah asked. "It only took our IT guy a few minutes to track down the commenter. They haven't gotten a home address, but it's coming from Columbia Heights. Right near where your thug of an ex-boyfriend lives now."

"Are you sure of that?" she asked. "How did they do that?"

"That's not important," Jonah said. "What is important is that you both failed, and DC Whisperings wants to know more."

"That's manageable," Alex said. He walked back to his desk and grabbed his cell phone. "It's just a gossip blog. They all try to break these stories, but they're not professionals. They can be dealt with. We can put a stop—"

"Not you," Jonah said. "You've done enough here. I've put Laura on it."

Alex looked extremely upset that he'd been passed over for this crisis. "But, sir, I know much more than Laura about—"

"You're out of this one," Jonah said. "Both of you!"

"If you'd just listened to me," Erica stated.

"Enough!" The force of his words startled her. Jonah was almost menacingly angry. "I fought in fucking wars," he said. "I'll be damned if I let some punk hustler make me weak. He's done!" He turned and stormed out of the office.

"Jonah!" Erica called after him.

"What is he . . ." Alex rushed over to her. "Erica, you're shaking again."

She turned to him. "You have to help me, Alex."

"With what?"

"He's going to hurt Terrell," she said. "I think he might do worse."

"Jonah?" Alex was shaking his head. "He'll probably just threaten him. I know how these things go. They threaten someone with exposing their own past or—"

"No, he's not going to do that." Erica grabbed Alex's hands in hers. "Please, you have to help me get Terrell somewhere safe before Jonah gets to him."

"But why—"

"Alex! You have to trust me! Just trust me. Will you help me?"

He looked apprehensive, but he nodded. "What do you want me to do?"

"We have to call his job," she said. "Tell him to get out of there now and we'll meet him."

He shook his head. "I'll bet he quit his job after he got the payment."

"Then his apartment," she said. "We have to get to him."

"If he's in Columbia Heights, my mom lives pretty close to him," Alex said. "We'll take him there for now."

"Let's go," Erica said. "I just hope we aren't too late."

16

Sherise's eyes were closed, her face looking upward to catch all of the sun on this beautiful early afternoon. She thought she was going to have to get back on the exercise wagon to control her weight gain with this pregnancy. Now that things were about to lighten her load, she'd have time to do that, like take a long walk in the sun with her husband.

"What is this shit?"

Sherise opened her eyes to the sound of Elena's fake Midwestern accent.

"Oh, hi, Elena." Sherise pointed to the chair across the table from her. "Have a seat."

Elena looked around. "I'm supposed to be meeting someone else here. The host must have sent me to the wrong—"

"You're at the right table," Sherise said. "Dennis isn't coming. A friend at the firm got ahold of his phone while he was in the bathroom and sent you that text. You're here to see me."

"No, I'm not." Elena placed her purse over her

shoulder and looked down at Sherise in a menacing
way. "I don't have to talk to you. I'm about to sue—"

"No, you're not," Sherise said impatiently. "Stop
making a spectacle of yourself and sit down."

"What I'm going to do," Elena said, with a pointing finger, "is call my lawyer and file a harassment
claim against you now."

"I'd think twice before doing that," a deep voice
said.

Elena's mouth fell open at the sight of Justin as he
came around the curtain and approached their table.

"What are you . . ." She was getting suddenly nervous. "You're not allowed to come near me."

"You don't have a restraining order against him,"
Sherise said. "There's no law that says he can't be near
you."

"This won't look good for the case," she said,
smirking.

"There's not gonna be a case." Justin sat down. "Your
lies have caught up with you, Elena."

Elena gave a haughty huff. "Is that what you think?"

"It's what we know." Sherise placed the file, which
was in her purse, on the table. "Now sit down, Ms.
Brown."

The smirk on Elena's face disappeared as she looked
from Sherise to Justin and then to the file on the table.

"What's that?" she asked.

"It's a copy of everything," Sherise said. "Yours to
keep."

"Everything?" she asked, finally taking a seat.

"Is this really all about revenge?" Justin asked.

"I don't have to justify myself to you," Elena said.
"I have a witness and—"

"Dennis isn't going to be able to help you after this,"

Sherise said. "We know that your dad worked for Okun Industries for, what, thirty-five years?"

Elena swallowed hard, not saying a word.

"When the executives at Okun realized they had mismanaged the company, they knew they were going down." Sherise watched with a smile as Elena's expression changed. "They had run out of money and the debtors were pounding on their door. They'd already laid off half the workers."

"It's not uncommon for companies to use pension funds to pay debts," Justin stressed.

Elena's expression hardened. "But they didn't use it to pay off their debt. They used it to pay themselves bonuses before declaring bankruptcy and shutting down the company."

"What they did was wrong," Justin agreed. "It's not supposed to be used like that, but it's not a crime."

"It was a crime," she said, "until you made it legal."

Justin shook his head. "This is sick, Elena."

Sherise continued her summary. "So your daddy lost his pension when Okun raided it, and you blame Justin?"

"I was doing my job," Justin explained.

"Your firm's aggressive lobbying changed that law," Elena said. "What you did, made it possible for them to get away with it."

"You could have sued them," Justin said. "There are recourses for employees who—"

Elena laughed and Sherise heard something in that laugh. Elena was an angry woman full of pain. She was bordering on the edge of sanity. Sherise wanted to feel sorry for her, but she couldn't. If she'd targeted anyone else, Sherise would try and find sympathy, but Elena hadn't.

"Do you know how you sound?" Elena asked. "You push for these laws, knowing the consequences can destroy lives, take away everything that decent people have worked for, and console yourself by saying that they have legal recourse. It all works out, right?"

"So you plot revenge," Sherise said. "You change your name. You get an internship on Capitol Hill. You did well, considering all the lying you had on your résumé."

"Dennis helped you," Justin said. "I know he did. How else would you get to the firm with such a shady background?"

"Men are stupid," Elena said flatly, as if not caring anymore.

"You wanted a big payday," Sherise said. "Justin was collateral damage."

"No!" Elena slammed her fist on the table.

"Take it easy," Justin warned, looking around.

"He wasn't collateral damage," Elena said. "He was the head of that lobbying effort. Justin and the firm made tons and tons of money making it possible for Okun to destroy my family's life. Dennis told me everything."

"You know that Dennis was supposed to head that up," Justin said.

"He was taken off that case," Elena argued, "because he told the heads at the firm that he didn't agree with it anymore."

Sherise laughed. "He played you, bitch."

"Dennis was taken off the case because he was showing up for meetings drunk," Justin explained. "The client almost fired us. He went to AA after that."

Elena's indignation slipped away as she looked from Justin to Sherise.

"I guess he used you too," Sherise said. "He wanted to get in your panties and get back at Justin for taking over his account. Did you promise to share the money with him?"

Sherise realized that Elena was still holding on to hope, and it was a waste of time.

"Look, honey," Sherise said, "it's over. We have all the evidence we need. Look in the folder. There's even a picture of you and Dennis making out in Bartholdi Park last week."

"Between that and his vendetta against me over Okun," Justin said, "he's not going to be any use to you."

"So stop holding out," Sherise advised.

"No," Elena finally said. "He was going to get ten percent. He was really just in it to ruin Justin's career and . . . be with me."

Sherise smiled slyly. "You were going to get rid of him after you got your money, weren't you?"

"So you wanted to get rich?" Justin asked.

"You don't understand at all," Elena said, with a disgusted expression on her face.

"There was one thing," Sherise said, "one thing I didn't have time to figure out, but I think I know now."

Elena turned to her; her eyes were beginning to well up with tears.

"Your sister, Rose." Sherise paused to gauge the effect of the name on Elena; it was massive. "Not long after everyone found out that the pension was raided and they'd lost their entire retirement savings, Rose committed suicide."

"Doesn't make sense," Justin said. "She was a twenty-six-year-old woman. She wasn't dependent on that pension. Your father was the one who lost all the money."

"You're right," Elena said in a shaky voice. "It doesn't make sense. It wasn't a suicide."

"So, what happened?" Sherise asked.

"I guess you could say she took Justin's advice." Elena wiped a single tear that trailed her left cheek. "She filed a lawsuit against the company right away. She was going to fight for Dad. She was just a teacher, but she knew the law and . . ."

Elena paused, looking down as she swallowed hard to maintain her resolve. "She started getting threats," she continued. "At school and at work. People would drive by her house and leave her untraceable notes."

"My firm didn't do that," Justin said. "We'd have no reason to."

"No, it was Okun," Elena said. "She was so scared that she bought a gun. Then one night, I showed up at her place and used my key to get in her house. Just like usual, but she was such a mess by then, she thought—"

Sherise gasped. "She shot herself."

"She just got the gun," Elena said. "She'd only taken a couple of classes. She didn't know how to use it and she was scared to death. She must have been fumbling with it in the dark and . . . I heard a shot."

"It was an accident," Justin said.

"It wasn't!" Elena directed her grief at him. "It was a result of what you and your firm did. Everything has consequences. None of this would have happened if you hadn't fought to find a way to help a company cheat its workers."

"Your sister is dead because of Okun," Sherise said. "Not Justin's firm."

"She's dead and my father has nothing because of both of you." Elena looked at Justin. "I couldn't touch Okun executives. They're superrich and they've all lawyered up. But you were free and clear, and I felt it was time that someone other than my family started suffering the consequences of what you did."

"Well, you failed," Sherise said. "And now you're going to suffer. You see how that works? If you live just to cause pain, you only get pain in return."

"I don't have to listen to your threats," Elena snapped.

"But we've had to listen to yours," Sherise answered. "We've had to listen to your lies, which could ruin our lives."

"He deserves it." Elena stood up and looked down at Justin. "I think you know you do."

Sherise looked over to Justin, who looked to be suffering inner turmoil, before turning back to Elena.

"By the way"—Sherise pointed to her smartphone, which had been sitting on the table the entire time— "I've been taping this whole conversation. Didn't really need to, but just in case."

"Go to hell" was all Elena could muster before snatching her purse and walking off.

Sherise sat back in her chair, a victorious smile spreading across her face. "That went easier than I expected."

"What did you expect?" Justin asked, sounding annoyed. "It wasn't as if she could deny any of the evidence. What was she going to fight?"

"She's a bitch," Sherise said, turning to him. "Bitches fight, whether or not they have a chance. It's what we do."

Justin shrugged, looking down at his lap. He brushed away lint that wasn't on his pants. Sherise was worried. She watched him avoid eye contact with her, and it bothered her.

Sherise reached over and placed her hand over his on his lap.

"This isn't your fault," she said. "You did your job. You didn't cause any of this. You would never want any of that to happen."

He looked at her with a solemn expression. "I know, I just—"

"You just what?" she asked. "You're a good man, Justin. You have a good heart. You would never do something that would hurt innocent people on purpose."

He smiled, but she could tell he wasn't really feeling it.

"You can't doubt yourself because some crazy bitch comes along and decides to blame you for something you could've never expected to happen." She took his hand in hers and placed it on her belly. "This is who you are. A father, a husband, and someone who— I thank God every day—loves me."

"I do love you," he said. "I love our family."

"And we just saved it," she said. "Together."

Billie waited anxiously outside his front door, waiting for him to open it. Her stomach was in knots because she knew this would start out ugly. But there was also a sense of calm because she knew what she wanted out of it.

But would he even give her a chance? She heard a commotion at the door, on the other side. He could see her through the peephole. She smiled and held up the white tissue she'd taken out of her purse, hoping that he would at least give her a chance and open the door.

She heard an annoyed sigh and a few more seconds of waiting before the opening of locks.

"What do you want?" he asked as he opened the door.

Porter stood in the crack of the door, his demeanor making it clear that there was no way she was coming into his condo.

Billie felt bad when she saw the defeated look on his face. He wasn't really angry as much as just unhappy. This was supposed to be what she wanted, what would make her happy. She got it, and she was more miserable than ever.

"I need to talk to you," she said softly.

"Tara is gone," Porter said. "She's back in Detroit and she's not coming back. I don't care what you do to my career, Billie. There's nothing left to say."

"I hope you'll give me a chance to apologize to her too," Billie said.

"No, I . . ." Porter paused for a second, thinking about her words. "'Too'? Are you trying to say that you're here to apologize to me?"

"I am." She offered a smile. "And it's sincere, Porter. I promise."

"I don't believe anything you say, Billie! You're not the Billie I was married to."

"You're not the Porter I was married to either," she said. "So I think we're even on that, don't you?"

He shrugged. "Why? I'm not going to change my mind about Tara."

"That's your right," she said. "Tara is your daughter. Even though I love her like a daughter, I know I have no right to her. It would break my heart if I couldn't speak to her again, but I'll respect that, if that's your wish."

He was clearly skeptical; his stance was still protective. "You've never respected my wishes with my daughter, Billie. Since we've split, you've undermined me and went against what I wanted."

Even though what Porter said wasn't true, she wasn't going to bring that up. Before this ordeal started, she'd bent over backward to stay in his good graces regarding her time with Tara. But today wasn't the day to point out anyone's failings except her own.

"It won't happen again," Billie promised.

"Apologies don't mean shit," Porter said. "They're just words. You've threatened to destroy everything I've worked for. You threw so much bullshit my way. You think you can just come here and apologize and it's over?"

"It will be over," she said. "At least for me. I can't answer for you."

"And I don't want you to!" Porter snapped. "You play nice now, but next week you come back with another threat. Why would I believe you?"

"You don't have to believe me," she said, trying to stay calm and not throw his mistakes in his face. "I just have to tell you the truth, and this is the truth."

He threw his hands in the air. "I don't know what the truth is anymore. This is so fucked."

Billie realized that Porter wasn't moving and letting her inside, so she decided just to go ahead.

"I feel awful, Porter. I really do. You may not believe me now, because I seemed so delighted at making you suffer."

"You were delighted," he said. "I saw your face. You were loving it."

"I was," she admitted. "You'd made things so difficult for me for a long time, and I'd always had piecemeal ways of getting back at you."

"By destroying my career?"

"You'd threatened to do the same for me, Porter. Remember . . ." Billie stopped herself and took a deep breath. "That doesn't matter. What I did was wrong and I let it get out of hand. There's no excuse. I'm just going to ask you to forgive me."

"The damage is done," Porter said. "I've been reprimanded, Billie. I made a fool of myself and I think I ruined my promotion."

Billie was surprised to hear Porter say this. He never, ever admitted he'd done anything wrong. Here he was admitting a role in his own demise. Maybe she wasn't the only person who was going to grow from this experience.

"I'll do everything I can to counteract that," she said. "I promised to make sure Gil and I would sing your praises, and I'll follow through on that."

Porter pressed his lips together and his brows furrowed. He seemed to want to believe her. His stance loosened as a few inches of space now existed between him and his front door.

"Why are you doing this?" he asked.

"Because I've lost everything," she said. "I know, that's not when it's supposed to happen. I should've known before what I was doing was wrong, but I didn't. I'm not perfect. But seeing Tara run out of that restaurant, and standing there feeling like the most wicked, selfish person in the world, really hit me."

Porter lowered his head, clearly upset over the topic. "She hates us both, if that makes you feel any better."

"It doesn't," Billie said. "I never wanted her to hate you. I know the role I played in this, hurting the person I love most in the world. But I'm grateful to her because it finally shook me awake."

Porter finally let his body calm down. His shoulders lowered as he stepped aside and opened the door. Billie cautiously walked into the condo that she once called home. It was an emotional moment for her. It had been a long time since she'd been here.

"*This* is what my problem is," she said, looking around.

"What about 'this'?" he asked.

"I lost my fantasy," she said. "The fantasy that we had and I never really got over it."

Porter's eyes widened and a hopeful expression came over his face. "Are you saying you—"

"No," she corrected immediately. "I'm not saying I want it back. I'm just saying I never got over losing it. I dealt with the pain, but not the anger."

He rolled his eyes. "Can you just say what you're trying to say so we can get this over with?"

"I've said it," she insisted. "I've apologized and promised it won't happen again. Also, I want to let you go."

"*Let me go?*" he asked. "What do you mean?"

"We failed," she said. "We both failed and lost our chance at forever with each other. I didn't want to accept that, but it's true. I just wanted to blame you, but doing that forced me to hold on to anger and resentment. The further I got away from you emotionally, the more I had to see what was coming."

"What?"

"That I'm starting over again." She sighed, feeling emotionally overwhelmed at the thought of it. "That I'm over thirty and I have to start over, and I can't use what you and I had as a crutch to pretend as if I'm not back at square one."

"So your plan is to ignore that we were ever together?" Porter asked. His eyes expressed a sense of pain at the thought. "We were married, Billie."

"I'm not ignoring that." She held her hand to her heart. "I would never want to forget our good years, but I'm letting it go. There's a difference. I shared my life and my hopes with you. I still share love for Tara with you, but you can't be a part of my life, my heart, anymore. It will only hold me back. I've got to start over and this is the first step."

"This is about that guy, Michael, right?" he asked.

She shook her head. "No, this is only about me. I thought it was about Tara, and then I thought it was about you, and then I thought it was about Michael, but it's about me. Just me."

Porter looked exhausted as his arms fell to his sides. His expression grew sad and Billie realized that she'd reached him. He got it. This was really over. After all of this time, it was over between them.

"I guess I have to say 'sorry' too," he offered, his voice choking a bit.

"You don't have to," she assured him. "Not unless you really mean it."

"But I screwed you over really good at times," Porter said. "I admit it. I was an asshole to you after you left me. I was so angry that I lost you."

"I was angry you lost me too," she added.

"I'm still angry," Porter said. "I look at you, Billie, and . . . Shit, I just fucked up my life when I cheated on you."

"You did." She smiled. "But you can fix it. You just have to move on."

He was shaking his head as if not ready to accept what he had to do. "I'm supposed to live a life that doesn't include you at all? I'd prefer to have you in my life and trying to ruin it than not to have you in it at all."

"No, you wouldn't," she said. "You've been miserable. None of your relationships have worked since, because of it. Trust me, you'll be much happier."

"What about Tara?" he asked.

"That's up to you, Porter. You know I want to see her. I love her desperately."

"I know," he said. "I've used that to my advantage too many times and look where it's gotten me."

"It's gotten you a daughter who still loves you, even though you might not deserve it," she said. "Just like me."

He frowned as if trying hard to figure this all out, and Billie felt her stomach tying in knots. She'd been at such peace letting go of Porter and telling him so. But where Tara was concerned, her heart still belonged to the girl. That wasn't as easy. It killed her watching Porter now. It was only seconds, but it felt like several minutes to her. She waited patiently, not saying a word.

"I need time," he said. "I need time to work on my relationship with her. I need you to stay away during that time."

She nodded, feeling her heart flutter. "Whatever you want."

"That might take a while," he warned. "I've fucked things up pretty good."

"We both did."

"I'm not like you, Billie," he said. "I can't do what you've just done. I'm not . . . good, like you."

"I'm not good," Billie said. "I'm just human."

He shrugged. "So, what now?"

"You call me when you're ready to let me see Tara," she said.

"What about work?"

"I can be professional," Billie said. "You won't have any more problems from me. Can I count on the same from you?"

He smiled and nodded. "I'll do my best."

That was the best she could ask for, and Billie wasn't going to ask for more. She couldn't control what Porter did; and from this point onward, she wouldn't try. She only could control how she let what he did affect her, and what she did in return.

After leaving Porter's apartment, Billie felt an amazing burden lift off her. She was amazed at how holding on to resentment weighed her down to the point where she could feel it physically. It was already a bright, sunny day out, but suddenly it seemed brighter. No, she wasn't stupid. She knew that everything wasn't as simple as one conversation, but she had crossed a threshold and felt like she was on the path to freedom now. She was walking into a world of possibilities.

The first thing that came to Billie's mind the second she stepped off the bottom step of Porter's building was Michael. Even though she'd known she wanted to be with him, with this burden behind her, she was seeing him in a whole new light. She was remembering all of the exciting moments and fun they shared and how he brought out passion, which was just pure and real. She felt great about herself when she was with him. He made her laugh and made her want to enjoy life again.

"Hobbies," she said to herself. He'd said that one had to have hobbies in order to really be living.

"This is bullshit," Terrell said. "I'm out of here."

"You can't leave," Erica told him. "I'm telling you, Terrell, this is not a game."

Erica was grateful that she and Alex were able to get to Terrell before anyone else could. Alex had his number from Jonah's investigators. When Erica called him, she had a hard time getting him to understand what was going on. He denied having done anything, but he finally agreed to leave his apartment and meet her at the drugstore two blocks away.

Once there, Erica pulled him into Alex's car. He was angry at seeing Alex with her, but he didn't have much time to complain. Gratefully, Alex's mother lived only three blocks from the store. They quickly hurried him up there. Once inside, Terrell was growing increasingly angry, making it difficult for Alex and Erica to concentrate and figure out what to do next.

"But I didn't do anything!" Terrell said for the one hundredth time.

He was pacing the living room of the modest apartment. Erica could tell that he was scared enough to give up the street bravado. She wanted to reassure him, but she wasn't sure how to do it.

"Jonah thinks you did." Erica was sitting on the sofa, trying to stop biting her nails off from nervousness. "We're just going to have to convince him that it wasn't you."

"I don't even know what that website is," Terrell said. "You know me, Erica."

"It's true," Erica said to Alex, who was standing in the archway between the dining and living rooms. "I didn't think about it before, because everything happened so fast, but Terrell wouldn't bother with a political gossip site."

"What is this DNA evidence he seems to think you have?" Alex asked.

Terrell and Erica looked at each other. Erica shook her head and Terrell responded with a sigh.

"I guess I don't know," Terrell said.

"What was that?" Alex asked. "That look! What the hell is going on?"

"We just need to figure out how to convince Jonah that—"

"I've brought him to my mother's house!" Alex yelled. "I have a right to know what this is about. I'm sorry, man, but there is no way you're a real threat to Jonah, not enough to make him want to break the law. You're both hiding something from me."

Erica got up from the sofa and walked over to Alex. She could see how angry he was. She knew that she had to do something about it.

"Just calm down," she said. "I need your focus, Alex."

"Hey," Terrell said, "I didn't ask for this."

"Yeah, you kind of did," Alex snapped. "Talking shit is considered asking for it."

"Look, man!"

Terrell started toward them, but he stopped. They all turned to the dining-room table as his phone, sitting on top of it, rang.

Terrell looked from the phone to Erica, wondering what he should do. She gestured for him to see who it was and he walked over to it.

"Oh." He laughed, picking the phone up. "It's just my boy, Chris."

"Chris who?" Erica asked.

"He's my . . ." Terrell halted for a moment. "He's my next-door neighbor."

Erica had a feeling this wasn't a friendly call. "Don't tell him where you are. Don't tell him anything."

"Hey, man," Terrell said casually as he held the phone to his face. "What's up?"

"I'm not playing around," Alex whispered to Erica. "I want to know what's going on. This isn't about some stupid infidelity rumor. I've put my career at risk for you, Erica. I've brought my mother into it."

She could see that Alex had reached the end of his rope. He'd been the understanding friend, who wanted to be more; but now, if she didn't come clean, he was going to back out of everything. Without him, Erica knew she couldn't handle this.

"Holy shit." Terrell placed the phone back on the table. "He—he said that two white guys in suits, wearing sunglasses, went into my apartment. They opened it with a key and everything. He says they're in there now."

Erica shivered at the thought of what those men were there to do.

"Jesus," Alex said, seeming to have the same thoughts as Erica. "Erica?"

"Sit down," Erica ordered.

"Just tell me," Alex said.

Erica pointed to the closest chair. "Trust me, Alex, you'll need to sit down for this."

Alex didn't have much reaction while she told him about how she came to meet Jonah and later, through Terrell, found out that he was her father. She also told him about the history of Jonah's relationship with her mother and the trouble Terrell had been causing for Jonah over it.

Alex ran his fingers through his hair as he sat back in the chair. He shook his head for a few seconds before saying, "Wow."

"Yeah, that was my reaction at first," Erica said.

"And he's keeping you a secret for his political career?" Alex asked.

Erica nodded, feeling the pain that always came with that fact. "I'm too much of a liability for his plans and the people who back him."

"I thought . . ." Alex seemed at a loss for words. He clearly wasn't happy.

"You're disappointed in him," Erica said. "You thought he was a better man than that. What he did with my mom, her decision to keep me a secret, isn't his fault."

"But his choice to keep you a secret after finding out is," Alex said. "He's not . . . Jonah's not the man I thought he was."

"No shit," Terrell added.

"There are other things about him," Erica said. "He's done things to people who have threatened him. He's threatened Terrell more than once."

"I don't need to know more," Alex said. "I get it now."

He looked up at Terrell with a confused expression on his face. "Why would you push him like this, if you knew what he was?"

"I didn't," Terrell said. "I mean, yeah, the first time, but I was just looking for the money. I got it. I'm telling you, man, I was ready to leave town. Especially now that Erica—"

Erica looked at him and they exchanged an understanding glance. There was nothing left there, at least not romantically for either of them. He'd finally realized that. She felt sorry for him and angry at the same time. He was finally over her. That was a good thing. However, as long as he was a threat to Jonah, he would always be in danger. Erica still cared about him enough never to want that to happen.

"Well," Terrell said, "let's just say I had no reason to stay here. I didn't do that shit in the blog."

"Then who did?" Alex asked. "Who else knows about this?"

Erica went down the list. "His wife, my friends Sherise and Billie. That's it, I swear. None of them would do this. You can trust me."

"Doesn't your friend Sherise work for Northman now?" Terrell asked. "That's a shady bitch. She would—"

"No," Erica insisted. "Besides, the trace was from your part of town, Terrell. How did that—"

Suddenly there was the noise of keys in a lock and the front doorknob started to move.

"Oh no," Erica said. "They've found us."

"Wait." Alex stood up. "I think it's . . ."

Erica sighed the second she saw Alex's mother walk in the front door. His mother gasped at the sight of the three of them standing in her living room and the keys fell out of her hand. Alex rushed to her and quickly spoke a few words to her in Spanish, seeming to calm her down.

She turned to Erica, who tried to offer the most appreciative smile she could under the circumstances.

"So nice to see you again, Mrs. Gonzales," she said. "Thank you for letting us use your home for a bit."

"I wasn't actually aware that I had." Leeza Gonzales looked awkwardly at Terrell. "So, what exactly is going on?"

"Long story short," Terrell said, "Jonah Nolan is trying to kill me."

"Is that supposed to be some kind of joke?" Leeza asked, not at all amused.

"Don't I wish." Terrell plopped down on the sofa.

"Mama"—Alex reached out and took her hand— "come with me to the bedroom. I'll tell you about it."

"What has that man done?" she asked, ripping her hand away.

"Mama, just hold—"

"I told you not to work for him," Leeza said. "I told you he was no-good. That man is no-good. I swear to you, Alex—"

"Enough," Alex said. "I get it now. You were right all along, Mama. All those times you warned me against him. You were right, okay? Please."

"I'm sorry," she said, trying to calm herself.

She reached out to him and took his face in her hands. He leaned down and let her kiss his forehead before they hugged each other.

Erica was starting to realize something as she watched the scene before her. She remembered the scene at headquarters when she and Jonah ran into Alex and his mother. The look she'd given Jonah. She hated that man.

Just then, her phone rang. She checked the ID. It was Jonah.

"Who is it?" Alex asked.

"Go ahead and talk to your mother. I'll be a second. Hello," Erica said cautiously as she stepped farther into the dining room for some privacy.

"Where are you?" Jonah asked immediately. "Don't screw around with me, Erica."

"None of your business," she responded. "So you're adding murder to your list of bad deeds? Or let me guess, this isn't the first time."

"You don't know what you're talking about," Jonah said. "The only people I've ever murdered were in combat during wars. I just want to make sure Terrell isn't a threat to me anymore."

"Well, you've done everything else," she said. "So what was left?"

"There is a lot left," he said. "Is he with you? Are you at your apartment?"

"No," she said, "but you probably already know that. How many men in suits and sunglasses did you send to my place?"

"Erica, I would never hurt—"

"Save it," she said. "This is the last straw, Jonah."

"Just come into the office and we'll discuss—"

"No," she said. "I'm not coming to campaign headquarters or the Pentagon. I'm not working for you anymore. I quit."

"You don't mean that," he said. "You're angry over someone who doesn't deserve your anger."

"Terrell didn't post that comment," she said.

"I know."

"He would never have . . ." She stopped after realizing what he'd said. "You . . . what? You know?"

"What I showed you earlier today was preliminary. That was my investigator's first stab at finding out who was behind the comment. Five minutes ago, I got more information. The commenter has a history and uses that same username at other sites. We locked in on an IP address and will probably know who it is soon. One thing we're sure of is that it's a woman, not some idiot thug."

"Is it your wife?" Erica asked, at least feeling like she could calm down a little now.

"Don't be stupid," he answered. "Just come back and we'll—"

"No," Erica said. "No matter how this turns out, I

can't come back. You were gonna do something awful to Terrell, and now you're going to do it to someone else—whoever this turns out to be. It doesn't change anything."

"It doesn't have anything to do with you anymore, Erica."

"That doesn't matter. It's who you are and I can't support you."

Jonah sighed and, after some silence, responded. "You don't mean that. I'm your father and you're my daughter. That means a lot."

"Not enough to tell the world, though, right?"

There was silence on the other end of the line for a few seconds and Erica's heart broke. This man was never going to acknowledge her. Even if he did win the White House, achieve everything he wanted, she would always be the dirty secret of a man who wasn't even worthy of her.

"Is Alex with you?" he asked.

"No," she lied. "I don't want him involved in any of this."

"But you do want to turn him against me," he said.

She didn't understand what he meant. "You're the only one who can do that."

"Stay away from him," he said, "if you really want him out of this."

"There's no more 'this,' Jonah. Terrell is leaving town. You've made your point. We're done here."

"You and I aren't done," Jonah said.

"Yes, we are," Erica said, her voice a little uneasy. "We finally, definitely, are."

17

When Billie stepped into the Downtown Boxing Club in the Shaw neighborhood of D.C., she was pleasantly surprised. Although she wasn't sure what to expect, having never been in a boxing club before, she thought it was nice that this place didn't have any bells or whistles. It was bare-bones and old-school. Men were in different corners of the main room, using different types of training equipment. There were two boxing rings in the center of the room. One had a practice bout going on; the other looked as if it was preparing for one.

That was where she saw Michael. He was standing along the side of the ring, looking at an older man who looked as if he was giving him instructions in an exasperated way. The man was making fighting gestures, left hooks and uppercuts. Michael was nodding, but the other man was clearly frustrated.

Billie had to say that Michael looked incredibly sexy. He was topless, in a pair of loose shorts. His smooth, dark chest was muscled and wet with slight sweat. His perfectly sculpted arms tapered into red gloves worn over his hands. She remembered those arms taking her, grabbing at her waist, and pulling her to him. She craved it now, and so much more.

Michael didn't notice her. He was focused on his instructor. The only reason he looked toward her was because every other man in the room had turned his attention to her.

She smiled as their eyes connected, but he just stared. He looked her up and down like every other man in the room. She wasn't stupid. She had no intention of getting him back because of her looks, but every little bit helped. She made sure to look amazing. As she stepped closer to him, she could see it was having the desired effect. He couldn't take his eyes off her.

"Hi, Michael," she spoke softly as she reached him and his instructor.

"What are you doing here?" he asked.

"You must be Billie," said the instructor, a Latino man in his sixties, with all-white hair and tired eyes.

"Hi," she said.

Michael reluctantly made introductions. "Billie, this is Joseph Tammer."

"Are you his coach?" she asked, shaking Joseph's hand.

"Yes, but I'm about to quit," he said. "You're to blame for this."

"Joseph." Michael nudged Joseph a bit and shook his head. "Don't."

"Don't?" Joseph asked. "I'm trying to save you from getting hurt."

"How am I to blame?" Billie asked.

"When he'd met you, he couldn't stop talking about you," Joseph said. "He was very happy."

Billie smiled, but Michael was getting angrier.

"That's enough, Joseph," he said.

"But since you broke up," the older man continued, ignoring Michael, "he's been hell on wheels. He thinks he's ready for a real fight, but he's only a recreational boxer. He's not ready yet. He's gonna get hurt."

"I know what I'm doing," Michael said.

"You know the moves," Joseph responded, "but you're hotheaded right now. The way you were hitting that bag the other day, you could've broken your hand."

"Joseph!" Michael pleaded. "Can you give us a moment, please?"

Joseph nodded, turning back to Billie. "Please talk some sense into him. A broken heart is not a reason to fight."

"Is it true?" she asked Michael after Joseph walked away.

"What are you doing here?"

Billie smiled softly. "I'm happy to see you again. I've missed you."

"Billie—"

"I've brought you something," she interrupted. She held out the gift she'd been holding in her hands the entire time. It was a painting.

"It's my first painting," she explained, "and it's you."

Michael looked at the painting and frowned, looking confused.

"It was the moment after we were on the grass at the outdoor movie theater and our shoulders touched." She looked into his eyes, hoping to see some effect from recalling that tender, yet charged moment. "Then you looked at me and . . . I remember it so fondly that I painted it."

"That's me?" he asked.

"Yes."

Billie smiled as she could see he was trying to suppress a laugh.

"I know it's amateur, but—"

"It looks like"—he squinted, leaning in–"a donkey in a polo shirt."

"I did it from memory," Billie said.

"You don't remember me looking like a human being that night?"

"Michael." She placed the painting down, leaning it against the base of the ring, and sighed. "Give me a break. I haven't painted in almost a decade. I tried."

He sighed, shaking his head. "Look, Billie. I don't want any gifts from you. I have to fight. I think you should leave."

"Is what I did so unforgivable?" she asked. "Do you really intend to ignore me forever?"

"I have to," he said. "Looking at you, hearing your voice . . . I don't trust myself to do the right thing."

"How is staying away from me the right thing?" she asked. "The time we had together was short, but it was right. It was definitely right."

"If it was right," he said, "we'd still be together."

"I know I screwed up," she said, moving beyond the hurtfulness of his words. "I messed up a great thing. But it was a mistake, and I . . . I really want you to forgive me. I need you to."

Michael was looking at her and she could see that he really wanted to give in, but he was cautious. He was seeing her as yet another disappointing relationship in a string of many and was trying to resist the truth—that she was much more than that. She wasn't going to leave until he faced it.

"I know I've done enough damage to make you want to run the other way," she said. "You met me at a time I was caught up in something that I wasn't prepared to handle."

"Are you saying this was just about timing?"

"No," she answered. "It was ongoing . . . inevitable. You got caught in the cross fire and I regret that more than you know."

"You want me to accept this back-and-forth between you and Porter," Michael said. "I'm not willing to do that. It makes me feel—"

"Secondary," she said. "I know. You were great to me and only asked one thing in exchange. I didn't give it to you. I couldn't at the time and you were right to dump me. But Porter and I have . . . We've worked it out."

"Just like that?" Michael asked. "I'm supposed to believe you and just jump back in?"

"This didn't happen overnight," Billie said. "It's been two years coming, my break from him. I'm grateful to you and Tara. You both turning away from me was the best thing that happened to me. I never felt so alone, and I realized how empty and unfulfilling this anger I held toward Porter was. It hurt the people I cared about and gave me nothing in return."

She reached out and softly placed her hand on his upper arm. She was glad he didn't resist.

"I've let him go," she continued. "I let my love for him go a long time ago, but I let my anger toward him go this week. It was a painful experience that I was avoiding, because I was dreading the thought of realizing that it was all a failure—my life with him. But letting him go—really go, this time—was more liberating than I could have imagined. You were right, Michael. I'm not fit for revenge. It was eating me inside and poisoning everything."

"I don't think you're weak, like you accused me of thinking," Michael said.

"I was the one who thought I was too weak," she said. "I just couldn't admit how much I doubted my own intentions, so I blamed you. Honestly, Michael, I wouldn't have even respected you if you didn't dump me. But I'm asking you to give me another chance."

Michael looked around as if debating the best words to say, shaking his head as if he'd doubt anything that came out, either way.

"Billie, I . . . The reason I broke it off with you was because you hurt me."

"I know I did, and I'm—"

"Stop," he said. "Just listen to me. I was more hurt than I thought I'd be. I knew I was falling for you, but I didn't know how hard, until I had to walk out on you. Just seeing you now, walking over to me, it was like . . . Being with you is dangerous."

She smiled. "No one has ever said that before. I wish it were a compliment."

He loosened up a bit with a smile. "If I'm willing to put a woman first in my life, I have a right to expect the same."

"And I'm ready to do that." She took one step closer to him; and with her free hand, she raised it to his cheek, looking into his eyes. "It's really all I want in this world. I miss you and I want you back."

She could feel his body soften from its initially tense state. He looked down, and his eyes were drawn to her in a helpless way.

"Someone once told me . . . and then showed me that there are much better ways than getting into a boxing ring to work out all that angry energy you have," she whispered.

He smiled, shaking his head. "This is why I stayed away from you. I can't resist you, Billie. You're—"

"Yours," she said. "I'm yours."

She leaned up and brought her lips to his in a tender, yet possessive kiss that claimed him. He offered no resistance. Within seconds, his lips were even more persistent than her own.

"Every lady is entitled to go a little nuts once in a relationship," she finally whispered. Their mouths were separated by just half an inch. "We got it out of the way in the beginning."

"I don't have any guarantees that you won't go nuts again?" he asked.

"No," she said, "but I'll have a good, strong man to keep me in line."

He frowned, shaking his head. *"I'm gonna keep you in line?"*

She tilted her head to the side with a flirtatious wink and answered, "Well, you can try."

When Sherise came home from work that night, she knew something was up the second she stepped into the house. It was quiet. Usually, when she came home or when Justin came home, Cady was having a fit or putting on a show loud enough to reverberate around the house and come through on the monitors, which were in various rooms. All she could hear was the low tone of soothing R & B coming from the stereo in the living room. The only light in the house came from the dining room and she headed straight for it.

When she arrived, the scene before her was beautiful. There were only two chairs at the table, which was covered in a white tablecloth. There were pink rose petals in an infinity figure at the center of the table, surrounded by five small candles in glass holders. The black trellis-designed china was set out; on top of each was a sterling plate topping.

"And what is all this?" she asked, getting excited.

"All this is for you." Justin, who had been standing at the head of the table, walked over to her, looking handsome in a suit.

"Cady is with the sitter." He reached out to her and wrapped his arms around her waist. He leaned in and kissed her softly on the lips. "Overnight."

"Overnight?" she asked. "You must mean business!"

He nodded and kissed her again.

"You're the only one who's going to be babied tonight," he said with a seductive grin. "And it starts with your favorite dinner. Pan-seared red snapper, with shitake mushrooms and leeks in lobster cream."

"When did you have time to make all this?" She walked over to the table, his arms still wrapped around her as he followed behind. She lifted up the sterling plate top and saw her favorite dish. It was perfect. "Weren't you at work today?"

She felt his arms slip away from her and she turned around. There was a hesitant look on his face. What could be wrong?

"What is it?" she asked. "Please, Justin, don't sugar-coat."

"It's actually good news," he answered, "but I was going to tell you while we ate, so sit down."

"Tell me first," she said. "The food can wait."

"I left work early today," he said. "I had a lot of thinking to do."

"Have you decided when you're gonna expose Elena?"

It irked Sherise to no end that Justin instructed her to wait on exposing all of that bitch's lies to the firm, but she obliged. It was his choice when to drop that bomb. She only hoped he'd make it soon and would let her be there when he threw in their faces the information that the firm should have sought out before putting him on leave.

"Elena rescinded her sexual harassment claim this morning," he said with a smile.

Sherise smirked. "I knew the bitch would. I was hoping we could expose her before she got the chance to run away."

"The office is bending over backward, apologizing to me," Justin said. "You should have seen them today. They want to offer me the world. They just hope I don't cause them any legal trouble."

"They're going to be bending over even more when they find out what we know." Sherise was salivating at this thought. "They'll realize what fools they were, and Dennis—"

"Wait, baby." He gently placed a finger on her lips to silence her. "Elena admitted her accusation was false. She also implicated Dennis. She basically plotted it as his idea to get back at me and the company for overlooking him."

Sherise wasn't happy with this. "I'm not gonna shed a tear for Dennis. Fuck him, but she can't get away with that. This was her idea from the beginning. We need to make sure she suffers."

"I don't know if I want to do that." Justin grabbed a dining-room chair and sat down.

Sherise looked down at him and placed her hand

gently on his head, caressing it. She could see his turmoil. He really let Elena's awful words get to him.

"Do I need to remind you that you didn't do anything wrong?" she asked.

He nodded, reaching his hand out to touch her thigh.
It was just a soft touch, just a call for contact.

Sherise bent down and got on her knees. She
placed her hands on his lap and looked up at him.
"What is it, baby?"

"I know that Elena had no right to do what she
did," he said, "but I don't want to destroy her life."

"She wanted to destroy yours," Sherise insisted.
"Ours."

"I know," he said, "but she suffered immense pain
from something I created."

"You were doing your job, Justin."

"You know this isn't the first time something like
this has happened," he said. "I mean, nothing as drastic
as someone accidentally killing herself, but—"

"If you could lobby for a bill that couldn't be
abused, you would," Sherise assured him. "You can't
control how Congress words a bill."

"I could have used my influence to make sure there
weren't as many loopholes as there were."

"If you had gotten rid of the loophole Okun used,
they would have found another one." She cupped his
chin with her hand. "Justin, you know what you're
doing is right. Others abuse lobbying power. You take
the cases you believe in."

"I never really believed in this one," Justin said.
"That's just it. I took this account because Dennis
fucked it up. I didn't want it, and I think that's why I
didn't give a second thought to how it could be used or
abused."

"So," Sherise said, "from now on, you make sure that you only accept causes that you believe in. No more leftovers from assholes like Dennis."

"I don't think you're hearing me," Justin said.

"Then make it clear to me," she said softly. "I'm listening."

He looked at her with uncertain eyes for a moment before saying, "I don't know if I want to stay with the firm. They've made it clear they want me back, but this experience has changed me. Not just what Elena put me through, but their lack of faith in me. I don't have the passion, especially not for that firm."

"Then you join another one," Sherise said. "Or better yet, you open your own firm. You have so many clients and you have tons of clout on Capitol Hill."

"You'd support that?" he asked.

"It's what you want, isn't it?" she asked.

"I think . . . I think it is, but I thought it would be impossible right now. Especially with the baby coming."

"I'd support you, no matter what. We'll do great, as long as we're happy and doing what we want. Just because you support a family doesn't mean you don't get to be happy. We'll make it work. I'm here for you, baby."

He took her cheeks in his hands and smiled proudly. "*This* girl. *This* is the girl I married—the one who made me feel invincible. I can't believe I almost lost her."

"Never." Sherise felt her eyes welling up with tears. She loved him so much. God, had she almost lost him? She shuddered at the thought. Never again.

* * *

Alex swung the front door to his mother's house open just as Erica reached the top step. Immediately she looked at his expression and saw a mixture of complete despair and anger.

"Get in," he ordered as he stepped aside.

She stepped into the house, looking around. It didn't look like anyone else was there.

"What the hell is going on?" Erica asked. "You send me these frantic texts, with ten exclamation points, telling me I have to come over right now. What is so wrong?"

"You're not going to believe this shit." His voice held a dark anger, with sadness coming through in flints.

"Is it Terrell?" she asked. "He got on a bus to Houston last night. I don't think Jonah is going to go—"

"No!" Alex yelled.

Erica jumped. "What's wrong with you?"

He pointed to the sofa against the wall with one hand as he ran the other through his hair.

Sitting down, Erica took him in and realized that he was still wearing the same clothes he'd worn when she'd left him from this very place yesterday. His eyes were bloodshot red. Had he not gotten any sleep? Had he been drinking?

"Were you crying?" she asked.

"I was." He fell onto the sofa beside her.

Erica was deeply affected as she watched him lean over and place his face in his hands.

"Fuck," he said. "Fuck. Fuck."

She reached out and placed her hand on his back. "Alex, please tell me what's going on."

He finally looked up. "Jonah didn't want us together. He told me a couple of times to stay clear of you. He told you as well, right?"

She nodded. "What Jonah wants doesn't matter. I quit, Alex. I'm not working for him anymore. I'm not going to have a relationship with him. I don't care if he is my—"

"After you and Terrell left," he said, "my mother and I really got into it. I mean, she lost it. Terrell really told her too much, but it didn't matter."

"She obviously doesn't like Jonah," Erica said.

Alex let out a dark laugh. "No shit. This has been brewing between my mother and me ever since I went to work for him."

Erica was searching hard for something comforting to say, even though she had no idea what was really going on.

"She used to work for his family," she said. "Maybe he wasn't nice to her. He's kind of a snob. Or maybe you working for him just reminds her of her life as a maid. She might want to forget that. She's moved on, and—"

"She wrote the comment," Alex said.

Erica was speechless.

"I can't believe I didn't even suspect it," he added. "She's always talking about those local gossip sites."

"Why would she . . . Oh, my . . . and she lives close to Terrell. So when they traced it, they just assumed it was from him."

"He knows by now, I'm sure," Alex said. "I haven't gone into work. He's been calling me nonstop. I'm sure he'll send someone over soon."

Erica looked around the room.

"She's not here," Alex said. "She's meeting with her lawyer."

"Her lawyer?" Erica asked, doubtful that Jonah would try to sue his family's former maid. It didn't look good. "Why would she write that? How does she know about—"

"It's not about you," Alex said. "She was talking about herself."

"Oh, my God," Erica said as she realized what Alex was saying. "Jonah had an affair with your mother?"

"Just after he was married," he answered. "My . . . Her husband had just died and she was staying with his sister because being home just made her think of losing him."

"Jonah took advantage of her." Erica's anger was bubbling over. "How could he?"

"She said they slept together three times, tops," Alex said. "But when she told him she was pregnant, he threatened her."

"When she . . ."

Erica suddenly felt as if an elephant had stomped on her chest. The realization was so hard that she actually fell back against the sofa, letting out a huge gasp. Then she suddenly felt sick to her stomach.

"No," she said. "No."

"My mother was scared to death," he said. "She knew how much money and power Jonah had, especially now that he was married to Juliet."

"No," she said again. "Alex, it can't be true."

"He paid her one hundred thousand dollars," Alex continued. "That's why my mother was able to stop being a maid and get an education. He paid her and he threatened her."

"Alex!" Erica grabbed him by the shoulders and shook him. "Focus! Are you telling me that you're . . . you're Jonah's son?"

He looked at her. His eyes were full of pain and regret. He nodded several times quickly.

Erica let him go and jumped up from the sofa. The first thing she saw was the garbage can at the edge of the kitchen island. She ran to it and bent over, just in time, and threw up.

"I'm sorry," he said. "I'm sorry. I'm really sorry."

After a minute or so, she finally stood up and looked at him. He was right at her side and he handed her a paper towel to wipe her mouth.

"My God, Alex."

"I know," he said. "But it's okay. It's not like . . . Well, we only kissed."

"Don't!" she yelled. "Don't even mention it. I'm gonna throw up again."

Erica felt disoriented, in shock and utter disbelief. She was barely able to stand up straight. She reached out for the counter to steady herself. She was feeling dizzy.

"It's not easy for me either," Alex said. "I was falling for you, Erica. I wanted to . . . Oh, my God, I can't even think about it."

"This is why he didn't want us together!" Erica exclaimed. "That son of a bitch. Instead of telling the truth, he was willing to risk us—" She leaned over the garbage again, thinking she might throw up once more.

"I think he believed we would obey him," Alex said. "Jonah thinks he's God, so he'd expect us to follow his rules."

"This is disgusting," she said. "He's disgusting."

"We didn't do anything wrong," Alex said.

She stood up straight, looking at him and seeing how tortured he was over this. "I know, Alex. It just seems like it."

"I thought maybe . . . that maybe you suspected this?" Alex said as more of a question than a statement.

"How could I possibly?" she asked. "I mean, now, looking back, so many things make sense, but I never thought this."

"You pushed away from me after we kissed," Alex said. "I thought you sensed it was wrong."

Erica reflected on her conflicted feelings to whatever extent she could without making herself sick again.

"It's possible," she agreed. "But really, there's no way for me to sense that you're my . . . I can't even say it."

"Half brother," Alex offered. "There, I said it."

She slowly, unsteadily walked back to the sofa. She needed to sit down. Alex stayed where he was, leaning against the counter.

"But maybe I was suspicious of the weirdness," she said, "and my subconscious was telling me to slow my roll before I could figure it out." She looked up at him. "Alex, this is awful. It's just—"

"How do you think I feel?" he asked. "I'm completely freaked out by lusting after my own half sister. Not to mention the fact that I found out that the man I thought was my father, who died while my mother was pregnant with me, isn't."

Erica realized she'd been so focused on her own shock that she hadn't thought of how much worse this was for him. This was about more than just the two of them for Alex.

"I'm so sorry, Alex. You must be devastated."

He was shaking his head in incredulity. "I can't believe all those times I saw him, met him. He knew and still treated me like just some other kid."

"Now you know why your mother hates him so much."

"And her," Alex said. "How could she have an affair with a married man?"

"Alex, you can't be mad at her. She was in grief, and . . ." Erica stopped midsentence as she realized what Alex was saying. It clicked in her head. "It's her!"

"What?"

Erica hopped up from the sofa. "The woman Juliet was talking about when she was accusing my mother of sleeping with Jonah after they were married. She knew he was cheating, but she didn't know with whom."

"Now you know all about it," Alex said.

"Does your mother know about me?" she asked.

"No, I didn't think it was a good idea, considering her plans."

Erica took a few steps closer to him, noticing the apprehensive look on his face. "What plans?"

"She's not here because she's . . ." Alex's brows highlighted his agonized expression. "She's with her lawyer. They're planning a press conference. They're gonna tell the press everything."

"Oh . . . my . . . God."

EPILOGUE

"**Y**ou're looking good, Sherise," Erica said as she sat across from her in the outdoor café on U Street. "You're . . . I don't know, glowing. It sounds so clichéd."

Sherise smiled as she took a sip of her virgin daiquiri. "I'm coming into this pregnancy, girl. No more morning sickness and my stress is now so low that I sleep through the night. It's great."

"Getting nice and . . . plump there too." Erica laughed.

"Fuck you!" Sherise laughed too. "I'm still smaller than you, bitch, so—"

"Oh no, you didn't!" Erica clenched her hand in a fist and playfully directed it at her friend.

"Fact!" Sherise pointed to her. "And I'll tell you something else—"

Before she could finish, a car pulled up on the curb. It was a maroon BMW and Billie was inside. Both Sherise and Erica leaned over to get a look at the driver. Neither of them had still seen him in person.

"He's handsome," Erica said.

"He's okay." Sherise rolled her eyes. "I'll make my formal assessment after a real encounter, not a drop-off."

The ladies watched as Billie leaned over and kissed Michael on the lips before hopping out of the car and waving good-bye as he sped off. She turned to walk toward the girls with a hop in her step.

"You're walking like a girl that's getting some," Sherise said as soon as she reached them.

"That's because I am." Billie sat down. "Long time, no see, ladies."

"It's been weeks since we've been together," Erica said. "I hate it. And now that you're spending more time with Michael, it's going to get worse, isn't it?"

"No," Billie assured her. "We've all had or have husbands and boyfriends and we managed to keep our connection. We'll figure it out. This has been an insane few months for all of us."

"What months aren't insane for us?" Erica asked. She could remember very few.

"So we're meeting him formally tomorrow night?" Sherise asked. "I have to give my blessing."

"Yes," Billie said. "You'll meet him at the fundraiser for Northman tomorrow night. You have to be nice."

"Of course," Erica said. "You already have my blessing. I can tell you're happy."

Billie smiled, feeling a sense of overwhelming joy, which she was starting to get very comfortable with again.

"He's great," she said. "I mean, we've only been back together for a couple of weeks, but things are just picking up where they left off. It's weird how happy I am."

"Why is that weird?" Sherise asked. "You deserve it."

"I know," Billie said, "but it's been so long. I just didn't think it was gonna happen. When I'm with him, I feel like I have a future, all over again. As if everything that happened in my past needed to occur in order to be here with him now."

"Oh, girl," Sherise said. "He got you sprung as hell."

Billie laughed. "I'm being serious. My whole life is back in a flow now. I'm gliding with it. It's good."

"I feel ya," Sherise said. "Now that that bitch, Elena, is out of the picture and this pregnancy is settling in, Justin and I are in heaven. You just know it, when things are back on track. It makes you laugh at all those other times you tried to convince yourself it was, but it wasn't."

"Is he still at the firm?" Billie asked.

Sherise nodded. "But he's shoring up his clients and his plans. Neither of you can tell anyone about his going off on his own."

"My lips are sealed," Erica said. "I wish him the best."

"I'm going to be the wife of the CEO now," Sherise said.

"Correction," Billie said. "He's going to be the husband of the press secretary for the president of the United States."

Sherise grabbed her phone from the table and held it up for the girls to see. "See this? The combination of polls has Northman up by five now. From being down seven, just a couple weeks ago."

"You can thank Jonah for that," Erica said. "Asshole. He got what was coming to him."

Leeza Gonzales went public the afternoon Alex informed Erica of the shocking news. Things had been crazy ever since. The press everywhere wanted more answers about the affair with Leeza and how Jonah could have known about his love child and ignored him. When Jonah held a press conference to try and put out the fire, Juliet was conspicuously absent, which led to even more rumors that the two were headed for divorce. Proof of this affair brought mistresses out of the woodwork. In a matter of days, Jonah Nolan went from being the future of America to the whorish deadbeat dad of America.

He not only withdrew as Matthews's vice presidential nominee, but he also tendered his resignation at the Pentagon. Jonah Nolan's legacy was over; and all it took was a former maid who decided it was time to end the charade.

"Is he still trying to contact you?" Billie asked.

"Not in the last few days," Erica said, grateful for that. "I'm never talking to him again. I just have to accept that I don't have a father. I survived without one."

"You have us," Sherise said. "You don't need him."

Sherise reached out and placed her hand on Erica's, squeezing it.

"He deserved every bit of what has happened to him," Sherise said. "With you, he has the excuse of not knowing until you were older. But with Alex, he knew all along."

"I'm still afraid they'll find out about me," Erica said.

"I don't think so," Billie said. "It's starting to die down. He's out of the limelight. This new woman Matthews selected is all everyone is talking about. The press has moved on to her. I think the worst of Jonah is over."

Erica only hoped so. She hadn't had as much as one call from a reporter during the weeks since this exploded. She was grateful to God for that.

"Are you okay?" Billie asked. "I mean, with . . . Alex and everything."

"I don't want to talk about it," Erica said.

"You have to," Sherise urged. "You know that's what we're here for."

"I still get sick thinking about it." Erica's hands came to her temples as she felt a headache coming on. "I think I will for a long time."

"You only kissed him," Billie said. "It's not the end of the world. You have to get past it."

"I know, and I will." Erica rubbed at her temples, wondering whether one day, thinking about this wouldn't give her a headache. "It's just gonna take some time. I feel awful."

"Why would you feel awful?" Billie asked. "You didn't do anything wrong."

"Not for me," she said. "For Alex. Since this all came out, his life has been turned upside down. He had to go into hiding with his mom."

Erica had wanted so often to reach out to him over the past weeks, but she couldn't. He'd texted her once, but she'd only told him that she needed time and wished him the best. He promised he'd never tell her secret and she thanked him. That was their last communication, over a week ago. Erica didn't know when she'd be able to look at Alex and not feel dirty, but she hoped the day would come. Alex was a good guy and needed as many real friends as he could use, now that his life was never going to be the same. She wanted to be that friend.

"They should be safe, though," Sherise said. "I mean from Jonah at least."

"Who knows?" Erica said. "He's gone underground for now. He's waiting until the fever dies down. But what happens when it does? He had plans for his future and they've been ruined."

"He won't blame himself," Sherise said. "He's not capable of that level of awareness. Before blaming himself, he'll blame Alex, Alex's mother, Erica, me, and anyone else."

"He wanted to sit in the Oval Office," Erica said. "He felt it was his birthright, and he'll never get there now. I refuse to believe he's just going to go away. I don't think we've heard the last of Jonah Nolan."

"That can't be good." Billie gestured for the waitress. "I need a drink."

1

Sherise Robinson took a look around and had to smile. At thirty, she was sitting on luxurious leather seats in the back of a driven car on her way to a meeting where she was going to be named one of the most powerful, influential people in the country. Not bad for a girl from the mean streets of Southeast D.C. who no one believed would ever amount to anything.

She checked her makeup mirror even though she didn't have to. She looked flawless. Her golden caramel skin was glowing against her silky dark brown hair that she'd recently cut to a few inches below her shoulders, adding more sophistication. She had perfect high cheekbones and full, sultry lips, but the highlight of her face was her piercing green eyes.

Her face and those dangerous curves framing her fit body created an image of beauty that Sherise used to her advantage. She wasn't afraid to admit that. She could make a man give her anything she wanted and make a woman concede defeat just at the sight of her.

But looks alone could never have gotten her where she was today; about to be named the press secretary to the next president of the United States of America. She'd worked her ass off for that.

Yes, she played dirty at times to get what she wanted, and to keep it. That was just the game of power and politics in D.C. She'd learned to play it as a teenager when she'd gotten her first internship at the Department of Agriculture. She was just making copies, but she made sure to leave an impression by being faster, more organized, and more presentable than anyone else. Sherise knew what most sixteen-year-olds didn't: in D.C., presentation mattered more than substance. She parlayed that into a college scholarship and several jobs on Capitol Hill.

Meeting and marrying an up-and-coming lobbyist didn't hurt at all, but Sherise put in the work and made a name for herself as one of the best message people in D.C. Her position in the communications department of the White House led to a job for popular Maryland Governor Jerry Northman's campaign as the Democratic candidate for president. He won the primaries and finally, two weeks ago, with Sherise running his communications, he won the highest office in the land.

And to think, just a year ago, it almost all fell apart. Everything was on the brink of being lost . . . everything.

She closed the mirror and placed it in her Furla purse. She had to always look perfect now that she was constantly in front of the camera, her face on newspapers and websites. She made sure her staff, now totalling five full-time and two interns, always looked perfect as well.

Her staff wouldn't be at this meeting she was on her way to at the campaign headquarters for Jerry. She'd gotten the message this morning when LaKeisha

Wilson, Jerry's campaign manager, texted her and only other core team members to come in for an announcement. It was just a formality. Everyone knew that Sherise would be named PS for the new administration, but she couldn't help but be excited.

The phone rang with that familiar ring tone reserved for the one person who made Sherise's heart light up. It was her husband, Justin, the father of her two children and the love of her life. She didn't even want to think that, a year ago, their marriage was barely holding on by a string after it was revealed that they had both been unfaithful and their oldest child might not be his. That Cady turned out to be his helped make their attempt to reconcile go a lot smoother than it would have otherwise. They'd weathered some horrible storms, but got through them.

Now their marriage was stronger than it had ever been. Sherise never hid from the fact that, although she loved Justin, she married him for the advantages he gave her. Over time, she'd lost sight of how good a husband he was and made some terrible mistakes. One of those mistakes came back to haunt her in the worst way, and Justin strayed. She'd gotten him back. She knew she would. Sherise refused to give up anything that mattered.

Now marrying for advantages was out the window. She loved the hell out of that man and appreciated him for everything he was. Her career had always been her priority, but she would give it up, even a position as powerful as PS to the president, for her husband and her two babies.

"What you doing, hot stuff?" he asked in a playful tone.

Sherise smiled. "On my way to the meeting. You know that. You saw me leave."

"I know where you're going, smartass," he responded. "I want to know what you're doing."

"Just checking out how hot I look in my mirror," she answered. "Why? Did you want me to say I was thinking about you and touching myself?"

"Considering how well I took care of things this morning," his voice shifted from playful to serious in a split second, "I expected you to still be trying to cool yourself down."

"Oh my God, the ego on you, boy." She laughed. "You start your own business and now you think you're cock of the walk."

It was true that he'd been great in bed this morning, and the night before. Their sex life was better than ever. Justin had a new confidence now that he'd left the lobbying firm he worked at and started his own. A false claim of sexual harassment against him turned the firm that he'd made millions for against him. After the truth came out, they were all apologies, but Justin had made up his mind.

Only three of his clients followed him, but in the last eight months, he'd gotten five more. He had an assistant and an intern and was about to hire a new lobbyist to join him. He was doing well and future prospects were all positive. With a new baby on the way, it was a risk, but it paid off. His confidence was through the roof and Sherise was reaping the benefits in their bank account and their bedroom.

Justin laughed in the self-assured tone of a thirty-three-year-old man who knew he made well with his life. "So we're celebrating tonight?"

"I know what you mean by celebrate," she said. "You trying to get me pregnant again?"

"God forbid." He laughed. "I think you've made it clear that the baby factory is closed after Aiden."

Aiden, their six-month-old son, was perfect in every way. He was starting to develop his unique personality traits and Sherise couldn't love him more. Their older child, Cady, was almost three now and as stubborn and difficult as ever, just like her mama. They had a perfect family now, made only more precious considering it had all almost fallen apart.

"We both barely have enough time for the kids we have now," Sherise said. "You know how guilty I feel with two babies and working nonstop?"

"You've been on a presidential campaign," Justin said. "You couldn't pass up this chance of a lifetime. We made it work."

"It's not changing any time soon," she regretfully admitted. "Ugh, how did we get on this topic? You wanted to celebrate?"

"Sorry," he said. "Jeniah is at home with the kids and she said she can stay until about nine tonight. I'll try and knock off early and we can just have a quick dinner somewhere nearby."

Jeniah was the nanny they'd hired just before Sherise gave birth. With her working on the campaign and Justin working overtime at the new business, there was no other choice but to bring someone in the house. Taking the kids to a daycare or a sitter was no longer feasible.

"You knocking off early? The tide is turning?" she asked.

"The calm before the storm," he said. "All the new

elections. Everyone has decompressed and it's about to get crazy, so we better take it while we can."

"I don't know how long I'll be, but you've got a date." She felt the car stop. "Oh, I think we're here. I've gotta go, baby. I love you."

"I love you more," he answered back before hanging up.

Sherise smiled and took a heavy sigh. She waited for the driver to come around and open the door for her. As she stepped out in front of headquarters, everyone on the sidewalk stopped to take a look. Maybe one or two of them might have recognized her, but most were just staring at the beautiful young woman in the sharply tailored heather gray suit who looked like she'd been stepping out of driven cars her entire life.

If they only knew.

Billie Carter leaned her petite frame over the balcony overlooking the Atlanta skyline as the day was coming to life. It was only her third day in the city, but she was starting to fall in love with it. This was mostly attributed to the personal guide she'd had since arriving. That same guide came up behind her, wrapped his arms around her, and placed his head on her shoulder.

She turned her head slightly to the right and his lips met hers with a tender morning kiss that warmed her chocolate body underneath the silk bathrobe she was wearing. She turned around to face him, their lips still touching as she wrapped her arms around his neck and gently caressed the back of his head.

"I'm mad at you," Michael said slowly as their lips parted. "I don't like waking up with you not next to me."

Michael Johnson was the man of Billie's dreams

and she'd almost lost him. They'd had a chance encounter on a train in D.C. and all she could see was a six-foot Adonis with cocoa skin, deep black eyes, thick dark eyebrows, and a smile that made her lose her balance. But when her stop came, she got off and thought she'd never see him again.

When she'd formally met the thirty-six-year-old executive headhunter just a few days later, it wasn't under the best circumstances. She was just trying to get her career as an attorney, which had derailed, back on track with a new job at Agencis. Agencis was one of Michael's clients, and he'd wanted someone else to have the job she'd gotten.

They got off to a bad start, but Michael was determined to break the ice that Billie had formed around her heart after having it broken by a cheating ex-husband and a lover who turned out to be a secret drug dealer. Her inability to get past the awful ex-husband almost cost her Michael's love, but she fought for him in the end, the way he'd fought for her in the beginning, and they made it through.

A year later, they were going strong and head over heels in love. Billie had never thought she'd experience this again. She was convinced her chance had passed. Yet here she was in the arms of this handsome devil.

She pouted and kissed his nose. "Poor baby. I'm sorry."

"Don't apologize," he said. "Just come back."

He took her hand and tried to lead her back into the bedroom of their luxury hotel suite, but she hesitated. He looked back at her, taking in the small features of her face, framed by her curly natural hair, cut close to her head. She wore her emotions on her sleeve and Michael seemed to notice.

"What's wrong?" he asked.

"I'm worried about lunch," she said. "I want things to go . . . better than before."

By before, she meant the night they'd arrived in Atlanta. It was the second time she'd met Michael's family. As his father had passed years ago, his mother, Dee Dee, and sister, Aisha, were all the family Michael had. They'd all had dinner at Michael's childhood home on the eastern side of the city.

The night had gone about as well as the first time she'd met Dee Dee and Aisha, when they came to visit Michael in D.C. four months ago. And by well, she meant not well at all. While Billie had bent over backward to be gracious to her new boyfriend's family, it was not returned. From the beginning, Dee Dee grilled her with question after question about her previous marriage. Apparently, Dee Dee still lived in the 1950s and believed that a divorced woman had to be to blame for not holding on to a man. It had gotten bad enough that a small argument had started, which Michael interrupted.

Aisha, on the other hand, had followed in Michael's activist roots. One of the things that Billie loved about Michael was that no matter how successful he'd gotten, he never forgot where he came from. He was active in the community in D.C., especially working with young black men in dire need of a role model. Billie related to him, as she spent most of her volunteering doing pro bono work, which stemmed from her past. Her father had been railroaded by the legal system and sent to jail for a crime he didn't commit. He'd died there and it had changed her forever.

But while Michael remained active helping the less fortunate, Aisha had taken it a step further. She was pretty militant and immediately pegged Billie, and her lifestyle, too bougie to be authentically black.

"Don't worry." Michael gently cupped her chin and lifted her face to meet his.

She was tiny and he was tall, always looking down at her in a way that made her feel protected . . . loved.

"Trust me," he assured her, "they will warm up. It's just how they are. How they've always been."

"I can't seem to say anything—"

The phone that suddenly rang was Michael's, which sat at the edge of the bed only ten feet away. They both looked at it and looked at each other.

"Go ahead and answer it," Billie said, knowing that Michael was seeking her okay.

"I don't have to," he said. "It can . . ."

"It could be your mother," Billie said. "If you didn't answer, she'd find a way to blame it on me."

"That's just silly." He quickly touched his finger to her nose before kissing her forehead and turning toward the phone.

It might be, she thought, but wasn't particularly far-fetched. The second meeting wasn't much different than the first. When Billie arrived in Atlanta three days ago, Dee Dee's first words were to ask Billie if she was planning to yell at her again. Billie hadn't been the first to yell in their initial argument, but apparently Dee Dee forgot that. She laughed it off, but Billie knew it was intended to insult. Aisha called her a princess twice, pretending to be friendly teasing, but the bite to her tone made it clear to Billie that she still thought she was a snob.

At thirty-one years old, Billie knew the best approach was to put on a brave face and remain as gracious as possible. She was in the woman's home, after all. But today, they were supposed to be eating lunch with them and Billie had been racking her brain trying to figure out how to make things better.

"Can you believe that?" Michael said to her as soon as she entered the bedroom. He tossed the cell phone back on the bed. "This is the third work call in as many days. Nobody respects vacation."

"Clients don't care about vacation." She fell back on the bed, loving the feel of the thick down bedding.

"That wasn't a client," Michael said. "That was my office. I need to fire someone."

Billie eyed him to see if he was serious, and it looked like he was. "That's a bit harsh. We all get called on vacation. It's not right, but it happens."

"It doesn't happen here," he said, pointing to the floor. "In Atlanta, people respect your vacation. Just another difference that makes Atlanta better than D.C."

"Don't knock D.C.," she admonished. "D.C. helped you build your agency. Most importantly, D.C. gave you this."

He watched with a wicked smile as she undid the top of her bathrobe, revealing her perfectly round, perky small breasts and flat stomach.

"I can't argue with that." He walked over and leaned on top of her on the bed.

He straddled her, leaning down so she could grab him by the collar of his robe and pull him closer.

"For all its faults," he said, "it gave me the woman I love."

Her heart leapt at his words. She would never ever get tired of hearing them and was warmed to her core at the ease with which he said them. There was no fear or hesitation.

"I love you so much," she professed, her hands coming gently to his face as she looked up at him.

"Show me," he whispered, before lowering his mouth to hers.

She closed her eyes as she tasted his lips and felt her body respond with a tingling sensation throughout. His mouth moved down to the place where her neck met her chest and she felt his tongue gently taste her soft skin. She let out as a moan as his lips kissed her again, this time lower. Then lower.

"Michael," she said, her voice already getting breathless. "The aquarium, remember? We're supposed to be going there this morning. If we start on this . . . Well, you know how long we can go."

He looked up at her, his mind already made up. "Do you want to play with fish or play with me?"

There was no need to answer. There wasn't anything she wanted more than his hands on her. And as he leaned back to remove the rest of her bathrobe, Billie had already forgotten the question.

When Erica Kent knocked on the door to her boss's office, she knew he wasn't going to be happy. She was late and the last thing she wanted was for him to think she took this job for granted. She had been arguing with her landlord over the phone because the toilet hadn't been fixed all week, and time got past her.

Still, that was no excuse and she wouldn't make any.

"Come in," he said.

She opened the door to the office of the CEO of Robinson & Associates, Justin Robinson, the husband of her best friend, Sherise, who had practically saved her life when he hired her eight months ago.

Erica was not in a good place in her life a year ago. She'd allowed herself to be suckered into working for Jonah Nolan's vice presidential campaign, believing that somehow she could have an actual relationship with the man she'd learned was her father at the age of twenty-five. He'd had a brief affair with her mother and the two parted ways with Erica's mother, who died when Erica was nineteen, choosing to keep her father's identity a secret.

He wanted to keep her a secret for the sake of his career. At the time, he was one of the highest-ranking people with the Defense Department and on the short list for the White House. Being selected as the Republican candidate for vice president in the last election was all part of the plan.

Erica wasn't part of the plan. She was often reminded of how lucky she was. Jonah was an awful person who wielded immense power and used it to hurt anyone who crossed him. He used people, innocent people, and thought nothing of it. Jonah's complete failure as a human being was made undeniably clear to her in the worst way. She'd found out that he was also the father of Alex Gonzales, a man whose mother was a maid of Jonah's sister.

The worst part of it was that Erica and Alex had started falling for each other before finding out the truth. They'd even kissed. When the truth came out, there were no words to describe how devastated they both were. Their lives were ruined—Alex's more than Erica's because while she was still kept a secret, Alex's relationship, or the lack of one, with Jonah was declared to the world.

Erica quit her job on Jonah's campaign. Things were rough, especially with her younger brother, Nate, deciding to get a place of his own. Struggling with money had always been a part of Erica's life, but she was down to her last penny when, eight months ago, Justin came to her and offered her the job of his assistant at the new lobbying firm he was starting up. She knew this was more of a favor than a genuine request, but she made a vow to make it the best choice Justin could make for his company.

"I'm so so sorry," she said as she rushed over to his desk.

Justin looked up from his computer and reached out to get the report she'd completed. "You're lucky that the client is late for the meeting. Otherwise, I'd be in deep shit."

"I know," Erica said. "I just . . . I'm sorry. It won't happen again."

He placed the report on the desk and looked at her with an analyzing expression. "Are you okay, Erica?"

"Um . . . well, yes." Erica wondered what she looked like. "Is something wrong with me?"

The twenty-eight-year old was still the same vivacious, curvy girl she'd been since puberty. Her fair skin and light eyes highlighted a pretty, full face. She had a girl-next-door look about her, but was now showing a little more sophistication in the way she carried herself.

"You look stressed," he said. "I need to know if this is too much for—"

"No," she insisted quickly. "This job is not too much for me. You know I've been doing admin jobs for the longest, Justin."

"This job is more than that," he said. "I know I require a lot of you, and if you think it's outside of your area . . ."

"I may not have gone to college . . ." Erica stopped herself, noticing that her tone sounded a bit defensive. Always being around people with college degrees, sometimes more than one, and not having any can make a girl that way. "I can handle it. Sorry I was late."

"Seems like everyone is late today." He glanced at his watch. "This meeting was supposed to start a half hour ago. Hopefully, it'll be quick."

"Would you like me to call them?"

"I think . . ." Just then the Skype ring came up on Justin's computer and he sighed. "Finally. It's them. It's fine, Erica. That'll be all."

"Let me know if you need anything," she said before leaving and closing the door behind her.

She needed this job. She had to make sure not to slip up. Money was extremely tight. She was paying for everything herself. Before, it was her, her brother Nate, and her fiancé Terrell sharing the rent of a two-bedroom apartment. Then it was down to just her and Nate. Then it was just her.

It didn't seem fair, Erica thought. While her friends Sherise and Billie were able to go off to college on scholarship, Erica couldn't afford it. Nate was only twelve when their mother died and Erica had to take care of him. Neither had she found a lobbyist or lawyer to marry. The girls had loaned her money in the past, but Erica hated that. She hated being reminded that she was always the broke one.

This job paid decent enough and now that Justin was doing much better, she was promised a raise. She needed it desperately, so now was not the time to start messing up.

As she turned to enter her office just a few steps away from Justin's she heard the office doorbell. Their office, located on K Street in downtown Washington, D.C., shared a receptionist with the consulting agency next door. When she was out, the front door was locked and visitors had to ring a doorbell for Erica to let them in.

She rushed to the front of the office, toward the glass doors. When she reached them, she was pleased with what she saw. A very good-looking brother, sort of a walnut brown color, a close fade, and a finely shaven goatee, in a dark blue suit that was tailored perfectly to show that he had a large, muscled body underneath, but not too tight to make it seem like that's what he wanted you to see. He was smiling at her and he had a dimple on his left cheek.

Erica had a thing for men with dimples, but she pulled herself together and approached the door as professionally as she could.

"Can I help you?" she asked as she opened the door.

"Yes." His voice was deep and confident. "I'm Corey James. I have an appointment with Justin Robinson."

Erica had a hard time looking away from those deep eyes of his, but after a few seconds, she glanced down at her watch. "Your interview isn't until eleven. It's . . ."

"Ten thirty," he said. "I know. I didn't expect it to be so easy to get here from the Hill."

The Hill was the word used to describe Capitol Hill with the U.S. Capitol as its centerpiece. It was where Congressional staff, which Erica assumed Corey was, worked.

"He's actually running kind of behind," Erica said. "It's not his fault. A client took too . . ."

Erica realized his brows centered in a frown. He

was looking at her weird and she suddenly realized why. She hadn't let him in!

"Oh!" She jumped aside, holding the door open for him to enter. "Sorry about that."

He laughed as he entered. "I was starting to worry I'd have to conduct the interview in the hallway."

"Please sit down anywhere," she directed.

The front of the office was sharply designed with a minimalist look of green and blue. The centerpiece was the large-screen television against the wall behind the receptionist desk. It was always on C-SPAN, the public affairs channel that covered Congress and the White House.

"So you're here for the associate position?" she asked as he sat down.

"Yes, I am." He had a generous smile that didn't hold back. "Are you an associate? I can tell you're not the woman I spoke to on the phone because she had a Midwestern accent."

"Don't tell her that," Erica warned as she sat down in the chair next to him. "She's from Minneapolis and hates it when people ask her about her accent. She thinks it makes her sound like a hick."

"I know the feeling," he said. "Being from Waukegan, Illinois, I got a lot of weird looks when I first moved here."

"Isn't that near Chicago?" Erica asked.

"A little less than an hour away," he answered. "Where are you from?"

"Right here in D.C.," she said. "Southeast, as a matter of fact."

She eyed him closely to gauge his reaction. D.C. snobs were predictable. If you came from Southeast D.C. you were considered ghetto no matter who you actually were. The elitist culture in the district would shun you right away. Erica wondered if Corey was a part of that culture.

But he didn't seem to react at all. Maybe he was a good actor. After all, he worked on Capitol Hill.

"Nice," he said. "I'm gonna need your help."

"With what?"

"Well." He placed his briefcase in the chair next to him. "First, I'm gonna need your name."

She laughed girlishly and was immediately embarrassed by it. "I'm sorry. My name is Erica. Erica Kent."

He held out his hand to her. She accepted and shook it firmly. His grip was strong, but not strangling. She liked it.

"Second," he said. "I'm gonna need you to show me around Southeast."

Was he asking her out? Erica didn't know how to react to this. After having been with the same man for five years, her one attempt at getting back in the saddle was with someone who turned out to be her half brother. Other than that, her dating experiences were rare and awful.

"Show you around?" she asked, trying to act unfazed. "How can you work on Capitol Hill and not know Southeast? You're in Southeast."

He shook his head. "I'm in Capitol Hill Southeast. You know that. I'm used to the hot spots to go eat and the food markets, but I don't know the real Southeast. The neighborhood. In the two years I've lived here, I've never been able to really explore the real D.C."

Erica liked what she was hearing, a man who saw past all the pretty regentrification that Capitol Hill always raved about. He wanted to learn about the D.C.

that was there before people decided to bring in all the cafés and candle shops.

"You know what I'm talking about," he said. "The family joints, the dives and mom-and-pop places that the transients don't know about."

"I'd actually . . . I guess I could." So was this a date? She didn't even know this guy.

"I don't want to put you on the spot," he said, reaching into his pocket. "Here is my card. Don't worry about it now, but think about it later."

She hesitated a second before taking the card. "I'll think about it, Corey. I'll let Justin know you're here. Like I said, he's running a little behind."

"I'm good," he said, holding up his smart phone.

She went to the receptionist desk and grabbed the remote to the TV behind the desk.

"If you want, you can watch something other than C-SPAN." She handed him the remote.

"Thanks." He accepted the remote, but frowned as he looked at the television. "What is this guy doing on? I thought he disappeared."

Erica turned to the screen and felt dread at the sight of Jonah. It was stock footage of him and his now ex-wife, Juliet, standing in front of their massive Virginia house waving to the media. It was taken after Jonah was named as the vice presidential candidate more than a year ago. The piece was just reflecting on all of the high and low points of the presidential campaign that had recently ended. Jonah's bit was obviously a low point.

Disappeared was a good word to describe Jonah these days. After the news of his affair with his sister's maid and his love child he'd kept a secret all these years hit, the once hero war veteran and future of politics was everything that was wrong with the world. The campaign dropped him from the ticket, choosing a female senator to replace him.

Erica had cut all ties with Jonah after that, even though he tried several times to contact her. She heard about him resigning from the Pentagon, his wife filing for divorce, and his general withdrawal from the powerful society scene. It was unavoidable, but she still tried to stay as far away from it as she could. It was too upsetting.

Unable to even stand the sight of Jonah, Erica snatched the remote away from Corey and quickly turned to a channel focused on the day's financial markets.

"Better?" she asked, smiling, handing it back to him.

"Much," he agreed with a nod.

A blank screen would be better than Jonah, Erica thought as she walked back toward Justin's office.